BLOOD
REIGN

NEW YORK TIMES AND *USA TODAY* BESTSELLING AUTHOR
JASINDA WILDER

BLOOD
REIGN

INTRODUCTION

Synopsis of Blood Bonds

FOLLOWING THE VIOLENT EVENTS IN MANHATTAN, Maeve has been taken captive by a lethal alpha shifter named Caleb. He shackles her in what he calls mage-cuffs, magical handcuffs that block her from using her magic.

He brings her to the Tribunal's secret headquarters—deep within a mountain in the Swiss Alps.

It's tense between them for most of the very long trip, but there's also…another kind of tension. Caleb, however, is anything but forthcoming, and Maeve is too scared of what's going to happen to dig into it too deeply. She feels twinges of something, but all too soon they're arriving at the headquarters.

A massive, powerful glamour hides the headquarters from mortals as well as any other unwanted prying eyes. Having been given access, the glamour disappears for Caleb, revealing massive gates hewn right into the side of the mountain. The whole face of the mountain has been carved into a castle.

Caleb deposits her unceremoniously on the floor of the giant staging area just inside the mammoth doors, quotes Hamlet at her, and then shifts into his wolf and vanishes.

Now alone, a captive of her enemies, Maeve is surrounded by immortals who seem curious more than anything. They call her the WorldBreaker, which seems to be a title of some sort, but no one explains what it means.

A huge guard escorts her deeper into the mountain; despite the castle exterior hewn into the rock face, the interior is more like a high-rise office building, complete with some sort of skylights that allow sunlight in.

She's brought to an interrogation room. Lightless, soundless—isolating and unnerving. At some point, a person enters the room.

This is Zirae, the oldest and most powerful fae and de facto president of the Tribunal.

He probes her mind and discovers that she has partitioned her magic: essentially hidden her fae magic from herself—and thus from the magic in the mage-cuffs. He warns her partitioning is easy, undoing it is the hard part—and she's worried he's right.

She tries to evict him from her mind, but without her full powers, she's helpless before his vicious might and skill. That's when the real fun begins.

Zirae subjects her to a series of glamours that function as torture: he calls it the Coil of Undying Death. She dies in an ocean of lava; she dies at the bottom of the ocean; she dies in a blizzard. Each new scene is utterly realistic, perfectly real and believable, complete with the accompanying agony.

When it's over, she asks what he wants—what was the point?

"'Want?' he says. 'Oh, nothing. I was just making a point.'"

"What point?' I whisper, trying in vain to stop trembling and gasping for breath. I can still feel the heat, the cold, the choking water, the driving snow, although not a mark remains on my skin.

'That you cannot hope to resist, child. You are here. Your little…rebellion…has failed and will die without you.'

"I'm bloodmated," I whisper. "Surely you know what will happen if you keep us separated."

"'As a matter of fact, I do not know, and neither do you. You are not a vampire and nor are you fae. You are both and neither. Some would call you an abomination, others a scientific curiosity. I call you a threat to global peace unlike any other in human history. And I should know—I've been around for most of it.'"

His point, eventually, is that he sees her as a threat. The events in Manhattan—the fight against the Tribunal's forces—were livestreamed by an unknown mortal who subsequently vanished, her memory erased by a memory-phage glamour. The recording went viral, and now, unbeknownst to Maeve, human society is discovering all at once across the globe that immortals are real. The pillars of civilization are trembling, Zirae tells her, and he cannot and will not allow her to topple them completely.

He's not just worried about how trying to integrate immortals into society would affect civilization as a whole; he's worried about her plan to promote reproduction across the lines of fae, vampire, and shifter, how it would eventually cause true-blooded immortals to go extinct. He apologizes to her for what he's about to do to her—he cannot let her leave, ever…and nor can he allow her child to live.

He leaves, plunging her back into darkness, alone.

She's brought to a cell, stripped naked, the cuffs are removed, and then a ward is placed on the opening. She quickly discovers that not only does the ward prevent her from leaving or even getting too close—she's burned badly in her attempt to breach the ward. She passes out.

She wakes up, and an unknown male vampire pauses in front of her cell. He calls her the WorldBreaker again, but with reverence. And then he calls her a new name: The Once-Mortal Queen. He vanishes as mysteriously as he came.

She tries to sleep and fails. Tries to reach Caspian or the others in her coven and fails. Tries to de-partition her magic and fails.

And then someone unexpected appears: her grandfather, Elias Sparrow.

He explains that the ward on her cell is the most powerful in existence—nothing can get out. He tells her about Zirae—old, powerful, but twisted and broken by the weight of his age. Elias also informs her that he is part of a faction within the Tribunal that believes she is the only way forward for humanity and immortals but that they aren't ready for a coup. He tells Maeve she has to unlock her magic, learn better control over it, and above all, she cannot allow them to sterilize her.

This is news to her. They plan on *sterilizing* her?

He says he will do what he can when he can, but that much will be expected of her.

"'You are my granddaughter,'" he says, "'and you are your mother's child. I believe in you.'"

Furthermore, he explains a few things she was confused by in Zirae's speech, especially the word "prana."

"'For centuries, thousands of years, even, Sanskrit was the official language of immortal research, much like Latin was the official language of mortal academia. The monks, ascetics, and healers of that era and region were at the forefront of understanding how energy systems work in living beings. To mortals, it's been diluted into trite concepts regarding yoga. But the reality is, much of the terminology and teachings are true, in reference to how our bodies and spirits function.'"

During their conversation, Maeve says that her mother wasn't into yoga, and Elias says no, she lacked the patience. The problem with this is that to Maeve, her mother was the most patient person she knew, which puzzles Elias, who refuses to explain further, until he has more information.

"'I forget you were not taught even the most rudimentary concepts. I must go back, then. There are four types of…energy, I suppose, which form the basis of all sentient life, mortal and immortal. They are known as The Three Sisters and The Fourth God. There was, at one time, a lengthier Sanskrit version, but it phased out of use even among immortals. The Three Sisters are: mana, or dream energy; prana, or life energy, which you know as vitality, and rakta, or blood. The Fourth God is maya, or magic.' He arches an eyebrow at me. 'Can you piece it together?'

I consider. 'Prana—vitality…used by fae. Rakta—blood, used by vampires. Then mana must be used by shifters. But magic is a separate thing? I thought my vitality *was* magic. I've been thinking about it that way.'

He smiles kindly. 'That is common, even among fae. The truth is more complex. The Three Sisters form a trinity. All living, sentient beings contain, consume, and require all three as an essential premise of sentience. Higher mammals, such as dogs, cats, primates, whales, and so on…they are not exactly sentient as we are, but close, and operate on a similar basis, although their balance of the energies more closely resembles that of shifters. See, it's the balance that defines us. A fae, for example, relies more heavily on prana, or vitality—the energy of life.'

'How is that different than blood?'

'Blood is physical, a solid, material manifestation of the energy here in The Waking.'"

He goes on to explain some of The Waking and The Dreaming:

"'Essentially, The Waking and Dreaming are sides of a coin. When sentient beings sleep, they venture into The Dreaming, which can be thought of as a kind of gradient. Mortals never pass the shallows when they dream, lacking the sensitivity to mana. We immortals can pass deeper—fae and vampires, I mean. Our heightened sensitivity to mana means we can pass beyond the shallows into deeper, more dangerous realms. Shifters are different. They are of The Dreaming, with dual selves—a Waking self and a Dreaming self. A shifter in animal form is embodying their Dreaming self here in The Waking—and they use magic to do so. In The Dreaming, they hunt and consume mana, usually from dreaming mortals. This does not harm the mortal beyond a bad dream or some such, occasionally…

'Magic is the transition between Waking and Dreaming. It is the fuel that allows us to manipulate prana, mana, or rakta. A vampire manipulates blood—the physical manifestation of life. That is what defines a vampire's physical self as different from fae, shifters, and mortals, whether blooded or unblooded: heightened speed and strength, the ability to lighten themselves, all that. But maya is that which allows the vampire to utilize rakta in that way. When you, as a fae, perform a glamour, you are using maya, not prana, if you wish to be technically precise, but prana is the physical manifestation of that maya, in this example. When a shifter shifts, he or she uses maya to perform the shift, even though it is mana that they utilize. You cannot manipulate, see, or feel maya directly, which is why it is termed thus—The Fourth God, instead of being The Fourth Sister. Maya is what underpins the supernatural elements that defines immortal existence. We immortals are just different—we are human, just different kinds of human, with different sensitivities."

He tells her that she is not the only one like her—she's the only vampire-fae, but there are others. He also tells her that there are answers, and allies, in The Dreaming. He cannot say more, however, because of oaths which magically prevent him.

She tries again and again and again to get out of the cell and to unlock her magic and fails every time. She grievously injures herself in the attempts and eventually gives up, just lying in pain on the floor of her cell.

Footsteps approach. A fae female, old and powerful, unlocks the ward, and Maeve, immediately seized by bloodlust, pounces. The guards shock her into paralysis and the female subdues her. They bring her to a medical room—they're going to force an abortion and sterilize her.

She fights—futilely. She's bound to a table.

Nothing she does stops it—she is given nothing for the pain, not that it would have worked. There's nothing she can do to stop it; immortal doctors abort the life in her womb.

Pain, grief, and rage distill within her, then, and sharpen, harden. Become something like a weapon, which she uses to pierce and smash open the hard marble of her partitioned prana. All at once, it all comes back to her, and she goes apeshit.

She vents—only just barely holding on to the core of her power so she doesn't kill herself in the process. What she does do, though, is vaporize the entire lab and everyone and everything in it. Gone berserk with rage and grief, mad with bloodlust frenzy, Maeve slaughters everyone who gets too close, shredding through them like tissue paper. She discovers she can yank the blood out of people without having to drink it. Same with prana.

It's a brutal, vicious rampage.

Eventually, sheer numbers win—she's so badly wounded that the Tribunal forces manage to knock her down long enough to get another pair of mage-cuffs on her and return her to her cell.

But at least she's de-partitioned now, right?

Unconscious, she finds herself in The Dreaming, where she encounters…someone. She's not sure who it is at first. The voice, the presence in The Dreaming, guides her up to wake and encourages her to get out of the cuffs and find them in The Dreaming. The presence is a wolf, but she still doesn't know them—him, she decides.

She wakes up.

She's back in her cell, badly hurt but healing. She took a lot of blood during the slaughter, so she will heal swiftly.

She sleeps dreamlessly. Suspects the wolf in her dream was Caleb but can't figure out why, since he captured her and delivered her to her enemy. He *did* say that they had his pack, which is a pretty reasonable explanation, but why help her?

Since there's no way to know until she speaks to him again, she focuses on the mage-cuffs. Working carefully, merely observing so as to not cause herself more pain, she picks apart the magic of the cuffs, deciphering how they work and how to approach getting out of them.

Turns out it's quite simple, which is not to say easy. She figures out that all she has to do is endure unimaginable pain long enough to destroy the glamour, and she has to do so before the pain causes her to black out and before her body uses all of her blood to heal herself, rendering her just as blocked from her magic.

Elias shows up and they discuss her mother, Elias's guilt, and the death and destruction Maeve caused in her rampage. He tells her that during the rampage she drained enemies of blood and prana without touching them—something no one had even considered possible.

And then, while expressing her remorse for the innocent researchers killed in the venting that destroyed the lab and everyone in it, Maeve says a phrase that just sort of bubbled up inside her: "'I sent my enemy into the screaming void.'"

Elias's reaction is immediate and intense. He demands to know where she heard that phrase—who taught it to her? She doesn't know. Her mother never said it, and no one taught her.

"After what feels like an hour, he speaks in a soft, quiet, thoughtful tone. He's reciting something. 'By this blade, I shall send my enemies into the screaming void.' A pause, heavy and significant.

Words pulse in my brain, unbidden. 'And the void shall sing the final song.'

His eyes cut to me. 'With this prayer, I shall send my daughter into the singing void.'

'And the void shall sing the final song.' The response

emerges from me, once more unbidden, and tears prick at my eyes.

It's part of an ancient fae ritual, he tells her. Words spoken before battle, or at the funeral of a loved one. It is impossible that she knows the words—they are never spoken outside of sacred fae rituals, which have not been practiced in centuries. There is simply, without a doubt, no way Maeve could ever have accidentally heard those exact words.

This leads him to finally understand the mystery of why Maeve is so different, why she can perform glamours she should otherwise not be able to: her mother, Eliza, cast what's called a demense, an extremely rare and powerful glamour similar to a horcrux from Harry Potter, wherein the glamourworker places a small sliver of their soul, their very essence, into an object, such as a sword or knife, giving that object a minuscule fraction of the caster's identity. One demense cast upon an object makes that object behave oddly, being loyal to the caster. It doesn't become sentient or somehow "haunted" by the person, merely imbued with a little something extra—in the case of the only known successful demense, a dagger owned by Emperor Charlemagne, the dagger never rusted or dulled, and always remained with its owner.

Eliza, Elias says, cast a demense on Maeve. And not just one—many of them. Perhaps countless, over the years. Maeve realizes that her mother had a ritual that remained consistent her whole life: Eliza would braid Maeve's hair before bed and sing to her. But, instead of merely singing and brushing, Eliza was, in fact, casting a demense on Maeve, imbuing her with fractions and slivers of herself. When Eliza died and Maeve came into her true nature,

Eliza's spirit, now a significant proportion, came alive, in a sense. It's not her mother's actual entire being within her, but enough that in times of desperation, some of Eliza's ability and knowledge as a glamourist comes through in what Maeve eventually comes to call Mother's Spirit. It explains why she had such vivid dreams of her mother after death—her mother's spirit allowed one last burst of sentience. It explains Maeve's unusual power and abilities—much of her mother's power and skill were transferred to Maeve.

Elias tells her again that she has to get out of the mage-cuffs and escape—now that she's shown how dangerous she is, they won't let her live. She will be executed, and soon. So now the race against the clock is on.

Maeve asks what children call their grandparents, and he tells her that when he was a child, he called his grandfather "Aeldfar," the Old English version of Grandfather. Maeve decides to call him that—she's come to understand that he's not evil, as her mother stated in the video. He was faced with a terrible, impossible choice, and that has haunted him ever since. She sees his essential goodness and compassion and is coming to trust him.

The last thing Elias says before leaving is an explanation of the titles she keeps hearing: WorldBreaker and The Once-Mortal Queen. They're a reference to an ancient fae prophecy, which he recites to her:

"When the eagles of iron fall from the sky, and those of the Blood cry war brother against brother, then will the WorldBreaker come. Her hair will be as white as the driven snow. She will wield her maya with the spirit of her mother. She is the WorldBreaker. She is The Once-Mortal Queen, and all shall bow, but not before the rivers run red and the streets flood scarlet. She shall know Death, and Death shall know her. She shall have a mate of fang and a mate of fur. She is the WorldBreaker, and the Once-Mortal Queen."

He emphasizes the importance of her role in everything, in the coming changes. She may not want or have asked for the responsibility, but she was chosen nonetheless, and she must be equal to the task, or the world is doomed.

No pressure.

He leaves, and Maeve spends the next few days examining the magic of the ward on her cell and the magic of the cuffs. What she comes to understand is that not even she possesses the power to escape the cell through the ward or to break the ward. So she'll have to find another way out. But first, she has to get out of the cuffs. After some experimentation, she begins to get a glimmer of an idea, but the pain causes her to pass out, sending her back into The Dreaming, where the Wolf tells her to find the weakness in the cuff's magic.

She comes up with a solution and successfully breaks the magic of the cuffs.

Back down into The Dreaming she goes, now finally free of the cuffs, de-partitioned, and ready to escape.

She's also sure now that the Wolf is, in fact, Caleb.

She sees him in wolf form. Then he shifts into manform and explains that he lied and never escaped cuffs. No one ever has. She could because the cuffs were designed specifically to work on fae, shifters, and vampires. She is not fully any of them, and the magic couldn't adapt to her differences, allowing her to break the magic and escape.

It's also obvious that he is attracted to her...and she to him. He tells her she called him to her for her whole life. When he thought she was merely a mortal, it was perplexing that this random mortal girl would call a powerful alpha shifter to her dreams. But then, when he saw her in the alley, he understood that she was far, far more. And that they were destined to be mates—bonded mates.

When she returns to The Waking, her grandfather is there with bad news. The Tribunal has voted to execute her—likely within the next week or two. This prompts the revelation that she was unconscious after venting for a month and has been essentially comatose trying to get out of the cuffs for a week.

He also tells her that unrest out in the world is increasing. Fighting is breaking out in major cities across the world as immortals break their masks and come forward with their true identities. Politicians, leaders, actors, celebrities, musicians—they're abandoning the pretense. Mortals, now aware that immortals exist—and are becoming aware of the threat that the greater power and longevity of immortals represents, are rioting, angry that they've been lied to for so long, and afraid. Meanwhile, immortals are beginning to demand recognition and acceptance...

It's a mess. Governments are crumbling as they attempt to cope with riots and unrest, as well as the loss of so many key personnel as immortals leave their jobs to join the fight for equality and inclusion.

He gives her a lesson in glamourworking. Teaches her the importance of a calm mind and control over the prana within her—which is not actually *within* her so much as it *is* her.

She practices or tries to. But she keeps hearing Caspian's voice—it can reach her, but the moment she reaches out to him, the magic in the ward strikes her down.

She transitions to The Dreaming and encounters Caleb, which is becoming normal. She has a physical body in The Dreaming with him. They walk together. Their mutual attraction becomes ever more undeniable, which is confusing for Maeve, as she is still suffering immensely from the bloodmate sickness. They talk of their pasts—his mate who died, her mother.

It's a time of bonding and connection.

She struggles with allowing herself to connect with him, to let herself feel her attraction, much less act on it. Having been raised mortal, it feels wrong to her. But Caleb tells her that she must make her own path. Choose for herself.

But really, there is no choice.

She kisses him.

They get carried away, but the echo of her mates' pain from the bloodmate sickness snaps her back to reality, and she returns to The Waking with renewed determination to break the cuffs.

Angry, she lashes out at the ward and is thrown into The Dreaming, near to death. Wolf—Caleb—saves her. He helps her understand that she's been letting others dictate her choices, even how she behaves with her coven—with Alistair, Fin, and Stirling. She loves them but has not made love to them. Why not? She's not a vampire and is not bound by their ways.

It's a long, philosophical conversation in The Dreaming, and through it, she finds a kind of freedom—to love who she loves, how she wants to.

And she stops fighting her need for Caleb.

She allows herself to give in. To make love with Caleb. In The Dreaming.

When she returns to The Waking, she retains a physical mark of their lovemaking—claw marks on her back.

So...what is real in The Dreaming is real in The Waking...

She thought The Dreaming wasn't real, that it was just very vivid dreams. But seeing physical marks transfer to the waking world changes everything. She feels Caspian across the bloodlink, feels his confusion at having felt her joy and pleasure, which smashes her with guilt...

But also with an idea.

The mark Caleb left upon her is a mate-bond. What they did was not just sex but a true, magical mating—fulfilling the prophecy that she would have a mate of fang and a mate of fur.

Aeldfar, her grandfather, appears, and they discuss her mating with Caleb. He explains that she should not feel guilty and guesses that even if they are confused, Caspian and her coven will come to understand and accept it. And that she must do whatever is necessary.

He confirms that her idea to escape *through* The Dreaming can work.

He leaves, and she goes back into The Dreaming to attempt it.

Caleb is there, and they talk about many things before she brings it around to her idea—to escape through the dreaming...but she needs him to do it.

He understands and agrees it's possible.

They make love again, but this time, it's different. The glorious fury of their mating brings them together into a place or state of being that is between The Waking and The Dreaming, and she breaks through, ripping a hole in the fabric of reality separating the two realms, and escapes her cell.

She finds herself on the mountaintop with Caleb. Physically, while they are still mating. The mate-bond is finished—shifters are bonded in two phases: in The Dreaming and then in The Waking. Now they are truly mate-bonded, and she is free.

Time to rescue his pack.

But first—she is finally able to reach Caspian.

She, Caleb, and Caspian have bond-mate tattoos.

Caspian is hurt and angry that not only did she mate with someone else, but it's also a wolf—a shifter. Bonding *him* to a wolf.

But then the Tribunal finds them, and the fight is on.

The coven is close and joins the fight.

Together, they fight their way into the mountain and down to the cells where his pack is being held.

Maeve learns how to break wards. They free his pack, a group of wolves that she feels a mental connection to, similar to a coven's bond, although limited since she's not a shifter.

And then…

Imprisoned along with Caleb's pack?

The other two like her: a vampire-shifter male and a fae-shifter female. Prisoners of the Tribunal—victims and products of the same experiment that produced Maeve. But where Maeve's mother escaped, allowing Maeve to live free, these two didn't. They're half-feral, but she's determined to free them.

There's another surprise down there, too: the male vampire who sired her, the last surviving victim of the experiment. Her father.

Once they're freed, Maeve's little army marches upward toward the top, where the actual Tribunal is. Along the way, they encounter more Tribunal forces, some of whom fight, and some who defect to Maeve's side, taking a mark of fealty—an ancient oath of loyalty that Mother's Spirit helped Maeve conjure.

Along the way up, she and Caspian come to an understanding—that Maeve loves Caspian, always has, and always will, and that her loving Caleb doesn't take away from her love for him.

It is revealed that Caleb isn't just a powerful alpha shifter, he's an Alpha Prime, capable of commanding just about anyone, even other alphas, to do his bidding. She gains several more very powerful new allies, and Connor, one of Caleb's pack, is killed.

And then, at long last, she enters the Tribunal chamber and faces the Tribunal, the six oldest and most powerful immortals to ever live.

She and Zirae fight—an epic battle of magic.

She wins, barely, with the help of Caleb, as well as Theris the vampire-shifter, and Aquilia the fae-shifter — but Zirae escapes, somehow ripping a portal through The Dreaming, like she did, sort of.

The rest of the Tribunal appears, seeming ready to snap out orders and take charge as they always have. Instead, Maeve, now beginning to understand the true depth and breadth of her power, subdues them easily and begins questioning them. She gives them an ultimatum: take her mark of fealty or be banished, but if they cross her or attempt to take up the fight against her to get control, she will kill them. In the process, it is revealed that the Tribunal has always known that the races can procreate and intentionally prevented it. Secundus—children that are products of such unions, like Maeve—are more powerful than Primi—the original races, fae, vampires, and shifters. The Tribunal feared the change, feared losing their power, feared the dilution of "pure blood" and the loss of culture, and so doomed all three races to extinction.

After thoroughly excoriating them for their selfishness and cowardice, she leaves them, the chamber, and the mountain.

Alistair reveals that he has an ancestral home estate in England, and she, Caleb, Caspian, Alistair, Phineas, and Stirling go there to be alone, to recover, reconnect, and rest before whatever comes next.

She mates with Caspian, cementing and renewing their bond, and with Caleb…and with them together. She also finally shares true intimacy and lovemaking with Phineas, Stirling, and Alistair, and with all of them. She bloodmates with the other vampires and receives an intricate tattoo marking the mate-bonds—a five-pointed star…one point for each mate.

Except…the interior of the star is empty of ink, suggesting…something Maeve isn't ready to think about.

As the mates bask in the afterglow, one of Caleb's pack barges in with an iPad, showing a news report: open fighting in New York between a collection of immortals and an organized army calling itself the Mortal Federation.

War has come.

ℙ<small>ROLOGUE</small>

𝕊<small>NOW</small> <small>BLOWS</small> <small>ACROSS</small> <small>THE</small> mountaintop in razor-sharp swirls and shuddering, billowing blasts. The sky is black, choked with snow-heavy clouds. The wind is vicious and relentless, scraping the rocky, jagged Alpine peak bare even as the white curtain of frigid flakes piles up where the wind just swept.

No living being could survive on this mountaintop, nor for long, not in this storm. Even an immortal would find it unpleasant.

Had there been anyone with eyes to see, they might, if they were sharp-eyed and knew what to look for, see a weird, shivery patch of deeper, darker shadows wriggling and writhing against the black backdrop of night.

Look closer.

Just shadows, perhaps? A trick of the wind and the blowing snow.

No?

Closer yet. Shift through the shadows and peer hard at the sliver of animate black.

Do you see it?

It's a line. Not so scary, right? The shortest distance between two points, that's all it is.

A line in the darkness, as if someone had taken a razor blade and sliced downward through the fabric of reality.

Watch it, now. Watch carefully.

There—do you see it?

Something is moving *within* that short, narrow gap in reality. You won't be able to make out its shape, no matter how acute your vision—it has no shape.

Not any kind of outline or form that you'd understand, at any rate. Or perhaps if it does have a shape, it shifts and distorts so constantly you might be reminded of the ocean as it rushes toward shore, rising and falling and rippling and writhing into waves, lifting into peaks and dipping into valleys.

The thing, if it can even be thought of as a *thing* at all, seems to be hesitating on the other side of the gap in reality.

You see, that line is a hole. A narrow slice in the veil between realities.

Picture it this way: pick up a coin and hold it between your thumb and forefinger; it has two sides—the front and the back, right? It also has the edge, the rim, which you only see when you hold the coin just so, edge-on. That rim, that thin, narrow edge is the veil between the front and the back of the coin.

The line of darker shadows here in the air above the blizzard-occluded mountaintop, then, can be thought of as a hole drilled through the coin of our little metaphor.

We, all of us, exist on *this* side of the coin. Occasionally, you might get a brief, vague, half-remembered peek at the reality that exists on the other side when you're asleep and dreaming.

But…just as we reside here, on the waking side of the coin, there are things that reside on the other side, in a version of reality where dreams are real, where fantasies can come true…and so can nightmares. It's a place where imagination and creativity are the stuff of magic.

These things, up until this precise moment, have *only* existed on the other side. The veil keeps them there. When you dream, you are not *there* on the other side. Not *you*, your body, your physical self—just your…ka. Your soul. Your mind. That part of you that thinks, dreams, wishes, imagines.

When you visit this other side in your dreams, you emit mana—the energy of dreams and creation, the stuff that powers your soul, the engine of fantasy. You, being mortal, lack the requisite sensitivity to see or feel the mana that exists within you. So, when you dream, that unused mana radiates from you.

And these things, the hungry denizens of The Dreaming, they crave mana. They *are* mana. And you aren't using it, so why not? They stalk you as you tiptoe across the surface of The Dreaming in your flimsy, weak, thin little mortal dream. They nibble and nip, taste and lick. You feel nothing. Perhaps your dream takes a turn for the bizarre—suddenly, the dream you're having of giving that speech tomorrow shifts, and suddenly, the audience is a school of fish; that shift in the substance of your dream is the moment when one of these things, these creatures of The Dreaming, takes a little bite out of your mana. You may have a nightmare—your teeth falling out or being chased by Freddy Krueger, who is, somehow, also your mother-in-law wielding that horrible meatloaf recipe on a yellowing, dog-eared 3x5 card. Or, you may have a lush, sexy fantasy about that fine as fuck blonde from 3C across the way who keeps giving you shy looks as you both bring in your groceries.

If you're physically here, in The Waking, and only visiting, then they can't harm you. You'll wake up and the dream will be firm for a moment or two, but then it fades until all that's left is a vague impression at best.

There are, of course, those who can visit The Dreaming in a more physical sense. And they do have reason to fear the creatures who live there—for if you're there in a more physical sense, the creatures *can* harm you if they think to take a bite of your mana—for mana is what you need to get back on the other side of the veil where you belong.

They can wrap you up in endless coils and drag you down, down, down…and what lies beneath? What's there, down in the deepest depths of The Dreaming?

The place called Death.

The veil has protected us, here in The Waking.

But now?

There's a hole. The veil is torn. And the creatures that lurk in The Dreaming have a window into our reality.

The Dreaming is a vast place—infinite, really, and even though the mysterious creatures that live there are numberless and beyond counting, this window is quite small. A sliver, at best.

Unfortunately, The Waking is ripe with mana. We're glutted with it. It flows like a river, rushes like currents. Every time you lie, you use mana. Every time you tell a story to your friends about that sexy hookup or fumbling boss or clueless parent, you dip into the well of mana within, scoop a little out, and put it into the world. The more energy used to create, the more mana that creation puts into the world. A feature film, then, is a geyser. A novel is a wellspring. A dreaming mortal, though? That's more like a lake.

To a thing that feeds on mana, The Waking is an all-you-can-eat buffet.

And with so much mana to eat, a creature might sniff out that minuscule hole in the veil, scenting a cornucopia of dreams to snack upon, fantasies to devour, stories to slurp up.

And these things, as has been stated, *are* mana. And where there's mana, there's maya—a kind of byproduct, you might say.

Maya is magic.

When a story pulls you in and captures your imagination and transports you to that world, you are experiencing magic—sort of. A small, weak version, but magic nonetheless.

This is where things get interesting.

Keep all this in mind as the following sequence of events unfolds. Remember what you've been told about mana, maya, and the creatures that live in The Dreaming.

Return your attention to this narrow gap in the veil between The Waking and The Dreaming.

Watch it closely once more.

See that thing wriggling on the other side? It's sniffing. Scenting. Nosing the hole like a fox investigating the space under a fallen tree, looking for a rodent to munch on.

Now it sends a tendril through, a bather dipping a toe in the water to test the temperature.

Seems safe—so far, so good.

The tendril is a thin tentacle of distortion, perhaps the size of your forearm; you can't see it directly, but if you sort of squint without looking directly at it, you'll see a shimmering outline. Think of the Predator when it's invisible, stalking Arnie through the jungle.

Keep watching.

First a tendril, then another. They touch the ground, prod the air. A third joins the first two, and then the tendrils merge to become a single thick arm reaching through the gap.

It's not an arm, really, that's just another metaphor to help you visualize this amorphous being.

More of the thing squeezes through the gap, very much like an octopus shoving itself through a gap in the rocks smaller than a quarter.

More, and more, and more.

The air above the peak shimmers wildly, now. If you can make out its shape through the curtain of swirling snow, you'd see it shifting and twisting and coiling, curling in on itself into a tight little ball, and then unfolding through at least a dozen dimensions beyond the most common three.

It's out, now. The thing has brought its entire shapeless, weightless, formless bulk through the gap. The wind does not affect it, nor does the snow. Or gravity, for that matter.

Speaking of matter, even that has no real effect on this thing. It's not of our reality, remember.

It floats in place, there above the mountain's peak, a mile or so above sea level, somewhere in the Swiss Alps.

It twists in on itself endlessly, swirling and coruscating in translucent distortion. And then…it moves. If you can picture a jellyfish, or perhaps more accurately, a Portuguese man o'war, you might have a rough approximation of the thing's manner of locomotion.

It shivers and wriggles its way down the mountain. It passes through trees and leaves no trace, not even a shimmy off pine needles as it passes. Further, and further.

It pauses briefly—sniffs a corpse. Female, naked, and headless. It's dead and so has no mana, which means the thing continues onward, downward.

It investigates the overturned wreckage of a snowmobile without any real interest. Another few corpses, these mangled and mauled—again, dead, and so without sustenance for the creature.

Further on, then. An outcropping of bare rock rises in its path—it goes through it.

After a few more minutes of travel, it comes to a ragged, gaping hole in the side of the mountain itself. Snow howls in the opening, catching in drifts against the hulks of machines and equipment. Into the darkness, into another hole. It is incurious, this thing. It has a singular focus: find mana. Here, it can scent the traces and old vestiges of mana as it lurks in corners and prowls through offices and labs and sleeping quarters. But there's nothing left—not anything it can eat, at least.

Down into the bowels of the earth it goes, following the scent of what was, at some point in the recent past, powerful mana. If it had a mouth, it would be watering—like walking into a kitchen where someone made chocolate chip cookies an hour or so ago—the scent isn't exactly fresh, but it's still pungent and delicious.

It passes discarded weapons, piles of bloody clothing, and patches of dried blood. Cells where living beings once resided, beings rife with delicious mana.

The thing is getting impatient, if such a sentient emotion can be applied to a brute, thoughtless thing. It is alive, yes, but is it sentient? Not really. Just hungry.

Keep thinking of that Portuguese man o' war. It's a fairly accurate way of picturing this thing—just…make it bigger in your mind. Much, much bigger. A man o' war the size of an orca, with similar predatory instincts. And without the cute, playful personality—cute and playful as long as you're not a harbor seal or Macaroni penguin, that is.

After exploring the vast space under-mountain, it decides in its rudimentary way that there's nothing to eat here, and so it passes through the side of the mountain and out into the open air.

It billows and haunts across wide, rolling fields and over and sometimes through the foothills. It's not interested in the two-lane road over which it passes—but remember, it is a predator, after all. So the road itself isn't of any interest—the faint hints of mana it scents near the road—just *above* the road…now those it *is* interested in. The strains of mana aren't static—they move. This way, that way. Back and forth, linear, following the vector of the road.

So, when the thing follows the road further down-mountain, it's just following the old, faint hits of faded mana from the cars that passed—cars containing people who dream, and lie, and daydream, and fantasize.

The road twists and turns and switches back and forth and carves down the mountain, and with it hunts the thing.

The road passes through a town. It's not much—a few bars, a few restaurants, a few shops, a library, a little school, a playground, and a few clusters of houses tucked in among the trees and foothills.

The road carries onward in its journey, but the thing pauses. It coruscates into a shop—cameras, film, tripods, bags, framed photographs—it munches on the faint trace of mana coming from the photographs, and perhaps its outline becomes a little more distinct as it twists into itself, but the photographs only contain enough mana that it can barely taste it. Kind of like running your finger inside the bowl after all the frosting has been used.

Onward, then.

A restaurant—more old traces but nothing it can really sink its teeth into. The library holds promise: so many books, so many stories—but it's a million little pieces, and this thing is ravenous. It wants a *meal*, and the library is a bag full of sunflower seeds—good for snacking, but nothing that'll really fill it up.

And then…ohhh yes. There. A mile away, as the crow flies, nestled against the flank of a hill, surrounded by towering pines swaying precariously in the wind…a house.

Small. Cozy. Steeply pitched roof—not quite an A-frame, but close. A wide front porch on stilts, a garage below, and sliding glass doors looking into a den.

Smoke curls up out of a chimney and is snatched away by the eager wind.

The thing slants and heaves and billows over the

landscape, rushing through trees and over roads and past a narrow, twisting, two-track through the trees. It pauses in front of the little house. If it were an animal, it would be sniffing, scenting. Nose twitching, ears swiveling, crouched low on its belly—assessing.

It inches forward to the base of the wooden steps leading up to the balcony. Pauses. It scents prey. After a moment or two, the thing dances upward, following the angle of the steps but not the form—it actually phases through the steps and pauses at the glass. Watching. Waiting.

On the other side, prey. And a choice.

On one side of the room is a large rectangular box that flashes blue and white—the thing shimmies to the side to get a better view. Pictures. Images. A story. Much mana. So, so much mana—the box of moving images fairly drips with pungent, powerful, delicious mana.

But…opposite the box is a figure. A being. Alive, like itself, but more dense. A native denizen of this strange place in which the thing has found itself.

The thing watches the being for a while. It seems to be almost but not quite sleeping—watching the images on the box. In one hand, the being holds a cylinder full of liquid, from which the being sips occasionally. On the other hand, it, or he—the thing has an innate, passive ability to comprehend the form and nature of things and to understand them in a non-sentient sort of way—holds a piece of paper rolled into a tube, inside of which is a substance made of plant matter, which this strange being has set on fire, the smoke of which it inhales occasionally. The thing notices that the more of the smoke the being inhales and the more of the liquid it ingests, the more powerfully the being reeks of mana.

A funny, odd, and delicious combination.

The choice, then: the box, or the being?

It writhes through the glass, neither noticing nor caring about the abrupt, drastic change in temperature. The thing drifts to a stop equidistant between the box and the being.

The being blinks his eyes and then rubs them with the back of a wrist. When his vision doesn't clear, he rubs them again and blinks harder. Still blurry, as if a film over his eyes. Maybe he should get his vision checked—his grandfather and father both had vision issues and had floaters that got progressively worse.

The thing watches the being—he seems to be consuming the mana coming from the box. Not directly, not as the thing would consume it, but still. Now, the thing watches the box.

On it, many beings like the one here. They are clothed differently. After a few minutes of observation, the thing understands that the box is a source of stories. The images on the box—or in the box—tell a story, and the being consumes the story for entertainment.

It watches more—the story is fascinating.

Ah!

There!

In the box, within the story, is a creature. Huge, violent, and powerful. The beings in the story fear it, and love it, and hate it—but mostly fear it. The being, watching, experiences a pulse of powerful mana when the creature soars and roars inside the box.

Yes.

The thing has chosen—it will consume the mana within the box.

It glides and tangles toward the box and the images that form a story—the mana that it so ravenously craves.

The thing goes through the glass—but not into the mechanics of the machine; it isn't interested in the wires and circuits. No, the thing goes into the story.

Consider the story, then, as the thing would view it:

A boy, perhaps one could consider him a man. His hair is blonde, almost white. Curly, almost ringlets. Perhaps not handsome, he is more…striking. He wears armor, fine, expensive stuff fit for a king—for the man-boy is, in fact, a king.

He sits astride the creature which has so raptly captured the thing's attention. The creature is massive and magnificent. It has a long, serpentine neck, thick hind legs, a long, wicked tail, huge wings which, when folded, it uses as forelegs, and sharp snapping jaws—and best of all, it breathes fire.

Within the story, the creature—the beast—soars through a blue sky and swoops down upon more of the smaller beings, catching them up and crunching them down, breathing fire upon them and crushing them with its tail and ripping them and tossing them with the sword-like talons on its feet.

Yes, yes, yes—the thing is going to feast, indeed.

The being, watching the box, sits up. He places his bottle on the table in front of him, stabs out the small red-orange coal of the tube in its other hand, and sets that down as well.

He rubs his eyes. Blinks. "What the fuck?"

The TV is…blurry. Not out of focus, but…he can't find the words.

He just knows it's freaky. Weird. Maybe the pot was

laced? Maybe he's more exhausted than he thought. Don't sleep-deprived people sometimes hallucinate?

Or maybe he's dreaming. That's it. He's just dreaming.

He pinches his arm so hard he leaves a bruise—but on screen, Vaghar is still oddly blurred and shimmery, as if outlined with Vaseline or something.

The scene continues—the assault on the castle, the men at arms, the arrogant young prince, and the battle-worn older Queen That Never Was…

And the other prince, the one-eyed one whose name he can never remember because this damn show and the weird fuckin' names, man.

The shimmering outline of the dragon goes funny—or funnier.

And then…the mightiest dragon of them all turns to face the screen. It seems to be looking *at him*. Its huge face fills the screen. Burning yellow eyes regard him with cold, calculating hunger.

He scrambles up onto the couch and huddles against the back, arms around his knees. "What? I'm dreaming. I'm dreaming. Fuck—I *have* to be dreaming. Wake up, Johannes. Wake up!" He smacks his face hard, leaving a red mark on his cheek.

Yet, on the TV—or *in* the TV—Vaghar is still staring at him, rumbling in its chest like boulders rattling down a mountainside.

The man spies the remote on the coffee table—he lurches forward, topples off the couch, and hits the floor with a painful thump, scrabbling at the smooth surface of the table. Knocks over his beer. Finally, his hand finds the remote—he stabs the power button with his thumb frantically, twice, six times, a dozen times. The dragon remains on the TV, huge head weaving side to side, tilting, great eyes blinking, occasionally snarling or chirping curiously, hungrily.

Moving with ragged, clumsy haste, the man crawls on all fours across his living room and yanks the power cord out of the wall.

Vaghar opens his jaws and roars—showing the fiery orange volcano glow at the back of its throat.

"The fuck? The fuck! It's fucking *off*!" The man is panicking now.

He kicks the TV—the expensive, seventy-five-inch LED screen cracks and splinters but does not change the fact of Vaghar—now all nose and eyes and teeth.

Then, glass splinters again—spitting *outward*. Shards sprinkle the carpet and pepper Johannes' face. He yelps in shock, touching his face with his fingers—they come away smeared with blood.

He scrambles backward on his ass, scrabbling on all fours, kicking at the carpet and chanting, "Oh fuck oh fuck oh fuck oh fuck."

The TV cracks—the plastic frame detonates at all four corners and the pieces of the frame rocket across the room with such force that they bury into the drywall like thrown knives.

Glass explodes, and then a giant, reptilian nose emerges, followed by a long, serpentine neck. One wing with a claw-like limb smashes into the floor, and then another.

The man screams. He's frozen in place, on his back halfway into the kitchen.

Behind him, the green numerals on the stove read 3:34.

Back in the living room, the dragon fully emerges from the wreckage of the TV, much as the thing emerged from the gap in reality less than an hour before.

Ceiling trusses shatter and shingles soar away into the blizzard, and drywall dissolves into dust and fragments.

Trees are swept aside like matchsticks by the vicious, careless sweep of the tail. Wings—450 feet from wingtip to wingtip—claw at the air, and the dragon lifts a few feet, talons seeking purchase on solid ground. Five hundred feet from nose to tail, the dragon—no longer exactly Vaghar from the story on the screen, now something else, something new, something *real*—crouches in the forest, and its neck curls and coils and cranes, lowering until it comes nose to nose with the being—the man, Johannes.

He's beyond weeping, beyond begging. His mind is broken. Even if he would somehow survive this encounter, the essential sanity of the man would be gone. He would live in this moment for the rest of his miserable life.

It's almost a mercy, then, when the dragon rears back, opens its mammoth jaws, and spews liquid fire.

Johannes is incinerated, but his muscles function momentarily—propelling him to his feet in an instinct to run, to stop being on fire.

Crunch.

The dragon tastes mana, juicy and potent.

Perhaps later it will find more of the tasty little mana-ripe beings to snack on. For now, though, it decides it wants to explore its new world.

It likes it here, it decides.

It's no longer the amorphous thing from The Dreaming.

See, once a creature from The Dreaming comes here

and finds a suitable source of mana, it eats it. There are certain laws of the universe which are immutable, magic or not. One of them is that things which exist cannot simply vanish, no more than anything is created out of thin air.

When a human is conceived, it doesn't come from nothing—it's the combination and propagation of parental DNA. When a piece of paper is burned, the essential matter is not erased, it simply changes—becomes ash, smoke, and carbon, and returns to nature to become something else.

The same law applies—here in The Waking, at least. Whether those laws apply in The Dreaming is anyone's guess—immortal scientists haven't found a way to study The Dreaming yet.

But, when the Creature emerged into our world, into The Waking, it became subject to the laws of nature—to a degree. It is still, after all, a creature made of magic, so there is much which it can simply ignore. But when it ate the mana of the story within the TV, specifically the great, powerful, dense mana of the dragon, it *became* that thing. Its essential nature is the same—it is the same hungry beast perpetually on the hunt for mana, but now it has a new form, and that form, the dragon, is fully informed by the lore of the greater framework from which it came.

It *is* the dragon, but yet, at its core, for all the intelligence and vicious cunning of that beast, it is still the creature that emerged from The Dreaming. It cannot go back. It cannot revert.

It is now part of this world, for better or worse.

If you were to post a watch on the mountain peak, you might notice an occasional shimmer. Some are as big as the one that became the dragon—these will find powerful sources of mana and, in devouring them, become weird, wild, and powerful new things: orcs, dragons, griffins, phoenixes, goblins, quaint little forest huts whose inside is bigger than the outside…the scope of human imagination is the only limit to what these creatures can become once they find their way here. Others are smaller, a barracuda to the great white shark of the one we observed. These smaller ones will become smaller things: a talking dog, a semi-sentient tree, a water sprite, a dryad inhabiting an ancient oak, a wyvern, a wisp.

Our dragon will soar the vast mountain ranges, perching on jagged peaks and satisfying its dragon's belly with goats and horses and the occasional wayward hiker or skier. People will see it and even take videos. Its existence will be debated and argued over.

It was the first.

It will not be the last.

And they will change our world in big ways and small, in ways no one can predict.

CHAPTER 1

THERE ARE FAR TOO MANY RED pins in the map.

Occupying an entire wall of the library—the only space not taken up by shelves overstuffed with books—is a map of the world. Since I have magic, it is not a normal, mortal, static, boring map. Oh, no. This map is…shall we say…interactive. It began as a regular old flat map, a Mercator Projection, if you care about such things. I had it copied, blown up to be a square ten feet to the side, and fixed to the wall of the library.

But then I stared at it and realized it was lacking something. So, I glamoured it. Now, it's no longer that wildly inaccurate Mercator nonsense, where Greenland is way out of proportion and looks much closer to the US than it is in reality. Now, the continents are represented in accurate proportion and position in a way only magic will allow. And, best of all, I can use the same pinch-to-zoom methodology as an iPad to magnify a particular place, and I'll see a real-time view of it as if I'm watching from a satellite.

I'm still not entirely certain how I managed it—a lot of imagination and even more willpower, perhaps. I have been practicing my glamours, after all.

But, back to the pins. There are three colors: yellow, orange, and red. The yellow pins represent reports of minor skirmishes—these are so numerous as to defy enumeration and are scattered everywhere, clustered most thickly around cities, primarily first-world cities; why that is, we're still not sure. The orange pins represent significant engagements between mortals and immortals—more than a hundred people involved in total. These are not as numerous as the yellow, but still, too many.

The red pins are the worst. The scariest. They represent actual pitched battles between organized factions. There are pins in New York City, London, Hong Kong, Tokyo, Paris, Rio De Janeiro, Bogota, Sydney, Melbourne, Singapore, Moscow, Berlin…just about every major city.

The reports are coming in from mortal news media as well as messages sent by my newly-minted representatives: Hesperion, Sorren, and Raphael.

Hesperio's messages take the form of a small ball of glamour light, which, when touched, opens to form a weird, distorted, miniature sort of hologram version of Hesperion—very much, in fact, like in Star Wars—giving what amounts to a recorded message. Very cool, very sophisticated.

Sorren's messages arrive by snake. I don't love snakes, and these are six-foot-long, wrist-thick cobras. They coil around my ankles and wind up my legs and then my waist, and then perch on my shoulder with their tails wrapped around my wrist, and they hiss in my ear, and somehow I hear Sorren's sibilant-heavy voice in my brain.

Raphael sends his messages to me via a process he calls shadow-link. Apparently, vampires have a certain affinity for and power over shadows—not at all unusual. But this…this is a little odd. The first time it happened, I freaked out.

I was here, in the library, staring at the map and trying to decide what to do—my new hobby, it seems. And then, out of the corner of my eye, a shadow seemed to grow in the corner, down between the edge of a bookshelf and the wall and the floor. I took no real notice of it at first. But when it seemed to spread, like an ink stain on fine linen card stock, I turned to peer at it, watching it. And yes, it blossomed—grew larger and larger almost imperceptibly. I was alone in the library, so there was no one to ask. Before I could reach out to Alistair or anyone else for advice or help, the shadow seemed to reach out and swallow me whole.

I was surrounded by darkness—but it was definitively *not* The Dreaming. I knew that much.

"Hello?" I called.

A swath of shadows detached itself from the gloom and became a figure—arms, legs, a head.

"Who's there?" I said again, staring hard at the figure.

It came closer, and I grasped at the prana.

"Just me, Maeve," came a familiar voice, rich, smooth, and powerful: Raphael.

"What—what is this?" I asked.

"A very old and nearly forgotten means of communication between vampires. It's called a shadow-link. If the bond that allows you to speak mind-to-mind with your coven mates is a phone call, then consider this a text message. Sort of. I don't need to be bonded to you, but I do need to know you personally, directly. I could link to Alistair since I've had a conversation with him, but not Phineas since I've not spoken to him directly."

I turned in place—there's nothing to see. Even Raphael, when I focused on him once more, was barely more than a man-shaped shadow among shadows and a voice more in my mind than my ear.

"So…how do I do it? How do I shadow-link with you? Or whomever."

"My time is short, so I'll have to teach you another time. I'm in Brussels, Belgium—it's long been a sort of gathering place for vampires—there are more havens here in Brussels than anywhere else in the world. This is…not beside the point, but anecdotal to my point. Which is that things are heating up here. I'm in contact with the leading figures in the vampire community here, and they are looking to come out of the shadows once and for all, as is happening around the world. What worries me is the temperature here, politically. Belgium is a complicated place, Brussels in particular, and the politics, just among mortals, is treacherous at the moment. Add in the vampires and you have a powder keg. If the vampires here make a public gathering, and it feels at all volatile, things will get very bad, very fast. You'd have another red pin."

I absorbed this in silence for a moment. "Suggestions?" I asked.

A pause. "At the moment, there isn't much to *be* done, unfortunately, but wait and see what happens. I am speaking to the coven leaders daily, and I am urging a cautious, peaceful approach to de-cloaking."

"De-Cloaking?"

"Oh, well, yes. That's the term that seems to be in vogue. Meaning, revealing their existence—I mean, at this point, it's common knowledge that immortals exist—that cat's out of the bag. De-cloaking refers to individual revelation."

"I see. Well, thank you for the report, Raphael. Continue to monitor the situation and continue to advise a cautious, peaceful approach. There is no reason for violence, yet it seems to be how everyone is responding."

Raphael sighed. "Yes, well, such is humanity, I'm afraid. Fear begets violence, and the unknown and unfamiliar begets fear."

"I wish I could say you're wrong, Raphael."

Something cool and insubstantial brushed against the outside of my arm. "I must take my leave now. I have a meeting with the coven leaders shortly."

"Thank you for the update."

"Of course. I'll be in touch again soon."

"And you'll show me how to shadow-link."

"It would be my pleasure. Until the next time, my queen." His shadow bowed, and then the shadows receded as gradually as they had swallowed me, leaving me staring at the map once more, blinking in the abrupt light.

"Maeve?" A voice behind me brings me back to the present.

I turn away from the map to find Stirling behind me, a cell phone in his hand. "Hi. What's up?"

He smiles. "I must admit, I enjoy hearing you speak more informally, sometimes. Queen Maeve is hot, but just Maeve, the girl, is a different kind of hot." He rakes his eyes over me, top to bottom, twice. "How does it feel to be wearing jeans again?"

I laugh, smoothing my palms down the front of my thighs and back up my hips, and then shove my hands in my back pockets, shrugging. "Weird, honestly. I mean, it's nice to be clothed at all, let alone in my own clothing. But…once you get used to it, there's a certain freedom in nudity."

He sidles closer, resting a hand on my hip, nosing my throat. "And if I'm being honest, there is a selfish part of me that likes you naked all the time." He inhales my scent. "And the blood armor? Sexy as hell."

I feather my fingers in his hair, tipping my head back to offer him my throat. "Are you here to seduce me? Or did you have something to tell me?"

His tongue swipes up from the suprasternal notch at the base of my throat, his long, elegant fingers holding my head tipped back. "Can't it be both?"

I knot my fingers in his hair, gasping as venom sends a sudden burst of heat billowing through me. "I suppose it could…"

"In truth, I came to tell you something, and then I saw you, and scented you, and forgot the real reason." He drags cool, smooth fingers down my neck, over my white V-neck T-shirt, and under the hem to find my skin at the small of my back. "And now, I can't seem to remember what it was I came to tell you."

I laugh, but the laugh turns to a moan as his tongue blazes a hot line against my jugular. "Perhaps a quick drink will help refresh your memory," I breathe.

"Perhaps it will…"

His fangs pierce with a delicious pang of pain that quickly becomes ravaging arousal. He pulls at my vein, and the rush of blood sends heat pooling in my sex. I feel my knees go weak, and his arm circles my waist, and then his hand cups my ass, and he's holding me up as my legs give out entirely. I moan, eyes closing, giving myself over to the pleasure of the moment—a brief distraction from my responsibilities.

His fingers pop the button of my jeans and tug down the zipper, and then his now-warm hand presses against my flesh to dive behind the elastic of my underwear. I whimper as he finds my clit and now I'm soaring as he drinks from me and sends me hurtling over the cliff into immediate climax.

Heat clenches and boils in my belly and radiates to my extremities, and his circling, pressing, long middle finger curls down and drives into me. I clutch at his nape with rough affection, holding him to me as he drinks and drinks, and I yank at the clasp of his slacks, drive my hand in to find him hot and hard and eager—

"Maeve, did you hear about—oh. Um." Saige's soft, delicate voice brings me abruptly back to reality. "Sorry, sorry, I'll—I'll come back."

Stirling lets me find my feet, withdrawing his hand from my jeans and his fangs from my throat at the same time. I give his manhood a quick squeeze before I pull my hand away as well.

"No, no. It's okay. We were just…" I laugh, trailing off and starting over. "Getting a little carried away."

With his back still to Saige, Stirling turns void-black, need-hot eyes to mine, sliding his middle finger, slick with my essence, into his mouth.

Later, I promise him, mentally. *We'll finish this later.*

He zips and buttons my jeans, leaning in to lick the wound closed and licking again to clean away the dribbles of blood trickling down my throat.

He turns to face Saige—whose eyes widen, a blush staining the soft, clear brown of her cheeks; his slacks are still undone, and his desire is quite evident.

"Stirling," I mutter.

He pivots back to me and zips up, then turns back and gestures at Saige. "Your report, Saige?"

I hold up a finger. "Wait. Stirling. Yours, first, please?"

He produces a phone from his back pocket, unlocks it, and hands it to me; on the screen is a paused video—a news report.

I tap the screen, and the video plays—it's the same unhelmeted British reporter from Colin's video from two weeks ago.

"The situation here in Manhattan is becoming quite dire, local residents tell me." He half-turns to indicate an elderly mortal female. "This is Abigail Henderson, a long-time resident of Manhattan's fabled Upper West Side. The Mortal Federation has blocked access to every bridge and tunnel from Midtown north and has erected barricades at every intersection along 31st Street from the East River to the Hudson, blocking access to the northern districts. Abigail came downtown for shopping and hasn't been allowed back to her home since—the barricades are guarded by armed soldiers who claim to have orders not to allow anyone past the barricades."

He turns back to the camera. "The Army of the Once-Mortal Queen, now referred to by most simply as the A-O-M-Q, have no plans to take this demarcation sitting down, they say. This reporter has spoken to several leaders of the AOMQ over the last two weeks, and I can tell you one thing for certain—the Battle for Manhattan is far from over."

"Shit." I hand him the phone back. "Any word on the response from the government? Or anyone?"

He shrugs and shakes his head. "Nothing. Reports from D.C. are sporadic and either exaggerated or under-stated, and sometimes both at the same time. A single re-port will say the White House is empty and the president has abdicated while also saying Congress is standing united against the specter of civil war. All I know for sure is that the President hasn't been seen in public since she came out as immortal. Several cities, including New York, have declared states of emergency and have requested the ac-tivation of the National Guard, but so far, there's been no mobilization."

I glance past him at Saige. "What do you have for me, Saige?"

Standing barely 5'5", Saige is petite and quiet. She's freshly razored the sides of her scalp, with the thick black coils woven into dozens of tiny braids smaller than my pinky, which are then braided together to hang down to her nape. Gold hoop earrings ladder down both ears. Amber eyes give away her shifter heritage, blazing with internal light. Even though she's a small, quiet, still sort of woman, there's a potent energy to her that speaks of a feral, wild, predatory core of steel. Out of everyone in Caleb's pack, she's the one I've clicked with the most.

She's dressed in a loose white sundress, the hem fluttering just above the knee, a wide, supple leather belt around her waist just beneath her small, high, firm breasts—she's braless and barefoot. If she needs to shift, all she has to do is whip off the belt and shrug out of the dress.

She approaches, smiling hesitantly. "Um, yeah. I heard from Sorren just a few minutes ago. He says his report is sensitive enough that he doesn't trust it to a messenger. The boys are off hunting, and Sierra is off being Sierra somewhere, so, you know, here I am."

"For a two-hundred-year-old shifter, you seem uncomfortable with our sexuality, Saige. Does it bother you?"

She shrugs, toying with the buckle of her belt. "Not really—it doesn't *bother* me. I just…our pack is different. We're close—we've been together for a very, very long time. But we're more like siblings, which is unusual in the shifter world. So I'm not uncomfortable with nudity, but sexuality is a different story." She blushes harder than ever. "I've had lovers, of course, but…it's always been a very private thing for me. Seeing you guys so open with it is… it's weird." Her eyes widen. "Not *bad* weird, just…I'm just not used to it. We all keep our…relationships, such as they are…away from the pack."

"I understand, believe me," I say. "It takes some getting used to. I mean, I grew up mortal, so it's extra weird for me. But you do get used to it, especially with five virile, immortal males who can't seem to keep their hands to themselves," I say, grinning at Stirling.

"Don't act like you don't love every second of it," he murmurs.

"Oh, I do. But it has taken some getting used to."

Saige rubs her face with both hands and then lets out a quick, steadying breath. "Anyway. Sorren's report."

"Yes, please."

"He says the immortal community as a whole is watching what happens in Manhattan. He's been in contact with Raphael and Hesperion, and they say the same thing—fae, vampires, and shifters around the world, and especially in the US, are watching Manhattan. He called it a…shit, what was the word he used? Bellwether. I'm not entirely sure what that means."

"It means a predictor of something—an indicator of how things will go," Stirling says.

Saige nods, shrugs. "Makes sense, then, in that context. He said to tell you that if you're considering making a move, his advice would be to do it in Manhattan."

I blow out a breath and turn back to the map. "It is where things sort of blew up in the first place," I say, as much to myself as out loud. "So it does make a certain amount of sense to make a play there, especially if that's what everyone is watching."

Stirling and Saige wait, watching me think.

"Let's get everyone together. We have a decision to make." I glance at Saige. "When will the boys be back?"

Saige shrugs. "They're not far." Her eyes go vacant. "They're heading back."

"And Sierra?"

This gets me a wince from Saige. "She, um…she says she doesn't answer to you."

I sense that she's not being fully honest. "What did she really say, Saige?"

Saige gives me an apologetic look. "She said she doesn't take orders from a half-breed child."

I laugh, which makes Saige's eyebrows raise in surprise. "I bet that went over well with Caleb."

I can talk to Caleb, and I can feel the pack—if I focus, I could probably communicate with the pack. But, since we're all still getting to know each other, I've opted to stay out of pack business and off the pack channel, so to speak. I could have summoned them directly or via Caleb, but my gut says to play it cautious and not give orders to the pack. Sierra has continued her campaign of what feels like outright hatred, staying away not just from me but the whole pack and the estate in general, largely roaming the forest in wolf form, with occasional forays in her human body to the nearby town. No one says so in so many words, but my pack-sense tells me she's…distracting herself with mortal males.

"Maeve, Sierra doesn't mean—"

I cut her off. "She absolutely does, Saige. And that's okay. She's entitled to how she feels. She owes me nothing. It's not my fault I'm Caleb's mate any more than it's her fault she's not. If she wants to hate me, that's her choice. I'm not threatened by her anger, but nor will I waste my time and energy chasing her. She'll just have to figure things out for herself." I shrug. "It's pack business, and while I'm Caleb's bonded mate, I'm not a shifter. So it's not my business."

I reach out mentally to my coven. *Can I have everyone in the library? Stirling is here, and Saige. The others are on the way, minus Sierra, of course.*

I receive an overlapping wave of mental responses, wordless acknowledgments in the form of intimate caresses from their mind to mine.

A few minutes later, Caspian, Fin, and Alistair arrive together. One by one, they greet me in their own unique way: Alistair with a soft, cautious brush of his lips against mine and a much less cautious but very much private caress of his mind against mine in a way that has me squirming and pressing my thighs together; Fin with an exuberant kiss and an affectionate squeeze of my ass with both hands; and Caspian with a nuzzle of his nose to my throat with his hands framing my face.

As Caspian pulls away, I hear claws clicking on wood, and Caleb, Colin, Callahan, and Channing pad into the library in their wolf bodies. Caleb trots over to me, shifting between one step and another with a brief, blinding amber glow. He hooks an arm around my waist and claims my mouth in a quick, rough kiss—he's flushed from exertion, his golden skin coated in a sheen of sweat, panting slightly.

"Have a good run?" I ask.

He grins, but it doesn't entirely reach his eyes. "Mostly."

"You miss Connor."

He nods, his jaw tight. "We all do. A pack run isn't the same without him. I miss his humor."

Saige's eyes glimmer with unshed tears. "You didn't get a chance to know him, Maeve, but he was *so* funny. Even in his wolf, he was funny. Caleb, remember when he ate that mushroom? He tripped balls for three days."

Caleb's lips twitch. "He was communing with the Earth Mother," he said. The lip twitch turns to a full-fledged grin. "Which was funny because, you know, he was as Irish as the day is long and never otherwise went in for what he called hippie mumbo jumbo."

"Even though he spent six months running with the

Apache coyote shifter clan back in, what was it, '67?" Saige says.

Caleb frowns. "Oh, shit. I forgot about that. He did, didn't he? He said he wanted a change of scenery."

Saige laughs. "I thought for sure they'd kill him. Those coyotes don't much like outsiders."

"It couldn't have been Sixty-Seven, though," Caleb says. "It was before the Russian thing."

I frown. "Wait, are you guys talking about *Nineteen* Sixty-Seven or *Eighteen* Sixty-Seven?"

Caleb chuckles. "Eighteen, babe. The year the US acquired Alaska from Russia."

"Also, that bullshit treaty," Saige says, her delicate, demure voice now a savage snarl.

"Yeah, that too," Caleb says.

Saige blows out a breath. "But yeah, you're right. It had to have been before that. Sixty-Six? It was after the war, I know that."

Callahan shifts, becoming a towering, dark-haired hulk of a man. "Sixty-Six." He grabs a stack of bathrobes we've taken to keeping in the library for this exact reason and passes them out as Colin and Channing both shift as well.

Caleb nods. "It was Sixty-Six, you're right. We were in Wyoming at the time. Red Cloud told us we'd best make ourselves scarce. We barely hit the trail when shit blew up."

"Still think we should've stayed," Callahan growls. "Could'a made a difference."

Channing smacks his shoulder affectionately. "Wasn't our war, brother. You know that. We may have been wolves, but we were still white men."

Callahan just rumbles in his chest, a sound that says

he hears him but doesn't agree—the whole argument has the feel of something that's been debated back and forth for, well, centuries.

Caleb does something—some sort of wordless alpha pulse of authority—and everyone falls silent and turns their focus to me.

I press a kiss to his bare chest—he doesn't bother with the robe. "Thanks, honey." I sweep my gaze around the group. "I appreciate everyone gathering so swiftly. We have a decision to make."

It's still weird to me to wield such authority over people who are all literally hundreds of years older than me. It's a constant thorn in my side, this feeling of being an imposter, and I do what I always do: ignore it and forge on.

"Saige heard from Sorren while you were out on your run," I say. "He says the immortal world has their collective eyes on Manhattan—according to him, Raphael and Hesperion report the same from the vampire and fae communities they've been in contact with. It seems like the mortal world is paying just as close attention to Manhattan if the news reports I'm seeing are any indication."

I gesture at Stirling. "And additionally, Stirling just showed me a news report from Manhattan, which only confirms how bad the situation is there—the Mortal Federation has divided Manhattan into half, barricading all northbound intersections at 31st street across the entire island, as well as blocking off the bridges, so no one can get into or out of Manhattan. But the immortals, operating under the name the Army of the Once-mortal Queen, are planning to fight back and try to retake territory."

Alistair scrubs his jaw. "Not a good situation, is it? With the US government all but disintegrated, things around the country will only go from bad to worse. Supply lines will stop, and the country will just shut down. Food will get scarce, anarchy will prevail, and people will die. To say the situation could go apocalyptic is not much of an overstatement, and I'm British."

I frown at him. "What does your being British have to do with it?"

He snorts. "We Brits are famous for understating things. Stiff upper lip, keep calm and carry on, that sort of thing."

"So if *you're* saying it's nearly apocalyptic, then it's really, really bad, is your point."

"Quite." Since being in England, his accent has become more pronounced, not surprisingly.

It's hot.

"So the question becomes what we do about it?" Caspian says. "I mean, Maeve, you can't take full credit for this whole shitshow. What happened in Manhattan wasn't your fault. None of it is."

I sigh. "We could argue fault till we're all blue in the face, my love. It's pointless to worry about how much blame I do or don't deserve. I feel a responsibility to do *something*. People look to me. I can't say I want that responsibility—I certainly didn't ask for it. But it's mine, regardless. I have a certain amount of power that others don't, as well as visibility, you might call it. People are identifying me as the Once-Mortal Queen. Do I think I'm a great choice to be some sort of queen over all immortals? Not really. I'm not even twenty yet." I shrug, lifting my palms and then slapping them against my thighs. "But, here we are."

I scan the room, looking at each face, tilting my head

to see Caleb upside down. "Recommendations? You are all vastly older and wiser than me."

"Go to Manhattan," Caleb murmurs. "Kick ass."

I laugh. "Perhaps we elaborate on what kicking ass looks like?"

"Show the mortals they're fucking with the wrong bitch queen," Saige says.

"Damn right," Callahan says.

I sigh. "Okay, I appreciate that vote of confidence, really, truly I do. But we want to de-escalate. We don't want this to become a full-fledged civil war. We want people to learn how to accept each other and live together in peace and harmony."

"Good fuckin' luck with that." Surprisingly, this is from Colin, who tends to come across as fairly sweet and innocent, making it easy to forget he's a 200-year-old shifter.

"No shit," Fin says. "Far as I know, there's never been anything but a scared sort of tolerance of us—and that from a serious fuckin' distance."

I groan. "I *know,* okay? I mean, I wasn't there, obviously, but I get it. We just…if we can't change that now, then when?"

"We're on the knife's edge of global war," Channing says. "How do you get mortals to stop trying to kill us?"

"By refusing to let war be the only answer," I say.

Alistair winces. "Unfortunately, dearest one, we may not have a choice but to fight. The Mortal Federation isn't going to just go away because you don't want to kill anyone else. I've heard of this Nathaniel Bridgestone, and he's not the type to just give up. He likes war and seems to hate immortals."

I scan faces again. "So...what? Go to Manhattan and take on Bridgestone and the Mortal Federation?"

Caleb squeezes me with his powerful arms. "Unfortunately, love, yes. I think that's the only play right now. Your people need to see you're willing to fight for them against the people who want to kill them. They're not going to follow you into peace if they don't know they can follow you into war. Bridgestone, at least, has to be handled."

I thump my head against his chest. "Fuck. You're right, and I know it. I just don't like it." A sharp exhale. "So. Manhattan, here we come. All of us?"

Alistair frowns. "As much as I hate to say this, I think Fin, Stirling, and I should stay here. We have Sorren, Raphael, and Hesperion working on gathering the oldest and most powerful immortals, including the former members of the Tribunal. Once you sort out things in Manhattan, you're going to need to address a system of governance to replace the Tribunal, and this estate seems to me to be the best place for you to settle as your seat of power someday. So we need to get this place ready. There's a lot to do."

I leave Caleb's arms and go to Alistair, taking his hands. "I don't want to be apart from you." I look at Fin and Stirling. "Any of you."

Fin sidles up behind me and rests his chin on my shoulder. "We don't like it either, babe, but Alistair is right."

Initially, we'd been assuming the Tribunal base in the mountain would be the best place for me to use as my headquarters, but the more I thought about actually going back, the sicker the idea made me. I just couldn't bring myself to go there. So, we abandoned it. Hesperion organized a systematic dismantling of the place, stripping everything useful from it. Much of the equipment has been steadily arriving here ever since, along with personnel.

The estate is vast, encompassing several hundred acres. Aside from the main house, there are several large barns, several fieldhouses, servants' quarters, storage sheds, and a store near the village where goods grown on the farm are sold. In the centuries of Alistair's absence, the property has largely functioned as a museum and tourist attraction, with the main house allowing guided tours by Harry, and—for an eye-watering sum—overnight stays. The various fields are still in use, producing hay, wheat, and potatoes, as well as an apple orchard and a variety of vegetable gardens—the agricultural work has been carried out, in long historical tradition, by tenant farmers—albeit Alistair is far more generous with the terms than in times past. It is very nearly a self-sufficient community all on its own, and with a bit of financial investment and hard work, it can be made completely self-sufficient. Which is Alistair's goal now that we've decided the state will function as my…home. Seat of power? My court? Call it what you will, I love it here and really have no desire to leave.

Especially not without my mates.

I gather Stirling close and inhale the intermingled scents of my beloved mates—Caspian and Caleb hang back, allowing me this moment with the others.

"I love you," I whisper. "Are we sure there's no other choice? I just got you guys back."

Alistair lets out a sound that's part growl, part sigh. "I don't see a way. If we're to host your growing court, there's work to be done. You'll need communications, logistics, housing for staff…and all that requires, well, a lot. Harry is competent, but this needs my attention. And honestly, it's long overdue."

I growl in frustration. "I'll just have to wrap things quickly, then, so I can get back here to you as soon as possible."

The four-way embrace breaks apart, and I step back. "Well then, it's decided. I go to Manhattan to deal with General Bridgestone and the Mortal Federation."

Caspian takes my hand. "I'll be with you every step of the way."

Caleb takes the other. "As will I."

I look at the pack. "You choose your own path. I'll welcome you, should you choose to join us, but I won't compel you, and I'll ask Caleb not to, as well."

Saige is the first to speak. "Like I'm gonna hang out here without my alpha? Hell no." She grins at me. "Plus, you need a girlfriend."

Callahan steps forward. "We're with you, Maeve. Where our alpha goes, we go." He's silent a moment, his gargantuan frame still and coiled. "You possess our alpha's heart, and so you possess ours."

"Thank you, Callahan." I smile. "Perhaps one day I'll have your love and loyalty simply for my own sake and not just because I'm your alpha's mate. But I do understand such things are earned. I promise I'll do my best to earn them."

I sense Sierra before she enters the room—she trots in and sits on Callahan's feet in wolf form, staring at me with open malice.

"Sierra, thank you for coming. I'll let the others fill you in on what you missed, but the short version is we're going to New York. Your pack has chosen to come with me. It is not compulsory, not by me and not by Caleb. Alistair, Fin, and Stirling are staying here to oversee the work on the estate."

She continues to stare at me—more like a OnceBlood Wolf than a shifter.

I shake my head and shrug. "I have too much of importance to worry about to bother with your jealousy, Sierra. Do what you want." I glance at Caspian and Caleb. "We'll need to make travel arrangements."

"That could be difficult, actually," Colin says. "Flights are getting canceled everywhere, especially international ones."

Alistair produces a cell phone from his pocket. "I can make some calls. I know some people."

"That would be great. Thank you, Alistair." I head for the door. "I suppose I should pack, then."

All it takes is a look at each of them, and Fin and Stirling follow me.

Caspian brushes my mind with his, a silent caress to tell me he approves of me taking time with Fin and Stirling to connect before it's time to say goodbye. I'll need time with Alistair, too, but my sweet, buttoned-up professor prefers to have me alone. He doesn't mind sharing and even enjoys it on occasion, but for the most part, our physical relationship is a private one.

Fin and Stirling catch up to me as we head across the house to my private quarters.

Even though it's not even midday, shadows swirl around us as we enter my bedroom. Prana surges in my belly, and a gust of wind blows the door closed. The shadows boil, emerging from corners and crevices to swarm around us, bathing us in cool, cloaking darkness.

"Can you smell her?" Stirling's low, smooth voice comes from my left.

"Smells like desire," Fin says on my right.

"She needs us." Stirling's nose grazes my neck.

"She's wearing too many damned clothes." Fin's finger grazes between the hem of my shirt and the waist of my jeans.

My breath catches my throat. I love it when they do this—play with me as if I'm a helpless little mortal thing.

I hold my breath and tremble, waiting for their next move.

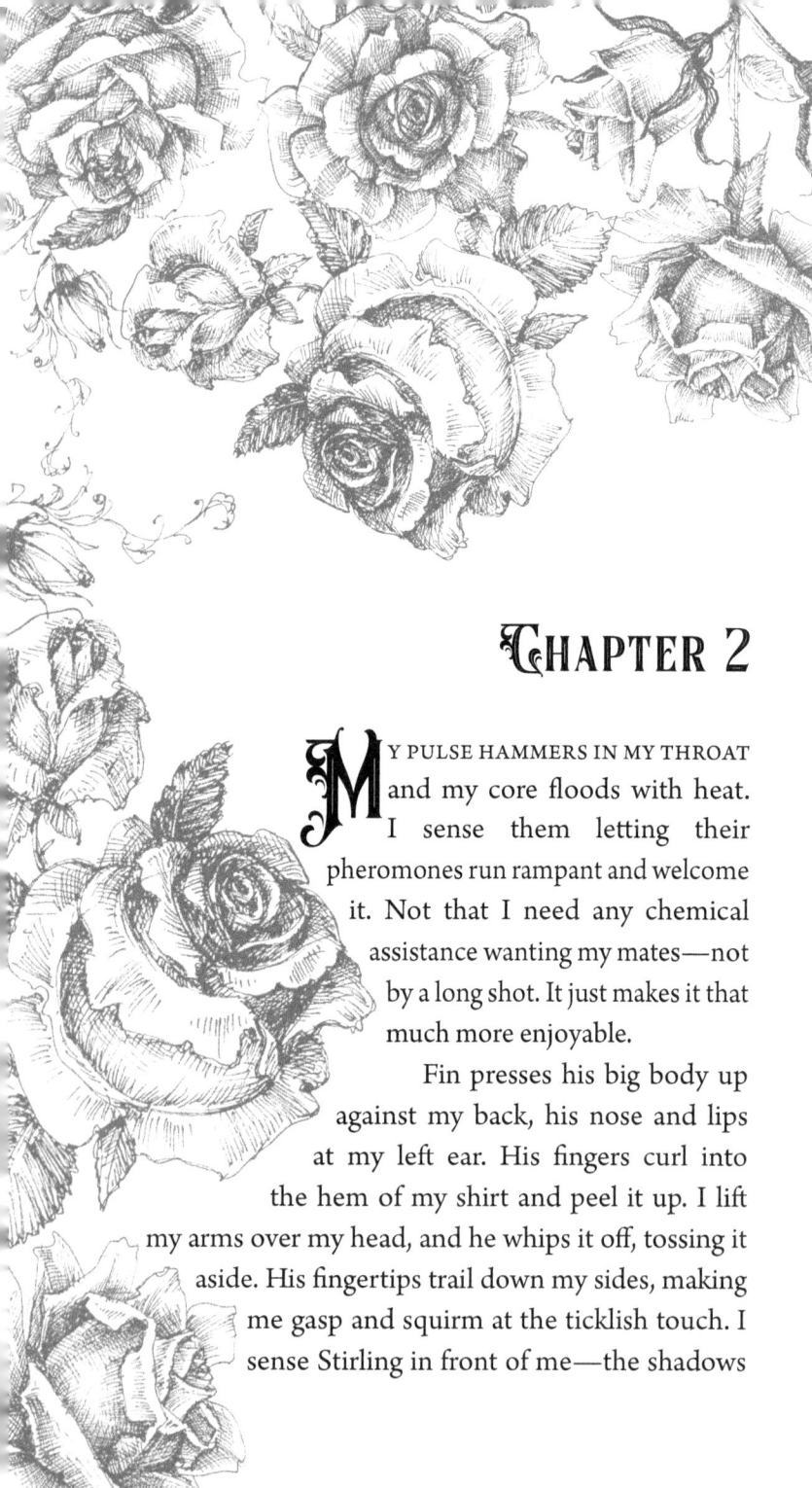

Chapter 2

MY PULSE HAMMERS IN MY THROAT and my core floods with heat. I sense them letting their pheromones run rampant and welcome it. Not that I need any chemical assistance wanting my mates—not by a long shot. It just makes it that much more enjoyable.

Fin presses his big body up against my back, his nose and lips at my left ear. His fingers curl into the hem of my shirt and peel it up. I lift my arms over my head, and he whips it off, tossing it aside. His fingertips trail down my sides, making me gasp and squirm at the ticklish touch. I sense Stirling in front of me—the shadows are so thick around us that we can't see anything at all. They're my shadows—a trick I discovered after trying to replicate Raphael's shadow-link: I can summon shadows, play with them, guide them, use them, and manipulate them.

Stirling's hand grasps my waist and his lips touch my navel, tongue dipping in, eliciting another shivering gasp, followed by a giggle. Fin works the clasp of my bra and the undergarment slides forward; Fin catches it and flings it away. Stirling unbuttons my jeans and drags the zipper down. I feather my fingers into his hair, scraping my fingertips against his scalp.

Fin's hands smooth around my sides to my belly and glide up to cup my breasts, lifting them and letting them drop heavily before pinching my nipples. I whimper as Stirling yanks my jeans down with sudden, rough aggression, turning them inside out as they catch at my knees. I jerk my foot out of one leg and then the other, and then Stirling is sliding my panties off, and I'm naked for them.

Stirling catches my left leg behind the knee, pulling it up so I'm forced to balance on one leg—Fin curls a strong hand around the back of my thigh, pinning my leg against my belly. And then, before I know what's happening, he has my other leg as well, and now I'm helpless in his arms, his broad hard chest at my back and his powerful, gentle hands holding me up with my thighs splayed open.

Stirling's mouth huffs a hot, blooded breath over my sex, and then his tongue laps against my seam. I whimper, launching my arms up over my head behind me and wrapping them around Fin's head and neck. Stirling's tongue dips inside me, probing deep, and his nose nudges my clit and his hands carve up over my belly to caress my tits.

"Make her scream," Fin murmurs.

"Then hold her still for me," Stirling growls. "She likes to fight."

I play along, fighting against Fin's hold. And the fun part is, we don't really have to worry about holding back. I can thrash and fight as hard as I want and I won't hurt him, and he can hold me as tight as he wants without worrying about the same. So, I really fight, trying to get away using purely physical strength.

But strength is still a function of biology and proportion, and Fin is far, far larger and stronger than me, so he holds me in place without effort.

There's no safe word because we don't need it. They feel me, mentally and emotionally. They know me, inside and out. If I stopped enjoying what they were doing, they'd probably know it before I did.

Stirling licks up my sex rhythmically, slowly, teasing, one hand pinching and rolling one nipple and then the other. I work my hips, seeking more pressure, more tongue, more heat—just *more*.

"Drink from her," Stirling breathes.

Fin kisses behind my ear, and then the side of my neck, and then his tongue laps against my jugular, and venom sears through me, sinking into my skin and soaking into my bloodstream, and then his fangs hit and pierce. At the same exact time, Stirling's tongue flits against my clit, making me thrash and jerk, and then his tongue weaves around the rim of my hood and pudendum, and then— fuck, fuck, god, his fangs sink into the soft plump flesh above my clit and his mouth fuses around me and he drinks from me and his tongue probes my clit between swallows.

I fight, then, bucking and thrashing as orgasmic

pleasure blasts through me. Stirling is busy—not just drinking, but touching, pinching, rolling my nipples until they ache and pulse, and his other hand traces under his chin, down my sex. He scoops a finger into my clenching channel, pulling wetness out. He smears it in a thick hot line down my taint to my asshole and then over the tight knot of muscle—pushes, gently.

"Oh, fuck, Stirling—god!" I cry out, already on the brink of climax.

Fin drinks from me, great, glutting gulps of my fae blood. I scrabble at his head, pull on his hair, tipping my head to the side to give him all the access to my throat he needs. I feel my body responding to him, feel my blood pulse hot and thick, rushing through my veins, eager to find his mouth—and Stirling's.

I groan low in my throat as Stirling's finger slips inside me, bit by bit—readying me for him. He sips my blood for a moment or two and then withdraws his fangs and licks the cuts closed, and then his tongue lashes my clit with hungry fury.

I come with a scream, thrashing wildly against Fin's implacable, loving hold. Stirling's knuckles bump against my bottom, and then he pulls it slowly outward, tongue flicking faster than ever. My orgasm bursts apart into a million individual quaking instants—Fin's lips against my skin, the aching pierce of his sharp fangs inside me, his hands keeping my thighs open for his brother, Stirling's finger driving into me and pulling out with gradually increasing speed, his other hand toying with my breasts, and his mouth worshiping my pussy, lips fused and tongue ravenous and wild.

I feel prana surge, and I give over to impulse—I

lighten my body. I feel Stirling and Fin do the same, and then I call upon the wind again, and we float up off the floor. The currents play beneath us in geysers and torrents, and we twist in mid-air. Fin rotates to his back and now we lay upon nothing, upon the air of my magic, and Stirling stretches out and the shadows boil and swirl, and there's only us, only the sensations of my mates around me, beneath me, loving me, worshiping me.

I fumble behind my back and find the fly of Fin's jeans. Rip at it. Shove the zipper down and plunge my hand behind his underwear to grip his hot hard cock. He growls against my throat as I caress him, forefinger and thumb sliding down to his root where I open my hands to cup his taut soft balls—this gets me a half-laughed groan as he drinks from me.

"Let me taste you," I whisper. "Please, Fin."

"Put us down," he answers, closing my skin where his fangs were.

I guide us over the bed and pull the wind back into me. We settle on the mattress, and I feel Fin pull away and undress. Stirling does the same, and I banish the shadows so I can see them. Naked, Fin kneels to one side, and Stirling, kicking away his jeans and underwear, rolls to his knees on the other.

I shuffle closer to them, cupping Stirling's face in one hand while pulling Fin in for a kiss with the other; Stirling palms my face.

"My turn," he growls and claims my mouth.

They playfully pretend to fight over me, then, pulling and pushing me back and forth, trading kisses until I'm breathless.

I pull back, and press my thumbs to both their lips, grinning. "*My* turn," I breathe.

I trail my hands down their chests and stomachs, over their hard, rippling abs, and clutch their cocks. Fin growls and Stirling groans as I caress their lengths. I stroke them in unison, licking Fin's nipple, and then Stirling's...Fin's navel, and then Stirling's...sinking to sit on my shins, I caress Stirling's length with a slow twist as I wrap my lips around Fin.

Stirling works my hair free of the braid and slides his fingers through my luminous white locks, sending it cascading around my shoulders before gathering it and wrapping it around his fist. He applies gentle, coaxing pressure, encouraging me to slide my lips down Fin's length. I pull up and work Fin's thick, throbbing root with my hand as I transfer my mouth to Stirling, swallowing around his pulsing length.

Back and forth, then, caressing one while taking the other in my mouth, teasing and teasing, only giving them each one slow, tongue-swirling slide of my lips around their hard, begging cocks.

When I taste the tang of pre-cum beading on their tips, I pull away, gaze up at them, licking my lips and pumping my hands around their cocks from root to glans.

"I think she's ready for us," Fin murmurs, caressing my cheek. "Are you ready, Maeve?"

"Maybe," I say, licking a bead of pre-cum from his tip. "Depends on what you're gonna give me."

He wraps a hand around my nape and pulls me closer to him, claiming my mouth and reaching between our bodies to hook a finger inside me, plunging it deep, smearing my essence against my clit before adding a second finger, and then a third. I moan into his mouth as he works me to the cusp of climax with his fingers, his tongue dancing with mine. Stirling kisses my shoulder between my shoulder blades and then shifts to kneel behind me and licks my throat on the opposite side of where Fin drank from me. The venom throws me over the edge and I come, squeezing hard around Fin's fucking fingers, and at the moment of climax Stirling smears his saliva against my asshole and presses a finger inside me, and I shatter even harder, screaming into Fin's mouth as I lose myself in wild rapture.

Shaking and shuddering, I topple down the other side of orgasm, caressing Fin's hot length. He pushes the fat soft head of his cock to my entrance.

"Want it?" he whispers into my whimper.

"Mmm-hmm!" is all I can manage, panting and gasping.

"How about this?" Stirling whispers in my ear. I hear a crack of a plastic lid and hear his fist sliding slick around his length, and then feel warm wetness coat my rear entrance, and then Stirling presses against me.

"Ohhhhhhhh fuck—fuck, yes. Yes. Please yes," I say, breathes with anticipation.

Fin moves to his back and brings me with him to kneel over him, knees and shins beside his hips; Stirling kneels tall behind me, hands caressing my back, my sides, my hips, my ass cheeks. I groan as Fin surges deep in a quick, powerful thrust—he bottoms out inside me, his hands cupping my heavy, aching, swaying breasts. Stirling, meanwhile, eases in with delicate gentility, gripping my hips. I whine high in my throat as Stirling fills me, and then his hips clap lightly against my ass and I can barely breathe, hyperventilating at the wild fullness of having them both inside me.

"Oh fuck, my loves," I breathe. "So good—you feel so good."

Stirling remains still, buried deep inside my ass, and Fin slowly pulls almost out, fluttering a few short, teasing strokes before driving in once more. I lean over him, crushing my breasts against the hard anvil of his chest, pushing my hips high and back—begging silently for more.

Fin carves his hands down my sides to grip my ass cheeks and holds me apart so Stirling can slide deeper. "She wants more, brother," he growls. "She needs you to fuck her."

"Is that true, my mate?" Stirling whispers.

"Y-yes," I stammer, aching with need. "Please."

"Please, what, my love? Tell me what you need."

"You," I answer, pushing back into him. "Fuck me. Fuck my asshole, Stirling. I need it."

He squirts more lube onto us where we're joined, and then slides almost out, pausing, and then driving in while Fin pulls out.

I cry out as they move, my fingers knotting in the sheet with desperate strength, so overwhelmed that all I can do is breathe and take it. Stirling slides home while Fin hesitates with just his tip nuzzled between my nether lips, and then Stirling pulls out, and now I'm almost empty and aching for my mates to fill me again. Before I can beg, they give me what I need—both of them thrusting deep in synch. I scream, pressing my torso lower and pushing back into them. I dig my clawed fingers into Fin's chest, dragging my lips against his sternum.

"Again," I whimper. "Please. Again. Don't stop, my loves. Please don't stop."

Moving in perfect unison, they draw back and this

time plunge in without pause, and the fullness chokes my breath and makes my pulse hammer. They bottom out inside me with a slap of flesh against flesh. Stirling braces his hands on my back at the top of my ass while Fin pulls at my hips, and now they find a new rhythm—alternating once more.

Fuck, I don't know which I like better.

"You're gonna come for us, aren't you?" Fin says.

"You're gonna come hard," Stirling orders.

"Together," I gasp. "All of us together."

But I can't help it. I can't stop it. The climax builds inside me with volcanic force, and I'm powerless to hold it back. I press my mouth to Fin's pec and envenomate him and sink my fangs into his muscle, tasting his blood as it floods my mouth in a slow hot sweet seep. I cry out and feel myself clenching and spasming as my orgasm builds and builds, and Fin and Stirling are losing themselves to their own individual releases, fucking me in alternation, and it's too much, so beautifully too much and I can't take it and I love it and I can't breathe can't scream can't move can only pull at Fin's blood and whimper between swallows.

Fin draws his knees up and levers into me harder than ever, driving and thrusting with mad abandon, grunting my name in a soft, ragged chant. Stirling drapes over me, gripping my hair and one shoulder for leverage as he slaps into me, his mouth stuttering at my spine, pressing slow desperate kisses as he reaches his release.

Mine is the trigger for theirs. I feel it. I lose myself to it, throw myself willingly over the edge, driving my ass backward to get more of them, to take them harder, deeper. Screaming, I come. I feel it explode in my core, billowing waves of heat that tingle through my fingers and toes and scalp, stars bursting behind my eyes. I feel myself clamp hard around them, and they grunt and groan at the taut pulsing tightness of me around their surging cocks.

Fin comes with a shout, throwing his head back and arching up off the bed, thrusting into me with rough desperation. Stirling is next, pushing me apart and leaning backward to push as deep as he can go, releasing while buried deep, growling as he comes, pushing deeper and deeper as he explodes inside me.

Through it all, my orgasm continues, each of their releases triggering me to come harder, or come again, until I'm fraught with a climax so intense I weep from it, sobbing as they slow their thrusts.

When we've all recovered, Stirling very slowly eases out of me, and then Fin. Stirling scoops me up in his arms and carries me to the bathing chamber. There, they wash me, soaping my curves, massaging my muscles, and cleaning away the spill of their seed.

Once we're clean, Fin wraps me in an oversized bath sheet and carries me back to bed. I lay on my back and pull them both close, cradling them to my breast, one on each side, and together we drowse in the midday warmth.

I must have dozed off because I wake to cold marble wrapping around me, Alistair's familiar pipe tobacco and coppery blood scent washing over me.

I blink awake, finding myself cradled in his arms, the bath sheet discarded. His fingers trace from jaw to temple and over my ear, nudging my hair away from my face. His eyes, laced with delicate swallowing black, fix on mine.

"Hello, love." His voice is quiet. "Okay?"

I nuzzle closer, slipping my thigh between his. "More than okay. I'm wonderful, especially now that you're here."

"It was good? With Fin and Stirling?"

I grin up at him. "It was incredible." I sift my fingers through his hair. "How long was I asleep?"

"An hour or so." He runs a finger over the lines of white-and-gold ink inscribed on my skin, following them as they arc over my shoulders and down my arms, back up to my chest, in concentric spirals around my breasts. "I've made flight arrangements."

"Mmmmm." I close my eyes and focus on the icy burn of his unblooded touch. "When and where?"

"A friend has a private jet that will fit you all. You leave at midnight from an airfield outside Manchester." He cups a breast, nuzzles it with his nose and lips. "You'll fly into Atlanta—that's the closest I could get you. Every other airport is closed, and I have a feeling Atlanta will close soon."

"Atlanta? Guess we'll have to find a car and road trip north."

"Mmmm. Sorry. I know it's not ideal, but international travel, by commercial air at least, is going to be difficult, if not impossible in the weeks and months to come."

"Thank you for arranging it, Alistair."

"Mmmm," he hums again, his mouth now otherwise occupied by kissing circles around my nipple. "Anything for you."

"Anything?" I whisper.

"Anything."

I roll to my back and bring him over me. "Then make love to me, Alistair."

He gazes down at me with void-black eyes exuding his love. "I really wish you didn't have to leave," he murmurs.

"Me too." I caress his lips and then prick my thumb

on his fang and slide it into his mouth. "How will you feed while I'm gone?"

We have a stock of pouches laid up, he answers mentally. *London isn't far, also. The chaos will make hunting easy.*

He captures my wrist and licks the pad of my thumb. His hand scoops under my head and his tongue slides over my pulse—the bubbling heat of his venom makes my pulse race and my sex gush with wet heat.

He's cold and unblooded, a frigid block of ice burning against my hot, flushed skin—a delicious contrast. I sift my fingers through his hair again and press him to my throat—with exquisite delicacy, he punctures my flesh and slides his fangs into my vein, and his fingers find my sex. I feel the first flush of warmth stain his stone-slick skin with the initial taste of my blood.

"Drink your fill of me, my love," I breathe, cradling him to me.

He growls in pleasure between swallows, an animal sound that sends ripples of arousal through me. Marble slowly softens to flesh, and I reach between us and find his manhood, the last part of him to receive the flush of blood. It warms under my hand, and I caress him, feeling him hardening. Within seconds, he's fully erect.

I guide him to me, nestle him between my lips—he sinks into me without hesitation, and we both groan in unison. I cup his ass in my hands and pull at him, then wrap my thighs around his hips and hook my heels behind his back.

"Love me, Alistair," I whisper. "Give me something to dream of while we're apart."

Now drawing slow, careful sips of my blood, he thrusts

into me. I gasp as he fills me, pulling at my blood in time with his thrusts.

Maeve, my love. You are my world. You know that, don't you?

I feel blood tears prickle at his words. "I do, my beloved. I know. And you're mine."

He loves me, then, with slow, delicate passion, taking my blood as he takes my body, groaning raggedly as if each sip and each thrust is a gift.

I bury my face in his throat and press my lips to his pulse, arms and legs wrapped around him, pulling him with each thrust, my hips rising to meet his.

My climax rises slowly, building by degrees. Time loses meaning. Alistair withdraws his fangs and closes the wound, and then his mouth finds mine, hot and ripe with copper; he kisses me deeply, and I feel him reaching his release. My own rises to meet his—he drives with increasing speed into me as he closes in on his climax, and I gasp in his ear and my fingers claw into his back as mine surges and pulses to a breathtaking crescendo.

"Maeve!" Alistair says, his voice shaking and breathless.

"God, Alistair!" I cry in answer.

When we come, it's in soul-shattering unison, his breathless moans matching my whimpering wails.

The stars shudder, and my soul winds around his, and I feel his mind tangle with mine, showing me the depths of his love for me with such direct, open vulnerability that I can only weep and show him my own, opening my mind to his.

I feel a connection to him that nearly eclipses the day we bloodmated—even without tasting his blood, his memories swirl through me—a childhood on these very grounds, chasing hounds and riding horses, a stern, cold, hard father and a distant, aloof mother, mortal servant men and women filling the halls with life and busyness—servants who doubled as playthings for his parents; Paris in a bygone age of carriages and powdered wigs, London by night, narrow streets lit by torches and fearful mortals scurrying through shadows, and Boston echoing with the tromp of redcoat boots; a beautiful blonde mortal woman with admiring blue eyes; that same blond woman curled in bed, listless with trauma; later, begging him for a child, consequences be damned; Libby swollen with child, skin pale and drawn tight to sharp cheekbones; a screaming, bloody birth; desperate months as she clung to life, fading into death as the baby grows; a mound of brown soil, a wooden cross, and wailing child on the hip of a vampire nursemaid; a towheaded young boy scampering through the forest, growing into a slender, thoughtful young man; a note from a friend held in trembling fingers, dropped to the floor as grief overwhelms; a much younger Stirling, and then Phineas, and then a vast, dim, wild forest and Caspian, naked, dirty, and feral...

Memory after memory flows through me, and I realize he's actively sharing them with me, giving me himself, leaving no secret untold.

Slowly, the flashflood of memory subsides, and once more it's just Alistair and me cocooned in silence, breathing in ragged gasps.

He gives me his weight, and I hold him.

"Thank you for that, Alistair," I whisper, toying with the slightly too-long hair at the back of his neck. "I love you so much."

"You deserve all of me," he answers. "Hearing me tell it is one thing, but seeing it for yourself…"

"It's a gift, Alistair. Your memories are a precious gift."

He rolls to his side next to me. "You're the gift. I don't know what I did to deserve you, but I shall not argue with the Fates."

"Nor shall I." A soft, contented silence follows. I break it with a question. "The Fates…are they real? Or are they like the old Greek gods, something people believe in and swear by?"

He shrugs and shakes his head. "Depends on who you ask. I've always believed them to be…myths based on some distant reality, like King Arthur. Are there real Fates out there? Maybe. I've never met them, and I've never heard of anyone who has, nor read any source even suggesting they're real figures. Are the Fates myth or legend? As far as I know, no one knows."

"This time with you means more than I can say, Alistair. I'll miss you."

"We'll be in touch via the bloodlink, of course," he murmurs, nuzzling the underside of my jaw. "But it won't be the same, will it?"

"Not even a little bit."

"Damned responsibilities, eh?"

"Damned responsibilities indeed."

We lapse into silence for a long time. Eventually, we make love again, this time even more slowly—there's no blood drinking or memory sharing. It's just love, shared and made, a union of heart, mind, and body.

When we're done, he sighs. "Best begin preparing for your journey, Maeve."

I growl in irritation. "I don't want to." I nuzzle closer. "I want to stay here, just like this, with you."

He laughs. "I know. Me too. But duty calls."

"Duty can go fuck itself."

Another laugh. "Maeve."

I groan. "Fine. But I don't have to like it."

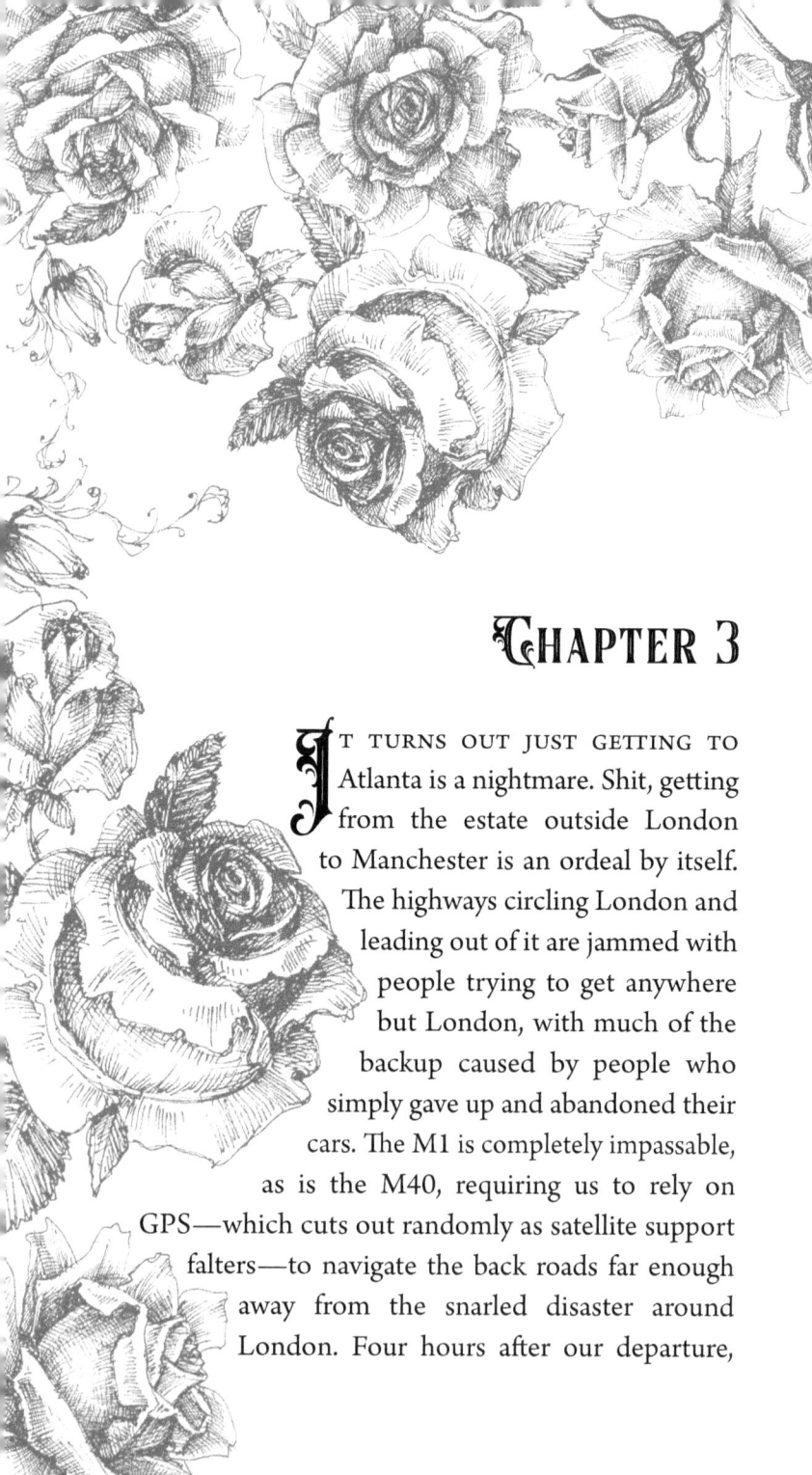

Chapter 3

IT TURNS OUT JUST GETTING TO Atlanta is a nightmare. Shit, getting from the estate outside London to Manchester is an ordeal by itself. The highways circling London and leading out of it are jammed with people trying to get anywhere but London, with much of the backup caused by people who simply gave up and abandoned their cars. The M1 is completely impassable, as is the M40, requiring us to rely on GPS—which cuts out randomly as satellite support falters—to navigate the back roads far enough away from the snarled disaster around London. Four hours after our departure, we finally can get on the M40 near Birmingham—a distance we could have covered in half that time under normal circumstances.

We make it to the airfield outside Manchester after seven hours of travel—fortunately, Alistair had foreseen this and we'd left ourselves eight hours for the trip, fully double what it should have been.

Along the way across the English countryside, we saw plenty of evidence of the troubles—smoke rising from villages and towns in the distance, a burned-out hulk of a semi—or as they call them here, lorry—overturned and hanging halfway off an overpass; groups of mortals trudge along the shoulder of the M40 here and there, carrying meager belongings on their back and in their arms, watching us pass with fearful suspicion. We pass a lone fae male near Birmingham, carrying nothing but a backpack, his hair hacked off, bruises staining his face, and his arm in a sling. When we slow to talk to him, he just stares at us without a word until we carry onward with a shrug.

Manchester burns in the distance—explosions and white-gold flares of magic light up the night sky.

The jet idles noisily on the single runway, a mobile staircase snugged up to the doorway. There's no one waiting, so we leave the vehicles parked near the hangar and board the jet. The pilot is a vampire, unblooded, about Alistair's age, a clean-cut male with short brown hair and a neat goatee, his eyes voided, wearing jeans and a T-shirt with a ballcap. He watches us board from the doorway to the cockpit, and then once we're all seated, he closes and secures the door.

"My name is Absalom," he says in a clipped, precise

British accent. "Please find a seat, buckle in, and prepare for takeoff."

With that, he closes the cockpit door and locks it, and then we hear the engines whine as they spool up.

The flight across the Atlantic is uneventful and long—the pack takes over the TV, playing an action trilogy back to back to back, chattering, laughing, and teasing each other. Even Sierra, as long as she doesn't accidentally look at me, engages with her pack with an easy, familial humor that surprises me; she's funny in a biting, sarcastic, acerbic way.

Caleb sits across from me in a rear-facing seat with my feet on his lap, idly massaging my feet and staring into space as if lost in thought—beside me, Caspian reads a thick fantasy novel while I practice simple conjurations.

The trouble starts when we get close to Atlanta. The pilot pops open the door and sticks his head out. "We've been ordered into a holding pattern," he tells us. "Hang tight; it could be a long wait."

A long wait indeed—we circle for two hours before they clear us for landing, and then we sit on the runway for another two. We can see a line of jets ahead of us and stacking up behind us, wing and taillights flashing. Callahan snarls something about getting out and walking.

And then the real fun begins. Once we're finally allowed to disembark, we carry our luggage—none of us packed more than a duffel bag—into the concourse and join the horde of travelers. The airport is utter mayhem. Gate agents have given up—the lines at every gate are so long one is indistinguishable from the next. Every seat is taken, with more people sleeping on the floor, backs against walls and pillars and family members.

A few feet away, between two gates, a couple of mortal males start shoving and shouting—I hear something about an outlet—and it quickly turns into a fistfight. No one stops it—not even the terrified-looking security guard less than fifty feet away, armed with a taser and pepper spray.

"Attention," a voice announces from overhead, "all outbound flights have been canceled. Gate agents have no additional information at this time. All flights, international and domestic, have been grounded. Repeat, all outbound flights have been canceled…"

Caspian glances at me. "Getting back to England could be tricky."

I scan the chaos. "Getting out of this airport could be tricky. Getting to New York could be tricky. Getting to England?" I shake my head. "There's gonna be a rush at the car rental counter. We should hustle and see if we can get one."

"One?" Caleb barks a laugh. "Good luck fitting all of us in one car, unless they have a church van."

We reach the rental counter, but judging by the mayhem, we're too late. There are two clerks behind the counter and at least sixty people in what could be termed lines but is more like an angry conglomeration.

"I'm sorry, sir," one of the clerks says to the man at the counter. "But we're sold out. We have nothing. No cars."

There's a sign made on MS Word, printed out, and taped to a piece of cardboard, stating "NO CARS AVAILABLE."

"Then why is the counter open?" The customer demands.

The clerk, a thin, reedy, acne-pocked teenager, throws

up his hands. "I don't fuckin' know, man. I'd LOVE to go home. All I know is we ran out of cars an hour ago."

"My brother is dying," the customer says. "This is my last chance to see him before he goes. You have to have something! Anything! I'll take a goddamn bicycle."

The clerk winces. "I'm sorry, man. I feel for you. I just can't give you what I don't have."

Caleb, beside me, leans forward, his nose twitching. "He's a shifter," he murmurs under his breath. "This could get messy in a second."

"FUCK!" The man—huge, at least six-six, with mountains of muscle under a thick layer of padding, shaggy black hair, and a bushy beard—grips the edge of the counter in his massive hands.

The counter cracks under his grip and his huge shoulders heave with ragged, straining breaths.

"FIND ME…A FUCKING…*CAR*!" he bellows so loudly that the cardboard sign wobbles and tips over.

The clerk, a mortal barely out of childhood, quails, paling, and staggers backward. "The fuck? Fuck! He's—he's—he's a fucking werewolf!"

The shifter's head snaps up. "What did you just fucking call me?"

"Oh, fuck." Callahan sighs. "Little mortal dude is dog meat."

The enormous shifter growls, a rattling sound that makes the floor shake. Around us, mortals press away from the distraught male. Fur sprouts on his neck and his shoulders bulge and swell. His jeans split down the thighs with an audible rip, and his shirt shreds into tattered ribbons of cotton. Amber light flares, momentarily blinding, and then an eight-foot-tall grizzly bear stands towering over the counter, claws like sabers, roaring in fury.

"Caleb." I gesture at the bear. "Go do your Alpha Prime thing."

Caleb glances to the side—tracking the cell phones recording what's happening. "Fuck." He steps forward into the open space around the berserk, roaring, slavering grizzly. "HEY!"

The bear pivots, muscle and fur shaking as he lands on all fours and stomps toward Caleb, growling and rumbling with each step.

"*HALT.*" Caleb's voice snaps, magically loud and quivering with authority.

Everyone, mortal and immortal, freezes in place. I glance left and see the mortals can't even blink.

The bear shuffles to a halt, its giant snout a foot away from Caleb. He snuffles in confusion and then makes a growling sound in his chest.

"Shift back." Caleb's voice is calm and quiet, conversational. "You don't want to do this, friend. Not here, not now."

"RRRrrrfffff." He sounds irritated in an ursine way; he plops down on his haunches as if the wind has gone out of his sails.

"Shift back." Caleb reaches out a hand and rests it on the bear's head. "You won't get where you need to go like this."

With a great snarling whuff of annoyance, the enormous bear seems to shrink—although not by much. Amber light blazes and the man is left crouching, naked, in the center of the open space.

"Callahan, give him something to put on," Caleb orders.

Callahan drops his duffel bag, unzips it, rifles through it for a minute, and then tosses the shifter a pair of big, baggy gym shorts. The shifter catches them, glancing around the room as if just now realizing how much an audience he has: there's an additional crowd beyond the doors, recording with cell phones raised overhead.

"Shifters, circle up." Caleb steps forward, and immediately, all the rest follow suit, circling around the shifter to provide privacy so he can put on the shorts.

When he's dressed, nominally at least, they step back. The shifter is visibly shaken up.

He turns to the clerk. "I apologize for my behavior. You did nothing wrong. Please forgive me, my friend."

The teenage clerk seems taken aback. "I…I…yeah, no—no problem. Forgiven. I wish I could help you, I just…I can't."

Turning back to Caleb, he drops to one knee, head bowed. "My thanks, Alpha. I wish your intervention had not been necessary. I am not myself, with my mother's death weighing so heavily on me."

Caleb claps the man on the shoulder. "We've all been there, my friend. Having a brother is rare in our world. You should be with him. What's your name?"

He rises to his feet. "Nico." NEE-co. "He's my half-brother, sort of. My father sired me on a female servant before the treaty, and my mother—my father's mate—bore my brother by a male stablehand, also before the treaty. We were raised as brothers."

"How does he come to be dying?" Channing asks. "I've not heard of a shifter taking ill."

Nico shakes his head. "Not ill. Wounded fighting the Mortal Federation in New York. Too wounded to survive."

I glance at Caleb, and we don't need to even speak mentally to come to an agreement. "We're bound for New York ourselves, Nico," I say. "Please, join us."

Nico frowns at me as if seeing me for the first time or as if weirded out by being addressed by a non-shifter. "Who are you?"

I smile at him. "My name is Maeve."

Saige steps toward him. "She is Maeve Sparrow, the WorldBreaker and the Once-Mortal Queen. We go to New York to address the Mortal Federation and bring an end to the hostilities."

Whispers and murmurs rise at her words. Part of me wishes she hadn't announced me here, like this, in this context.

"Thank you, Saige." I move toward Nico and place my hand on his forearm. "She speaks truly, Nico. And we would be honored to have you with us."

He stares down at me with an inscrutable expression. "They shot him. He wasn't shifted. He wasn't doing any-thing—he was just there. It was a protest."

"I know. But if you come with us, do not think this is a mission of revenge. I will avoid open warfare if at all possible."

"They say the immortals there are calling themselves the Army of the Once-Mortal Queen."

I nod. "So they say. They fight in my name, but I've not commissioned them to do so. That's the other reason I'm headed there—to find out who is organizing armies in my name."

He glances at Caleb, then at me. "You command an Alpha Prime?"

I shake my head. "Not command, no. He is my true, bonded mate." I rest a hand on Caspian's shoulder. "As is he."

Nico's eyes widen. "A shifter bonded to a fae?"

I grin. "Haven't you heard? I'm no fae, Nico. I'm a vaer—half vampire, half-fae. And yes, I'm bonded to an Alpha Prime." I gesture with a sweep of my hand at the pack. "And this is his pack."

"Not your pack?"

I shake my head and shrug. "I'm not a shifter. I can feel them through my bond with Caleb, but no. They're not *my* pack—they're his."

"Yet they follow you?"

Saige answers. "We do follow her—not because our Alpha commands it, but because we choose to. She fought the Tribunal itself to rescue us. She saved our Alpha, she saved us, and I believe she will save our world. You can do no better than to follow her."

Conjure the mark, Caleb says mentally.

I conjure the mark of fealty with a flourish. Saige is the first to place her palm on the glowing golden-white ball. "I swear my eternal fealty to you, Maeve; I pledge my life and death in willing service to your cause and your court."

I hold her eyes. "Thank you, Saige." I swallow hard. "And you're right—I do need a girlfriend. I'm happy it's you."

She blinks a few times and then slams into me, her strong smooth arms wrapping around my neck. After a moment, she lets go and backs up, smiling.

Colin repeats Saige's vow as he takes my mark. One by one, the rest follow suit—Channing, Callahan, and Colin.

Sierra is last, standing slightly apart. She's dressed in skintight black leggings with a black tunic belted at the waist, the hem hanging just below her backside, and calf-height, well-worn combat boots. Her waist-length raven-black hair has been intricately braided into a crown around the top of her head and then falling loose and glossy down her back—Saige's handiwork, I'd guess.

She's a stunning, intimidating woman, I admit. Powerfully built, immensely strong, curvy, and breathtakingly beautiful, she radiates feminine lethality. Right now, she's glaring at me with a hard, cold expression that outright dares me to fuck with her.

I face her with the mark hovering above my right hand. I smile. "The mark is voluntary, Sierra. I offer it to you even though I know what you will answer."

She uncrosses her arms and flips me off with both hands. "Fuck your mark and fuck you." She spits at my feet and slings her bag over her shoulder with a hard look at Caleb. "Compel me, Alpha. I fucking dare you."

Caleb only stares at her with sadness in his eyes. "Your jealousy is eating your soul, Sierra. You weaken the pack with your anger." He strides over to her, and touches the index and middle finger of his right hand to her forehead. "I free you of your bond to this pack, Sierra Mackenzie Hendricks. I command you no more. Choose your own path."

The entire pack gasps audibly as one.

Sierra's eyes widen, her mouth flaps open and closed, and then tears spurt from her eyes and trickle down her cheeks. "Caleb—no. No."

I look around and realize this entire exchange is being live streamed—I throw up my hands to waist high with a flourish, casting a glamour that envelops us in a dome of light, shielding us, giving us privacy.

Caleb holds her gaze. "I have known of your feelings for decades, Sierra. I have done nothing to encourage them, hoping you would understand." He softens, steps closer, and cups her biceps in his hands. "You are a good woman, a powerful, skilled shifter, and an invaluable member of our pack, Sierra. I haven't broken the bond…yet. You have six months to choose your path—get over your jealousy and anger and rejoin the pack, or cling to your feelings and reject the bond." Sierra opens her mouth to speak, but Caleb cuts over her, silencing her without magic or compulsion. "I love you, Sierra—as a friend, as a sister, and as my pack-mate. But you *will not* disrespect my mate again. *Ever*. She has done nothing to you. She has been endlessly understanding and forgiving—far beyond what your behavior warrants."

"Caleb—Alpha, please." She sounds…broken.

"Figure your shit out, Sierra. Six months." He looks around, seeing the shield I cast. "Even now she considers your feelings, after you cursed her and spat at her. You're better than this."

He nods at me, and I lower the dome. The crowd remains, watching, rapt. I wonder if the glamour shielded sound as well as sight—I didn't specify, so I don't know.

Caleb scans the crowd. "*DISPERSE*." The word is laced with authority none can ignore, certainly not mortals. Within seconds, we're alone at the rental counter.

He shoulders his bag. "We'll have to walk for now. Pack—move out."

Callahan, Channing, Colin, and Saige follow him away from the counter and toward the exit. Caspian eyes me—I nod at him, and he follows them. Caleb goes with him, as does Nico.

That leaves me alone with Sierra. She stares at me, tears in her eyes. She looks lost, stunned.

"You've taken everything from me," she whispers. "Before you came along, at least I had hope, even though I knew he'd never love me back. Now, not only do I not have that, I don't even have my pack."

I sigh. "I'm not one of the Fates, Sierra. I didn't choose to be his mate. I had no more choice in that than you had in *not* being his mate. I'm truly, truly sorry."

Her lip quivers. "Why are you so fucking *nice* all the goddamn time?"

"I never had friends growing up. It was just me and my mom, and because she was hunted by the Tribunal we moved every few months. Having a coven, having mates… and now having a pack around me? It's a gift, Sierra." I hold her eyes. "I'll tell you a secret: I have no fucking clue what I'm doing. I'm just…I'm trying to be a good person. I'm trying to make the best decisions I can with what's in front of me. All of this just…it got dumped in my lap and I'm just trying to figure it out. I never wanted to take anything from you. I can't change how you feel, or Caleb. He's my mate. I didn't ask for it or choose it, but I do love him. I know that hurts you, and I'm sorry. I don't want you to leave. They're your pack—your family. We can be cordial or even just ignore each other. But I can't keep dealing with your anger—I have too much else on my plate. If you can't get over hating me, you'll have to make a choice and deal with the consequences—it isn't my place to tell Caleb what to do with his pack."

"But you could. You could ask him to take me back."

"Perhaps, but I wouldn't. And I don't think you would want me to, in the long run. And besides, Sierra, he didn't kick you out—he gave you the time and freedom to sort yourself out. If you can't be around me or him, leaving the pack might be the kindest option. I don't know. Maybe you just need some time. And if time is what you need, then he gave you that time away from the pack without risking bond-sickness."

She winces, nodding. "He did that for Connor after his father died. That's why he went down with the Apaches." She rubs her face with both hands. "I've been with the pack since my first shift. I don't know what to do or where to go."

"Whatever you do and wherever you go, Sierra, just be careful. It's dangerous out there for immortals. And just know that as far as I'm concerned, you're always welcome. I'm only speaking for myself." I glance after the others—Saige trails behind, watching our conversation with concern. "We all must choose our paths, Sierra. Now, you choose yours."

I move past her and trot to catch up with the others, my bag bouncing off my hip.

Saige stares after Sierra, walking backward, eyes misting. She waves once, and Sierra waves back, and then the current of hurrying mortals moves between us.

"She's my sister," Saige whispers. "She's my girl—my ride or die. I know she's difficult, but…"

"I have a feeling she'll join us sooner rather than later," I say. "I think she just needs some time alone to figure herself out. Caleb knows what he's doing, Saige. He values her. I think what he did was the kindest thing he could have done."

She turns to walk forward, nodding. "I trust my Alpha. I just…Sierra puts on a tough front, but deep down, she's a very sensitive person. I worry about her alone."

I clasp her hand in mine and we walk like that, following the pack and my mates as we weave through the chaos of the Atlanta airport.

I find myself worrying about Sierra too—I can't imagine what it would be like having a pack, a family, constantly surrounding me for two hundred years and then suddenly being alone.

I don't envy her, that's for sure.

We reach the exit and emerge in the bright hot humidity of an Atlanta morning. Crowds cluster waiting for taxis—another fight breaks out, and a gun is drawn and fired. Someone screams.

Overhead, a passenger jet howls—too low, too fast. More screams.

I look up just in time to see the jet bank sharply, wings tipping precariously—before I can even consider doing anything to help, its nose angles down, and the engine whines—

WHUMP!

Heat billows like a hot breath from Hell as the jet smashes into the ground in a massive fireball.

Caleb's arms circle my waist, and he hauls me off the ground, hurrying me away. "You can't do anything, Maeve. You can't help them. It's a mortal affair."

I realize my hair is glowing—my skin, my tattoos. The crowd around us is torn between horror at the crash and confused, awed fear at me.

When eagles of iron fall from the sky, and those of the Blood cry war brother against brother, then will the WorldBreaker come.

The eagles of iron have fallen.

Now, I suppose, those of the Blood—immortals— will cry war brother against brother.

The rest of the prophecy echoes in my head:

"Her hair will be white as the driven snow. She will wield her maya with the spirit of her mother. She is the WorldBreaker. She is The Once-Mortal Queen, and all shall bow, but not before the rivers run red and the streets flood scarlet. She shall know Death, and Death shall know her. She will have a mate of fang and a mate of fur. She is the WorldBreaker and the Once-Mortal Queen."

I glance back: the dead mortal lays in the middle of the road going past the Arrivals area—a river of blood runs away from him, painting the road red.

I never really believed in prophecies, I realize.

I suppose now I might have to start.

CHAPTER 4

I T TAKES US HOURS OF WALKING TO LEAVE the chaotic, violent hell of Atlanta behind us. Caleb leads us—naturally enough. Colin uses his cell phone to monitor the various newsfeeds from around the world. He catches up to walk beside me.

"Here. You may want to see this." He hands me the phone.

It's an article. "Maeve Sparrow, self-styled Once-Mortal Queen, leader of a breakout faction of immortals, arrives in Atlanta, chaos ensues."

"Well that's bullshit," I mutter. "I'm not a self-styled anything, and I'm not a leader of a breakout faction."

He snorts. "No shit. Mortal media has a way of distorting the truth. But the video is good. It shows the whole thing—makes you look great." He blushes. "Um, politically speaking, I mean."

I laugh and elbow him. "What, you don't think I look great?"

He glances at Caleb nervously, and then at me. "No, um, no! I just…Caleb, and Caspian, they—"

I laugh again and touch his arm. "I'm teasing. He's not going to tear your head off for complimenting me. And also, I knew what you meant."

He arches an eyebrow at me. "Shifters are notoriously territorial about their mates, especially a bonded one. That's what makes your relationship so…um, unique."

"Having five mates, you mean?"

He snorts. "Having five mates…none of whom are shifters. It'd be less weird if they were all shifters, but sharing a bonded mate with four vampires? Yeah, that's fucking weird, dude." He glances at me. "Um. Ma'am, I mean."

I laugh. "Dude, relax. You're fine. We're friends, right?"

He glances down at the sparrow symbol emblazoned on his chest. "Yeah…friends."

"Well, friends with layers, then. My point is you can relax around me."

"Oh. Right." He walks beside me, phone in hand swinging at his hip. He glances at me. "Can I ask you a question?"

"Sure. Shoot."

"The, um…the other two like you. Where are they?"

"Oh, Theris and Aquilia? Aquilia is called an Aeshir, and Theris is a Fomori. Zirae coined the terms, and despite my dislike for him, it doesn't make sense to create new ones when these are suitable. I shrug. "And I don't know where they are—they spent their lives locked in those cells. So when they got out, I think they just wanted to explore the world and…I dunno. Figure out…life? Themselves? I told them they were welcome to come with us, but they chose to go their own ways. I admit I'd love to have them with us for what's coming in New York. But after everything they went through, I wasn't about to do anything to infringe upon their freedom."

"Couldn't you have made them?"

I shrug. "I mean, no? I'm coming to believe that true authority works best when people choose to *give* you that authority. Ruling in fear is wrong. Forcing people to obey you because you're more powerful than they are is wrong. I only want people who choose to follow me. If the Fates have chosen this role for me, so be it, but I'll fill the role my way."

He's quiet awhile. "I respect that, Maeve. I think the Fates chose you for a reason, and the more I get to know you and see the things you do and why you do them, the more I get why they chose you."

I bump him with my shoulder. "Thank you, Colin. It means a lot to hear you say that."

He blushes. After a minute or so, he shoots me another look. "You think the Fates will give me a bonded mate?"

I blow out a breath. "I wish I could answer that. I know very little about the Fates and the immortal world in general." I give him a warm smile. "But what I do know, Colin, is that any woman would be lucky to have you as her mate."

He grins. "You think so?"

"I know so. You're sweet, handsome, smart…yeah. You'll make some woman a hell of a mate. Just…look beyond shifters, Colin. I know what the world has instilled in you, but the world was wrong. I'm only guessing based on my own experiences, which are very limited, but I think if you open your mind and start thinking about fae and vampires not as enemies, but just *people*, then you open yourself up to a whole new world of possibility." I lower my voice and lean close. "And from what I hear, the sex is even better with someone from one of the other races. I mean, when I thought I was a mortal, things with Cas were *really* intense. Way more so than with my previous mortal boyfriends. Way, *way* better."

"For real?" His voice sounds faint.

"Oh yeah. For real. I mean, ask Caleb, sometime. Tell him I told you to ask. All I know for sure is that love is not meant to be limited. Would you refuse to be with someone because her skin was a different color? Or his?"

He widens his eyes. "No! Of course not. And…hers. Not that there's anything wrong with being gay, I'm just not." He shakes his head. "No, I….people are just people. We're all the same when it comes down to it. Different cultures, religions, morals, music, whatever, but all that's just… surface stuff. Once you get to know someone, you realize we're all just people."

I smile at him and shove him playfully. "Then how is it any different when it comes to a fae girl or a vampire girl?"

He blinks. "I…we have different needs."

"Sure, but that actually makes things easier, in my experience. Caleb needs mana—it's how he powers his abilities as a shifter. And you know what I don't need? Mana. So he can feed from me and it won't make any difference.

But Caspian and me, we're both vampires, right? Well, he can feed from me and it'll sustain him. Because as a half-fae, I produce my own blood. But I can't feed from him even though I need blood as a vampire. I know—it's almost counterintuitive. I make my own blood as a fae, but as a vampire, I need outside blood. I'm not sure how it works, and I don't think anyone does—my grandfather maybe. But I do know that Caspian feeds from me, and his body uses that blood—if I then drink his blood, I'm getting my own back, stripped of nutrients. See how that works? I need blood that is not my own. And guess who I can get it from without causing any problems?"

"Caleb. Because he doesn't use blood—not, like, for his magic."

"Exactly." I look at him. "I'm not a shifter, Colin. Am I so bad?"

He frowns at me. "No, of course not. you're amazing."

"Well, thank you. But knowing what you know about me, if I wasn't already mated, would you be able to think about me, in that way? I ask hypothetically, for the sake of the discussion."

He shrugs and nods. "Of course." He thinks about it. "Yes. I could. You're…well," he blushes. "You're beautiful, obviously. But you're a good person. You care about people. You're brave and powerful."

"And there are fae and vampire women out there who are beautiful and good and brave and powerful, Colin. You just have to let yourself see them that way. As *women*, rather than fae or vampire." I frown. "Well, you have to see them for who they are. Being fae is part of who a fae woman is. She's a woman, and a fae, and part of whatever culture she's from. Being fae is just another part of who she is, but you can't see her as *just* fae, any more than you can see a person of color as *just* that—nor can you *not* see that part of them. Make sense?"

Colin doesn't answer for quite a while—a glance tells me he's thinking deeply so I walk with him in amiable silence.

After a few minutes, he shoots me another look. "How did you know he was your mate?"

I shrug. "I didn't. With Caleb, I mean. Or with Caspian, for that matter. You have to remember, I grew up in the mortal world. Mate bonds don't exist for mortals. All mortals have are emotions—spending time with someone and deciding you like them enough to spend your life with that one person. But it's a flawed system, you might say, not that there's any other option. There's no way to *know*—you're trusting that person with your heart, your body, and your life. And you're hoping they love you and are giving themselves to you in the same way. But you don't *know*. There's no magical bond linking your minds and souls."

"Sounds scary."

I laugh. "I suppose it must be. I was never in love with anyone, before I became immortal—or before my immortal nature came out, I suppose I should say."

"Do you think we have the mate bonds because there are so few of us? Like, to balance out the fertility issues?" He kicks a chunk of concrete, catching up to it and kicking it again.

Around us, the streets are eerily silent. Behind us, the Atlanta skyline is wreathed in a haze of ozone, smog, and tendrils of sick black smoke. We pass a gas station— the windows are boarded up, the glass shattered; a large brownish-red stain mars the concrete beside one of the pumps. The sign advertises premium, mid-grade, and regular unleaded for $4.29, $3.99, and $3.49, respectively, as well as cigarettes and lottery tickets.

"It does make a certain sense when you put it in that context, doesn't it?" I say after a moment. "I suppose the real question you're getting at is what does it feel like to be mate-bonded, right?"

He grins at me. "Yeah, pretty much."

I consider it for a few moments. "It feels...like inevitability."

Colin laughs. "Yeah, no clue what that means."

"I mean...being with that person feels inevitable. Like, even before we were bloodmated, I just...*knew* where Caspian was. There was no bloodlink, no mate-bond, none of that. But I just *knew*, down to my toes, that I was meant to be with him. And that was scary as fuck for me at the time because I didn't know vampires were real, I just knew he was *really* freaking different and really, *really* frightening, even though I also knew he'd never hurt me. I couldn't *not* be with him—and he couldn't *not* be with me—he fucking tried, too."

"So you didn't know he was your mate? You just... knew you had to be with him?"

"Exactly. And because Cas and the others didn't realize what I am—not just an immortal, but a new and different kind—Caspian was hesitant to let anything physical happen. But it reached a point where neither of us could deny what we needed—because by that point, it wasn't desire, it was a real, undeniable, physical need. We *had* to. And when we finally did, we bloodmated and my immortal nature was revealed, or the glamour hiding my immortal nature was dissolved once and for all, however you want to put it." I look at him, smiling. "I guess all that is to say that when it comes to a mate-bond, the magic is undeniable. It can't be mistaken. If and when you find your mate, bonded or otherwise, you'll know."

Colin laughs self-consciously. "This is a little backward, isn't it? This whole conversation?"

I laugh with him. "Yeah, it kind of is, isn't it? Here you are, two hundred and fifty years old, asking me, not even twenty, about mate-bonds." I glance at him. "Why not ask Caleb?"

He watches Caleb, striding with that confident, powerful swagger. "Yeah, that's not the kind of conversation I'd feel comfortable having with him." He watches his toes for a moment, still kicking that pebble. "Also, I'm only one-ninety. I was, um, illegal. My mother…" he sighs. Starts over. "She was headed west with her mate. Outlaws, bandits, whatever you want to call them, they captured her. Killed my father and took turns raping my mother."

I frown. "How did a group of mortal bandits overpower a pair of shifters?"

"Surprise, I think. And numbers. There were a lot of them. Mom and her mate fought like hell, but they were so outnumbered they didn't really stand a chance. By the time her mate died, Mom was half-dead. So they took turns raping her until they'd had enough, figured she was gonna die, and took off, taking all of her food, ammunition, and supplies. Well, being a shifter, she didn't die. She shifted to her animal form and carried me to term that way. She raised me more animal than human, out in the wilderness west of Tennessee—which, back in 1834 was pretty much just forest inhabited only by the occasional tribe of

Indians—Native Americans, sorry. They knew who and what we were and left us alone. Caleb came along when I was sixteen and took me into his pack. Mom went west to California."

"Is she still alive?"

He shakes his head. "Nah." A tip of his head to one side. "Well, I don't know for sure. We made our way to California a few decades later and I looked for her. I talked to people who knew her, but they all said she vanished in the 70s—1870s, I mean. I scoured hundreds of square miles around where I knew she'd been living, but only found traces of old campsites. She probably got lonely and tired and just died of age-sickness, I guess."

"I'm sorry, Colin."

He shrugs. "I never knew her before, obviously, but my whole life she was just sad. Seemed to me like she was only hanging on for my sake. She was relieved when Caleb approached our fire and asked if I wanted to join his pack. I think she only lasted in California as long as she did out of sheer stubbornness."

I hesitate before asking my next question. "The men who attacked…"

He grins at me, a shockingly savage smile on such a boyish face. "Oh, I found them. That was the first thing we did after Caleb bound me to the pack. We hunted them down and killed them, very, very slowly. I knew the one who sired me, too. I scented it on him."

"What did you do to him?" I ask out of morbid curiosity.

"We herded him like a moose. He was in the Hudson Valley area, trapping. We herded him into Iroquois territory—right into their camp. And then we let them have him."

I frown in confusion. "I don't understand."

"Oh. Well, the Iroquois were one of the most feared tribes in North America. They had torture tactics Europeans couldn't even conceive of, and they *hated* the white trappers. Guys like him, especially. They knew of him and had been looking for him—my mother wasn't the only one he'd done that to. He'd raped and killed several of the tribe's women. The worst thing we could have done to him was give him to them. They knew we were there and why we'd done that, and they gave us a hell of a show. They made his death last over a week. It was fucking brutal, and no more than a goddamned monster like him deserved." He laughs. "If it had been an option, I'd have hauled his ass down to Apache territory and left him for them. Those dudes were *super* creative when it came to torture. They'd cover you in honey and stake you over a fire ant hill. Found the remains of a guy they'd done that to, once." He shrugs. "The way white settlers treated them, though? I don't blame them."

"Callahan expressed a similar viewpoint."

"Well, we lived out in the wilderness of the unsettled west before Europeans made it out there. We treated the land and the local tribes with respect—we were living on *their* land. We respected their ways and their space. They had immortals in their tribes, but they treated them no differently than anyone else. Of course, many of the chiefs were immortal—being the most powerful and whatever, it just made sense, I guess. But they…they accepted us. As long as we were polite and respectful, they left us alone. We'd trade with them once in a while or go on hunts with them." He goes silent for a while. "We took this land at the end of a gun, and it hasn't been for the better, from my perspective. I'd go back to the old ways in a heartbeat."

Ahead, Caleb has paused at the railing of an overpass, watching something on the freeway below. Colin and I jog to catch up.

The expressway is, like all the others we've seen, a jammed, snarled, tangled-up mess. Abandoned cars litter the lanes, making travel so difficult as to be nearly impossible. That doesn't stop people from trying, of course—mostly desperate mortals.

Caleb is resting his forearms on the railing of the overpass, watching a situation unfold below—a pair of squabbling mortal males. One rear-ended the other, it looks like. The argument is about to turn violent—even as I think it, one mortal slugs the other in the nose, and blood spurts. Even from here, I smell it, and my vampire tries to convince me to jump down there and get a taste. I squash that impulse. Within moments, the two men are duking it out clumsily, getting in awkward hits and clinching, shoving away. Around them, a dozen or so other mortals watch from open car doors, but no one interferes.

Except for one man. Tall and lean, neatly dressed in chinos and a polo, carrying a briefcase as if headed to a business meeting. He sets his briefcase down and approaches the fighting men. He tries to defuse the situation verbally, at first, but the men ignore him. So, he pulls one apart from the other and shoves him backward with surprising strength from such a slender figure. This backfires almost immediately. The one he shoved lunges at him, connecting with a hard punch to his jaw. The other charges into the fray and connects as well, and then somehow the two men who'd been fighting each other are suddenly ganging up together on the well-intentioned stranger.

But something seems off. Or…smells off. I scent the air, but it's faint. Honey?

Oh, shit.

Understanding hits, too late. The man who intervened does something with his fingers, and then gold light swells, and the other two men are flung backward. Bleeding from the nose and mouth, holding his ribs, the male—a fae, clearly—straightens, and wipes his lips and nose with the back of his wrist. Holds out his hands to the two men in warning.

"He's one of them!" A bystander shouts. "One o' them freaks! He's gonna magic us all to death!"

"Get him!" Another shouts.

And then the crowd of bystanders, none of whom had the courage or fortitude to even try to stop the fight, swarm around the lone fae male. Before he can cast another glamour, several men have him by the wrists and ankles. He thrashes and flails, and I can feel him fighting to make his prana answer without his hands—

Before I have time to even think about it, I'm leaping over the railing and landing on the freeway—the asphalt cracks and splinters as I land.

I fling out a hand, sending a wave of power out. "*STOP!*"

Everyone freezes, even the fae. I approach the mob of a dozen or so mortals, whose eyes track me with fear. I pry their hands off of the fae, help him to his feet, and guide him away, putting him behind me.

I glance at him. "Are you all right?"

Released from the grip of my glamour, he nods. "I'm

fine, thank you." He winces. "I haven't been struck like that in centuries. I'd forgotten how unpleasant it is." He extends his hand to me. "Philemon Argent."

I shake his hand. "Maeve Sparrow."

His brows draw down. "Maeve Sparrow..." and then his eyes widen, and he drops to one knee. "My queen. I'm at your service." He glances up at me with hope and awe. "I've heard you can conjure a mark of fealty."

I produce the mark with a roll of my hand, and he palms it without hesitation. "I pledge my life, my blood, and my abilities in service to your cause and your court from this day to my dying breath."

Light swells and my sparrow mark inks itself on the front of his navy-blue polo. He grins as he rises to his feet. "Saved by the queen herself!" He glances at the men he tried to help. "Ungrateful mortals."

I place my palm on his shoulder. "I'll have a little talk with them. I'm glad to have you." I gesture at the overpass. "The rest of my party is up there. We're headed to New York."

"I was just trying to get out of Atlanta before things got any worse. I would be honored to fight alongside you."

"Well, we do hope to find a path forward without fighting, Philemon."

He sighs and shakes his head. "The way mortals are behaving right now, that seems an unlikely outcome. But one worth pursuing, I suppose. it is the more noble endeavor, certainly."

I nod and turn back to the still-frozen mortals—not frozen as in cold, I should point out—frozen as in temporarily deprived of voluntary movement.

I send a tendril of prana swirling around each of them,

using it to rotate them and rearrange them so they're all facing me in a line abreast. "Now. I'm going to let you go, but you will remain as I have arranged you, and you will listen to me."

I pull my prana back to myself, and the mortals slump, gasping, hands on knees, shaking heads, and eyeing me with fear and suspicion.

A tall, overweight, balding man drags a huge handgun from the small of his back and aims it at me. "Arrange this, bitch."

I sheathe myself in prana, turning it into a thick armor of jellied air. I wait calmly as the man pulls the trigger once, twice, three times, four, six…each of the bullets lodges in what to him must look like the air itself, and then drops to the ground with a tinny clatter.

I watch as he looks at his gun as if it's somehow responsible, and then at me. I let him fire the rest of the clip or whatever at me. I drop the sheath of armor and wrap a thread of maya around the weapon, causing it to heat up. It glows orange and then red, and then he drops it with a shocked yowl.

"Are you quite finished?" I ask, arching an eyebrow at him.

Someone, another mortal, has joined my party up on the overpass and is livestreaming the entire event—Caleb allows it, so I allow it as well.

The man who shot at me stares at me. "What satanic black magic is this?"

I laugh. "I'm no Satanist, and it's not black magic. Just plain old magic." I walk up to him—he freezes in place without my help—and touch two fingers to his temple.

Pull prana from him—just a hint, enough to catch a

glimpse of his memories—an abusive father, bullied for his weight all his life, a wife he abuses as his father did his mother and him, a secret proclivity for visiting young male prostitutes while spouting homophobic hate all over his social media and in real life.

I wrinkle my nose and withdraw myself from his memories—they feel oily and filmy and disgusting.

"You aren't a very nice person, Geoffrey Allen Liebowitz. Not very nice at all." I hold his eyes. "Secrets have a way of finding the light, you know."

"Y-you—you don't know a thing about me, devil woman!"

"Oh, but I do." I lean closer. "I know your father was a monster, and you have become him. I know you claim in public to hate gays…but in private? Well, Andrew, Isaac, Patel, Hector, Tommy…they all have a different story to tell, don't they? You're the worst kind of hypocrite, Geoffrey. You are what you hate. You hate them because you're too much of a coward and a weakling to hate yourself, much less accept them or yourself and less yet love them and yourself." He opens and closes his mouth, but I speak over him. "Sit down, Geoffrey. And be silent. I can make you, but I'd rather not waste any more time or energy on the likes of you."

He plops heavily to his buttocks, right there on the ground at my feet, looking up at me with horrified confusion.

I look around at the others. They're all watching with a mixture of fear, confusion, suspicion, and awe. "Not that any of you are any better." I point at Philemon, still standing a few feet behind me. "He alone out of all of you had the courage to do something. You all stood there and watched those two—" I gesture at the two men who started the whole business, "fight in the street like feral dogs. And you did nothing. He, someone with more to lose than any of you, as you so clearly demonstrated, stepped forward and tried to stop the violence. And when these two mindless thugs turned on him and he nonviolently defended himself, what did you do? You attacked him."

I feel their shame rise like a miasma.

I let the silence do its work.

I look from face to face. "It is responses like that that's causing *that*." I point at the skyline of Atlanta. "You fear what you do not understand. That's human nature. You don't understand us—we are different, and we can do things you can't, things you don't understand."

I conjure a rose and send it floating across the space. One of them, a young woman, reaches for it. I smile as she plucks it from the air, marveling as she spins it between finger and thumb, and then sniffs it.

"It's…it's real?"

I nod. "It is."

"Will it die like…like a real rose?" She asks.

I shrug. "I don't know. I suppose you'll find out. It may just vanish, or it may die, or it may not. I don't know. I've never kept one long enough to find out."

"What else can you do?" A man in the back asks.

I laugh. "Many things."

"That guy," another man says, pointing at the fae. "He called you queen."

"Among the immortals, there are some who believe I am what's called the Once-Mortal Queen—a figure from a prophecy from a long time ago."

"Are you?" he asks.

I shrug. "I do seem to fit, yes."

"So you're…what? Trying to become…fuckin'… queen of America or some shit?" This is another person, an older male with a long gray mullet.

I laugh. "No—gods no. My purpose is to stop *this*," I gesture at them, and the area around us, "from happening. To help our world transition to the reality of immortals being real. We've always been real, and we're not going anywhere. We don't want to take over, we don't want to rule or anything like that. We just want to live our lives, same as you. We're humans. We're people. We have friends, we have parents, we have boyfriends and girlfriends and husbands and wives…we're just different than you. We live longer. We age differently. We have abilities you don't, but those abilities come with downsides, just like everything else in life."

"Like what?" The mullet man says.

"Like, we can't have children with people from our own race. A vampire can't have children with a vampire. It's very difficult for us to have children, and that's at the heart of everything to do with the conflict between my people and yours." I pause. "That, and the very idea of there being a *your* kind and a *my* kind, when we're all just people living together in the same country."

"But you can do anything you want," mullet man says. "You could turn us all into frogs. Put a curse on us. What can we do? You stopped bullets like it was nothing."

I laugh. "Turn you into frogs? I'm not an evil witch from the Brothers Grimm. Perhaps it's possible, but I wouldn't know. I've never tried." I point at Philemon. "You were about to kill him with your bare hands. He could have done any number of things to defend himself in ways that would have hurt you, but he didn't, not even when his own life was in jeopardy."

Silence.

"Yes, I can do a lot of things. I can stop bullets. I can freeze you in your tracks. I could have hurt you, but I didn't. We're here, together, talking like rational human beings. Maybe next time you see something you don't understand, try to understand it instead of trying to kill it. Especially when it's a person."

"My brother and his friends were killed by a vampire," someone says, voice shaking—I identify the speaker, a young Hispanic woman. "It drank their blood and they died."

"He, or she," I correct. "We are not an *it*. And yes, there are immortals who aren't good. Who will do bad things. Hurt people just because they can, or because they're afraid."

"What would a vampire be afraid of? They ain't even had a stake or garlic or nothing."

I laugh. "Forget everything you think you know about vampires—ninety-nine percent of it is wrong. A vampire *would* be afraid of people, especially a big crowd of angry, scared mortals. If you were surrounded by people who wanted to kill you just for existing, what would you do? Defend yourself? Even if in so doing you confirmed their fears of what you are? Or just let them kill you?" I hold my hands out, palms up. "I don't know the circumstances of your brother's death, so I won't try to justify or defend the actions of that vampire. Maybe it was unprovoked. But you mortals do plenty of that to each other, don't you? In fact, you kill each other over nothing at all far more frequently than any mortal has ever been harmed by one of my people. It does happen—of course it does. But by and large, we're just people who want to be left alone to live our lives as we see fit."

You've said your piece, Caleb says to my mind. *Time to go.*

I turn and glance at him. Nod. Turn back to the small crowd. "I have to go, now. Goodbye."

I leap back up to the overpass and watch the crowd slowly disperse. Most get back into their cars and weave around the abandoned vehicles while others head away on foot. After a few minutes, the area is deserted, except for one mortal.

Caspian wraps his arms around me. "Good speech, babe."

I glance at the mortal who was recording it. "Hello."

She stares at me—a pretty, young Black woman with an enormous duffel bag at her feet. "Are you really a queen?"

I shrug. "To some, yes, I suppose I am. But I'd consider it more of a...position or role than anything. I'm certainly not royalty, like King Charles or whoever."

"Oh." She glances at her phone. "Lotta views already."

She shuffles her feet without looking at me—she wants to ask something.

I move closer to her. "What is it?"

"I got a brother up in Boston. I'm tryin' to get up there to be with him while all this shit is goin' down." She waves in the direction of Atlanta. "But it's scary out here on my own. Flights are shut down, trains ain't runnin', busses ain't runnin', and I don't have a car."

I sweep a look at my people; Caleb nods. Caspian just offers me a shrug and a smile. I look back at the woman.

"Well, we're going to New York. You can travel with us for as long as our paths are aligned."

She grins, relieved. "God, that would be amazing." She arches an eyebrow, looking at Caspian in particular—he's nearly unblooded, looking pale and hard-skinned, his eyes laced with black. "Um, not to be, like, ungrateful, but…he ain't gonna eat me, is he?"

Caspian laughs. "I'm a vampire, not a cannibal." He indicates me. "And I get what I need from her. No one here will harm you."

"Long as you don't harm us." This comes from Callahan.

She widens her eyes when she sees him. "Good lord, you're a big one, ain't you?"

Callahan just shrugs. "Yeah."

Saige steps forward with a welcoming smile. "I'm Saige. Don't worry about Callahan. He's just grumpy."

Callahan snorts. "I'm not grumpy."

Colin elbows him. "You are kind of grumpy, dude."

"I'm Sharon," the woman says.

Introductions are made all around, and Caleb starts heading onward.

Channing, however, remains at the railing, staring down at the freeway.

Caleb notices. "Channing? What's up?"

Channing points down at the freeway. "Why couldn't we, um, borrow a ride from down there?" He shrugs one shoulder. "They've all been abandoned. I don't see anyone coming back for any of them."

Caleb nods. "Not a bad plan. Maeve?"

"Makes sense to me." I scan the immediate area below

us and then point. "There—that van. The big white one. The church van?"

Channing hops over the railing and jogs to the van, which is blocked in by half a dozen other abandoned vehicles. He shimmies into the driver's seat—the engine rolls over, catches, and sets off on a rattling hum. "Runs okay and has a half tank of gas."

Caleb hops down. "Everyone, check the other cars for gas cans. If we can find something to siphon with, even better."

Saige and I help Sharon scramble down the embankment to the freeway, and we all spend the next thirty minutes going through trunks and truck beds and back seats. We do find three red gas cans, two empty and one full. Colin finds a coiled-up garden hose in one truck bed, and Channing cuts a section of it off and siphons enough gas from the other cars to fill the two empty cans. It takes several more minutes for the men to shift the cars away so we can get the van out—Sharon watches them shove cars out of the way with an expression somewhere between awe and shock.

Finally, we're able to navigate the van off the freeway, up the ramp, and onto the road we've been traveling along—a more circuitous route, but with the freeway in the condition it's in, it's simply not an option.

Even more than not having to walk, I'm grateful for air conditioning. Georgia is *hot*.

CHAPTER 5

SEVERAL HOURS LATER, IT BECOMES clear we have to stop. Callahan, in the very back row, spies a deer running toward the tree line a few hundred yards from the road—Caleb has to use his Alpha compulsion to keep Callahan from shifting right there in the van and jumping out the back.

Callahan growls, half-feral, before regaining control. Sharon, sitting in the second row between Saige and me, looks shaken.

"We need to stop for food," Caleb announces. "Maeve, you and Caspian don't need food the way we do. If we go much longer, we'll all be acting like Cal."

"Um, there's a little town not far from

here," Sharon says. "I came through this way on a road trip with my ex. There are a couple diners and a gas station. I dunno what it'll be like now, of course."

"How far?" Caleb asks.

Sharon shrugs. "Few more miles, maybe? It was two, three years ago, now."

Philemon, in the third row with Colin and Nico, clears his throat. "I, um…I have a few protein bars. I'd be willing to share them, should anyone…" Callahan leans over the seat, his chest rattling in warning. "Oh, oh, yes, um…here, please, take it." He fishes a bar from his bag and shoves it at Callahan, who rips it open with his teeth and devours it in three bites.

"Appreciate it," Callahan rumbles between bites.

Sharon giggles. "You're not you when you're hungry."

"I'd kill for a Snickers, right now," Callahan says.

"You and your sweet tooth," Saige says, laughing. "It's a wonder you don't have cavities."

"I'm a shifter. Don't get cavities." Callahan is grinning, now. "If I did, I wouldn't have any teeth, I don't think."

"Can you imagine a shifter with a mouthful of crowns?" Colin says, cackling. "Or…or dentures?"

Callahan's laugh is unexpected, a deep, genuine belly laugh. "A wolf trots up to you with dentures in? Oh god, that would be a great prank."

"Connor would have been the first to do it," Caleb says.

The van goes quiet, then.

Sharon looks at me, confused. I lean close and whisper. "Pack-mate. He died recently."

"Oh," she whispers back. "I'm sorry to hear that."

"Thank you," Caleb says, responding to her whisper.

Sharon starts. "You heard that?"

"I'm a wolf. I can hear your heart beating in your chest. I can smell the last thing you ate—chocolate." He grins at her.

She frowns. "They say animals can smell fear. Is that true?"

"Oh, absolutely," Saige says. "Fear, anger, arousal, any strong emotion, hormones, pheromones, stuff like that, we can smell it."

"We can also smell lies," Callahan says. "Not a hundred percent of the time, but nearly."

"Okay, that's bullshit. You cannot," Sharon says, twisting in her seat to look at him.

She's short, an inch or so taller than Saige, with a beautiful, bouffant natural afro, delicate, fine features, dark, lovely skin, and a curvy build. She's wearing khaki shorts, hiking boots, a close-fitting red V-neck accentuating her ample chest, and a black raincoat tied around her waist. A long fixed-blade hunting knife is sheathed at her right hip.

I think of *The Walking Dead* for some reason. She seems like she could be a character from that show—a badass survivor.

Callahan rumbles. "It's true. Two truths and a lie. You and me, let's go."

Sharon eyes him for a minute or two. "My father is a licensed auto mechanic," she says. "I've never owned a television. In the third grade, I accidentally ate rabbit poop because I thought it was chocolate."

Callahan answers immediately. "Lie, truth, truth."

Sharon gapes. "Lucky guesses."

"Try again."

She considers a moment. "I rode an elephant in Thailand. My mother is a congresswoman. I can't whistle."

Once again, Callahan answers without hesitation. "True, true, lie."

Sharon blinks. "Starting to think maybe you're tellin' the truth. "

"Your mom is a congresswoman?" Saige asks.

Sharon nods. "Georgia State House of Representatives." She sighs. "Least, she was, before all this mess. I don't know where she is now. We had a falling out a few years ago about my brother and we ain't spoken since. I tried callin' her about a hundred times over the last few weeks but never got through."

"Yeah, cell phone towers were one of the first things to stop working, for some reason. It's weird. Cellular data still works here and there but phone calls don't." Colin holds up his phone as he speaks. "No one really knows why. Sorry to hear about the falling out with your mom."

Sharon sighs and shrugs. "My brother came out and she went through the roof. Kicked him out of the house, deleted him off her phone, changed the locks, got rid of any photo in the house with him in it." A shake of her head. "I told her he's my brother, I love him, and I will *not* go along with that mess. If she wants to disown her boy for being gay, she can damn well disown me, too. And she did."

"Bullshit," Callahan mumbles. "That is some grade-A pussy-ass bullshit."

"Any parent who will not accept their child's differences is no parent at all," Nico murmurs in a low, quiet, angry rumble. It turns out to be his only contribution to the entire conversation—he's a man of few words, it seems.

Sharon smiles at him. "I'm glad you agree, big man."

Callahan seems uncomfortable, for some reason—the way she's looking at him, smiling at him? I don't know. It's cute, though. "You're telling the truth, by the way. Just in case you were thinking the whole story was another two-truths-and-a-lie thing."

Sharon laughs. "Nah, two for two is proof enough for me." She looks at Philemon. "So what's your story, morning glory?"

Philemon hesitates. "I, um…"

I laugh. "You can tell her. The days of hiding and lying about the truth of who you are, are over. We're all just people in this van."

Philemon nods. His brownish-blond hair is cut in a classic side part, neatly combed. He's dropped the glamour mask, so his features are sharp, angular, and handsome in a geeky sort of way. "Well, um. My father sired me on his mate's handmaiden. It was 1680, I believe. She survived breastfeeding, believe it or not. She lived to see me take my first step, I'm told. I don't remember her, obviously."

Sharon holds up both hands. "Hold up, hold up, hold up." She points an accusatory finger at him. "You're tryna tell me you were born in the year of our Lord One thousand six hundred and eighty? As in, you're…" She frowns, thinking. "Math ain't my strong suit. Three-hundred and forty-five years old?"

Philemon gives her a quizzical expression. "Well, yes? That's what immortal means."

Sharon throws her hands up. "Well excuse me! Ya'll are the first I've met in person. Hearing the word immortal is one thing, but hearing someone claim to be older than this whole damn country is a whole other ball of wax, my geriatric friend."

Philemon frowns. "Um, by fae standards, I'm barely into adulthood. What you might consider early thirties, in mortal terms."

Sharon pinches the bridge of her nose. "You *do* look about thirty-five, don't you?" She scans the car. "So, you're all hundreds of years old?"

Colin raises his hand. "I was born after the Treaty—I'm only one-ninety."

Sharon's eyes widen. "Well ain't you just a baby! *Only* one hundred and ninety!" She shakes her head, hair bouncing. "How do I know y'all are tellin' the truth?"

Saige laughs. "You don't. It's not something we can prove. I mean, I could tell you what San Francisco was like during the gold rush years—I was there. But then, I could just be making that up."

"Well? What was it like? What were you doing?" Sharon turns to face her, expression eager and interested.

"It was wild, dirty, smelly, chaotic, violent, and amazing. You met all sorts of people from all over. Everyone came to San Francisco thinking they'd hit it big in the gold fields, but most didn't. It was a lot like people going to Vegas thinking they'll change their fortunes at the slot machines. A lot of men died broke and starving. There were a lot of diseases because most people didn't bathe or wash their hands, and you lived crammed in cheek-by-jowl, in the cities at least." Saige's eyes take on a faraway look. "Folks fighting over a few grams of gold flakes. Someone would ride into town dragging some poor horse thief along behind them, string 'em up, and hang 'em without so much as a how do you do." She glances at Caleb, meeting his eyes in the rearview mirror.

"Your story to tell, Saige," he mutters. "Don't look at me."

Saige ducks her head and fidgets with her fingers, picking at her nails. "I was a prostitute, actually. My father was a mountain man—he felt the war coming and headed west into the wilderness. The man who sired me was just some mountain man who came by my mom's cabin one winter. She made him leave before the frenzy could take over. Or, so she always claimed. We lived alone in a cabin in the middle of the forest most of my life. This was in what's now Ohio, I guess. Back then it wasn't even a territory."

"Sorry, but when are you talking about?"

"Oh, um, late seventeen hundreds. I was born in 1780. Makes me a young adult." She lets out a breath. "Anyway. I left home when I was twenty or so. Went east, spent time in the cities—hated it, and went back west. Spent as much time as a wolf as a woman. I didn't even know packs were a thing. Mom was…well, today, she'd probably be diagnosed with clinical depression and agoraphobia or something. She hated people, hated crowds. Wouldn't get out of bed for days at a time. So, she didn't really teach me much about who and what I was. Being a one was just what I knew."

She's quiet for a few moments, thinking.

"Ended up in San Francisco in the early thirties. I'd…I was…" She swallows hard, starts over. "I was a virgin when I arrived in San Francisco. I'd just wandered around alone, hunting when I needed to eat, only occasionally venturing around people. I was more than half-feral if I'm honest. So then, when I decided to see what Frisco was like…it was overwhelming. Not at all like the cities back east. I was a kid when I went east—by mortal standards, not just ours."

I reach across Sharon and take Saige's hand. "Saige... you don't have to talk about it."

She smiles at me. "I'm not ashamed. It was something I chose. Most people just don't understand—mortal or immortal." She shrugs. "It's hard to make sense of a decision like that."

"You don't have to justify it. It's no one's business but yours."

She flips a hand. "Short version is, I went what you might call boy crazy. I liked the mortals. I wasn't in a frenzy, it was just...sort of like when a mortal raised in a super controlling conservative Christian home moves out and starts discovering her sexuality. Well, I was a virgin, had no experience around humans basically, let alone men, much less yet *mortal* men. And back then, you couldn't just sleep around. There was no hookup culture like there is now. Things were...*very* different. I obviously had no intention of marrying in the mortal tradition, or even courting, nor did I have or want a mate. I just wanted sex. So, I scoped out all the brothels in the city, picked the one I liked best, and worked there. I only did it for...a year, maybe? Not even. It got old. The men were smelly and rough and the pay wasn't great. Once I'd had enough, I left San Francisco and headed north, which is where I ran into Caleb. I didn't have a pack and I wasn't interested in a pack with the usual sexual politics."

Sharon clears her throat. "You may have to elaborate because I'm not sure I understand what you mean about pack sexual politics."

Saige laughs. "That's not exactly a quick answer, but I'll try. Basically, what you need to know is that immortals in general are less fertile. We don't conceive easily.

Relevant to you, as a mortal, is that we cannot conceive with someone from our own race—our own kind of immortal, I mean. I can have a shifter mate, even a bonded mate, and we can get it on all we want and we'll never, ever conceive. You've heard us mention The Treaty, well, the super, super, *super* short version is that what you know as the Revolutionary War was a much more complex event. It was about immortals. See, up until now, the only way for immortals to reproduce is with a mortal."

Sharon frowns. "How does that end up in a war?"

"Because when a mortal woman conceives an immortal male's child, the process of pregnancy, birth, and breastfeeding is fatal to the mother," Saige answers. "There are no exceptions. Vampire children tend to kill their mother the fastest due to their blood needs, and mothers of shifters tend to live the longest, but no mortal mother has ever lived past the first year of their child's life."

Sharon doesn't answer. "Damn. Really?"

Saige nods. "Really. Obviously, mortals don't tend to like this. Never mind that a lot of mortal women have chosen of their own volition to have a child with an immortal, even knowing that it *will* kill them. There's no magic involved, no compulsion, nothing."

"And what about a mortal man puttin' a baby in an immortal woman?" Sharon asks. "Does he die, too?"

"Very often, yes," Saige answers. "Not as uniformly as a mortal mother. With a mortal mother, she dies because immortal children have vastly different biological needs, coming from our different physiological makeup—the magic that lets us shift or do glamourwork or drink blood. Those needs are just too much demand on the mortal body, and she can't support it. Even now, with modern medicine, I'm not sure a mortal woman would survive. Maybe through a late-term C-section? *Maybe*? With a mortal male and an immortal female, it's different. When an immortal female conceives, she goes into a frenzy. It's uncertain, scientifically, if the frenzy comes before the conception or after, but the understanding is that the frenzy is meant to ensure she conceives."

"I'm sorry…frenzy?" Sharon says.

"Sexual frenzy. Just what it sounds like. She wants sex, needs sex, can't get enough sex. It's not just a want or need, though—it's way worse than that. She has no control, mentally or physically."

"So, you're saying she'll just fuck the poor man to death?"

Saige laughs with a nod and a shrug. "More or less. What actually ends up killing him is not the sex but the drain. Mana, prana, or blood."

"What now?"

"Elements of magic," Saige answers. "Shifters use mana to shift, fae use prana to create glamours, what you'd think of as magic spells, and vampires, obviously, need blood to be human." She gestures at Caspian. "See how he's pale and his skin looks kinda hard? He needs blood. Eventually, he'll be totally white and his skin will be hard as stone until he gets blood."

"I'm always human," Caspian says, sounding a bit perturbed. "I'm just unblooded."

"Right," Saige says, wincing. "Sorry." She looks at Sharon. "Interracial dynamics are still touchy."

"Wait, y'all don't even get along with each other? And you want *us* to get along with *you*?"

Callahan snorts. "Exactly." He waves at the window.

"Thus, all that. It's a big damn mess, and it's been a long fuckin' time coming, too."

Sharon looks at me, then. "I thought all this was your fault?" She holds up her cell phone. "I had data connection for a bit, a while back, and I looked you up, and people sayin' this whole big mess is your fault."

"It's not," Caleb snaps. "What she did was the tipping point, sending things that were already boiling over the edge."

I lean forward and touch his arm. "It's okay, Caleb. It's a fair question."

Sharon eyes Caleb somewhat fearfully. "Sorry, I don't mean to insult anyone, I just—"

I put my hand over hers. "No, no. Not at all. He's just protective. I did set it off, but like Caleb said, it was going to happen one way or another. Immortals were, and still are, on the verge of extinction."

"Wait, I missed something. Y'all are going extinct? How?" Sharon looks to Saige for the answer.

"Well, that's what I didn't finish explaining. The war— we know it as The Mortals' War, and you know it as the Revolutionary War, was about reproduction. It was mortals hating us for killing their women. It was about a lot more than that, but that was the heart of it. We lost and signed The Treaty, which states that we cannot reproduce with mortals."

"But if the only way you can have kids is with mortals…" Sharon says, understanding dawning in her eyes.

"Exactly. It was signed in 1784. For 240 years, it has been illegal for us to have children. Immortal men don't just go around raping and knocking up women willy-nilly, as a rule. They get into relationships. They fall in love.

Things happen. Contraception doesn't work on us, either. And then suddenly she's pregnant and you can do nothing but watch her die."

"My mate Alistair went through that," I say.

Sharon looks at me. "Hol'up. You've got him, and him...both your mates." She points at Caleb, driving, and Caspian in the front passenger seat. "How many other mates you got?" She pauses. "And what's a mate, anyway? Like a husband?"

"I have five mates. Caleb, Caspian, Alistair, Phineas, and Stirling. Caleb is a shifter, the others are all vampires and form a coven."

"I thought that was witches."

"A common misconception," Philemon answers. "The notion of a coven of witches came from fae women forming groups—and they did call them covens, but it was a kind of joke, needling the vampires. They weren't witches, they were just...knitting circles, more or less. Pre-modern versions of a book club. They would get together and share glamours and prana manipulation techniques, and complain about their mates, children, and chores. And obviously, vampires have formed covens for most of human history, and the two got conflated."

"I didn't know that, Philemon," I say. "Thank you for sharing that."

He smiles. "My mother was in one. I was young enough that they let me sit in with them, until I was too old, at least."

"So a vampire coven is like a family," Caspian says. "A chosen family. It can be all men, all women, or a mixture. It can be three people or fifty. You become a coven and you share a bond. I can talk to my coven mentally from any-where in the world."

Sharon's eyes bug out. "Y'all are blowing my damn mind." She rubs her face with both hands. "And I still want to know about pack sexual politics. But we keep gettin' off track."

Saige laughs. "It's a lot to take in. Immortals don't view sex the same way you mortals do. We're more…open about it, even more so than Europeans compared to Americans. But it's…" she looks at me. "You might be better off an-swering that than me."

I consider the question. "It's weird, honestly. I wasn't, like, promiscuous as a mortal teenager. I had a few…not boyfriends—we moved around too much to get too deep into feelings. But I had sex, and I liked it. But I never even thought about multiple partners or any of that. I liked sex, and that was about the end of it. And then it turns out I'm immortal, and everything changed. I mated with Caspian and felt attracted to the others. Now, that's not usual, but there are rules. Nothing worth getting into, but suffice it to say that actual penetrative sex is generally reserved for mates. When a vampire is feeding from a host—a mortal, usually—it's a sexual thing. But it's limited to foreplay—most vampires don't even *want* to have actual sex with a host, it's just that the act of drinking blood is an intimate, physical, and erotic thing—and sexually pleasurable."

"For the vampire, you mean."

"No, for the mortal. I'd recommend trying it. Not with my mate, of course, because we're exclusive—me and my mates. Caspian and I don't feed from mortals. Caspian feeds from me, and I feed from Caleb."

She stares at me. "If I let a vampire drink my blood, I'll get off?"

I nod. "You will. It will feel like nothing you've ever experienced before. But do be careful—you might not go back to boring old mortals." I say this with a wink.

"So, pack politics," Saige says. "Most packs are mixed gender, like ours." She sighs. "We have another female, but she's…not with us. For personal reasons." She shakes her head. "Anyway. Most packs do have sex with each other, but it's complicated. See, shifters especially produce more males than females for unknown reasons. Most packs only have one or two women, so the sexual politics can get complicated, keeping everyone happy. It's not…it's hard to explain because that's not how our pack works. But usually, a pack forms a very complex multi-directional marriage, you might say. It's unique to shifters. Fae tend to form more traditional single-mate relationships. Vampires too, but that's complicated by feeding habits."

Sharon shakes her head. "My brain is spinning. So… if I fall in love with some immortal, and we bang, I'll die?"

"Only if you get pregnant. And the conception rates are about the same, I think, so you have the same chances as with a mortal male."

"And condoms, birth control, none of that works?"

"Nope," Saige says. "Condoms, maybe, for a while, but they tend to fail. Immortals cannot take birth control—it doesn't work. It may as well be a sugar pill. And in mortal women, birth control just… doesn't work either—immortal semen just…overpowers it or something. It's not very well understood because it's hard to study."

Sharon just nods. "Good to know." She stares at nothing for a while and then shakes her head. "It's absolutely *wild* that I never knew any of this. That *no mortal* knew any of this till a few weeks ago."

"Well, it was less of a mystery before the Treaty. We weren't forced into hiding then," Callahan says. "People knew we were out there, that we existed, and some of the details of how we function and what we are, but mortals have always been afraid of us. That was most of human history. It's just the last couple hundred years that things have been like this. Older immortals remember the old ways, how it was before. But we younger ones were born too close to the Treaty to know the difference."

Caleb pulls the van off the two-lane highway, following a sign for a local cafe. A few minutes later, we reach a junction. On one corner, a gas station. On another, a small cafe—a few cars are parked at it, mostly beat up old pickups. At a third corner, a small local history museum. The last corner is a general store advertising cold beer, pizza, liquor, and the like.

Caleb parks at the cafe, and we all pile out.

It's a tiny place with a black-and-white tiled floor, Formica counters, cracked vinyl booths along the front wall with a window at each, and a bar opposite. A handful of locals are at the bar, eating burgers and sipping coffee. The proprietor leans over the counter from the other side, a pot of coffee in one hand and a lit cigarette in the other.

He hears the little bell over the door ding as we enter. "Come on in, y'all," he says, without looking at us—he's examining something a man across from him drew on a napkin, grinning.

And then his eyes flick to us, narrowing. They land on Caspian. "He sick?"

"No." Caspian lifts his chin. "I'm not sick."

"Then what's wrong with you? You don't look right." He scans all of us. "Somethin' off about all'a you."

"We just want something to eat," Sharon says. "Our money's green, same as anyone else's."

I touch her shoulder. "It's not your responsibility to defend us."

She shakes her head. "I been refused service because of the color of my skin, Maeve. I know how it feels. I know where this is going." She shakes her head again. "Feels like the same damn thing to me, and I don't like it."

The proprietor's eyes narrow to slits, and he straightens, wedging his cigarette in the corner of his mouth and crossing his arms over his chest. "Y'all are them...whaddya call it. Freaks. Immortals. Them weird, magicky fuckers from the news."

"I'm a vampire," Caspian says. "They're shifters." He gestures at the pack and then at me. "She's a vaer—fae and vampire."

"Well, I ain't' servin' no damn bloodsuckers."

Caspian growls. "I have no interest in your blood. Trust me. I wouldn't touch you with a ten-foot pole. I'll drink coffee and mind my own business. Talk to my... friends. Pay good money. They just need to eat."

Smoke skirls in his eyes. "Y'all can get the fuck out. Ain't servin' you. Keep your money."

I step forward. "We're no threat to you or anyone. We're passing through and we just want some food. You don't need to be like this."

"I'll be however the fuck I wanna be, bitch. Take your ass outta my restaurant 'fore I call the sherriff."

Caleb and Caspian both snarl viciously, and he takes a step back, paling.

I catch their arms. "Stop, stop, stop. Not helping. I've been called worse as a mortal." I sigh. "Let's just find somewhere else."

One of the patrons speaks up, then—an overweight, balding man in denim overalls. "Try Brutus's place, down the road about half a mile." He jerks his thumb north, indicating a county road heading away from the highway we've been following. "He's a weird, freaky fucker, lives way out in the sticks with a bunch'a folks. Might be one'a your kind. Least, he'll prolly serve you."

"Thank you, sir," I say. "I appreciate the information. Have a nice day." I nod to the proprietor. "You too."

He just snorts smoke out of his nostrils.

Outside, Sharon groans in anger. "That shit makes me so mad. It ain't right."

"It's a part of life," I say. "Something I imagine you have far more experience with than us. Or me, at least."

She nods. "Yeah, maybe. Ignorance is ignorance, though, no matter what it's about. But I guess it just goes to show bigotry ain't just about skin color or who you're bangin.'"

We pile back in the van and head north in the indicated direction. The van is quiet.

"I should have stayed in the van," Caspian says after a moment. "You'd have gotten served without me."

"Fuck that shit," Callahan grumbles, his voice tense and pissed off. "That's exactly why we're doing what we're doing." He lifts his chin at Sharon. "Once upon a time, that dumbfuck redneck would've refused her service. Fuck, he still might have. But overall, this country's made progress, right? Progress like that didn't come from people staying in the goddamn van, Caspian."

Caspian sighs. "But I don't even need food."

"That ain't the point, sugar," Sharon says, reaching over the back of the bench to pat his knee. "You oughta been able to walk in and sit with your friends while they ate."

"Can I play devil's advocate for just one second?" Colin says. "There *is* a slight difference between racism based on skin and what we're dealing with now. Sharon is just the same as any other mortal. No more dangerous or different than anyone else. But to mortals, Caspian *is*, conceivably, dangerous. They don't know he won't go flying into bloodlust and kill everyone. And the problem is that it *is* a possible scenario. Perhaps not likely, but *possible*. They don't know anything about us, so their fear *does* have some amount of merit."

I tip my head back with a rough sigh. "You present an unfortunate truth, Colin. So not only do we have to combat the human fear of *otherness*, but we also have to fight the very rational fear of us because we are, in fact, dangerous to mortals."

"We can't present it like we're just a different sort of human," Channing says. "It's more complicated than that."

"It will be a long, uphill battle for acceptance and inclusion." I rub my face. "I think the best first step is the one we're taking right now: stopping it from becoming another all-out war."

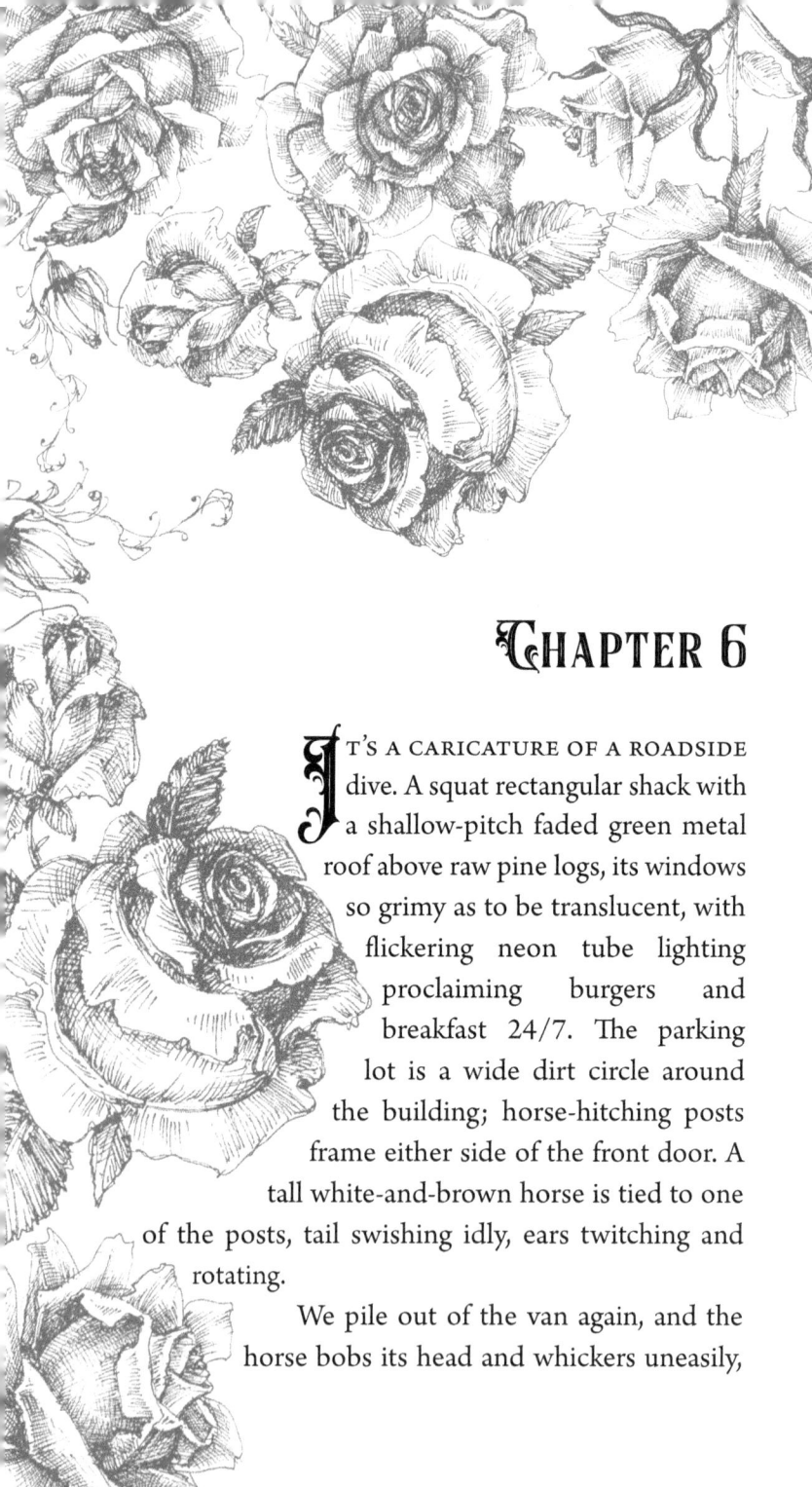

CHAPTER 6

I<small>T'S A CARICATURE OF A ROADSIDE</small> dive. A squat rectangular shack with a shallow-pitch faded green metal roof above raw pine logs, its windows so grimy as to be translucent, with flickering neon tube lighting proclaiming burgers and breakfast 24/7. The parking lot is a wide dirt circle around the building; horse-hitching posts frame either side of the front door. A tall white-and-brown horse is tied to one of the posts, tail swishing idly, ears twitching and rotating.

We pile out of the van again, and the horse bobs its head and whickers uneasily, nostrils flaring, dancing around on its hooves. The shifters give the horse a wide berth.

"Horses can smell our animal," Caleb says to me, catching my hand in his. "We make 'em nervous."

Inside, the floors are faded and worn wooden planks, the walls are the same raw pine logs, and the ceiling is the underside of the metal roof, sprayed with black insulation and crisscrossed with girders supporting HVAC and lighting. A handful of round four-person tables dot the interior, with a pair of two-way double doors leading to the kitchen opposite the front door. A window with a wide stainless-steel ledge shows a glimpse of the kitchen—a shelf lined with white ceramic plates and Styrofoam clamshells and bags of buns. On one side of the kitchen doors is a small counter with an antique cash register, a credit card machine from sometime in the 80s, and a glass case with a rotating cake display featuring a few sad slices of days-old carrot cake. On the other side, another short stretch of the counter with a few stools, opposite which, under the window, is a low stainless-steel table with an industrial Bunn two-pot coffee maker and the various coffee-making necessaries, as well as thermoses of milk and half and half.

A single male sits at the counter, a dirty white cowboy hat sitting crown-down on the counter beside him, sipping coffee and picking at fries.

On the other side of the counter, a gargantuan man leans thick forearms on the counter, chatting with the customer in a low, familiar tone. He's only six feet tall or so but built like an industrial freezer. Broad, bulging shoulders, cliff-like chest, tree-trunk arms straining the sleeves of a dirty white T-shirt. His lower half is hidden by the counter.

His hair is brown, curly, and shaggy, and he wears a thick, bushy, chest-length brown beard, well-kept and clean.

He sees us enter, straightens, and passes stiffened fingers down through his beard. "Welcome in. Sit wherever." His voice is a slow, syrupy Georgia drawl. His nostrils flare, and his chin rises. "TwiceBlood brothers and sister."

Caleb steps forward. "TwiceBlood brother. Will you welcome our OnceBlood companions and our mate?"

The burly shifter's nose twitches, his upper lip with it, making his drooping mustache twitch. "Vampire and…" His eyes widen, fixing on me. "You're her."

"I'm me," I say with a smile. "My name is Maeve."

He rounds the counter and stops in front of me, expression inscrutable. "You're the one they call the Once-Mortal Queen. They say you're fighting for our kind."

"They do say those things about me, yes." I take his hands in mine, silencing Caleb's growls with a quick glare. "Will you welcome me?" I gesture at Caspian. "My vampire bloodmate?" At Philemon. "Our new fae friend?" At Sharon. "Our mortal friend?"

"If you bring peace, I welcome you." He drops to one knee. "Honored to have you here. Please, be welcome."

I tug him to his feet. "We're very hungry." I wrap my arm around Caspian's waist. "Except him."

The huge shifter eyes Caspian warily. "A hungry vampire makes anyone nervous, m'lady." For a brief moment, his southern drawl becomes something more European, but it's there and gone so fast I doubt my ears. "My name is Brutus."

"Well, Brutus," I say, taking a seat at the bar next to the silent customer. "Caspian isn't hungry."

Caspian chuckles. "Not exactly true. I *am* hungry."

He nuzzles my throat. "But yours is the only blood that will satisfy."

The customer beside me turns his head slowly to eye Caspian, seated on the other side of Caleb, who is beside me. "Good answer," he says in a raspy smoker's drawl; his eyes flash golden white, and a thumb-size fireball dances across his knuckles. "Hate to have to interrupt my lunch."

"Jeremiah," Brutus says in a deep, warning rumble. "Unnecessary."

Jeremiah just grins, flicking the fireball from knuckle to knuckle, fingertip to fingertip in an impressive display of magical control. "Just making myself known."

The pack puts two tables together and we sit all together, along with Philemon and Sharon. Brutus takes orders all around, stopping last at Caspian. "I do keep some bags in the back. I'm the only immortal-friendly place in the county, so I keep 'em on hand for emergencies. You want one?"

Caspian grins. "That'd be great, Brutus, thank you."

I eye him after Brutus has vanished into the kitchen—a series of sizzles announces the burgers hitting the grill. "I thought you didn't like the bagged blood?"

He shrugs. "It's better than nothing, and who knows when we'll get privacy to feed the way I need? Plus, refusing hospitality is rude."

I nudge him. "You know we'll find a way."

He leans close and kisses the corner of my jaw behind my earlobe. "I know." He sips the coffee in his hands—more for appearances in case a non-immortal were to come in, and for something to do while the rest of us eat and drink.

Behind us, the pack makes desultory conversation

with each other and Sharon and Philemon, trading unlikely stories.

Jeremiah finishes his fries and slides off his stool, sidling around the counter to refill his coffee and ours with
a familiarity that speaks of being a long-time regular. "So."
He glances at me. "Once-Mortal Queen, huh? When's the
coronation?"

"Nothing like that," I answer.

"Hear Atlanta is a real warzone." He peers at me sidelong through a haze of steam. "Immortals roving around in
gangs, openly doing magic and shifting and feeding. Scared
mortals are forming their gangs, I hear, and attacking anyone reported to be different."

"So I've heard," I answer, noncommittal.

"Seems like a queen oughta do something about that."

"I'm working on it. I can't settle things one city at a
time. I can't fix everything on my own. We're making our
way to New York, where I'm hoping to sort of…set an
example."

He nods. "Hear it's a real mess up there. Not just petty
squabbles between civilians, but actual organized fighting."

"So we've heard too, which is why I'm starting there."

He nods. "About time somebody did something." He
examines me. "Figured it'd be someone a little more… experienced, I'll admit, but if you're willing to take on the
job…"

I laugh ruefully. "The job was sort of thrust onto me,
but I won't shirk it. You have my word I'll do my best to
see our people accepted and included, no matter what it
takes or how long it takes."

He nods again. "You've got some good answers, girly."

Caleb growls. "Do *not* address my mate as 'girly,'" he snaps, his voice crackling with Alpha Prime authority.

Brutus emerges from the kitchen with a long, black-handled flipper in his huge paw. "You're a Prime."

Caleb nods. "I am."

Brutus bows his head. "Alpha."

Caleb waves him off. "All good, Brutus. Thanks."

Jeremiah tosses a $20 on the counter. "See ya 'round, Brute."

Brutus waves with the flipper. "See ya 'round, Jer. Say hi to Mags for me."

Jeremiah nods, plopping his hat on his head and exiting to swing onto his horse. Hooves clop, and then he's out of sight.

Brutus makes several trips, dropping off plates of burgers and fries for everyone, except Caspian, for whom he brings a now-familiar white pouch of blood.

Once we've all dug into our food, Brutus leans on the counter by Caleb. Caleb sniffs the air. "You're a bear?"

"I am. But my pack is…complicated."

Caleb takes a big bite of his burger. "Damn good burger, my friend," he says between chews. "All packs are complicated."

Brutus hums a noncommittal sound. "Mine especially so."

Caleb finishes his burger and turns to catch Nico's eye—the other male lifts his chin and brings his plate over to the counter.

"You doing okay with the pack, Nico?" Caleb asks.

Nico nods. "I get along with most people." He sighs. "My behavior this morning was extremely out of character."

Caleb claps him on the shoulder. "I understand.

Worry for a loved one will do that to the strongest male. Especially one without a pack."

Nico eats his fries four at a time. "Bears don't tend to form packs, Alpha. Not like you others. We bears like to keep our company. Family units are as big as things get, usually."

I glance at Caleb—the question must be in my eyes because he answers it before I ask it.

"In the TwiceBlood world, we refer to any group of shifters as a pack. But not all shifters even form true packs. It falls roughly along animal species lines. Wolves obviously form packs, because we're wolves. Hyenas, lions, the social predators all form recognizable packs. But solitary hunters like bears, tigers, and serpents do not. At most, they form family units and occasionally large but loose groups of family units. Which is what I suspect our new friend Brutus is calling his pack—a group of families." He gestures at Nico with his head. "Bears are territorial and don't usually get along well with unknown bears in their territory."

"How would they know? Usually, I mean?" I ask.

Nico answers. "Smell. I knew we were in a bear's territory before we got out at the last place. I knew he was a bear before we entered the restaurant."

"Remarkable." I sniff the air, closing my eyes, drawing on my senses. I shake my head. "Nothing."

Nico laughs. "You're not a shifter. And it's a certain scent only another bear would recognize. A wolf might smell it but wouldn't necessarily know what it means. Just like I might recognize a wolf's mark on a tree somewhere, but it doesn't register to me as 'here be wolves' like it would to another wolf." He indicates me. "You wouldn't smell it at all."

"How does your human brain translate your animal senses?" Sharon asks from the other table. Been wondering that."

Caleb answers. "I'm not sure we do, exactly. How a shifter's two selves co-exist isn't very well understood. For a long time, it was thought our animal lives inside us, and we let it out. But recent studies and experiments show a new understanding—we co-exist in different realms: The Waking and The Dreaming. When we shift, our selves switch. But we are always whole, always ourselves. So, I think the answer to your question is that my animal self still processes the sensory information that my human brain cannot conceive of—how the world looks to a canine, for example. Our nose gives us more information about the world around us than sight or sound. Bears too. But the human brain cannot perceive it that way. So I think the magic does the translation."

Sharon laughs. "That makes sense, logically, but part of me is kinda thinking it sounds a little like you're using magic to explain things you just don't understand."

Colin laughs. "I think you're right. But then, magic *does* explain a lot of things."

Sharon just shrugs. "I wouldn't know. I thought magic was just some Harry Potter shit till about last week. I thought all the news reports were just some bullshit, and then I saw some old dude flick his fingers and a dude across the road caught fire and burnt up in about fifteen seconds flat. Freakiest shit I've ever seen."

"You'll see freakier," Callahan says. "Just stick with us."

Sharon's eyebrows rise toward her hairline. "I got all sorts of jokes lined up, but I know you're not kidding, big boy. And that's what scares me."

He indicates me. "You're in good hands. She's the most powerful glamourworker alive."

I shrug. "That's not known to be true."

"You defeated Zirae, who was acknowledged by every elder to be the most powerful fae to ever live," Philemon says. "I believe that makes you more powerful than him."

I bob my head from side to side. "Perhaps. I didn't defeat him—he still lives, and I have to assume he's planning his revenge."

Philemon nods in accession to my point. "You still did what many thought was impossible, however. Zirae is no longer in power. He knows fear. He knows someone out there can challenge him."

"And that makes him even more dangerous," I say. "Now he has something to prove."

Onward and northward.

Callahan's burgeoning connection with Sharon. I know he knows better, but what am I supposed to do or say? She's beautiful, smart, funny, and accepts all of us without hesitation. So, I get it. But it worries me, for both of their sakes—I have Alistair front of mind as I think about this.

Given that, I check in with him mentally. ***How are things there?***

Quite well. Sorren has arrived with several elder shifters of various tribes. Updates to the property are progressing apace. How is your journey going?

Slow. We have to take all back roads and surface streets because the freeways are mostly impassable. We've

encountered some resistance from mortals, but we've also been joined by a mortal, as well as a shifter and a fae.

Collecting an army, then. That's good. I fear you'll need it to get into Manhattan. The news reports from there are not good. It's a volatile situation and it's only getting worse.

Awesome, I reply, with a mental sigh. **It's not going to be a quick trip up there, either.**

You can only do your best. And I think what you are doing, collecting people along the way, is just as important and necessary.

I hope so because I don't see any other way. But I'm actually hoping you can give me some advice on another issue.

I can certainly try. What's going on, my love?

The mortal we've adopted, Sharon? She and Callahan are developing a thing. And I don't know what to do about it, or if I SHOULD do anything or say anything. I mean, is it my place? He's a couple hundred years old and I know he knows the risks. We've made Sharon aware of the reproductive situation with immortals, so she knows, too. Do I say and do nothing and let the situation play out? Talk to Callahan? Talk to Sharon?

Alistair's response is slow in coming. That is quite a difficult situation, Maeve. On one hand, they're both adults. They are both aware of the risks. But emotions have a nasty tendency to override reason. I suppose my advice would be to talk to the mortal first. Make sure she really understands the risks in getting involved with Callahan and that you're only coming to her out of concern for her wellbeing.

That does make sense. Thank you, Alistair. I miss you guys.

We miss you, too, dearest one. Be safe.

I'll do my best. You too!

The risk here is minimal at best. But we will keep watch.

I resolve to get Sharon alone at some point.

The actual driving is easy enough—we made good time and didn't hit any obstacles. We're on a low-traffic county highway going through rural Georgia, so our progress is good.

And then we reach a small village around sunset and decide to stop for the night, and that's when things get interesting.

We top off our fuel tanks and then gather at a diner. Caspian fed from me discreetly on the drive, a quick but intense drink from my wrist as we pulled into town—enough to put some pink to his skin and make him less obviously a vampire.

The diner is mostly empty, with only a few tables being used. The waitress is a short, stout, older mortal woman with curly gray hair and the raspy voice of a lifelong smoker. With so many of us trooping through the door, we're worried she'd turn us away simply due to being overwhelmed, but she counts us silently and begins shoving tables together without a word.

We order quickly, and she sets about getting everyone drinks while the cook started our food. So far, so good. The food, understandably, takes a while to come and does so in waves since there's only one cook.

The trouble starts when one of the other customers, a teenage girl dining with who I assume are her parents, recognizes me.

Which is weird enough for me on its own—I certainly didn't have nationwide—if not global—fame on my bingo card. It's when she comes over to me that the trouble begins.

"Um, hi?" She shuffles over to me, her phone in her hands.

I blink, startled. Look up at her, confused. "Hi."

She turns her phone to face me—it's a screenshot of me from the viral video that began all this. "Is this you?"

The hum and hubbub of chatter and clinking utensils quiets. "Uh, yeah." I sip Diet Coke. "I'm Maeve." I hold out my hand for her to shake.

She stares at my hand like it's got some contagious disease visible on it. "I'm Tilly." She's about fifteen or so—only four years younger than me but somehow seems like a baby after all I've been through. "What are you doing *here*?"

I drop my hand. I can't tell if she's excited, awestruck, disgusted, confused… "Well, I'm headed to New York. Do you live around here?"

She shrugs. "Yeah. Can you really do magic? Like, *real* magic? Not, like, illusions or whatever?"

"Um, well, yes."

She looks at Caspian. "And…he's a real, actual vampire?"

"Yes, he is." I take Caspian's hand in mine. "He's my mate. Kind of like a husband."

"Can you show me some magic?"

"Tilly! Get back over here!" Her mother says in a low, venomous hiss. "*Now*! Stay away from those…those… *things*!"

"Mom, god, *stop*!" Tilly turns to look at her mother over her shoulder with a bug-eyed glare of embarrassment. "Don't be such a bigot. Geez."

I try to smile, but it's wobbly and weak. "Um, well?"

I look at her parents: her mother is red-faced with anger, sporting an impressive "I'd like to speak to your manager" super-Karen bob, and her father is muscular but big-bellied, wearing camo cargo shorts, a black "wifebeater" style tank top, and Crocs with calf-high white tube socks. "Your mom may not like that."

She rolls her eyes. "She doesn't like anything except rosé wine and *The Bachelor*." She smiles at me, bouncing up and down a couple of times. "Please?"

I flourish my hand and conjure a rose. Present it to her with a smile. "Here."

Her eyes widen and she slaps her palm over her mouth. "SHUT—UP! That was *so* cool!"

I shrug, grin. "Thanks. It's just a little trick."

"Can I learn how to do that?"

I wince. "Well, no, probably not."

"I heard you were mortal like me, once, though."

"Well, it's a little more complicated than that." I try to decide how to explain it to someone without an understanding of magic. "I wasn't *actually a* mortal. There was a glamour, what you might think of as a spell, making it *seem* like I was. It stopped working, and I became who I really am. So, I didn't *become* immortal, really, I just stopped *looking* and *feeling* like a mortal."

Her face falls. "Oh."

"Sorry." I gesture at the rose. "You can keep that, though. It was nice to meet you."

"Can I get a selfie with you?"

I hesitate, thoroughly weirded out by this whole situation. I force a smile. "Sure!"

Tilly lowers herself into a crouch next to me, phone held out at arm's length, and snaps a few quick selfies.

"Tilly Margaret Alanson!" Her mother screeches loudly, irate, marching over to us. "That is *quite* enough, young lady. These *creatures* are dangerous."

She reaches for her daughter, snatching the phone with such abrupt violence that the device clatters to the floor, the screen shattering.

"MOM!" Tilly yanks her arm away. "You're *such* a bitch!"

The father lurches out of his seat and takes two stomping, lumbering steps toward his daughter, hand raised.

Caspian is a blur of shadows even to my eyes—to the mortals, he'll have simply appeared between the father and Tilly. "Strike your child, and I strike you," he snarls, venomous and vicious. "And trust me, *mortal*, I strike *far* harder than you."

"Fuck you, *punk*," the father grunts, and lashes out with a punch.

He's a big man and probably cut quite an intimidating figure twenty years ago. As it is, had Caspian been a mortal twenty-year-old, the punch would have broken his jaw. But since Cas is what he is, the man only succeeds in breaking his own fist.

Caspian chuckles. "Is it my turn now?"

"Cas," I warn, muttering quietly.

He sighs, annoyed. "So I *can't* rip his arm off and beat him to death with it?"

"No," I say. The man looks pale and worried, cradling his broken hand, looking from me to Caspian. "Maybe just a finger or two as a lesson."

Caspian is barely holding back laughter—it's wrong, I know, but so am I.

Caspian picks up a glass from their table—empty,

but for melting ice and the dregs of Diet Coke. He stares at the man as he slowly closes his fist. The glass cracks, just hairlines and spiderwebs at first, and then a chunk splinters away and tinkles on the floor; he squeezes harder and shards rain down. He clenches his fist closed, grinding, and the glass becomes dust trickling from the bottom of his hand. He opens his hand, showing a multitude of cuts dribbling blood, which heal in real-time.

Tilly turns to look up at Caspian. "Please don't hurt them," she whispers. "I know they're assholes, but they're *my* assholes and they're all I've got."

Caspian brushes his palms together and then dusts them on the thighs of his jeans. "No one is hurting anyone." He smiles. "I admire your bravery and open-mindedness, Tilly." He stares hard first at the father then the mother. "You could learn something from your daughter, the both of you. It's not smart to antagonize someone who offered neither harm nor insult, especially when that someone could end you before you could blink. Remember that I didn't harm you, even after you struck me."

A tall middle-aged mortal male, thin and scrawny everywhere but with a protruding potbelly, scurries over. "I think you should leave. All of you. Now. I'll comp your meals—just leave."

Caleb rises to his feet and towers over the mortal. "Why?"

"You're causing a scene and scaring my customers." He pales but holds his ground before Caleb.

Caleb arches an eyebrow. "*We're* causing a scene? *They* approached *us*. She yelled at her daughter in public for talking to us. Her father would have struck her. Yet *we're* causing the scene?"

I sigh. "I won't argue with recalcitrant mortals, Caleb." I rise to my feet. "I believe most of us are finished anyway."

Tilly stomps her foot. "This whole thing is stupid! You're supposed to be adults, but you're acting like scared little children!" She glares at her parents and then the manager. "You're going to comp their meal? Which has to be, what? A hundred dollars? Two hundred? You're an idiot." She turns back to me. "I'm sorry, Maeve. I didn't mean to cause you trouble."

I smile at her. "You did nothing wrong. This is what we're facing. People don't understand us. We just need more people to be like you."

She smiles, twirling the rose between her finger and thumb. "I'm glad I got to meet you."

"So am I, Tilly." I use a tendril of prana to scoop up her broken phone and fix it, floating it into her hands.

Her eyes widen and shimmer. "Ohmygod. THANK YOU!"

I hear her mother gasp in outrage.

My eyes go cold as I regard her. "Did you have something to say?" I reach out a tendril of prana and wrap it around her—she can't see it, but she can feel it, a warm, invisible coil. I taste her, feel her. "Your name is *actually* Karen? Wow." I drop my voice to a whisper only she can hear. "Does your husband know about the lawn boy, do you think? I know your daughter does."

Her eyes widen. "No, please. It was…it was just once."

I smirk. "You can lie to yourself, Karen, but you can't lie to me."

"It…it doesn't mean anything."

"You're religious, Karen. You read your Bible, don't you?"

She swallows hard. "Y-yes?"

"Maybe you should read the part where Jesus tells the Pharisees that whichever one of them hasn't ever sinned can be the first one to throw stones at the prostitute." I saw a TikTok about that once, in LA before Mom died. I guess it stuck with me for some reason.

"I…I…"

I pull my prana back in and walk away. "Someone pay for our meal. Let it be known that the Once-Mortal Queen pays her debts." I sweep out of the restaurant without looking back, hoping my exit is as dramatic as I intend.

Sometimes, you just have to make a statement.

A few minutes later, the rest of our crew has left and is piling into the vehicles.

A small crowd has gathered—curious locals who've heard about some hubbub at the restaurant. They record us with cell phones and snap photos with their phones held over their heads as if I'm some A-list actress.

There's a motel a mile or so down the road, a sad, dilapidated place that's probably thirty years past its best days, such as they may have been.

"Maybe y'all oughta let me negotiate," Sharon says.

I scan the motel—a long, low, single-story building with a dozen rooms. I frown, realizing that at some point, I stopped thinking about money; I have no idea who paid for our meal, or how, or how we paid for gas.

Caspian touches my mind with his, feeling my question and answering it. *We're a wealthy coven,* he says. *You don't need to worry about money.*

A few minutes later, Sharon emerges from the motel office with a handful of tarnished brass keys attached to oversized white plastic squares with room numbers printed beneath peeling lamination.

"They're all the same," she says, "So take a key and pick a room, y'all."

Another few minutes later, the keys are distributed, and the rooms have been claimed. I have one with Caleb and Caspian. We set our bags on the king-size bed, looking around at the room.

Faux wood-paneled walls, dirty, worn green shag carpeting, a TV that would have been cheap thirty years ago.

"The Ritz it is not," I murmur. "But it's somewhere to sleep for the night."

"Sleep," Caspian says, sidling up behind me. "Right."

Caleb cups my jaw in a hand. "My pack and I need to run," he murmurs. "Don't wait up."

I tug on a lock of his messy, over-long blond hair. "Wake me when you're back."

A small smile touches the corner of his lips. "Maybe." He glances at Caspian. "Take good care of our girl."

Caspian grins, already unbuttoning my jeans. "Oh, I will."

Caleb's eyes track the movement of the zipper, and his nostrils flare as he scents my sex when Caspian tugs my jeans down past my butt. "Dammit," he mutters to himself. "Fuck it. The run can wait."

He peels off his shirt, shucks his jeans and underwear, and prowls toward me, dropping to his knees in front of me. Caspian tugs up my shirt—I lift my arms, and he tosses it aside. Caleb drags my jeans around my ankles, helps me out of them, and then hooks one finger in the front of my panties. Caspian unhooks my bra, and Caleb pulls down my underwear.

I reach behind me, grasping for Caspian's manhood, but he snags my hands and lifts them up over my head and behind me; I find his hair and hold on.

My bra vanishes, and my panties, too. Caleb's beard tickles my thighs as he kisses up from my left knee; Caspian's lips kiss behind my right ear and then down my neck. I shiver and widen my stance.

Caleb traces a finger down my seam, teasing me as his lips slowly kiss upward and then go to my other leg. Caspian kisses my throat, my jugular, and then licks…and licks…and licks, and venom sizzles into my flesh and into my veins, bubbling in my blood. My sex heats, pulses, and floods with the wetness of need.

Caleb catches the scent of my desire, rumbling in his chest. "Now, bond-brother," he whispers.

His tongue laps against my clit and his lips fuse around it, and at the exact same time, Caspian punctures my flesh with his fangs; my blood sings, and ecstasy surges through me.

I cry out, going limp as release blasts through me, plunging me into throes of heady bliss. Caspian draws at my blood, and his hands cup my breasts; I feel his erection nestle between the globes of my buttocks, still hidden behind the clothes he still wears.

Meanwhile, Caleb is devouring me. He tongues me eagerly, ravenously, as if I'm his last meal. The first initial foray into orgasm was a mere precursor to what's building, now.

Caspian pinches my nipples, squeezing hard and pulling them away and then releasing, timed in synch with his slow suckling of my blood. Caleb, in counterpoint to Caspian's slow deliberation, is hungrily feasting upon me, licking, flicking, sucking, while his hands grip my ass, toying, teasing his touch closer and closer…

But then, as I hover, gasping, on the edge of the orgasm, Caleb pulls away and gets to his feet, wiping his lips with his wrist.

"No-no-no," I whimper, "I was right there!"

Caleb doesn't respond in words. He waits until Caspian withdraws his fangs and closes the wound, and then steps into me. He palms my ass in his hands, claims my mouth with his, and lifts me while kissing me. I moan into his mouth, tasting myself on him—I draw prana from him and feel him opening to me, offering it freely; I, in turn, hold myself open so he can pull at my mana.

Caspian knots his hands in my hair and kisses the back of my neck, between my shoulder blades…licks down my back, touching each knob of my spine with his tongue so his venom spikes into me, sending white-hot lances of need shivering through me. The orgasm I'd been on the cusp of swells through me once more, building rapidly to a shuddery new intensity.

Caleb's cock nuzzles my opening, and I cling to Caleb's neck, taking his tongue into my mouth and drawing at his prana, tasting his soul as he offers it up to me. Life billows through me—a wild, manic energy. Need shatters, a desperate starvation for my mates.

And then, with a sharp thrust, Caleb is inside me, pushing deep, stretching me apart with his huge, hot, hard cock. I cry out into his mouth, whimpering into the kiss. He pulls me down onto him until I'm seated on him as deep as he can go, and then he thrusts even deeper until I ache with him, can't kiss anymore, can't breathe, can't think, can only scream silently as the orgasm smashes me into shaking, shivering paroxysms.

All the while, Caspian kisses my flesh everywhere—shoulders, throat, spine, sides, hips, thighs…pushing venom into me until I'm writhing and gasping breathlessly.

Caleb sinks to his knees, sitting on his shins, and then thrusts—I scream, finally catching my breath.

Behind me, Caspian lets my hair go to spill down my back, caressing my cheek. I open my eyes, see him standing next to me, watching. His cock stands at attention, begging. I reach for him, holding Caleb's neck for balance with one hand and clutching Caspian's cock with the other. Caress his hot length and pull him closer. My vampire takes over for a moment, and I tilt his cock away, softly stroking him, licking the soft, tender skin next to his balls, and then suckling one delicate egg-like weight into my mouth, let it go, and lick his inner thigh. My venom makes him groan, and his cock pulses in my hand. I puncture his femoral and blood spurts hot and sweet into my mouth, and the blood-bond spreads through me. I feel him, feel his pleasure in my veins, in my body. The hot, taut, hard pulse of his cock, the tight weight of his balls, the anticipation in his belly, I feel it all—it's as disorienting as it is erotic because it's layered over and through my own pleasure. I feel my pussy split open to a throbbing hot ache by Caleb's cock, the wild line of climax rising from my core, my breasts heavy and my nipples hard.

I stroke Caspian's length and feel his pleasure at my touch spread through me, making my own pleasure multiply; I squeeze around Caleb, and he thrusts into me. I feel Caspian moan, and I know he feels my sensations as I feel his.

With his blood warm and sweet in my mouth, I close Caspian's flesh and find Caleb's wrist and waste no time licking his wrist and sliding my fangs into his vein, and now…oh, fuck, oh fuck, I feel him too, I can feel the tight wet heat of me clenching around him, the pulsing pressure of orgasm building inside him, the flow of prana leaving him and mana flooding in.

Three-way ecstasy pounds inside me, confusing and overwhelming and incredible. Our united sensations weave through us, uniting us in a whole new way—I stroke Caspian's cock, and Caleb moans as well. Rise up and slam down, squeezing as hard as possible the whole way, and Caspian growls at the same time as Caleb.

Caleb presses a thumb against my clit, and all three of us gasp.

Whenever I think I have this multiple mates business figured out, the magic of it goes and does something new—like this.

Caleb drives up into me, and I gasp and caress Caspian's length. We all shudder as orgasm shivers and hovers just out of reach.

"Need your mouth, my love," Caspian murmurs. "Please."

I lick Caleb's wrist. Pull Caspian's cock toward me and wrap my lips around him, slide my tongue against him— we all groan, and my sex tightens involuntarily, and Caleb thrusts into me.

And, oh god, it's wild, then. Caleb fucks me soft and slow, and Caspian stands with the statue-like stillness only a vampire is capable of as I take him to the back of my throat, and both men growl and gasp and groan, and I whimper.

When I feel Caspian reaching his edge, I pull away. "Need you inside me, my love," I whisper, leaning into Caleb.

He takes the cue and moves to his back on the floor. I crush my breasts against his chest and tilt my backside high. Caspian vanishes for a moment and then returns with a cracking click of a plastic lid, and warm wetness floods down my ass and his fingers smear it over me and into me—one finger delves in, and then two, and I hear the slick squelch of his hand on his cock—I turn to watch over my shoulder, biting my lip in anticipation and desire. His cock glistens with lube, and his fist slicks down it.

"Oh fuck, please," I whisper. "Please."

He presses the tip against me. "This? You need me?"

"Need you," I agree, writhing on Caleb with eager flutters of my hips. "Please, my love."

I crane my head to watch over my shoulder as he presses in, slowly, gently; his eyes are subsumed with black as he penetrates me, and I cry out, feeling the ecstasy of it threefold—my own, as well as his and Caleb's in rippling echoes.

An eternity later, he bottoms out inside me, and I'm so full it hurts, but it hurts beautifully, perfectly. The rippling echoes of pleasure shudder through me, and I have to move. I shift forward, taking Caleb deeper, and Caspian withdraws...and then Caspian pushes in and Caleb slides out, and the slick slide of them is too much, and feeling it echoing and echoing and echoing is almost more than I can handle—more than my brain can process.

I whimper and let them take over. All I can do is keen in my throat as my men take me, love me. They move in unspoken synch, our spirits united in a way I never knew possible, and tears sting my eyes, glowing with prana and tinged scarlet with blood.

Faster, then, and I feel Caspian's orgasm pulsing at the edge of my mind and feel it throbbing inside my body, and Caleb is losing control of his thrusts, and now I feel him break apart first, with a loud guttural shout—I feel it in my pussy and in my soul, and Caspian feels it too, and he snarls with a dark, primal release, and now I'm coming, we're all three of us roaring like beasts, and our interwoven orgasms build upon each other and I see myself through Caleb's eyes and Caspian's at the same time, with my eyes closed, and then I open them and see Caleb beneath me, watching me, shocked wonder on his face, and turn to watch Caspian go through the same emotions, and I know my face must show them as well.

I feel Caleb's spirit, and Caspian's, and mine, a distinct union, three souls made one, and the physical sensations, as intense as they are, pale in comparison to the wonder of the spiritual.

Slowly, we settle back to earth, and the distorting, triplicate sensations fade, and I'm only me, feeling only my body and only my spirit.

For a moment, I'm lost without them.

They pull out, clean me, and cradle me between their bodies.

I sleep, and do not dream.

CHAPTER 7

NOISE WAKES ME. SLOWLY, AT first, a white noise without distinct form or meaning. Then, as I come out of the trance-like fog of sleep, the noise resolves itself into a cacophony of voices beyond the door.

I blink my eyes open—Caspian lounges on the bed beside me, staring at the noise with a pissed-off expression. "What is it?"

"Reporters. A fucking lot of them."

"How did they find us?" I ask.

He shrugs. "Who the hell knows? That mortal girl's parents, maybe? Or one of the rubbernecking local yokels outside the diner yesterday. Doesn't matter. They're here now."

"How many are there?"

He shrugs again. But then his gaze goes vacant and his nostrils flare, scenting. "Twenty-seven."

I rub my eyes. "Sorry, not awake yet. I could have done that."

He just chuckles. "You still sleep like a mortal. Not sure what to make of that."

I laugh, too. "Seems like I do, doesn't it? As a vaer, I shouldn't need sleep at all. Maybe I just like it?" I look around. "Caleb is running?"

He nods. "Slipped out a couple hours ago, not long before those jackals out there showed up."

"Mortals like a story," I say. "And we're a good one."

"No way to get out of this room without facing them, though. So you'll have to make some kind of a statement."

I nod, mind racing. "A statement, yes." A slow smile blossoms on my face. "This might actually end up working in our favor."

Caspian frowns at me. "How so?"

"Well, much of the enmity we're coming up against is ignorance-based fear. What's the best way to combat that?"

"Educate people," Cas answers.

"Exactly." I gesture in the direction of the noise. "And they'll be doing us a favor in helping us get the truth out there, helping us educate the public as to who we really are."

Acting on impulse, I slip out of bed and head for the door, my speech already forming in my mind.

A strong warm arm hauls me away from the door before I can open it. "Maybe some clothes first? American mortals are weird about public nudity."

I glance down, realizing only as he points it out that

I am, in fact, stark naked—I'm so used to it at this point that I forgot. "Oh, right—clothes." I lean back into him. "Thanks, love."

He kisses my temple, one arm slung low around my waist, the other across my chest midway between breasts and chin. "The shower has surprisingly good water pressure."

"Mmmmmm. Sounds good. Be right out."

Twenty minutes later, I'm showered, dressed, and my damp hair is braided, the tip dangling past my shoulder blades—it seems to grow faster after the incident in The Dreaming that turned it white than it ever did as a mortal. Another oddity without explanation.

I can make them leave, Caleb says, mind-to-mind. *I'm watching them from the tree line.*

It's okay, I answer. **I see this as an opportunity to expose mortals to the truth about us that isn't getting enough publicity.**

His answer is a wordless rush of warmth, pride, and approval.

Have a good run? I ask him.

We did. Made a kill. Felt good after days of not shifting.

Did Nico go with you?

A rush of amusement hits me. *Bears and wolves hunt very differently. He shifted when we did but went his own way.*

I brush his mind with a quick, loving caress, a wordless end to the brief conversation.

I head for the door, but some vague, indefinable instinct has me going back for a towel from the bathroom. Caspian quirks an eyebrow at the towel slung over my shoulder but says nothing as I pause at the door, hand on the knob.

"Ready?" I ask.

He nods once. "Ready."

I suck in a deep breath, hold it a moment, and let it out slowly, and then open the door and step out into the bright morning sunlight.

Immediately, the cacophony of voices erupts into a mad, deafening barrage of shouted questions and blinding flashes and cell phones and digital recorders being shoved at me.

I'm stunned at first and then claustrophobic as the crowd of reporters closes in around me, shouting and shoving.

Caspian snarls, stepping in front of me protectively, and I feel Caleb's protective anger boiling.

I lash out with a wave of prana infused with my will, and shout a single word: "*SILENCE!*"

Immediately, all noise halts—not just the voices, but *everything*. Birds, bugs, wind, traffic.

"Now. Everyone take three steps backward."

Because they have no choice, they do.

I see fear in their eyes, written on their faces—their mouths move frantically, but no sound emerges.

I hold up a hand, fist closed. "Now. Your attention, if you please." I keep my voice at a conversational level. "I will release your voices in a moment, but we must have order and calm. Behave like rational adults. Speak one at a time. I will answer questions *after* I've explained a few things." I scan the faces. "No shouting, and no interrupting—me *or* each other." I open my fist, splaying my fingers wide, and let the silence glamour fade.

There are a few coughs and some muttering as the reporters try out their voices, just to be sure.

"Now. As I'm sure you're all aware, I am Maeve Sparrow. The immortal community has given me titles: The WorldBreaker, and the Once-Mortal Queen." I hold up my hand to forestall the inevitable questions. "As I said, I'll take questions at the end. I am not royalty of any kind. I am not seeking to become 'queen of America,'" I use air quotes around the phrase, "or anything like that. Those immortals who follow me do so of their own will. As for WorldBreaker—while I didn't set out to break anything, I cannot deny that the events in Manhattan involving me, my mate, and my coven certainly did seem to set things in motion."

"Miss Sparrow," a young male mortal in the front says, "there are reports that you have more than one mate. Can you speak to that?"

I nod. "I can. It's true." I wrap my arm around Caspian's waist and lean into him. "This is one of them— his name is Caspian Taylor, and he is a vampire. Another mate, Caleb, is around here somewhere and might join us at some point—he's a shifter. The word you'll be tempted to use is 'werewolf,' but I'd advise you—and any mortals watching or listening—to never, *ever* refer to a shifter as a were-anything. It's a derogatory term—a slur, and a bad one." I glance at Caspian, smiling, and then at the crowd of reporters. "I have three other mates—all vampires, but they're elsewhere at this time."

I glance at the young man who asked the question. "One follow-up question, and then I'll move on."

"Polygamy is illegal in the United States, Miss Sparrow. Does that concern you?"

I shrug. "Not really. We aren't married in the legal, civil meaning of the word. And a mate is…" I trail off, thinking. "It's not marriage as you'd understand it. It's far more. More complex, and much deeper in every way—mentally, physically, and emotionally. But, if the letter of the law is your concern, then no, I'm not worried about it because we aren't married and I have no intention of worrying about such things. That's a mortal concern and has nothing to do with us."

"So mortal laws don't apply to you?" Someone near the back shouts.

I arch my eyebrow as more questions are shouted in overlapping chaos—at my quirked eyebrow, they all fall silent once more.

"Do not twist my words, mortal." I put some hardness into my voice. "Marriage is a mortal concern—that's what I said and it's what I meant, and you know it…" I send out a tendril of prana and find the one who shouted the question, tasting her mind and soul. "Britney Rogers, of St. Louis, Missouri, daughter to Ken and Eileen, girl-friend of Michael Krasinski."

I find her eyes. She pales.

"I…I'm sorry, M-miss…"

"Then don't ask stupid questions and don't twist my meaning."

No one speaks. I nod.

"The information available to mortals regarding who and what we are," I gesture at Caspian and then the other rooms, inside of which I feel the others listening and watching, "is scant and is either misleading, grossly inaccurate, or simply false. For example, vampires, such as my beloved mate, Caspian. I grew up, like you, thinking vampires, shapeshifters, all that was just…fairy tales. Stories. Tall tales. And much, if not all, of what you think you know about vampires from books or movies or comics, is laughably wrong. Caspian, clearly, is not a mindless, bloodthirsty monster. He has no interest in your blood, for the most part. And if, by some chance, he did decide to feed from you, you would not turn into a vampire. You wouldn't even remember it happening. It would not hurt you. It would not leave a mark or a scar. Crosses, silver, garlic, stakes through the heart, none of that is real."

A hand raises on my left and near the back. I point. "Yes."

"So…what *is* true, then?"

"Vampires do drink blood—human, fae, shifter, or animal. There are circumstances where a vampire in desperate need of blood can experience what's called bloodlust. But even then, the vampire is very, very, *very* unlikely to drink so much blood that the host is harmed because that is how you create what is called a nosferatu, which *is* a mindless, bloodthirsty killing machine. But such an act is expressly forbidden, and any vampire who does so will be hunted down and executed."

I exhale, gather my words, and continue. "Here's the delicate truth. Blood drinking, for vampires, is a sexual thing. They—we—release certain pheromones which cause sexual arousal in the host. This arousal erases fear and creates desire. Before piercing a vein the vampire will lick the host's skin. Our saliva contains a very powerful natural analgesic, which also creates intense physical pleasure, so even the piercing of flesh with fangs becomes a pleasurable experience. I can testify to this firsthand, as I was with him before I became what I am now." I hold up my hand once more. "Yes, there are questions of consent, which historically speaking was…not something most males ever really considered, mortal or immortal. This is the truth. You may have been fed upon by a vampire and wouldn't know it. If you remember anything, it would it be a vague memory of fooling around with someone. The important thing to remember is that while the feeding experience *is* sexual, the sexual component always ends at what you would consider foreplay. Immortals consider true, penetrative intercourse to be sacred, reserved exclusively for private, intimate moments between mates."

"There have been a few posts on various social media platforms claiming that if an immortal reproduces with a mortal, the mortal dies," an older man near the front on my right says. "Is there any truth to that?"

"There is. And that's why we are in the situation we're in. For most of human history, mortals and immortals lived together, aware of each other, in a tenuous sort of peace. There have been conflicts, of course, but for the most part, we have always lived among you, whether openly, in disguise, or merely quiet about our true nature. But then, around the time of the French Revolution, there was a movement among certain factions of immortals to be more open, to live among mortals freely, without hiding our natures or abilities. This movement spawned a small group of radicals who thought that because they were immortal and possessed abilities mortals did not, that immortals should be rulers or something. It's idiocy, and the vast majority of immortals did not believe that and condemned the breakaway faction. But the harm was done. The extremist faction took mortals against their will, openly. Wives, sisters, and daughters were taken and subjected to horrible things, which, understandably, caused fear and anger among mortals. It grew and spread here, in what was then the colonies. This conflict became mixed up in the larger political situation—the American Revolution. It became a war, a very messy, complicated one that mortals only remember part of. When the immortals began to lose the war, they signed a treaty. You see, despite our long lives, greater strength and senses, and magical abilities, we are very few and reproduction is difficult, which I will explain shortly. Mortals, with their greater numbers and technology, were able to sway the war against the immortals. In order to prevent any more lives from being lost, the elders of the time—elder immortals, I mean, those in positions of power and authority—signed what is only known as The Treaty. It was an agreement between mortals and immortals ending the war, with several conditions—chiefly, that immortals cannot under any circumstances reproduce with mortals. The other part of The Treaty was that a great spell would be cast—a glamour, as we fae call our works of magic. The glamour would erase all knowledge of immortals from mortal minds and memories, past, present, and future." I pause. "The Treaty was a death warrant for immortals. Why? Because we cannot create children with our own kind. A vampire cannot create a baby with a vampire. A shifter cannot create a child with a shifter. A fae cannot create a child with a fae."

"So when a mortal has a child with an immortal, the mortal dies?" This is from the elder male who posed the last question.

I nod. "Yes. But not as you might think. A male vampire, for example." I gesture at Caspian. "When we first began seeing each other, he resisted being with me for fear of impregnating me and thus causing my death. Because I was, then, seemingly mortal. Had I *been* a mortal, and had we mated resulting in pregnancy, I would have carried that child to term, given birth, and been a mother to that child. But being mortal, my body would not have been able to supply everything the baby needs. Even in utero, the baby would be siphoning away nutrients from my body, weakening me. A mortal body cannot survive the creation of an immortal. The host mother always, always dies, usually somewhere around breastfeeding or weaning. Immortals researched for centuries to find a way around this—because immortals are still people. They would fall in love with a mortal, and then that mortal would die. Loss of a loved one is devastating, no matter who you are."

"So…" the elder male speaks up again. "You can't procreate with mortals according to The Treaty, because it kills the mother. And you can't procreate with your own kind…" I see him putting two and two together. "You'll die out as a people, or species, or…I'm not sure how to put it."

"Exactly." I smile at him. "We are every bit as human as you. We're just…different. And I'm not sure how to put it either. But you're right. That's the problem. We can't reproduce. We live a very, very long time, but without children, eventually, there will be no more immortals."

"But there are three kinds of immortal, aren't there?" A woman asks.

"And what about an immortal woman with a mortal male?" Another man asks.

"Good questions," I say. "I'll answer the second first because the first question requires a more in-depth answer. A mortal male can impregnate an immortal woman, but the majority of the time, the process results in the immortal female going into a kind of blind lust called a mating frenzy, and the male is killed. She has no real control over this, and from what I've heard, it is devastating for the immortal female to come out of the mating frenzy and discover she's killed her lover. Now, unlike with mortal females, this is *not* uniformly fatal. The female *can* resist the frenzy. More usually, however, she must be restrained by her friends or family until the frenzy fades. But it is still very, very risky for the male."

"Seems like a good way to go, if you ask me," a young male in the front mutters.

I can't help a laugh. "Until she rips your head off, yes, it would be." A few scattered laughs greet this. "Now. The first question: there are three kinds of immortal—well, until recently this was true, but it is not any longer. That's next. For now, focus on the three I've mentioned: shifter, vampire, and fae. A quick explanation of the other two, since I covered vampires."

I feel Caleb approaching and pause. At first, my unexpected and extended silence confuses the reporters, and then there are shouts of fear and surprise. The crowd parts like a stage curtain. Caleb pads on silent paws toward me, a massive wolf the size of a male lion and approximately the same color.

He ignores the crowd entirely, stopping in front of me. I drop and wrap my arms around his neck, inhaling his warm, familiar scent and burying my fingers in the thick, soft lushness of his fur. He growls in his chest, a low rumble of approval.

I sense the shift coming, and then amber light blazes bright, and I open the towel to accord him some element of privacy—more so for the mortals than for him. When the blinding amber light dulls and fades, Caleb stands facing the crowd, nude and mammoth and carved from marble.

I don't miss the gasps of awe—mostly from the women.

"Show off," Caspian mutters under his breath so only the three of us can hear him.

Caleb chuckles as he wraps the towel around his waist.

In pure Caleb fashion, he curls me against his body, wraps my braid around his fist, and kisses me thoroughly and deliciously, and then he lets me go and assumes a casual stance beside me.

Once I've gotten myself under control, I clear my throat. "This, ladies and gentlemen, is a shifter. As I said before, he is *not* a werewolf." Caleb's snarl at the word is vicious, and those in the front take an involuntary step backward. "As with vampires, forget what you think you know. None of that applies. He won't bite you, and if he did, it wouldn't turn you into a shifter *or* a werewolf." I glance at him. "Stop the growling, my love. They have to understand." To the reporters, then. "Again, silver bullets won't work. Most of the time, you have nothing a shifter will be interested in. They don't drink blood, and they don't eat humans. What makes them a shifter is not some disease or mutation. Like vampires, they are *born*, not *made*. A shifter is a being who is fully animal and fully human." I gesture at Caleb. "He is always his wolf, and he is always his man. They coexist within him at all times. He always has a wolf's senses—smell, hearing, everything. He cannot speak in wolf form, but to his pack and me, his mate, he can communicate in other ways."

"Do they prey on humans like vampires?" A voice from the back calls.

"No," I answer. "Not as you would understand it. Shifters primarily value the same things their animals do: space to roam and to hunt, mates, and friends. You wouldn't know a shifter if you met one. Vampires, you might, if they're unblooded—a vampire in need of blood appears different. Hard, stone-like skin and eyes that are black from edge to edge."

"Not as we would understand it? What does that mean?"

I shake my head. "It means there are elements I do not have time to explain, and that is one of them. The short answer is that they feed on dream energy. You won't know, feel, remember, or care if a shifter was to consume some of your dream energy."

Caleb speaks then. "If you have ever felt a dream that sort of…changes…somewhat randomly, that's a shifter consuming your mana, your dream energy. You produce mana in huge quantities naturally but even when dreaming only use a fraction of it. We feed on the excess, in a place known as The Dreaming. As Maeve said, the shift in a dream is the only effect you'd notice. It cannot harm you."

A dozen questions are shouted, but once again I silence them with a look. "Fae," I say loudly, moving on. I glance to my left. "Philemon? Can you come out, please?"

A moment later, a door opens a few doors down from mine, and Philemon emerges. He's dressed like an accountant, again—creased-front khakis and a neat, pressed, baby blue button down, tucked in, with a slim leather belt and sensible low-profile sneakers. He has a glamour on, which works for my purposes. He moves through the crowd to stand with me—Caspian and Caleb step back to make room for him.

"This is my friend Philemon. He's a fae." I rest my hand on his shoulder.

He waves. "Hi."

"He looks..." a woman near the front starts, trails off. "Well...normal."

I meet his eyes. Nod. "Go ahead."

With a quick, sharp gesture, Philemon removes the mask, and his fae features emerge—sharp, aquiline, a little too perfect, somehow. His eyes glow with fresh prana, and his hair a little, too.

There are a handful of gasps and murmurs.

"Any fae who lives among mortals assumes what we call a mask—a glamour that makes him or her look mortal. It's a simple bit of magic, sort of like putting on makeup, I suppose. I've never used one, though."

Philemon nods. "Essentially, yes, although it's a bit more complex than makeup." He frowns and tilts his head to one side. "That may not be true, as I'm a man and do not wear makeup, which does seem like a very complicated process itself."

"Do you feel it?" someone asks.

Philemon shakes his head. "There's a brief tingle when I first apply the mask, but after that, no, I don't feel it. I do feel the drain on my prana, however."

"Prana is our word for magic, or rather, the energy which we use to create magic," I explain. "A fae is not a fairy. Nor are fae elves. Fae are fae—and the word is both plural and singular, by the way—one fae, many fae. Fae require prana, not just for magic, but to live, similar to how vampires require blood and shifters require mana—dream energy. Prana is...life-force. The energy that provides sentience. Mana is the energy of creativity and dreaming. Prana is life, metaphysically speaking, and blood is...well, blood, the force that animates the physical body. Gleaning prana is not always inherently sexual the way blood drinking is, but it can be. It *is* very intimate and very personal. In moderate quantities, it does not harm the host any more than drinking blood does—one thing I forgot to mention is that the pheromones and venom created by vampires also cause the body to overproduce blood, so you are not left weakened by blood loss, as long as the amount is moderate."

"Intimate but not sexual? What does that mean?" This sounds like the same person who asked Philemon if he feels the mask, but I'm not sure.

I glance at Caleb first and then Cas—they both nod, feeling my intention across the link.

"If you care to volunteer, I can show you. It will not hurt or cause harm; you have my word." I hold out my hand.

A moment of silence, and then a mortal male in his late thirties shuffles through the crowd and stops in front of me, eying my hand warily. He's fit and good-looking, wearing faded jeans, vintage Nike high tops, and a Ramones T-shirt.

"What…what do I do?" he asks.

I smile reassuringly. "Nothing. Just take my hand." He reaches for my hand, but his shakes. I can't help but laugh a little. "No tricks, I promise. You will come to no harm."

My laugh, or perhaps something in my eyes, convinces him, and he slips his hand over mine. I wrap my fingers around his palm and hold his gaze. I flex that muscle in my mind or spirit or wherever it is, and pull prana from him—just a trickle, a hint, enough to get a taste of the man.

An old house, dirty and cluttered, worn carpeting, stinking of cat pee, and musty decades of neglect. A postage stamp backyard with a rickety, splintery swing set-slide combo—the slide is warped and faded yellow plastic. Two young boys romp in the yard, playing war with sticks and rocks. A tired, over-weight woman with hair the color of old dishwater watches them, listless and lifeless, from a white plastic outdoor chair; a cigarette smolders between her index and middle finger, dangerously close to singeing her fingers.

One of the boys—the one whose memory I'm in—falls and scrapes his knee and runs to his mother, crying. At his tears, she transforms. She stubs the butt out in an overflowing ashtray sitting on an upturned milk carton next to her chair, on which is a warm, half-finished 20oz Mt. Dew. She lights up from the inside, life entering her features. She gathers him onto her lap and hugs him and kisses him and reassures him with whispers and gentle thumbs upon his cheeks. She brushes the dirt from his skinned knee, kisses her fingers, and touches them to his war wound, and then sends him back to play, pretending to be a stern general, with a snappy salute and a last-minute tickle.

My eyes sting as I withdraw from the memory, releasing his prana.

His eyes are hazed with tears.

"Your mother took wonderful care of you and your brother. She loved you with everything she had." I pat the back of his hand.

He nods, clearing his throat gruffly. "She…yeah. She was amazing. Worked three jobs to take care of us. Never had time for herself. We didn't have much, but it didn't matter. Mom was…" he blinks hard. "She died six months ago. Heart attack." He frowns. "That…that was it?"

I nod. "That was it. When we draw your prana, we feel your memories. It's…in my experience, it's random, what I see. Just hints, glimpses. A sort of taste of the person. That's why it's intimate but not sexual."

Philemon clears his throat. "It's actually not random, you know. It's usually the memory or memories that are top of mind for that person."

I blink at him. "Oh! Really?"

He nods. "Yes. It's taught in more formal fae educational settings, but obviously, you didn't receive that."

"No, I didn't. Thank you, Philemon, I appreciate it."

The mortal male looks at his hand, then at me. "So... you took...what did you call it? Prada?"

"Prana," I correct. "It's a Sanskrit word. Much of the terminology used by immortals comes from Sanskrit. And yes, I did—just a very small amount, for demonstration purposes. I prefer to get mine from my mates." I gesture at Caleb and Caspian.

"And we, mortals, I mean, don't use prana? Or mana?" he asks.

I shake my head. "As far as I'm aware, no. Or, so little as to be negligible." I glance at Philemon. "Anything to add?"

He tilts his head to one side. "I'm hardly an expert, mind you. But you're correct, Maeve. Mortals do use each of the Three Sisters, but only in very small amounts. Prana drives sentience, mana drives creativity, and blood drives physicality. Of maya, mortals have next to none, or simply cannot manipulate it—the difference is academic at best."

"Thank you, Philemon," I say. "Now. Questions. One at a time, please." I point at a hand near the back. "Yes, you, near the back."

"You're immortal, so you can't die?"

"We're immortal, so we cannot die of *natural causes.*

We don't get sick, not physically. We do not age, or just very, very slowly. But we can die by violence. It just takes a lot more damage than a mortal." I point at another hand. "Yes?"

"You're different than them? You're not fae, shifter, or vampire?"

"Correct. I'm what's called a vaer—V-A-E-R, half-vampire, half-fae. And I'm the answer to the questions about there being three kinds of immortal, in reference to reproduction. You see, historically, fae, shifters, and vampires do not get along. It's an age-old enmity going back literally thousands of years, ingrained in our natures. It's more than…well, racism, I suppose you could call it. More like how cats and dogs just naturally don't get along, but when taught to and raised together, they can. It was simply not an acceptable notion throughout history for the three races to mate with each other. You just didn't do it. It was not an option."

"If it's that or die out…" the asker prompts.

"Exactly my position," I say. "It's what I'm trying to accomplish. I want to bring mortals and immortals into society together as equals, and I want immortals to let go of the enmity for the good of immortal-kind. I do not want war. I do not condone violence—although the situation in Manhattan may require it, unfortunately." I scan. "Anyone else?" A hand goes up. "Yes?"

"Is there a way to undo the spell that makes us forget about immortals?"

I blink. "Wow. Um. I don't know. I'm not sure how it was done, but it's worth looking into. An excellent question, and unfortunately, I just do not have an answer." Pause. "Next? Yes?"

"How old are you?"

I laugh. "Don't you know better than to ask a woman that? I'm nineteen."

"You seem older."

"I've been through a lot and have had to learn how to lead." Among other things. I think Mother's Spirit has aged me. "Plus, the white hair."

"How did your hair turn white?"

I smile and shrug. "That's a story for another time. But it did turn white. It's not dyed and it's not natural, as in I wasn't born with it. The Spark's Notes version is that I went into The Dreaming with my physical body, which many, if not all, immortal researchers and academics believed to be impossible. The trip turned my hair white for reasons I can't explain."

"Are you the only vaer?"

I nod. "So far as I know. There are two others similar to me, however: a fomori, which is a shifter-vampire, and an aeshir, which is a shifter-fae. And again, so far as I know, we are the only ones like us. But, hopefully, not for long. I believe we are the future of immortal-kind. We face an uphill battle getting mortals to accept us and not fear us, and to not attack us out of that fear, but even more challenging than that, I believe, is convincing immortals to let go of their own internal bigotry and learn to accept each other."

There are a few more questions shouted at me, but I hold up my hands. "We have to get back on the road now. Thank you for your time and attention." I scan the crowd of reporters. "One last thing, though. Please, do not misrepresent what I've said to you or quote me out of context. Our world has enough to deal with without media manufacturing drama. Believe me, there's already more than enough. Thanks again. Goodbye." I stare at them, then, waiting.

No one moves.

"This is where you leave," I stage whisper. "Now."

Another moment, and then one by one the reporters drift away with backward glances and more than a few last-minute photographs.

Once I'm sure they're all going to actually leave, I slip back into my room, put my back against the door and let myself hyperventilate.

I just held a press conference. Holy shit.

CHAPTER 8

THE NEXT FEW DAYS ARE blessedly uneventful…in terms of the road trip, at least.

My press conference garnered a few hundred thousand views that first day, and then several million by the end of the second day, and by evening on the third day, it was officially viral. Restaurants no longer kicked us out, so there's that, at least. Reporters seemed to find us wherever we went but kept a respectful—or perhaps cautious—distance, content to snap photos with zoom lenses.

Those original reporters probably warned them about how I handled their assault on my privacy.

We're sticking to back roads, county highways, and state highways—every time we cross an interstate overpass, the lanes are clogged with abandoned cars, especially near more populous areas.

It's not all good news, though: Sharon has elected herself our social media guru. She made a few "official" accounts on various platforms and posted candid snapshots, short videos, and confessional-style interviews. This is good and fine. We needed an official social media presence, and she's most qualified to handle it. The less good news is that for every positive comment and like on the posts, there are half a dozen haters, inflammatory and derogatory comments, and downright heinous and vile posts attacking us by ignorant mortals and faceless keyboard warriors. It's nothing new, of course, but disheartening, nonetheless. Mainly because many of the comments and posts are dedicated to tracking our movements and hinting at retaliatory action. Retaliation against what, we don't know.

And then, a week after the press conference, we get our first taste of true resistance from an anti-immortal faction.

I'm not entirely certain where we are—one of the Carolinas, maybe; the hours and miles and days are blurring together. At every stop, our caravan grows a little bit larger as immortals find us and join our northward journey. I try to greet each new arrival that night as we stop. We have eight new fae—five males and three females, none of whom know each other. Six new vampires, four in a coven—two males, two females—and two individuals, both males—five shifters, a pack of coyotes, four males and one female—the female is the alpha, which Caleb claims is highly unusual. We also gain a dozen mortals—it's not clear if they're supporters or just traveling with us for safety in numbers—I welcome them with a warning that we expect them to keep the peace and be respectful, and so far, they have been.

So now, stopping for the night is a major undertaking. We let the majority of the caravan figure it out for themselves, and my inner circle finds a motel of some sort. A couple of nights, there's nowhere to go, so we pull off into a vacant parking lot and just sleep in the vehicles.

Our van is in the lead, Callahan driving. I'm in the very back row with Caspian and Caleb, resting and chatting mentally with Alistair, Fin, and Stirling. We discuss the updates to the estate necessary to make it my eventual permanent residence, and the reports from Sorren, Hesperion, and my grandfather—Sorren is making a lot of progress with the shifters, but Hesperion is having less success with the fae, who seem hesitant to throw their lot in with me; no one has heard from my grandfather.

"Shit, shit, shit, shit," I hear Callahan grumble from up front.

I mentally sign off and sit up. "What's wrong, Callahan?"

I peer through the windshield and see the issue for myself: an overturned semi blocking both lanes, with a jumble of burned-out wrecks, refrigerators, piles of scrap metal, old engines, school busses…

"It's a blockade," Callahan murmurs. "Placed intentionally."

"I smell mortals," Caleb says. "A lot of them. Very close."

I send out a tendril of prana, seeking, seeking.

Finding.

Ten…a dozen…twenty…forty…not just heartbeats, not just the lush, fresh scent of mortal blood but intentions, also.

Violence.

Anger.

Hatred.

I release the tendril. "It's an ambush."

"No shit," Callahan growls.

Caleb snarls, a purely wolf sound of warning.

"Sorry," Callahan murmurs.

I glance at Caleb with an eye roll. "He's allowed to be sarcastic, my love."

Caleb ignores that, kissing my temple as he squeezes past me for the side door. "Pack. With me."

Moments later, there's a pile of clothes and a flare of amber light, and then a handful of wolves are bolting away from the van, leaping over the median, and vanishing into the tall grass on the far side of the highway and into the trees—several gunshots crack across the silence.

"Did they just shoot at my pack?" I ask.

"It would seem so," Nico grumbles.

I sigh. "What do they expect to accomplish?"

I climb out of the van and stop midway between the hood of the van and the blockade. With a flex of prana, I conjure a thick curtain of jellied air around me.

"Who is in charge?" I call out, using a thread of prana to amplify my voice.

A quick trio of gunshots rings out—BAMBAMBAM! the rounds bury in the curtain.

I sigh. "This isn't going to go the way you're thinking,

mortals. Will the leader of this little…faction…please come speak with me? You can keep your little guns."

B A M B A M B A M ! — B A M B A M B A M ! — BAMBAMBAM!

More rounds are buried in the curtain—little bits of metal trapped in nothing at all.

"Very well, then," I say. "The hard way it shall be."

I summon roots from the dirt and cause them to grow, to thicken, to multiply. Send them into the blockade, long, wriggling green shoots that wrap around tires and axles and beams and handles, becoming thick as arms, and then pythons, and then tree trunks. I use the roots to pull the blockade apart bit by bit—first the semi, scraping across the blacktop with a screech and howl of metal on stone, pulling it aside until it rolls to rest in the median. Then, piece by piece, I remove the rest of the objects—or most of them, at least.

Enough to see the huddled cluster of mortals crouched with their guns, watching as a waist-thick root moves with serpent-like sentience, coiling around the mangled ruin of an old pickup truck, lifting it over their heads.

"Guns down, mortals," I call out. "Now."

I watch them turn toward me, level their guns at me, and fire—a deafening barrage of semi-automatic weapons fire, barking and chattering and cracking.

"I have no reason to hurt anyone," I say.

"Die, bitch-witch!" A male voice, in a thick southern drawl: *bee-yitch wee-yitch.*

"Bitch-witch," I repeat. "How creative."

"Want me to scare them a little?" Caspian says, coming to stand next to me. "Flash over, take a few guns, maybe draw a little blood?"

I shake my head. "Not yet. They're just scared, ignorant mortals doing what they think is necessary to protect themselves. We aren't threatened by them, only inconvenienced."

Caspian chuckles. "I see. So, what's your plan, now?"

I shrug. "Not sure yet, still thinking."

A howl erupts from the woods on the right, answered by another on the left…the howls echo and move and seem to multiply until even I'm not sure where the wolves are or how many there are. I mean, I know how many there are, obviously.

"I'd put the guns down, mortals," I say. "Those wolves aren't likely to listen to me—not after you took unprovoked potshots at them."

Another barrage of gunfire, and now my curtain of air is riddled with bullets. I infuse it with more prana, thickening it and making it more solid. I don't need the hassle of getting hit right now.

Time for a slightly more aggressive action, I suppose. I walk forward, pushing the curtain ahead of me. BAMBAMBAM! Yes, yes, yes, you have guns. You'd think they'd realize they're only wasting ammunition.

I halt on this side of a bullet-hole-riddled school bus, which is on its side halfway across the righthand lane. Roughly thirty feet away, the mortals have arranged themselves in a series of ranks, like you'd see in a Revolutionary War movie—the ones in front on one knee, the ones behind standing. All the mortals have aimed their guns directly at me.

All I can smell is mortal blood and fear.

I fight the urge to sample the blood. Instead, I get creative. Send prana into the ground, causing a ring of boiling soil to crack up through the blacktop. I hear frantic shouts of panic and fear as the ring becomes a wall of thick black soil; another burst of prana and the dirt solidifies into the hardpan of an old dirt road.

Shouts echo—curses, pleas, screams, epithets.

A gunshot echoes from inside the chamber, accompanied by irate shouts—I can't help but laugh.

"Are we done?" I ask.

Silence.

I allow the wall to soften once more, and then slowly lower it until I can see faces—dirty, fearful, and pissed off. "Put your weapons down and show me your hands."

Rifles and AR15s and handguns and shotguns clatter on concrete and hands go up. I let the wall subside back into the earth and use a sharp gust of wind to scatter the weapons out of reach.

No one moves. No one speaks.

"Well? Explain yourselves." I stand facing them from a few feet away with my hands clasped behind my back, hoping I'm channeling an irritated teacher who has just said, "I'll wait."

Still, no one speaks.

I fix my gaze on a man—middle-aged, faded jeans sagging under a beer belly, wearing a battered, sweat-stained green John Deere cap. "You." I probe him with prana, gleaning a few pieces of information. "Eric Packard. You actually seem like a somewhat decent sort, Eric. What's with the blockade? Why attack people who have done you no wrong?"

He shuffles his feet. "Heard y'all was heading this way. They're sayin' you're eatin' souls, and your vampire slaves

are turning everyone you meet into more vampire slaves."
Vamp-AH-r

I cackle. "Wow. That's a shocking amount of stupidity in one sentence, Eric. What evidence did 'they,'" I emphasize the word with air quotes, "provide that convinced you it was true?"

He scuffs the blacktop with a toe. "Well…"

"You saw a post on social media and just assumed it was true?"

"Naw, I just…they said there was firsthand accounts. They had quotes an' everythin.'"

"Oh, they had *quotes*?" I can't help the sarcasm. "Wow. I'm *sure* those quotes were a *hundred* percent real and not at *all* invented."

He points behind me. "That there is a vampire. I seen pictures of him."

I nod. "He is indeed a vampire." I look back at him. "He doesn't seem to be making vampire slaves out of you, though. I mean, I'm in the way, sure. But…well, so far, no souls are being eaten, either. Sure seems like maybe you jumped to some very wrong conclusions."

He clears his throat. "Could be."

"Notice how I didn't hurt anyone? Notice how my vampire mate hasn't burst into flames or drank your blood or made slaves out of you? See, here's the thing, Eric. I could have done all sorts of horrible things to you. But I didn't. I don't eat souls. No immortal that I've ever heard of does. Vampires are not made, they're born. And there's no such thing as vampire slaves."

He frowns hard. "You don't know everything, bitch-witch. Maybe y'all ain't interested in hurting us, but not all of the other freaks like you out there are as nice as you."

"You have an excellent point there, Eric. The question is this: Why provoke unfriendly fae, vampires, and shifters? See, I think even most mortals, if someone is shooting at them for no reason, would respond in kind. You're trying to kill me? Fine. I'll kill you, too. But, with immortals, you're only gonna get a few shots off. And then you're dead." I point at Caspian. "You could hit him a dozen times, direct, close-range hits, and he'd still rip your head off." I gesture to my left and right, and the wolves prowling toward us. "Same with them. Your little guns aren't going to save you, Eric. If an immortal decides to kill you, there isn't much you can do. Even *with* a gun. Luckily for you, we're not interested in killing you." I move closer to him. Let my prana flare within me so my eyes, hair, and tattoos glow. "My advice to you, Eric? Start thinking for yourself. Try to look at facts before jumping to conclusions. And maybe don't go around attacking innocent people without provocation."

I let the ocean of seething prana swell, boil, and surge into my hands—I slice both hands down and away in a sharp, hard gesture. A swirling gust of white fire-laced wind billows outward, away from me, with a deafening hurricane roar. The makeshift roadblock is swept away in a searing torrent. When I release the magic, there's nothing left. No school bus, no wrecks, no fridges, no semi.

Gone. Incinerated.

I flip my hands at them. "Now shoo. I have places to be."

I spin on my heel and head back to the van. I hear yips and howls and growls and barks from the pack as they follow—pausing to circle around the mortals, who still stand frozen in place, shaking, as five giant wolves prowl circles around them, snarling.

"Caleb!" I call. "Leave the mortals. They've learned their lesson, I believe."

The pack trots back to the van, shifting on the run.

A minute later, the caravan is rumbling past the huddle of frightened mortals in their camouflage gear and their homemade banner proudly proclaiming—in dripping red spray paint letters—*MORTAL MELITIA*. With an E.

Ai-yi-yi-yi. Really?

Something tells me that what waits for us in Manhattan is going to be a whole different kind of beast than a handful of scared, misinformed, uneducated "Melitia" country boys.

CHAPTER 9

THE JOURNEY TO MANHATTAN takes nearly two weeks in total. We deal with three more ambushes. During the last one they managed to hit Callahan with an errant shot—he had his arm hanging out the window as he drove and the round creased his forearm.

In discussing it, though, Caleb, Caspian, Nico, Philemon, and I decide the ambushes serve a valuable lesson: without overwhelming numerical superiority or armored vehicles and heavy weapons, mortals don't stand much of a chance.

But, according to reports from mortal

news outlets—those still operating via the increasingly spotty internet, at least—the Mortal Federation operating out of Manhattan boasts exactly that: armored vehicles, heavy weapons, and a steady stream of mortal volunteers bolstering their numbers every day.

We reach the distant suburbs south of the five boroughs thirteen days after leaving Atlanta—a drive that should have taken a day or two at most. The farther north we got, the closer to larger metropolitan areas we got, the worse travel became. Even surface streets and county and state highways were cluttered with abandoned vehicles. Gas stations are increasingly empty and looted, as are grocery stores, convenience stores, army-navy surplus stores, hardware stores...

The farther north we travel, the more things resemble the early seasons of The Walking Dead.

So far, no zombies, thank fuck.

Now, a few miles outside NYC proper, things have changed again. Here, in the endless maze of quiet, tree-lined streets with neat sidewalks and mid-century ranch homes with detached garages and postage-stamp yards, things seem almost normal. Cars are parked in the driveways; people sit on porches smoking cigarettes and watching us suspiciously as we glide through the quiet neighborhoods.

In the distance, however, you can make out the muffled chatter of automatic weapons fire, the occasional crump of explosives, sirens, and shuddering booms that Caleb tells me are the sound of tanks firing their cannons.

Tanks.

Fuck me. *Tanks?*

North, north, north. Slowly. Watching each intersection as we pass through. Gradually, neighborhood streets with houses and yards become wide two- and four-lane thoroughfares lined with shops and restaurants—closed, dark, boarded up, windows shattered.

A body hangs halfway out of a second-story apartment window; blood pooled on the sidewalk below in a tacky, drying, reddish-brown pool. At one intersection, a city bus lies on its side, charred, still smoking; the underside is riddled with bullet holes, and the brick wall of the apartment building opposite the bus is charred, pocked, and scorched by magic.

There's a tang in the air—acrid and sour, somewhere between curdled milk and burning hair. Philemon tells me it's the scent of spent magic—battle magic, in particular. One spell, or two, or even several cast in quick succession in a localized area won't leave a scent, he says. But dozens, or hundreds? The kind of rapid-fire aggressive glamours used to end lives, all cast in a small area? *That* leaves a scent.

The farther into the city we go, the more apocalyptic it gets. A Walgreens on a corner is little more than a blasted-out shell—a direct hit from a tank, Caleb tells me. In another place, a circular hole ten feet across is cored through several city blocks at ground level—a hastaxi orb, but larger—Philemon says it's sort of like an artillery version of a hastaxi. I stood in the hole and stared through the neat, precise core to a street half a mile away. Desks, walls, bookshelves, clothing racks, displays…bodies— all sliced and cauterized when the orb passed, leaving not even ashes behind.

A pile of bodies lies in the middle of another intersection—mortals, soldiers, wearing camo and armor. The bodies burn with white fire but are not consumed.

We skirted through New Jersey, Callahan informs me,

into Brooklyn, and then cut north again. We're approaching the East River now, apparently. My knowledge of NYC geography is essentially zero, so I'm relying on others to guide us. In this, I feel more like a nineteen-year-old than any kind of a leader.

Caleb calls a halt. Our caravan, now thirty-some vehicles long and boasting over a hundred immortals and half that again in mortal numbers, piles up behind us. To our left, the intersection is blocked by the now-familiar sight of a makeshift barricade—cars, trailers, box trucks, street vendor carts, but here the barricades have been erected by people with engineering skills and heavy machinery, each piece fitted precisely, the whole bound with chains and barbed wire and razor wire. This is not a makeshift barricade for an ambush by backwoods bumpkins playing wannabe militia. This is a blockade erected by people who know what the fuck they're doing to force people to go where they want them to go. There's another barricade opposite, leaving the only path the back way we came or the way we're going.

Caleb gathers the pack. "We need to do some recon. Saige and Colin, get around the barricade to the left; Callahan and Channing, to the right. I'll head forward. The rest of you, hang tight. Nico, check our backtrail. Philemon, Maeve, if you have any kind of defensive measures, get them ready."

"Alpha!" A young female shifter calls from behind us. "Alpha! A moment, please?"

Caleb, in the act of peeling off his shirt, turns as he tosses the shirt onto the hood of the van. "A moment only. Speak your mind and be swift."

She inclines her head in a gesture of respect. "If you're

doing recon, I can help. I'm a hawk. Aerial reconnaissance could be valuable."

"Your name?"

"Emily."

Caleb nods. "Excellent suggestion, Emily, I thank you, and your queen thanks you." He gestures in the direction of the river—or so I assume. "See where they've barricaded and if the barricades are manned anywhere. If you can get even a rough estimate of how many tanks or whatever this Mortal Federation has, that would be fantastic. Be safe and be careful."

I rest my hand on her shoulder. "I appreciate you volunteering, Emily. Your contribution is valuable and welcome."

Emily is, going by appearances, another so-called "illegal," an immortal born in secret after the Treaty. She's medium height and svelte, with pixie-cut platinum blonde hair. She smiles at me, eager and full of energy. "I'm just glad to be doing something! If I have to sit in the back of my dad's stupid RV listening to Creedence Clearwater Revival for one more fucking second, I'll go feral."

I grimace. "Ooof. I understand—it's been a very long trip. When did you join us?"

"North Carolina. My uncle, my mother's brother, was part of that ambush. He blames Dad for Mom's death. He never knew why she died, meaning that Dad's a shifter, but he knew Dad got Mom pregnant and that she didn't survive the birth. When Uncle Paul found out about immortals, he went nuts. Tried to kill Dad and me both and then when that didn't work, he joined that so-called Militia because he now hates immortals. I guess he and Mom were close."

Caleb rests a heavy hand on her shoulder. "Emily. We need to go."

Emily rolls her eyes with a sigh. "Sorry. Dad calls me a jabber jaw."

I smile at her. "We can talk more later, Emily. For now, Caleb is right. We need information so we can make a plan."

"On it." She does a weird half-curtsey, half-bow thing and then turns and jogs down the street, peeling her clothes off. A glimpse of her back and buttocks, and then amber light flashes, and a red-tailed hawk digs at the air with her long wings, soaring upward with that distinctive piercing screech.

The pack has long since vanished, leaving behind piles of clothes. Caleb is last. He cups my jaw and kisses me. "Back soon. Defensive measures, babe. Around here, anything could happen, so be ready."

I caress his jaw. "Will do. Love you. Be careful."

He winks at me, shucks his jeans, and shifts on the move, already a wolf loping away before his jeans hit the ground.

Philemon looks at me. "A dome, you think?"

I nod. "Go to the back of the caravan and cast forward. I'll link up with you midway."

Philemon jogs toward the back of the lineup of cars. I cast a line of prana toward him and feel his meet mine—I've never done anything like this before, but the actions come instinctively—Mother's Spirit, perhaps, or maybe I'm actually learning things. We weave our prana stream together into an unbroken line connecting us; I feel his movements, his deft manipulations of the warp and weft in the ley lines, spinning the single thread into a thick rope of dozens of braided strands—needle-thin strands that are braided together, and then those are braided together, and so on. I mimic his actions until the link is braided from end to end. And then I feel Philemon begin to push. It's the only word. He pushes toward me, and so I push toward him, forcing the ley line to belly open in the center, slowly becoming a bubble of woven prana that gradually envelops the caravan. Technically, it's not a dome but a long, ovoid bubble surrounding the caravan above and below. Maya glimmers between the threads, shimmering dimly in the bright sunlight. I anchor the tip of the structure into the earth and feel Philemon do the same, severing the connection between us. A few minutes later, he rejoins me near the front.

I can feel the pack, and Caleb, quite clearly—he's moving slowly, creeping. The others are harder to pinpoint since our connection isn't as strong or deep, but I feel them moving nonetheless.

I even feel Nico, now that he's been added to the pack— I'm not sure when Caleb formally bonded him to the pack, but that portion of pack politics isn't any of my business since I'm not a shifter. Oddly, though, I feel someone else back there with Nico…

Sierra?

Ten minutes later, the giant, shaggy, lumbering brute that is Nico's grizzly shambles along the line of cars, vans, RVs, pickups, and busses. And beside him? Sierra, in wolf form. She's limping, her fur bloody and matted, one ear split halfway down the middle.

Caleb?

I know. She's been trailing us at a distance the whole time.

She's injured.

She's tough. She'll heal. If you believe she's come to some sort of understanding, she can return to the pack. Otherwise, the separation remains.

I'll talk to her.

She may not be able to shift if she's hurt. We heal much faster in our animal form, and if we're injured badly enough, we cannot shift at all until our human body can withstand the injuries. A quick pause. *The situation in Manhattan is not good, Maeve. I'll debrief you fully when I get back, but… it's not good. The Mortal Federation has cut the island in half and controls the whole northern half. They have the equipment, leadership, and personnell to make this very, very difficult.*

Great, I growl. **Finish the recon and get back here so we can make a plan.**

I feel a wordless assent and leave it at that, assuming he needs to focus.

I watch Nico and Sierra approach. Nico stops a few feet away from me and collapses backward with a gruff moaning whuff onto his butt.

"All clear back there?" I ask him.

He nods, lets out a groaning whuff, and then indicates Sierra with his chin.

"Thank you for escorting her here."

He bobs his head, whuffs again, and then pushes to his feet and ambles away on all fours, thick fur, and great muscles swaying.

Sierra is sitting on her haunches, her front left paw held off the ground—it's mangled horribly. She's skeletal, shaking, and visibly weak. She's sustained several gunshot wounds to the torso. Her jaws are stained pink with old blood.

She looks up at me and whimpers pitifully.

"Jesus, Sierra," I whisper. "What the hell happened to you?" It's a rhetorical question since she can't answer. I can feel the pack across the bond, but since I'm not a shifter, I can't communicate mentally with anyone but Caleb when they're in animal form. "Can you shift?"

She just whines.

I crouch warily. "Can I try to heal you? I'm not great at healing, but I'll give it a shot."

She shifts toward me, whimpering again. I take that as permission. I cradle her injured paw in my hands, close my eyes, and access my prana. As always, I visualize it as a seething, roiling ocean of blinding golden-white liquid light at the center of me, behind my navel. I pull a needle-thin thread of prana and focus on her paw—just the paw. It's been broken—not just broken but shattered beyond all recognition. A trap, I assume. God, the pain must be unimaginable. I have no clue how to ease her pain other than healing her, so I focus on that.

In my mind's eye, I wrap her injured paw in prana, coating it in the golden-white light; the prana acts as a sort of magical X-ray, almost, letting me see in more acute detail the breaks in the bone and the tears in the tendons and ligaments.

Slowly, focusing all my will, intent, and attention on each specific break, I use as little prana as I can manage, knitting each little piece of bone back together one by one. I lose track of time. My head pounds. Sierra doesn't move and seems to be barely breathing. Once the bones are knitted, I do the tendons and ligaments next, which are much easier, and then the fur.

When the paw is as good as I can make it, I release her and sink backward onto my butt. I'm sweating and panting, I discover.

I've destroyed mountains, ended hundreds of lives

at once, and fought a six-thousand-year-old fae tyrant and haven't felt this drained.

"It's the detail work," I hear, and I open my eyes to see Philemon watching from a few feet away. "Something about close work, healing something as delicate and complex as a canine paw is much more demanding in some ways than a major glamour." He shakes his head. "This is why you're the queen, though—a healing like that would have taken any other healer several times longer."

Sierra gingerly tests her paw, resting a bit of weight on it. It holds, and she seems surprised. Her amber-glowing wolf's eyes look up at me, full of very human emotion.

"I can help with the gunshot wounds," Philemon says. "They're older and simpler to heal, and this is something I have dealt with, albeit a very long time ago."

I nod, glancing at him. "That would be good. That really took it out of me."

Sierra tenses and growls when Philemon crouches at her side, fingers reaching for her fur.

"Hey, he's going to help, okay? I know he's a fae, but he's good people. You can trust him."

Sierra lets out a long, low rumble, teeth bared; Philemon, eyeing her warily, touches her fur with careful, delicate fingers, barely making contact with the red, crusted wounds. I feel his prana surge. At first, nothing happens. And then the wounds, three of them, all seem to enlarge at once, the holes stretching—Sierra whines in her throat. One by one, spent, misshapen rounds emerge from the wounds and tink onto the asphalt.

Philemon breaks out into a sweat, now putting his other fingers onto her fur, his whole body shaking with exertion. First, the crust, tinged with what is surely an infection, softens and turns pink, and then, even more gradually and almost imperceptibly, the seeping wounds grow smaller and smaller and smaller. Last, they begin to close, the flesh knitting back together, then scabbing over, and then turning pink.

Philemon sags backward to his butt, panting. "Sorry, I—I can't manage the fur."

Sierra twists and licks at the patches. A moment later, amber light swells, first from her eyes and then more nebulously, and then the glow blinds us, fades, subsides, and Sierra is lying nude on the ground, fresh pink healing round wounds on her side—one just beneath her breast, another just below her ribcage, and a third closer to her hipbone. Her ribs show, her cheekbones are prominent and sharp, and her skin is tight and papery. Her eyes are hazed with unshed tears.

She squeezes her eyes shut. "Why?" she breathes, her voice a hoarse whisper I have to strain to hear.

Philemon presses a cold, sweating bottle of water into my hands. I twist the top off, scoop my hand under her head, lift, touch the bottle to her lips, and tilt.

"Slow," I caution. "Small sips."

She wets her lips first. Licks. I tilt again, and she allows a few drops down her throat this time. Gasps raggedly. Another sip, this time a bit more.

She tilts her head away, swallowing. "Not…my first… rodeo," she whispers.

Someone else—Caspian—hands me a large white T-shirt. I help Sierra to a sitting position. She struggles into the shirt, groaning in pain. She accepts another sip, this time taking the bottle and drinking as she settles the shirt around her hips.

Her eyes go to Caspian and then Philemon. "Thank you." She swallows hard. "Thank you."

Caspian nods. "Good to have you back, Sierra."

Philemon just smiles. "I'm glad I could be of assistance, Miss Sierra."

We're alone then. I sit cross-legged near her and wait. She takes tiny sips, staring at the ground between her thighs. Finally, she turns her gaze to mine, hers watery and fraught with emotion.

"Why, Maeve?"

I frown at her. "Why what?"

"Why heal me? Why help me after the way I treated you?"

I shrug. "Why wouldn't I? It hurt that you hated me so much for something out of my control, but I always understood it. I have nothing against you, Sierra. I didn't before and I don't now."

"I was horrible to you."

"Yes."

She looks at me. "Being separated from the pack…it was…" tears trickle, finally. "I'd rather die than go through that again." She shakes her head. Sighs. "I know Caleb isn't meant for me. He never has been. But I thought…I thought maybe even if we weren't bonded mates, we could still…" A shuddering sob. "And then you came along, and…I couldn't handle it. The jealousy, the pain of losing something that was never mine, the embarrassment…it was all too much."

I squeeze her knee. "I'm sorry, Sierra. I mean, I love Caleb. But I…ever since my mom died things have just been happening to me. Things I have no control over. But I'm sorry that what the Fates have thrown at me has caused you pain."

She snorts. "God, you're *really* hard to dislike, you know that?"

I grin at her. "Sorry?"

She takes my hands in hers. "Forgive me, Maeve."

I squeeze hers. "Of course, forgiven."

Her head swivels, and I follow her gaze—Caleb is trotting toward us, tongue lolling, ears perked and swiveling. Channing, Saige, Colin, and Callahan join him, emerging from shadowed doorways and shattered windows. Everyone shifts back to human form as they approach us, clustering around Sierra, hugging and laughing.

Caleb stands removed, still in his wolf body. Sierra wobbles to her feet, a task that requires a visible effort. She totters toward Caleb and drops to her knees. "Alpha. I've learned my lesson. I've apologized to Maeve. Please, Alpha. Caleb, please. I can't live without the pack."

Caleb sits on his haunches and regards her for a moment, and then he licks her forehead, once. She collapses forward, pressing her face onto the back of her hands, sobbing and shaking. "Thank you, thank you, thank you."

Caleb transforms and crouches beside her. "Welcome back, Sierra." His voice is low and gentle. "You've been through a lot, I see."

She works herself back up to sit on her shins, nodding. "Caught my foot in a fucking bear trap. I should have seen it, I know, but the bastard hid it really, really well, and I was dizzy with hunger. I had to keep up with your trail so I couldn't stop to hunt. I couldn't stop to sleep because that's when I made up time. So I…I missed the signs. It wasn't some old, forgotten trap, either. The fucker who set it came to check it. I played dead until he opened the trap, and then I…" she sighs, shrugs. "I wasn't trying to kill him, just get away. If I'd have just killed him, he wouldn't have been able to shoot me, but I...I thought since we're trying to make things better with mortals, I probably shouldn't go killing one, even in self-defense."

Caleb chuckles. "You might have erred a bit too far on the side of caution on that one, Sierra." He rises to his feet, regal and imposing despite being nude. "Go get something to eat and rest."

She fights to her feet, and Saige hooks her arm through Sierra's with a backward smile at me.

Caleb's attention turns to me. "I made contact with the Army of the Once-Mortal Queen. Their leader is coming here."

"When?" I ask.

"Now," he answers.

At that moment, a cloak of darkness sweeps over us, a thick, black, impenetrable bank of shadows surging and roiling.

It tastes of magic...and it smells familiar.

"No one move," I call out, magically amplifying my voice. "Remain calm."

I hear boots on stone. A snarl of a lion. The groaning whuff of a bear. A chorus of yips and howls of wolves. The clack of wood on stone—spear butts on asphalt.

I feel Caleb move to stand beside me, Caspian on the other.

I stand, waiting.

I smell blood—fae, shifter, and vampire.

The cloak of shadows swirls in reverse, becoming black threads that vanish into the palms of the fae who cast the glamour.

Andreas.

CHAPTER 10

GONE IS THE MORTAL MASK; HIS features are full fae—sharp high cheekbones, perfect bone structure, symmetrical features, and wide almond eyes glowing white without iris or pupil. His hair is long and wild and unkempt and thick black, shaggy around his jaw and collar, windblown and unwashed. A sparse black beard shadows his jaw, more than stubble and less than a full beard—apparently fae *can* grow beards, which in my mind seems to go against popular media tropes, not to mention my own observations. He wears faded and worn blue jeans, heavy black combat boots laced tight, and a black T-shirt fitted tight around his lean, hard, muscular frame. The letters A-O-M-Q adorn the front of the shirt in large, bright white letters.

"Andreas?" My voice quavers. "It's you!"

He swaggers toward me, his gait powerful and confident, his entire aura blazing with authority. He slings his arms around me, lifts me in the air, and swings me in circles, laughing. "Maeve! Gods and blood, child, I've missed you."

I squeeze his neck and laugh. "Andreas, god it's good to see you. I thought you were dead or something! You just vanished!"

"I had to. The Tribunal knew damn well that I was a threat—I know a lot of people in the fae underground." He sets me back with his hands on my waist and then frames my face. "This is what I could do for you, Maeve. I couldn't help you on your journey. I couldn't show you who you are. I couldn't defeat the Tribunal or Zirae. What I *could* do is build an army for you."

"You knew I'd need an army?"

He nods. "I've been a soldier more than anything else in my life. Even being a cop, I look at as being a soldier. If there's one thing I know, it's war. And I saw this war coming."

"I don't want it to be a war, Andreas." I step back and scrape my hair back.

He shrugs. "It is, whether you want it or not. Is it another Mortals' War? Not yet. That's avoidable, maybe. But it's not going to just go away. Things aren't going to just fix themselves. And like it or not, immortals look to you for leadership. You've only reinforced that since showing Stateside and doing pressers and gathering all of them." He points at the caravan behind me. "And mortals are divided on you—some admire you and look at you for leadership as much as the immortals do, but others fear and hate you."

I sniff a laugh. "I've noticed."

Andreas sighs, looking past me—I feel the crowd gathering. "We aren't safe here. The real battle is for Manhattan, but Nathaniel Bridgestone and his Mortal Federation control most of the boroughs surrounding Manhattan. We've secured this corridor as an approach to the territory we control, which is the southern half of the island."

"Is it open fighting?"

He nods. "Bitter, brutal, door-to-door, and street-by-street. They have superior numbers and technology. We have magic that almost counteracts their numerical and technological superiority. Almost." He juts his chin past me at the caravan and the crowd, watching us. "They will give us an edge that we badly need to drive the Mortal Federation off of Manhattan."

"And then?" I ask. "After we drive them out of Manhattan…what then? Take the fight into the Bronx?"

He shrugs. "That's tomorrow's worry. Today, we drive them out and establish Manhattan as a foothold. Secure the bridges and control ingress and egress. My inner circle and I have been discussing it, and we feel that once we control Manhattan, we turn it into what we've been calling the Immortal Enclave."

I sigh. "A foothold, huh?" I pinch the bridge of my nose. "Sounds like the first step in a war to me."

"You can't make reality go away by closing your eyes to it, Maeve." His voice is gentle but stern. "The Mortal Federation is real. They're well-armed, well-funded, and well-equipped. They're a real army with capable, ruthless leadership and a stated goal of running immortals out of New York entirely. If we let them run us out of New York, what's next? They move on to Jersey City? Atlantic City? Boston? Philly? They expand and turn the Mortal Federation into cells, into anti-immortal army franchises nationwide. If we let them win, here, it's over. Immortals will be persecuted. We'll have entered the mortal public awareness for the first time in almost two hundred and fifty years, and we'll be forced onto registries and into camps or reservations. The whole cause? Immortals being an accepted part of human society? It's won or lost *here*, Maeve."

At that moment, there's a piercing screech high overhead—I look up to see a red-tailed hawk stooping at full speed toward me. Emily. She hurtles toward me like a rocket, wings folded, talons trailing. She scoops her wings forward at the last second, abruptly arresting her momentum; ten feet above the ground, amber light flares, obscuring her form.

Her nude human female body emerges from the fading amber glow to land lithe and light in front of me, panting. Blood trickles down her left arm from a long, angry crease on the outside of her bicep.

"They're coming. Now. A fucking lot of them," she gasps. "They almost got me, the bastards. But we have to go, *now*."

Andreas stares at her. "Who are you?"

"She's Emily, a hawk shifter who volunteered to do some aerial recon."

Andreas's eyes light up. "I've been hoping for a shifter who can fly. So far, we've only got quadrupeds." He snaps his fingers, and magic amplifies the sound, so it echoes like a gunshot. "*IMMORTALS! MOVE OUT!*"

Caleb eyes me, shoving his legs into his jeans. *Gonna let him command your people?*

Yes, I am. I know nothing of war, Caleb, and it's all he knows. I trust him.

He nods his head, a bow of acquiescence. *Very well.*

Andreas doesn't miss this silent interaction. "What?"

"My mate doesn't like you giving orders to my people," I tell him; before he can open his mouth to answer, I continue. "I was telling him that I know absolutely nothing about conducting a war, and it's all you've ever known, and I trust you."

Callahan, Channing, Colin, Saige, and Sierra arrange themselves in a semi-circle behind me.

"What are your orders, my queen?" Caleb says, dropping to a knee in front of me.

Andreas frowns in Caleb's direction and then looks at me thoughtfully. He drops to his knee. "Forgive me if I overstepped…my queen."

I shake my head. "You're the commander of the Army of the Once-Mortal Queen, Andreas. I may not want war, but as you've correctly pointed out, war is here. Best to do everything we can to end it swiftly." I look at Emily. "How many, which direction, and how are they set up?"

She dresses as she answers. "Several hundred, but I wasn't counting." She points to our left and right. "They're going to try to cut us off from the bridge. I don't know shit about tactics or whatever because, like, I'm just a kid, but it looks like a—what do you call it? A pincer sort of thing, where they're coming from two directions at once. They're mostly on foot, but they have a few jeeps with guns on the back, I saw one tank and, like, three things that looked like tanks but with wheels and no cannon thingies."

"APCs," Andreas mutters. "Armored personnel carriers." He looks at me. "With your permission, we need to move, as our new scout suggested."

I turn to face the caravan and the scattered, growing crowd. "We are now officially part of the Army of the Once-Mortal Queen." I allow a pause. "We march on Manhattan, where we will fight against the forces of the Mortal Federation, who seek to drive all immortals out of New York—if we let them drive us and our brothers and sisters out of Manhattan, we've lost before we've begun." I scan the faces. "You've all joined me voluntarily. You've followed me here. Now, I ask you to follow me into war. I will never command or compel. But, if you do choose to continue to follow me, you do so as soldiers in my army. As such, you have a commanding general: this man." I point at him. "Andreas Bouras, a fae warrior and a father figure to me. If you follow me, you follow him. Andreas?"

He nods at me and then addresses the…troops, I suppose they are, now. "I've fought wars all my life. I've been on the winning side and the losing side. I've fought mortals and immortals. What we face is hatred and bigotry, plain and simple. The Mortal Federation, led by a man named Nathaniel Bridgestone, wants all immortals out of New York and, preferably, dead. Barring that, he wants us all counted, registered, and monitored as if we're criminals. He wants all immortal reproduction rights stripped—all human rights, all constitutional rights, for that matter. He does not see us as human. Those with him may not all believe as he does, but he doesn't hide his beliefs—quite the opposite, rather. He proclaims them, announces them, advertises them, and the men and women who follow him voluntarily take orders from him. The Mortal Federation is not a government army, it's a collection of volunteers. So in the coming fight, you fight for your right to exist. Follow me—follow your queen—and we will show them the errors of their ways. What that means is we have to be better. We have to be smarter. We can't commit atrocities against them. We can't give in to hatred, as they have." His eyes glaze over, and his attention goes unfocused. "They've passed through my first layer of wards. To Manhattan—double time. Stop for nothing. Choose your targets if and when fighting breaks out. No collateral damage. Now, we move. My forces form a rearguard. Move out!"

Andreas' eyes flare white and gold as he lifts his hands palms facing forward—shadows stream from his palms in fist-thick ropes. Some fifty feet from his hands, the ropes begin to fray into hundreds and then thousands and then millions of thin strands that soar skyward, left, right—every conceivable direction, streaming and seeking and boiling and roaming with semi-sentient eagerness, criss-crossing, joining and merging and splitting again. Each time the strands and streams merge and split, they multiply and expand, creating larger pockets and pools of seething dark. Soon, the whole caravan is swallowed by the shadows, and then the buildings around us, and then the sky.

Engines rumble and cough and strain. Caleb and Caspian guide me to our van, where we are joined by the pack and Nico. We roll forward at the head of the caravan as Andreas's small squad of soldiers jog down the line—I barely noticed them initially, shocked by the sudden re-appearance of Andreas. They wear something approaching a uniform: jeans, combat boots, T-shirts, bulletproof vests, and black ballcaps with the letters AOMQ across the front. They carry weapons, too—assault rifles for a few, handguns for most, and a few carry what look like regular spears—six-foot-long wooden poles with diamond-shaped spearheads of black metal—the metal, however, is glamoured, glowing dull purple in the shadows. They must be something like hastaxi, I decide. A few others carry shock-stick pairs. They're funded, I realize. The hats, the armor, the weapons…the AOMQ is not just a rag-tag bunch of immortals calling themselves an army. They're a real army with weapons and equipment and a command hierarchy.

It makes me feel a bit better about our chances.

I feel something tugging on my awareness—the shield dome Philemon and I created. I'd anchored it to the ground, and now we're leaving its protection. Hurriedly, I yank the anchor free from the ground and re-attach it to the hood of the van, hoping Philemon remembers to do the same.

Mere minutes after I re-anchored the shield, I hear the cracking rattle of automatic weapons fire and feel the shield work to absorb the impacts. I look out the window, but we're obscured by shadows. The mortals must be taking potshots at the moving pool of darkness, hoping to hit something.

So far, the shield is holding. I reach for the glamour and attach a thin thread of prana to it, feeding it to keep it strong.

More gunfire, close now. On our right. The shield shakes and I hear rounds clatter to the ground as they're stopped by the shield.

A thin beam of purple lances past my window from behind us, lighting up the shadows in a blinding blur.

A moment later, I hear a scream. The rattle of automatics cuts off momentarily and then renews with redoubled intensity. I feel the shield shaking and shuddering and pour prana into it—I focus my will and intent, thickening the dome, reinforcing it. I feel Philemon doing the same.

Another purple laser beam streaks past me on the left, and I hear metal on concrete and shouts. Overlapping gun chatter rattles and echoes off of buildings, oddly muffled by the shadows.

Ahead, I see the bridge arching over the East River. Immortal sentries stand guard in clusters of six on either side—a heavy steel I-beam lays across the road. As we approach, four immortals—two shifters and two unblooded vampires—pull on a thick guide rope attached to a series of pulleys; the beam rotates skyward just enough to let us through. They tie the guide rope off to the railing of the bridge but hold it, ready to drop the beam as soon as the last immortal is through. The immortal guards drop to their knees and fire assault rifles. Return fire zings over their heads. One of the immortal bridge guards jerks and topples to the ground and then crawls toward the bridge. One of the shifters on the beam detail breaks away, grabs the fallen immortal, and hauls him to safety.

I turn to peer out the window—shadows subsume the bridge and the guards, obscure my sight of the water below and the sky above, and the sound of weapons fire fades behind us.

A few minutes later, the shadows begin to clear, and I see Andreas about a hundred yards ahead of the van, standing in the back of a pickup truck, braced inside what looks to be a custom-rigged cage, hands outstretched, wielding the shadows. As I watch, the shadows stream into his hands, boiling black ribbons absorbed by his palms. I shove open my door and stand on the edge, peering back—our whole caravan made it unscathed. I can just make out the far end of the bridge—I'm just in time to see two of the guards hurriedly erecting a ward, plugging the bridge and cutting off access to the island.

And now I understand what the coming battle will be.

We'll fight for the bridges.

Andreas, once the ward is in place, slumps, exhausted, sweating, panting, and pale from the effort of holding the swarm of shadows that got us here.

But only for a moment. I watch him rally, forcing himself straight and tall once more. He wipes sweat from his brow, inhales deeply, holds it, shakes his hands, rolls his shoulders, and then exhales.

And then we're on the move once more. This time without shadows. I relax my grip on the dome, tying off my prana feed to it.

Twenty minutes later, Andreas is directing our caravan into an underground parking garage, above which is a squat office building of glass and metal—much of the glass windows are shattered and blasted out, but I also sense glamours hiding and disguising various elements. I squeeze my eyes shut, send a thin coating of prana over my eyeballs, and then open them. The prana acts like a filter, so I can see the glamours—screens of magic hiding the actual facade of the building, making it look blasted out and broken. It's perfectly intact, except where certain windows have been removed intentionally, replaced with blocks of concrete—sniper nests with firing lanes down the approaches from every direction.

Our van trundles underground into darkness, the sound of the engine dopplering off the walls and ramps, echoed by the vehicles behind. Down, down, down we go, in wide concentric circles. We reach the bottom and are directed to a parking spot near Andreas's truck. He hops out, swiping his hand through his sweaty, messy black hair.

"You'll have to teach me that trick with the shadows," I tell him, exiting the van.

He grins. "Neat, huh? Learned it from a sepoy sergeant in India, back in, oh shit, when was it? 1883? Somewhere around there. It's not hard." He strides purposefully toward the door. "Come on. You need to meet my command group. We have to plan our next move now that you're here. They're pushing hard from the west and encroaching south. We've taken two bridges in the last month and lost one."

"Andreas?"

He halts, holding the door. "Yeah?"

"I need to meet with Bridgestone."

Andreas frowns. "To what end? I've spoken to the man on the phone, and he's not gonna budge. There's no diplomacy, no bargaining. No deals. We push them off the island, or we surrender."

I shrug. "I'm sure you're right. Nonetheless, I shall meet with him. Face to face. Neutral territory."

Andreas barks a laugh. "There is no such thing. Mortal-controlled territory is everywhere that's not the southern half of Manhattan. The only truly safe place for immortals is right here, in this building."

"A contested bridge. One that is not controlled by either side. As soon as possible."

He eyes me, curious, calculated—this is not Andreas the cop, not Andreas the father figure—he's Andreas the soldier, purely and entirely.

He bows at the waist. "Very well, and as you wish." He pulls a walkie-talkie from his back pocket. "I'll set it up.

Meantime, let me show you and your mates your quarters. I've been expecting you, so I've got a place ready for you."

I rest my hand on his shoulder. "Thank you, Andreas. I can't tell you how good it is to see you."

He pinches a lock of my hair. "You too, honey. We've got some catching up to do when we get a second." He brushes a soft, quick, fatherly kiss to my cheek and then keys his radio. "Zeke—get me a line to Bridgestone."

I follow him up a stairwell, my mates with me, our pack tailing behind us.

We've made it to Manhattan, and yet it feels like the real work has just begun.

CHAPTER 11

I STAND IN THE CENTER OF A SQUARE of immortal soldiers, each wielding a shockstick shield and one of those spears. Caleb and Caspian are beside me, and Andreas is in front, outside the square. We're on the Manhattan side of a bridge, midtown, west side. There's a ward on this side, erected by yours truly. On the far end of the bridge, mortals gather. They're uniformed in basic camo, wearing body armor and wielding assault rifles. About a dozen, perhaps, milling around and waiting. A moment or two later, a huge Humvee arrives, and a figure unfolds from the rear. The soldiers swarm into formation.

I drop the ward and nod at Andreas. He gives no verbal command, just marches forward and the formation around me follows in perfect synch. I move with them, casting a shield around us. Our soldiers notice, glancing at me gratefully. Opposite, Bridgestone and his men move forward as well.

We meet in the middle. Andreas halts and steps aside, putting his back to the railing. The box around me flows to either side, becoming a corridor—Bridgestone's men do the same. I pull the shield inward, so it forms a barrier between the mortals and our men and then step forward to where our forces meet.

Nathaniel Bridgestone is exactly as I pictured him, mentally. Tall, broad-shouldered, heavy-set—a man who was once a powerhouse but for whom age has taken a toll. His hair is graying and thin, cropped close on top and shaved to the skin on the sides. He's clean-shaven and wears combat fatigues—the hems of his trousers are tucked into his boots and bloused. A sidearm is holstered to his thigh, a long combat knife on the other side. His eyes are hidden behind mirrored aviators. He's tanned and leathery, hard-faced, exuding cold authority.

"General Bridgestone," I say, nodding at him. "Well met."

He spits on the ground at my feet. "Freak bitch. You're the one calling herself the queen of immortals or some shit, ain'tcha?"

I sigh. "Your reputation precedes you, accurately," I say. "A foul-mouthed bigot."

"You called the meeting, freak bitch. What the fuck do you want? Surrender? I accept. All of your freaks can report to the Barclay's Center. You'll be counted and registered, and you'll stay there until you can be relocated to an immortal internment camp."

I stare at him. "Leave the island. Give us Manhattan. There's no reason to fight. We're not freaks. We are not interested in war, General Bridgestone. We want equal treatment. We want to be left alone."

"Give you Manhattan?" he repeats and then bursts into raucous laughter. "Just like that, you want us to just concede *all of Manhattan* to you fuckin' freaks? So you can, what? Turn all the poor innocent mortals on the island into frogs and eat us?"

It's my turn to laugh. "Seriously, where did you people get the idea that *anyone* is turning *anyone* into *frogs*? It's ridiculous. You sound like a moron. Even if I *could* turn you or anyone into a frog, which, as far as I know, I cannot, I don't eat frogs, General."

He stares at me—I feel his gaze like creepy fingers on my skin. "If you're not here to surrender, there ain't' shit to talk about. I am not conceding one single square inch of mortal territory to you freaks, mutants, and abominations. Our way of life, our cities, our people. You fuckin' filthy savages don't belong in our world. You never have, and you never will."

"The funny thing, Nathaniel, is that we've always been a part of your world—*our* world. We are every bit as human as you. We are not freaks, mutants, abominations, or savages. You, Nathaniel, are the savage. You and all your bigoted ilk." I wrap myself in a thick, dense shield like a cloak and step toward him, nose to nose. He stinks of body odor and cigarettes. "You have no clue what you face, Nathaniel. You will surrender. You will concede the island."

His hand drops to his gun. I see it but don't flinch.

"Draw it, Nathaniel. You fear me. And you should."

I feel Andreas getting nervous.

"I don't fear no freak bitch. Especially not a white-haired child like you. I'll squash you and your whole mutant army like bugs."

Anger bubbles inside me. Rages. Boils.

Calm, Maeve. Don't do anything rash. Caleb, in my mind.

We don't need a fight here on the bridge, my love. Caspian, too.

I ignore them.

Consider my options. End the meeting and go back to the island—the logical, safe, wise choice.

Or, give in to my rage and make a point. Irresponsible, rash, and foolish.

I draw prana, and my eyes flash. Bridgestone draws his pistol with remarkable speed, the barrel inches from my skull.

I grin. "Cute." I reach up, put my index finger over the hole of the barrel, and send prana into the metal. Bit by bit, I melt the insides. He doesn't feel it at first, but then the barrel and slide begin to glow a dull orange-red.

He squeezes the trigger—click, click. "The fuck?" He turns the gun sideways, staring at it in confusion, and then drops it with a hiss as the handle burns his palms.

Lances of prana lash out of me and swirl around each of the rifles held by Bridgestone's guard squad. They drop them with shouts of pain—those, I merely heated the outsides.

One of the mortal soldiers draws a pistol from his hip and levels it at me.

"Hold," I murmur to the men around me. "Do nothing."

I just stare at the man and his wobbling, wavering pistol. "Go ahead." I hold up my hands, arms out, palms up. "Shoot."

BLAM!

The round halts an inch from my face as if caught in invisible jelly. I pluck it, holding the shooter's gaze, and send prana into the round. It melts, dripping to the surface of the bridge, where it cools and hardens into a puddle of metal.

I turn my attention back to Bridgestone, who does look a little green around the gills. "I am the Once-Mortal Queen, the WorldBreaker. I do not want war, Nathaniel Bridgestone. But neither will I allow my people to be treated worse than cattle. If you bring war, it is war you shall get." I flip my hand at him, chin high, eyes blazing with anger. "You are dismissed, mortal."

I draw a line across the bridge from one side to the other with my finger in a single sharp, fast swipe. Prana ignites into a wall of white fire, heatless and harmless—but they don't know that. They stagger backward with cries of fear, shoving Bridgestone ahead of them as they scurry back to their side of the bridge.

I watch them go for a moment and then turn on my heel and stomp back to Manhattan, fury boiling in my veins. "I should have turned him into a frog," I snap. I glance at Andreas, trailing a bit. "I assume it is possible."

He shrugs. "Probably. Temporarily, maybe." He sighs. "I'm not sure that little display helped the cause much, Maeve."

I snort. "Against a man like that, there is only one

recourse—winning. You said it and you were right. But I had to see for myself before I committed my people to further violence. But now, yes. We fight." I stop so Andreas can catch up, and I hold his gaze. "We fight, and we do not fight fair. We do not harm innocents, and we do not commit the type of war crimes I assume they will. But we use every tool and tactic at our disposal. We fight for the Immortal Enclave, and we show no quarter."

Andreas is silent for a moment. "As you command."

"You disagree?"

He shakes his head. "I do not."

"Then let us plan our next move." I move forward once more. "But first, I need to see more of the city. What we have to work with. How many immortals do we have and what kind, what manner of arms and what equipment? How many mortals are in our controlled territory? Do they wish to flee to mortal-controlled areas? What is life like for non-combatants? If we're going to make this a true self-sustaining Enclave, we have to start setting that up now. What do we need?"

Andreas shakes his head. "I don't have answers for many of those questions at this time. We have roughly fifteen thousand immortals at last count, fairly equally divided between the three races. I have no idea how many mortals. We do have immortals joining us every day. Some mortals flee, some stay."

We walk down the middle of the road, heading east. Towers and apartments and offices rise to create canyons of glass all around, reflecting the early morning sun—we arrived last night and got settled into our quarters—a former corner office once occupied by some wealthy mortal executive. A large bed occupies the middle with a couch opposite. The glass facing the hallway can be turned opaque at the touch of a button to afford privacy. The windows overlook Manhattan—a stunning view. Smoke rises in a few places here and there in the distance.

At ground level, where we are, things are more dire. Trash is piled up on the curb, mounds and mountains of stinking refuse crawling with ants, rats, pigeons, and gulls. I see faces in windows, but most windows are dark, hinting at a lack of electricity.

I glance at Andreas again. "Where does the island stand in terms of electricity, gasoline, food, plumbing, all that? Trash is not being collected."

Andreas scrapes a hand through his hair. "I don't *know*, Maeve. I've been focused on building, funding, and organizing an army and keeping Bridgestone and the Federation at bay. I haven't had time to think about infrastructure. And for that matter, I'm a soldier, not a politician. You want me to be your commanding general? I'm your man. Running the city? You need someone else."

"Fair enough. In that case, we'll need to find someone suitable for the job."

Andreas's walkie-talkie squawks, then. "Andreas, HQ."

He keys the device. "Go for Andreas."

"We have a visitor. Several of them."

"Okay?" He pauses, waiting. "And? Who? How many? What do they want? Why are you telling me?"

"Leader is an elder fae. Calls himself Elias. He's looking for you."

I stop walking. "Elias?"

Andreas glances at me. "We'll be there ASAP."

We pile into the pickups we took here—once for

Andreas, Caspian, Caleb, and me, and another for the guards.

A few minutes later, we're parking in the underground garage and jogging up the stairs. Andreas leads the way through the maze of identical hallways to a conference room. The door is warded from the outside—the ward extends on either side of the door to cover the floor-to-ceiling windows. Andreas deftly unlocks the ward with practiced ease and precedes me into the conference room.

Seated at the head of the table is Elias, my grandfather—tall, lean, narrow-shouldered, graying hair that's gone a bit shaggy from its usual neat, clipped, classic side part. His jaw is shaded by silver stubble. He's wearing faded blue jeans and a black polo—as casually dressed as I've ever seen him. Usually, he wears a full three-piece suit.

He sees me enter behind Andreas and shoots to his feet, eyes lighting up as he hurries to me.

"Maeve! By the gods and blood, you look well! And you're here!" He wraps me in a hug before I can get a word in—I go stiff for a moment, unused to being hugged, and then I relax into the embrace, wrapping my arms around his middle and hugging him back.

"Aeldfar. You're here." I ease back and glance at the table. "With companions."

He smiles at me. "I'm here. I tracked down Andreas, as you requested, but I see you found him first." He indicates the four fae males, one vampire female, and one male shifter arranged around the table. "These are the elders of the Blood and loyal to you. Outside of the former members of the Tribunal, they are the eldest." He gestures at each in turn as he names them. "Arcturus, a Roman, and an expert in wards; Gaius, of a Germanic tribe I've forgotten the name of, and a tactician without peer; Hector, Athenian, a peer of Plato, and a battle-magic master; and Kanatase, a Mohawk warrior, chief, and a close, personal friend of mine from another life." He gestures at the vampire. "Elena, origin unknown to me, a master of shadows." The shifter, last. "Matthias, an Alpha Prime, and the only wolverine shifter I've ever heard of, from central Europe somewhere."

Arcturus is on the shorter side, barrel-chested and broad-shouldered, with jet black hair graying at the temples, his face lined and weathered and leathery. Gaius is huge, a muscular man with a generous layer of padding that does nothing to hide the mammoth strength of his frame, with blond hair in a double braid down his back and a long braided beard, both shot through with silver. Kanatase is tall and lean, clean-shaven with no sign of stubble, long black hair braided down his back, sharp-featured and hawk-eyed. Hector is medium height and trim, visibly the oldest, wearing a neat, short silver patrician beard and short, neatly parted hair. Elena is short, slender, and pale—unblooded, with blacked-out eyes and a hard, roving expression that takes in everything and gives out nothing. Matthias is built like the animal he turns into: short, powerfully built, with impossibly broad shoulders and huge arms, massive hands, thick forearms, brown hair left messy, and a shaggy, unkempt beard.

Elias drops to one knee in front of me. "At your service, my queen."

Chairs squeak, and a moment later, all six elder immortals are kneeling in front of me, rayed out behind Elias, heads bowed.

"Rise." I feel like an imposter, as always, speaking that way to immortals who are hundreds if not thousands of years older than me. "Let us sit and discuss the situation," I say. "I'd like everyone's input so we can plan accordingly."

We all find seats around the table; I notice Andreas sits far from Elias.

"The Mortal Federation is a powerful enemy," Elias says. "We did some recon on the way in, and they have a lot of men, a lot of vehicles, and a lot of weapons. And Nathaniel Bridgetone, as reprehensible as he is, is an excellent commander with battlefield experience in Iraq and Afghanistan. Controlling the bridges is key, obviously, to controlling Manhattan." He glances at Andreas. "I know we've had our differences, Andreas, and I know I cannot expect you to forget what I've done—I do not ask you to. Nor do I ask for forgiveness—the only one who could forgive me is my daughter. She is gone, and that's something I have to live with." He exhales slowly. "If you have anything to say to me on that score, say it now. I have nothing to hide."

Andreas is silent for a long time, staring at Elias. "I spent a long time hating you. Once upon a time, if I'd been in the same room with you as I am now, I'd have killed you. Or tried, at least; I admit I'm not sure I could, magic to magic, and I'd not like to test it. I've moved on. What's done is done. I'll never like you. I'll never be your friend. But I recognize the impossible position you were in, and I recognize that your decision did lead to Maeve, who I believe will save us all. As do you, unless I miss my guess." He spreads his hands out, shrugging. "We do not have time for grudges. All our resources must be bent toward defeating Bridgestone and establishing Manhattan as a safe haven for Immortals—we're calling it the Immortal Enclave."

Elias nods. "If you can put the past behind us, then we can work together as professionals. Agreed?"

Andreas nods. "Agreed."

Elias lets out a breath as if a weight has been lifted. "Now. You've done a remarkable job here, Andreas. The army you've built is admirable, and you've done well holding territory against a foe who is superior in several ways. But with Maeve being here, having brought her own small force, and now that I and my friends are here, I think we can make even more progress."

"I have named Andreas commander-in-chief. He reports to me, and you all report to him." I scan the faces for signs of disgruntlement but see none. "Gaius, as a tactician, I think you're best utilized as Andreas's second-in-command. Andreas?"

Andreas nods. "I've heard and read of your exploits against the Roman armies. It is my honor to fight alongside you, Gaius."

Gaius nods once. "I know you too, Andreas. Your stand against the Ottomans at the Battle of Dervenakia is legendary."

Andreas seems uncomfortable. "I did not stand alone. But I thank you, Gaius."

Arcturus taps the table with a thick finger. "I saw some decent wards at the bridges, but they can be improved. Wards can be an excellent offensive weapon as well, especially against mortals."

I smile at him. "Wonderful, thank you. I must rely on all of you—your wisdom and experience are without parallel."

Elias indicates Hector and Kanatase. "They will be invaluable in the coming battle. Being outnumbered and facing superior war technology, we are committed to guerilla warfare. We simply cannot win in a head-to-head slugging contest. Man to man, being immortal, we are superior. But in this age of tanks, machine guns, and grenades, that edge is significantly reduced."

"I'll leave the strategy to those whose province it is. One thing that must be understood, however, is that I am not a figurehead. I will lead our people into battle. It is how I am most effective. I'll leave strategy decisions to the generals, but I will not be told I am more valuable behind the lines. Are we understood on that score?" Everyone assents. "Next. Infrastructure."

Elias frowns. "Meaning?"

I wave a hand at the window. "We have to think beyond battles, Aeldfar. We have to operate on the assumption that we will win, and when we do, we will need things in place here to make this city livable. The central government seems likely to topple completely sooner than later—I have no interest in trying to rule a whole country. I will not be the queen of America, so if anyone is harboring secret notions of installing me as a puppet or some such nonsense, let it go now. My idea is for Manhattan, as the Immortal Enclave, to set a precedent for how mortals and immortals can live together. For how we can establish a city that can provide something like the comforts of civilization we are all used to." I point overhead. "We have lights. We have plumbing. But not everyone out there does—the power grid is spotty at best, from what I've seen. I assume the same is true for most services—people need toilets to flush, lights that turn on, and ways to communicate. Without the systems in place that have run these things for, well, ever, we will need to come up with alternate solutions." I look at Elias. "I'd like to task you, Aedlfar, with that problem. Provide services for the people of the Enclave. Trash collection and what we do with it. Electricity. Plumbing. Food production. We have to be self-sustainable. How do we get there once we have driven Bridgestone and his band of bigots off the island?"

Elias frowns thoughtfully. "That is quite a task, granddaughter."

I nod. "It is. But if anyone is equal to it, it's you. You solved immortal reproduction, after all."

Pain crosses his face. "But what a cost," he murmurs. "You honor me, Maeve. I will see it done. Do you have any ideas or thoughts?"

I shrug. "I mean, not specifically. But if we can glamour a spear to produce a laser bolt," I gesture at Andreas, "then we can surely find ways of merging magic and technology to create necessary services. Power stations, for example. Surely there are power generation stations of some sort in Manhattan? How can we use glamours to make them work after the larger grid goes down? How can we use magic to deal with trash? As for food production, I know in many cities, urban gardening has gained a lot of traction. And now that there will be far, far fewer people living here, we can utilize the vertical space to grow food—again, using magic to bridge any gaps. I know nothing about growing food, but out there we have people who lived much of their lives doing exactly that—all of you who lived in the time before the industrial revolution and modern food production standards can lend your knowledge to this. Rooftop gardens, vacant lots. We can even consider demolishing unused buildings to make room for larger plots. We are going to have to be creative—and just like the world is watching how we deal with the Mortal Federation, they'll be watching what we do after."

Elias regards me with a small, soft smile. "You have grown in wisdom since I met you in that cell below the mountain, my dear." He slaps the table. "I have some ideas where to begin." He glances at Andreas. "I'll need some introductions and some manpower. People with engineering experience and education and others with magical talents. A small task force to start researching."

Andreas nods thoughtfully. Keys his mic. "Zeke? Andreas, over."

"Go for Zeke."

"Find me twenty people. Engineers, glamourworkers, builders, especially people with knowledge of utility infrastructure—put out the call among mortals, as well."

"Yes, commander. I'll have a list for you in twenty-four hours."

"They'll be working with Elias Sparrow, creating a working infrastructure system. Emphasize how important the job is."

"Understood."

The door to the conference room bursts open, and a sweaty, red-faced young woman with ginger hair and freckles skids in. "Andreas! We're under attack. Federation forces are at the Kennedy bridge. We have a small force there, but the ward won't hold for long."

Andreas bolts to his feet, sending the rolling office chair hurtling backward into the wall. "Time to find out how our new leadership works together." He works a quick glamour with experience of long practice and speaks into his index finger as if it were a microphone. "AOMQ forces, all hands. Bridge attack. Repeat, bridge attack. Battle stations, all hands." He glances at me. "Coming, battle queen?"

Caleb draws a knife from his pocket, a small folding knife, and drags it across his palm. "Blood armor."

I draw his blood to me and coat myself with it, over my clothes, forming the skin-tight blood armor I wore under the mountain.

Elena, the vampire, whistles. "A neat trick, my lady. Does it provide protection?"

I grin. "You're about to find out."

CHAPTER 12

WE MAKE OUR WAY EAST AND NORTH to the RFK bridge—a small advance force comprised of Andreas, myself, my mates, our pack, Nico, Philemon, Emily, twenty-five of Andreas's handpicked warriors— roughly half fae, the other half evenly divided between vampires and shifters—and another twenty- five volunteers from my caravan, again being mostly fae and the rest evenly split. Not quite seventy-five of us. The messenger who brought word of the attack couldn't tell us how many mortals were attacking.

We need a reliable communication sys- tem—we can't rely on technology—even radios are unreliable because they need energy, which is currently in short supply and unreliable. I make a note to add that to Aeldfar's list of tasks.

We have four pickups packed to the brim—five in each cab and another eight to ten piled in the beds. The rest, the shifters, follow in animal form, a chaotic swarm of lions, tigers, bears, coyotes, wolves, lynx, bobcats, and jaguars…they growl and whuff and roar and snarl, easily keeping pace with our slow-moving trucks. The roads are clogged with abandoned cars and wrecked hulks, making progress slow.

I glance at Andreas, driving. "Need to get these roads cleared."

He nods. "Been on the list, but the fucking Federation keeps attacking, and it's been all I can do to keep repelling the attacks and holding our territory."

"I'm not criticizing, Andreas. I haven't been here—I don't know what you can and can't do, what you have and haven't done. I'm just pointing out what I see."

Andreas wipes his face with one hand. "Yeah, I know—sorry. I'm just…stretched thin and stressed out. Getting vampires, fae, and shifters to work together as an army? Fuck, it's damn near impossible. What authority I have has been hard-won." He glances at me. "To be perfectly honest, I'm relieved beyond expression that you're here so I can leave the political leadership to you. I'm an old soldier, Maeve. That's what I know. That's what I do."

I squeeze his shoulder. "You've done an amazing job here, Andreas. Truly. And I'm here now. We're all here. It's not all on you anymore."

He inhales slowly, holds it, and lets it out…not

shakily, exactly, but definitely with some emotion. "It hasn't been easy, I'll tell you that much."

We approach an intersection—the north-south avenue is blocked on the north side of the intersection. We have to keep going east anyway, but the barricade causes Andreas to halt, staring hard at the ten-foot-high amalgamation of overturned trucks, cars, semi-trailers, food carts, garbage trucks, and barbed wire. "That's new. I don't like that."

I look at him—his eyes are whited out, signifying that he's using maya. "What is it?"

He shakes his head, his eyes returning to normal. "I don't know. A feeling. Intuition. Something is wrong." He glances in the rearview mirror. "Emily—are you up for a quick flight?"

She's in the back seat, between Caleb and Caspian. "Yes! What do you need?"

He shakes his head. "I don't know. Something just isn't right. They're attacking at the RFK, numbers unknown, but there's a new barricade here. Head west along the Hudson and make sure the attack on the RFK isn't a feint."

"Who's fainting?" Emily asks, puzzled.

Andreas snorts a laugh. "Not faint, f-*a*-i-n-t, like passing out—feint, f-*e*-i-n-t, as in a fake out."

She blushes. "Oh. Sorry. My father didn't think education was necessary."

Andreas just smiles at her. "No worries. We can address that later. For now, the fact that you can fly, count, and assess is far more valuable than your vocabulary."

Caspian opens his door and lets her out—she climbs right over him with excited exuberance, peeling out of her clothing—loose, baggy sweatpants, a T-shirt, and a zip-up hoodie, no underwear, no bra, and Crocs on her feet. She tosses the clothing into the cab without a hint of self-consciousness.

"Hudson River, west. Got it. Be back ASAP." She says the acronym as a word rather than spelling it—*AY-sap*.

She takes half a dozen hard, sprinting steps, and then, much like a long jumper in track and field, a pair of long, extended-stride bounds, and then a wild skyward two-foot leap. Amber light flares, and her hawk swoops low, beats her wings furiously, and rockets skyward. Within seconds, she's gone.

"Hell of a talented shifter," Caleb says. "Shifting on the fly like that, literally? Takes a *lot* of confidence and a *lot* of practice."

Andreas glances over his shoulder at Caleb. "Can you and your pack see what the deal is at the bridge? What are we facing? Don't engage—just assess and report back to Maeve."

Caleb nods. "Certainly." He leans forward between the seats and kisses my jaw. "See you."

And then he's out of the truck, stripping, tossing his clothes in with Emily's. The pack, in the truck bed, do the same, having heard the order through the open window panel in the back of the cab.

Moments later, six wolves stream east, howling and yipping. Sierra, after a night's rest, a lot of food, and renewal of her mana reserves, is almost back to normal. I wouldn't classify us as friends yet, but she seems to have let go of her hatred of me, which is a huge step forward.

I hear gunfire to the east—sporadic bursts punctuated

by an occasional explosion. We wait for several tense minutes before Caleb's voice fills my mind.

They're hitting the bridge pretty hard. The ward is holding for now, but a few more direct hits from this damned tank, and it'll blow out. One tank, no APCs. A few HUMVEEs and roughly a hundred men, probably fewer.

I relay the report to Andreas, who curses floridly and extensively. "It's a feint—I'd put money on it. They're gambling that we'll take the bait—the tank is the real hook. But less than a hundred? We can repel that easily and he has to know it." He smacks the steering wheel with the heel of his palm. "Ask him how the defenders are faring. Can they hold out?"

I relay the question.

They have two fae who are doing their best to keep the ward up, but that tank is pummeling it—and the small arms fire isn't helping. Once the ward goes down, they're going to be in trouble. Ten fae, one shifter, and three vampires. I'd say they have minutes at most.

"We have to help them," I say. "I need to help them hold the ward."

He shakes his head. "Not yet. We need to know where the real attack is happening first."

I hear Emily's piercing screech high overhead—I look up in time to see her tuck her wings back and stoop toward us. She bellies her wings at the last second, abruptly arresting her incredible speed before gliding forward a few feet above the ground—she shifts back and lands lithely on her feet, trotting off the last of her momentum.

"The Lincoln tunnel," she says, panting. "Big time. Three tanks, two of the…whaddya call'em, armored personnel things, and at least, like, five hundred soldiers. That's just an estimate. There's a ward on this side of the tunnel but no defenders."

"I fucking knew it. With three tanks, that ward will fall in minutes." Andreas goes perfectly still, thinking. It seems like an eternity, waiting for his decision, but in reality, it's less than ten seconds. "We play along. Act like we've taken the bait. Maeve—you and Caspian take twenty or so to the bridge. Be visible, be showy. Give them something to talk about. Defend the bridge at all costs—that's not fake. Meantime, I'll take the rest to the tunnel, let them break the ward, and push through. We've already blocked off north-south access around the tunnel with warded barricades that even their tanks will have a hard time breaking through." he looks at me. "This is where you push your powers to the limit, Maeve. You have to wrap shit up at the bridge and get over to reinforce us. We're gonna hit them from behind and keep them busy while you handle the bridge and join us and hit from the front."

I blow out a breath. "Risky." I look at him. "You're putting a lot of faith in me."

"I am—because I believe in you. Now go. Just…keep the bridge intact if at all possible."

I shove out of the car, followed by Caspian. Andreas calls out for twenty volunteers to go with me—within seconds, two trucks are continuing east with the volunteer force while the rest re-route south and west.

I summon prana and leap skyward, lightening my body and launching myself with a blast of wind. I feel Caspian below and behind me a few feet, leaping from rooftop to rooftop, soaring nearly weightless for long seconds. Below, the trucks make slower progress, having to weave through the messy maze of streets.

With the river and the bridge in view, now, I hear the chatter of gunfire and the slow, regular *BOOM!......BOOM!......BOOM!* of the tank's cannon.

Blue-gray steel towers sway and shudder as the ward absorbs the concussions—the ward flares white, crackling and sparking like a downed powerline, visible even to the mortals. The ward is on the island side and the tank is a hundred yards away, rocking backward with each blast, yellow flame belching from the long barrel. Three HUMVEEs are ranked in a line abreast beside the tank, two on the left and one on the right; the HUMVEE on the right has a machine gun mounted on the top, which fires in cacophonous three- and four-round bursts. Soldiers kneel beside the vehicles, rifles to their shoulders, firing steadily.

The defenders huddle behind the girders of the tower, helpless to do anything but hope the ward holds long enough for reinforcements to arrive.

Which is me.

I float myself along with another blast of wind and then soar in a downward diagonal toward the bridge. I feel my prana boiling, eager and wild, seething in my gut, begging for release.

I guide my descent with brief directional gusts, aiming to land between the ward and the attackers.

As I fall, I summon a shield in front of me. Wind howls past my ears as I hurtle toward the bridge; I let my prana flare so my eyes, hair, and tattoos glow bright, blinding white-gold, turning me into a beacon.

Go low, I tell Caspian. ***Stay with the defenders. Tell them to be ready to drop the ward and attack on my signal.***

Got it. What's the signal?

You'll know.

I land on the bridge hard, shield in front of me. There's a moment of silence as the attackers stare at me, confused. I hear a squeaking of metal—the tank training its cannon on me. I pour prana into the shield until it's almost three feet thick.

"Stand down and retreat or be destroyed," I call out, amplifying my voice. "This is your only warning."

Their response is to open fire on me. All at once, my shield is subjected to a barrage of small arms fire, and then the tank booms and rocks backward; my shield absorbs the impact and sends me skidding backward a dozen feet.

My turn.

Holding the shield in one hand, I shoot a lance of prana at the tank—the mortals won't be able to see it, but they'll feel the effects shortly. I set the prana on fire— no heatless flame this time. The tank ignites—prana does not need combustible material to burn. Within seconds, screams echo inside the tank as the metal heats and turns orange and then red.

The foot soldiers recover from their shock quickly, shuffling away from the burning machine and pouring fire at me. The shield holds, but the effort is exhausting, draining my prana swiftly.

I can't sustain the shield like this for much longer—a shield is an active glamour, unlike a ward, which is passive. Active glamours require constant feeding and control to sustain, the tradeoff being a shield can withstand far more damage. A ward, being passive, only needs to be reinforced occasionally but cannot take the same kind of pounding a shield can.

I draw prana and launch a quick series of one-handed

fireballs—they're slow-moving, about the speed of a thrown ball, and do little damage to objects but can wreck a human. It's a distraction. And it works.

The gunfire cuts off abruptly as the soldiers scramble out of the way. I stretch the shield across the width of the bridge.

"*NOW!*" I shout.

Running footsteps echo on the bridge behind me. I feel Caspian beside me.

"Form up behind me," I call out. "I'll push forward to close the distance, drop the shield, and then we attack. Two of you fae, work with the shifter, protect his flanks. Vampire—you get into the HUMVEEs and take out the drivers. Ready?"

I don't wait for an assent. I push the incredibly dense shield forward—when a shield is this thick, it's like pushing a car in neutral: the density of the shield creates a physical sense of weight, requiring me to tap into my supernatural strength.

I strain, snarling. Foot by foot, I push the shield across the open space of the bridge—gunfire resumes, and I feel each bullet impact like the sting of a bee. I'm losing the shield—they can only be held for so long, no matter how much prana you have; the physical toll of maintaining the shield is greater than the drain on prana.

We're within a few feet now, and the impacts of the bullets on the shield are more than mere bee stings, now—truly painful. Nothing I can't withstand, but immensely unpleasant.

Now comes the tricky part. I focus on propping up the shield for a few more seconds while dividing my attention—I'd like to be able to reproduce Andreas's trick with the shadows, but I haven't had a chance to parse that glamour. So, instead, I do the opposite. I summon a flood of prana and channel it into the shield—but instead of reinforcing the density of the jellified air, I create light. Blinding, searing, brutal, punishing white light, like staring into the heart of a nuclear detonation.

The gunfire ceases; I drop the shield.

No order is necessary—the moment the shield goes down, those behind me attack. Four fae surge past me, wielding shocksticks in pairs—these are former enforcers. One stick as a shield, edges overlapping, the other as a weapon set to kill, crackling with savage electricity. Before the mortals can open fire again, the fae are among them, smashing with shields and lashing out with shocksticks. Screams echo and overlap and electricity buzzes and crackles. Four more fae, similarly armed and in the same line abreast formation, enter the fray behind the first set, and now they work in well-trained synchronicity, the first line smashing through, making way for the second, who spread apart, creating a wedge opening in the mortal forces.

Gunfire rattles and cracks, but we're too close now. The second line pushes outward, huddling behind their shields and stabbing around with their shocksticks, widening the wedge in the mortal line.

I feel a rush of air and catch a blur of shadows—the vampire leaping over the scrum and to the ground beside a HUMVEE. He rips the driver's door off and hurls it aside like a frisbee, decapitating several mortal soldiers and disemboweling several more. And then he's in the vehicle and body parts fly.

Refocus.

I move into the opening with Caspian at my side. "Go help with the HUMVEEs," I tell him. "I'm fine here."

He's gone in a flash of shadows, and then more screaming abruptly cuts off as he decimates the occupants of the second vehicle.

The shifter, a huge Black male with long dreads, shifts into a tiger nearly twice the size of a normal OnceBlood tiger; he leaps past me, pouncing on a mortal who attempts to get his gun up in time. No such luck—he's erased in a gory splash of red. The two fae tasked to guard his flanks follow the tiger into the melee, shocksticks crackling and stabbing.

I'm last into the fight. I relax into instinct, let my body and my spirit take over—Mother's Spirit, now as much a part of me as my magic itself. I lash out with my power and yank rakta and prana to myself, watching mortal bodies desiccate and wilt as their life force flows into my palm. The more power I draw from the enemy, the more powerful I become; I can feel their heartbeats, their souls, I can locate them without looking, reaching for prana and rakta and jerking it out of them with vicious, merciless violence. I feel myself glowing white-hot and blazing with an overload of energy.

"DOWN!" I shout.

My forces obey instantly, dropping to their bellies without question or hesitation.

I let the power explode out of me, formless and uninhibited. It's a wave of pure, undiluted destruction. The tank is washed away, dissolved in a flash in golden-white light with the awful acrid scent of burning hair and the tang of spent magic.

Mortal bodies, now corpses, are blown away, turned

to ash. The two closest HUMVEEs are blown over with a deafening squeal and crunch of metal.

Silence.

A dozen mortals, clustered together beyond the limited range of the blast, drop their weapons and sink to their knees. Caspian, the other vampire, and the shifter crouch in front of them, ready to attack.

"Wait," I say. I stride toward them. "Take their weapons and armor into the remaining vehicle and head for the tunnel. I'll deal with these remaining mortals."

I taste their terror in the air, a sharp, sour scent like old urine. I must be quite a sight for them: wrapped in blood armor that flows over my body, still liquid but somehow solid, glowing with an inner incandescence. My hair, skin, eyes, and bondmark tattoos all glow blinding white, and my hair flutters in a nonexistent wind.

"P-please," one of the soldiers whimpers. "Don't— don't kill us."

I remain silent as Caspian and the others strip them of body armor, weapons, ammunition, and other useful gear, pile it into the vehicle, clamber in themselves, and take off back across the bridge.

I regard the mortals with a long, silent stare. "Why do you fight?" I ask after a while.

The one who begged me not to kill them answers. "Bridgestone—he…he offered ten grand per head for a two-month stint. Another grand if you bring a friend with military experience."

"Money?" I stare at him. "Was it worth it?"

He shakes his head. "We…we didn't know what we were signing up for. He made it seem like we were a private security force, like Blackwater. We thought we were gonna be deployed overseas somewhere. And then we were shipped here to New York. We weren't briefed on anything. Just given unit assignments and told to follow our squad leaders, and I don't think the squad leaders even knew what the orders were till the last second." He shakes his head again, his voice quavering. "We didn't sign up to exterminate people, and that's what he has us doing. But the noncoms, they're loyal to him. They're the ones who share his beliefs, that you guys are…" he trails off.

"That we're what?"

"Subhuman." He whispers it. "Freaks. Savages."

"And what do you think?" I ask him.

"I didn't sign up to kill innocent people. But the noncoms will fuck you up if you refuse orders. I've seen people shot for refusing to carry out a raid."

I scan the rest of the faces. "I have no interest in executing prisoners. You face a choice now, mortals—return to your units and carry on the fight against me and my people, who have offered you no harm until you attacked us; flee this place and go home; or join us and fight for equality for all people, all humans, mortal and immortal."

"If we go with you…what will happen to us?" It's a young woman, her face tear-streaked and dirty.

"That will be up to you. There will be plenty of work for everyone. We need soldiers, of course, but I will not ask you to fight against your own kind. You are welcome to do so if you choose, but it will not be asked of you. The future of this place—Manhattan-That-Was—is changing. We are creating something new here. You can be a part of it. You will not be harmed or treated as anything other than an equal to everyone else, regardless of race or lifespan."

I summon the mark of fealty. Their eyes bug out with

shock and awe. "This is a mark of fealty. Touch it, and swear fealty to me, and you will be marked as one of mine. Head west, and one of my people will find you and show you where to go." I float the mark toward them. "It will not hurt or cause any effect on your body. It merely identifies you as belonging to my army—with one added element: if you betray me, I will know it, and you will die instantly." I don't remember if that's true, but it serves its purpose.

"What if we don't take the mark?" Another one asks.

I shrug. "Nothing. But my people won't necessarily know you've sworn fealty to me, and I cannot guarantee your safety since you're dressed in the uniform of the Mortal Federation. Do as you wish. I have no authority over you and claim none. I have other matters to attend to. Take the mark, or do not."

I leave the mark hanging in the air in front of them, a grapefruit-sized globe of swirling white and gold light. Turning on my heel, I launch myself into the air without a backward look. I feel, one by one, the mortals take the mark.

On to the real battle.

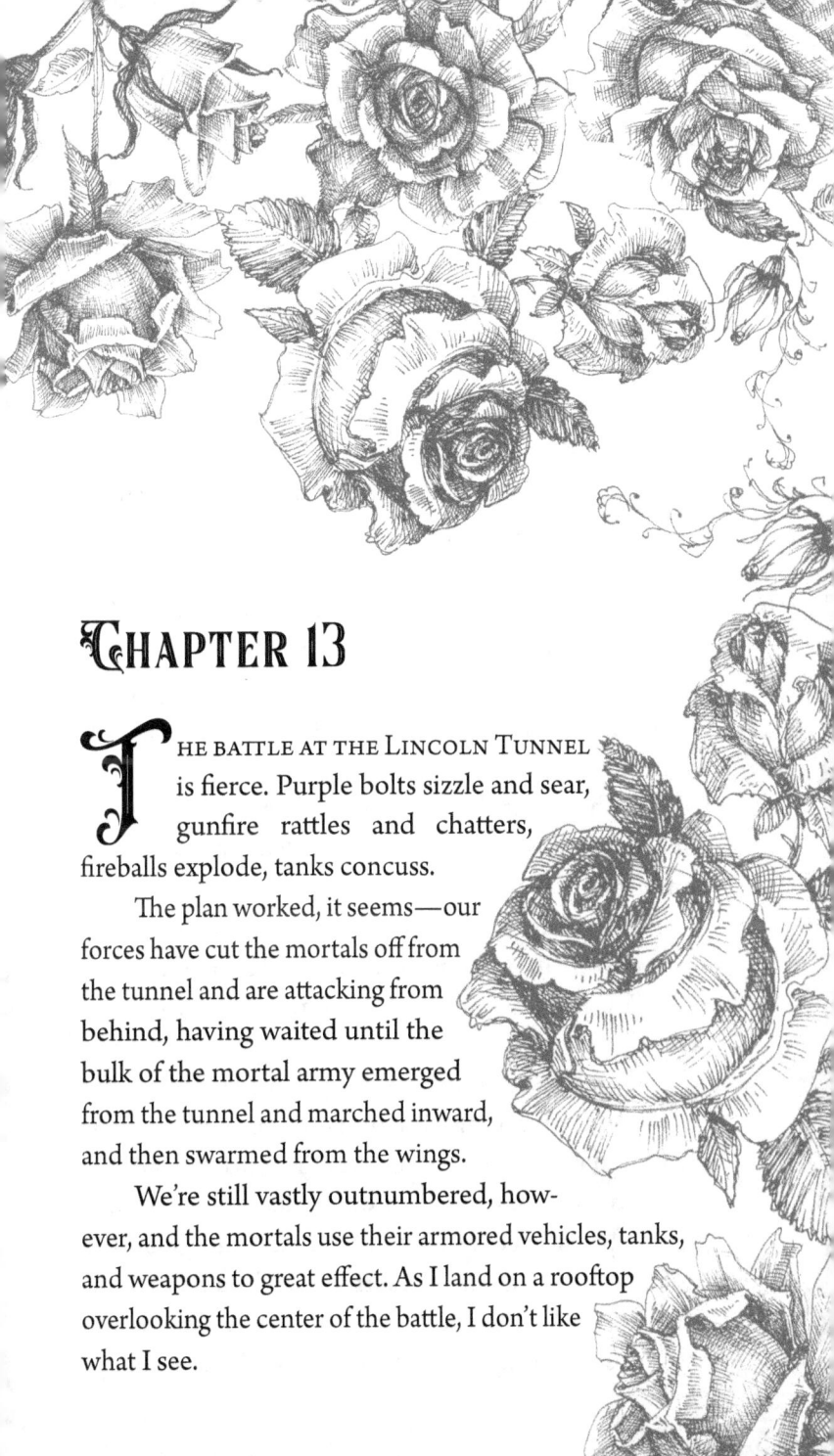

CHAPTER 13

THE BATTLE AT THE LINCOLN TUNNEL is fierce. Purple bolts sizzle and sear, gunfire rattles and chatters, fireballs explode, tanks concuss.

The plan worked, it seems—our forces have cut the mortals off from the tunnel and are attacking from behind, having waited until the bulk of the mortal army emerged from the tunnel and marched inward, and then swarmed from the wings.

We're still vastly outnumbered, however, and the mortals use their armored vehicles, tanks, and weapons to great effect. As I land on a rooftop overlooking the center of the battle, I don't like what I see.

I watch an immortal die, a shifter gunned down by half a dozen mortals. A vampire goes down as well, taking a tank's round to the chest; the mess is immense.

Andreas is using guerilla tactics, keeping his forces harrying the mortals and then vanishing back into the blown-out and abandoned office buildings. The tanks comprise the bulk of mortal destructive capacity, blowing buildings apart and eradicating hiding places as fast as the immortals can scurry from place to place.

What's *not* happening here is teamwork. I watch for a few minutes, assessing from above. What worked for us at the bridge was teamwork—the element of surprise that is me aside. The fae drove in with their shields, the shifter followed, and the vampire cleaned up around the edges.

I see Andreas on another rooftop, wielding one of the spears as a projectile weapon while directing the battle from above.

I wish again that we had a way of communicating—I don't have a walkie-talkie, and I cannot communicate with him mentally. It's an issue.

With nothing else to do, I leap across the road, using a gust of wind to boost me further. I land beside Andreas.

"You need to regroup," I tell him. "We need new tactics."

He ignores me, watching as a pair of bear shifters tear into a squad of mortals. The bears take multiple rounds each but shrug them off as they rip the mortals apart.

"Assign a pair of fae with shocksticks to each shifter. The fae provide cover for the approach and guard the flanks." I point at a vampire, surrounded by a dozen mortals who are trying to kill the vampire with knives and fists—it's not going well for the mortals. "The vampires take out the vehicles—their strength allows them to rip doors off and take care of the occupants."

Andreas eyes me. "The bridge attack went well, then?"

I nod. "I sent a dozen mortal survivors into the Enclave with my mark of fealty. Have someone collect them and give them work." I hold Andreas's eyes. "They were offered money to join the Federation and weren't told ahead of time what the mission was. I doubt most rank-and-file soldiers in the Federation are truly here for the cause—just the money. And fear—the noncoms, whatever those are—kill anyone who doesn't obey commands."

Andreas's expression darkens. "That changes things." A glance at me. "Noncoms are non-commissioned officers—they're the ones running the army."

"The fae who have been trained as enforcers are an excellent resource," I tell him. "They can get close and keep the mortals from being able to use their guns. Once we're inside their range, the edge provided by their guns and armor is gone."

Andreas nods thoughtfully. "Adjusting tactics mid-battle is difficult. We'll have to train them on that for the next one."

I give him an annoyed glare. "Fine. I'll do it myself."

"Maeve!"

I leap off the roof and land on the sidewalk below. Immediately, gunfire is directed my way, round whizzing, whining, and snapping past me.

"*FAE!*" I shout at the top of my voice, magically amplified. "*TO ME!*"

I throw up a shield as dozens of fae warriors disengage and swarm in my direction. Within a few seconds, they're forming up on either side of me—round snap overhead and slam into my shield, and then I can lower the shield because my fae warriors have their shocksticks in shield mode, edges overlapping.

The column of mortal soldiers inches forward—and then halts as Caspian and the others from the bridge arrive and form a line across the Federation's route. My line of fae extends parallel to the Federation column; the warriors huddle behind their shields as automatic weapons fire chatters and rattles and cracks.

An ominous sound echoes over the battle: the squeak of the tank's turret rotating.

"*VAMPIRES!*" I shout. "*GET INSIDE THE TANKS! FAE! COVER THEIR APPROACH!*"

Andreas lands beside me. "You're crazy!" He shouts in my ear. "I love it! Lead the vampires! I have the fae."

Caleb, have the shifters distract the soldiers. Wait for the fae to make their move. I feel him but can't see him—he's with the others from the bridge.

At once, my love, he answers.

Seconds later, I watch shifters break away from skirmishes, reacting to Caleb's Alpha Prime command. They form up in an alley-mouth with Caleb at the lead, waiting for the fae.

Twenty-some vampires have answered my call, flashing in blurs of shadows across the battlefield to hunker behind the shield wall. I look left, look right—blacked-out eyes watch me intently, waiting. Andreas watches. Caleb watches.

The mortals have halted the column—at the front, the fae shield wall holds up under withering gunfire from the mortal vanguard. The tanks are working in concert, adjusting their aim—all at me.

It's been a matter of seconds—less than thirty—since I landed on the sidewalk. It's felt like an hour.

"*NOW!*" I shout, hurling myself over the fae line with a blast of wind.

Andreas leads the fae charge, pushing the shield wall forward—these are armed with a spear and a shockstick, and the spears belch purple bolts with an audible crackling sizzle. The bolts are not as powerful as hastaxi orbs by quite a margin—they hit the tanks' sides and char and dent the metal but can't break through; mortals they sear through without so much as slowing. The sudden onslaught has its intended effect, distracting and slowing the gunfire from the mortals.

Vampires soar around me, blurs of shadow in the bright sun. A tank's cannon roars in the instant after I leap, the round whistling over the shield wall and blasting the brick building into spewing shards. I land on the nearest tank's turret. Two more vampires touch down with me. Mortal soldiers on the ground beside the tank whirl, draw aim, and fire. I throw up a shield, but not in time—several rounds hit the vampire nearest me, dropping her to her knees—she's unblooded, so the rounds crack and smash her stone-like skin, leaving bloodless pocks and divots. The other vampire scrambles up onto the turret, wrenches the circular door off with a scream of protesting metal, and then drops in.

Screams echo briefly and cut off abruptly, and then the tank rumbles to a halt.

I drop off the tank, grab the nearest mortal soldier, and fling him away—he bowls over several other mortals, and they all topple to the ground. A pack of coyote shifters seizes the opportunity and swarms over them, and blood flies.

The wounded vampire, one arm useless and missing an eye, lands beside me. She snarls viciously, rips the arm off one mortal, and uses it to club another. The other vampire leaps up out of the tank, scrambles down, and grabs the body of a dead mortal, hauling it to himself. He snags a pair of grenades from the mortal's equipment webbing, rips the pins free, and tosses them into the turret—seconds later there's a muffled *CRUMP* and a pillar of smoke boiling up from the opening.

The lead tank swivels its turret forward and draws aim on the fae shield wall. I fling myself toward it, but it's too late—the cannon booms, the tank rocks backward, and the shield wall is broken as fae bodies are scattered, blood spraying and limbs going in every direction. The mortals seize the opportunity and redouble their fire. The tiger shifter attacks, soaring over the shattered shield wall and pouncing on the mortals. Caspian and the other vampires with him blur toward the tank, and we four land at the same time. Caspian rips the door off and he and the other drop in. I ride the slowing tank, assessing the battle. Two tanks down, one still operational—but not for long. More vampires swarm over it now that the tactics have been proven.

Shifters of all kinds harry the mortal foot soldiers, dodging among the ranks and ripping and tearing and biting before leaping away, confusing the mortal ranks.

Still, as effective as the tactics are, we're still losing too many—shifters fall, wounded or killed. The fae shockstick shields can only take so much before they falter, and then the fae wielding them go down.

The third and final tank is taken out, and now the vampires go to work on the APCs, wheeled, armored tank-like vehicles bristling with weapons protruding from portholes.

The wounded vampire is down. The coyote pack has lost three. I feel Sierra take a hit—I hear the yelp.

I need to do something—this has to end. We're winning, but the cost is too high.

A surge of fury energizes me—these mortals are killing my people. For what? Why?

No.

I lash out with prana and yank the lifeforce from the dozen or so nearest mortals, a sudden flood of blood and prana swirling around me and soaking into me. The abrupt influx of energy cascades through me, and I immediately redirect it. I send a blinding lance of prana horizontally through the mortal column of men and machinery. Instead of igniting it, however, I keep pouring prana down the line, making the lance thicker and denser and more volatile.

With a snap of my fingers, I turn the prana in on itself—an implosion rather than an explosion.

Panic seizes me—that's not what I intended...at all.

All along the column, there's a sound like rushing wind, and a dense black line of nothingness appears where my prana was. It's razor-thin at first—thin but dense. Tanks, APCs, and HUMVEEs all sink down on their suspension, metal groaning. The line thickens, widens—the roaring of wind becomes a deafening freight train blast of noise, and the machinery tilts, wobbles, tips inward, denting, crushing inward.

The wind screams and dust swirls and blasts, chunks of rock and dirt and debris charging the air with deadly projectiles hurtling toward the expanding line of sucking blackness.

Fuck—what did I do?

A sense of wrongness pervades my spirit, a sourness, bitter and dark.

Slowly at first and then all at once, the sounds of the battle fade. The black line expands and expands, now the width of a tank—the vehicles are sucked in, twisting and twirling and toppling end over end like toys kicked aside by a careless giant foot.

Mortals are sucked in as well, screaming into the void.

My people are drawn toward it—what did I do? How do I stop it?

Panic shudders through me. I withdraw my prana, but there's nothing to draw in—it's been consumed by the void.

Shouts, screams. A shifter vanishes into the void.

"*RETREAT*!" I shout, amplifying it. "*RUN*!"

Immortals scatter, mortals with them, differences forgotten as the vortex of nothingness seeks to consume everyone and everything alike.

And then I hear a sound that chills me to the bone: laughter. A dry, mad cackle of deranged amusement.

It comes from everywhere and nowhere.

I whirl, see nothing.

Another bark of laughter from above, behind, all around.

The vortex expands.

The air above it shimmers, coruscates. Something immense and not quite visible crawls out of the vortex—it's only seen by the absence of light, or the refraction of light, perhaps. Words fail, but there it is. A creature. Too many legs, too many arms. Or not enough. Eyeless. Faceless. It slithers out of the vortex and oozes across the concrete of the road, glomming over corpses. Where it goes, the corpses vanish, and the thing gains reality—definition. Form.

A corpse becomes a spider-like leg—two, three, four…eight legs, but fashioned out of gore-dripping corpses, arms flopping, eyes sightless and staring. The thing scuttles with deceptive speed over the ruined hulk of a burned-out taxi—the scorched and blackened metal becomes the spider's torso. Bones crack and crunch, each step leaving a nauseating trail of gore. Dropped weapons become snapping pincers, discarded helmets dropped from dead mortal skulls become eyes, glittering and alien.

Before I can register what's happening, another shimmer catches my eye—a second *thing* emerging from the vortex. From the void, The Dreaming.

A dozen feet from the howling, sucking void is an abandoned city bus, windows shattered, two tires blown out, folding door sagging open. The thing from the void congeals onto the bus, and for a moment, nothing happens. And then one wheel wiggles, creaks, and extends, the axle becoming a long, thin, stretching leg. Another, and then all four, becoming legs. The tires dig into the ground and support the creature's weight as it stands up on all four legs. The windows along the sides are dark, showing only shadows writhing inside; twin red points of light glow behind the windshield—demonic, alien eyes.

The bus-thing scuttles forward, metal protesting, clicking, screeching, creating a spine-shuddering noise of insectile movement.

A squad of mortal soldiers huddles against the wall,

kicking and scrabbling as the vortex sucks them toward it; the bus-thing pauses near them, hunkers down, pauses… and then pounces forward.

There's an audible crunch, and blood pools beneath the bus-thing, running toward the curb. It scuttles forward, leaving only a smear of blood and shards of bone.

The corpse-spider, leaking and trailing gore, clambers with awkward, horrifying speed up the sheer, slick glass side of an office building.

Another shimmer from the vortex—this one shudders up the side of a brick apartment block and in through a window. Seconds later, the window and a ten-foot-wide chunk of brick surrounding it explodes outward in a shower of glass and masonry, and a ten-foot-tall bipedal monster leaps through the opening. Fat and bulbous with a thick greenish-gray reptilian hide, the creature has two small beady stupid eyes, saggy flesh jiggling and sagging around massive shuddering muscles. The sight of it tickles something in my memory:

It's the cave troll from that iconic scene in The Fellowship of the Ring—"They have a cave troll!"

Not just *like* it—it *is* it.

Real life. Huge, violent, and hungry. It picks up a wrecked taxi in one huge hand and hurls it at me with petulant rage. Shocked into motion, I throw myself to the ground, rolling out of the way as the hurtling taxi smashes through the air where I was.

Gunfire erupts, and purple bolts fly—the troll bellows defiantly and stomps toward the cluster of mortals firing at it. It picks one poor mortal soldier up by the legs and uses him as a club to bludgeon the others, sending them flying like bowling pins.

My attention is stolen, then: a figure emerging from the vortex. This one is solid and real—and recognizable.

Zirae.

Naked but for a scrap of cloth covering his groin, his flesh is sagging and wrinkled and papery, his long white hair tangled and loose and fluttering behind him like a pennant. His eyes glow with a weird, alien, disturbing greenish-white light.

He cackles, perched on the edge of the vortex like a gargoyle, toes hooked, fingers clutching. He has a blade clenched in his teeth, a foot long, S-curved with a wicked point, the hilt made of human skin wrapped in copper wire—the pommel features an eyeball, the iris red as blood, alive and roving and seeking.

"I found you!" he screeches. "Like my new pets?" He grips the knife in his fist as he spits at me. "*COME*! Come, Once-Mortal child." He gestures with the knife, a come-hither circle of the tip.

I make my feet. The vortex howls and sucks, but the range of the vortex seems to be limited to six or eight feet from the center. The tanks, APCs, and HUMVEEs have been sucked in, along with several wrecked cars and trucks, and several mortals, as well as a few immortals.

I scan the scene—my army has vanished, thankfully, except for Andreas, Caleb, and Caspian, who watch from the intersection where the bridge crew made their stand.

Zirae cackles. "The longer you wait, the more of my pets come through."

As he speaks, the air around the vortex shimmers again, and another of the things emerges—this one is long and serpentine, slithering in six-foot-thick coils of shimmering air like heat waves. Its huge, wedge-shaped head smashes down through the road itself—through a manhole cover, I realize. The concrete around the manhole splinters and cracks as the huge mass of the thing shatters it apart. Water splashes and something small and brown and chittering in fear scrambles up out of the hole—a giant sewer rat the size of a small dog.

Fifty feet away, another manhole cover explodes upward as the road around it crumbles away, and the void-serpent reappears, now coated in a skin of sewage and trash and wriggling rodents. It streams out of the sewer, its body six feet thick, its head the size of a car. Glowing green eyes scan and roam, hungry and alien. Its jaws yawn wide, revealing fangs the size of sabers which drip with venom the same glowing green of its eyes.

"Come to me, child!" Zirae screeches, cackling. "My pets are hungry, and this world is ripe with prey."

I look at Caspian. Caleb.

DON'T! Caspian shouts into my mind. *We can do this together!*

Caleb stares at me; he knows.

Love you, I say to both of them. **Finish the Federation. Create the Enclave.**

Maeve No! Caspian lurches forward, but Caleb grabs him and holds him back, presses his mouth to Caspian's ear, and murmurs something.

Caspian reaches for me, eyes haunted.

Caleb's mind brushes mine with soft, delicate affection. *Do what you must, my love.*

I beat him once, I tell Caspian. **I'll beat him again. It's okay.**

I touch his mind, press my love into him.

Zirae wiggles his fingers at my mates in a demented wave, cackling madly. "Ta-ta!"

He leans backward and lets himself fall back into the void, vanishing. I summon a blade of prana, solidify it in my hand until it's real—a transparent crystalline short sword with a straight, double-edged blade, circular guard, and heavy, pointed pommel. I snag a dropped shockstick and switch it to a shield.

Zirae's mad cackle echoes, echoes. And I realize that I didn't cause the vortex at all—Zirae did, somehow. A trap?

He must have been watching the whole time, waiting for the perfect moment to strike.

I hop up—the edge of the vortex is solid, somehow, a mushy, shifting surface like sand. Stare down into the abyss—it's a gray world of dark, shifting shadows. Not The Dreaming, but like it, or a part of it I've never seen.

Things move in it—vast, leviathan shapes lurking and flowing, shuddering and soaring, circling near this vortex. They see our world, and they want it. I feel their hunger—not for flesh but for mana. Ideas. Dreams. Nightmares. Stories. Daydreams.

One of them billows toward me, fluttering and twisting like a bedsheet ripped from a clothesline by a tornado. I duck, and it sears past me—I feel it, a cold, slippery, greasy touch of icy malice and alien hunger.

Malice is the wrong word; there is no intent, no sentience. Just flat, emotionless, algorithmic purpose: devour.

A mortal soldier, seeing the thing, or perhaps merely sensing it, runs. The thing swarms over him, wrapping itself around him. The mortal slows to a walk, then a zombie-like shuffle, and then drops to his knees. His head droops, his chin touching his chest. All fours. His back arches upward.

The knobs of his spine erupt through his back and lengthen into spikes. His bones crackle and snap, twisted into abnormal shapes—curved, sectioned, crablike. His jaw splits vertically down the lower mandible, and a long, spiny tongue slithers out, impossibly long and freakishly prehensile. It wraps around the ankle of a mortal soldier ten feet away, snapping out faster than a lizard's strike. Drags the mortal, kicking and screaming, into its maw. Here, physics doesn't seem to apply. Bones crunch and gore splatters as the deformed creature devours the mortal, slurping up every last bit of gristle and blood. Its skin, now mottled in a bizarre distortion of camouflage, ripples, and the thing grows, limbs lengthening, spine-spikes curving longer and sharper, its tongue dragging on the ground, twisting and writhing with a life of its own like an unattended firehose.

Zirae cackles, the laughter echoing. "Come, come, come." More daft, shrill laughter. "The portal won't close until you come through."

I look back at my mates. Caleb meets my eyes, grins, and then shifts, his wolf loping toward the long-tongued thing.

He pounces on it, claws shredding it back, teeth closing on its neck.

Caspian touches my mind with his once more, and then he blurs away, landing on the serpent, fingers clawed and ripping.

Andreas salutes me with his spear and then charges the cave troll.

That's the last thing I see: Andreas charging, spear raised, teeth bared in a rictus, preparing to do battle with a ten-foot-tall cave troll out of a fictional story.

I have no choice—I *have* to follow Zirae.

I leap into the void, hearing Zirae's mad cackling below me. I glance up as I fall into nothingness—the vortex is narrowing, narrowing, my view of the sky and the tops of buildings now a thin slice of blue, and then a razor-thin line of light, and then nothing at all.

I'm falling, and all around me is the echoing, reverberating madness of Zirae's manic laughter.

CHAPTER 14

THE DARKNESS CLINGS TO ME like a sticky resin, as if the shadows are a substance akin to pine sap. There is no sight—no motion, no direction.

"Best not dally," Zirae says, his voice so close to my left ear I can feel his breath huffing hot. "This isn't a very hospitable place, especially for silly girls."

I lash out with my sword, but it meets no resistance.

"Now, now—temper, temper." He giggles, breathy, lunatic. Something cold and sharp pricks the back of my neck. "Got you!"

I stab backward hard and fast, without thought—I hear a yelp.

His laughter echoes, doubles, trebles, overlapping until I'm surrounded by the mad cackling of a thousand maniacs.

Wind blows past my face, stinking of rotten meat and coffee breath. Something titanic slithers past my ankles, its touch colder than ice, making my bones ache.

"*ZIRAE!*" I scream, hating the hate in my gut like acid. "What do you want?"

"Oooooohhoooo!" he giggles in a demented singsong. "Someone is getting cranky. What do I want?" That cold hard touch slices across my armor at my bicep—hot and then cold. "I want your suffering. I want your madness. I want your hate. I want *you*, Maeve Sparrow, Once-Mortal Bitch, WorldBreaker, whore. I want you—I want to devour your pathetic little soul."

I can feel my prana within me—I can't use magic in The Dreaming, but perhaps here I can. I conjure a small ball of light, a bright globe the size of a baseball hovering over my palm. It illuminates the area immediately around me—there's nothing to see but more darkness…and a flickering, moving shadow.

There, to my left. I hurl the ball of light at the shadow—it sticks to him like a burr to dog fur. I lunge at him, swiping with my sword. He parries, turning my sword aside with ease; my light-ball adheres to the center of his back, casting long shadows of his form on this world of nothingness. Zirae whirls away from me, dancing lithely. He stabs at me with his knife—I dodge, twisting my torso aside, spin on my heel, and swing my sword around in a flat arc. He sucks in his belly and bends forward, just barely avoiding the sharp, whistling tip.

He dances backward, grinning, doing a wild, mad little jig while wiggling his knife at me. "Almost got me with that one!" Abruptly, the grin vanishes, the jigging stops, and he glares at me with baleful intensity. "Enough."

He flips the knife around so the point faces down, holds my eyes with his, unblinking, and stabs backward. His eyes flash greenish-white with a flare of power—I catch another whiff of rotting meat and coffee breath, the stench of his twisted magic. The knife blade buries into the blackness up to the hilt; he twists the handle 90 degrees and then rips it horizontally sideways with a hard, violent wrench of his arm, his whole body twisting with effort.

Wind howls and rushes, and a splinter of light pierces the darkness. Heat billows through the rip, heat that smells of hot sand and stale wind.

There's a soft, distant groan behind me, and the air around me shudders. I feel my heart pound—I feel like a small, defenseless mouse, and behind me is a huge, hungry predator with a morsel in plain view.

Zirae cackles again. "They smell the mana out there, you know. They smell it and they want it."

He yanks his knife free, spins it on his palm, and gestures at me with it, a repeat of the follow-me gesture.

I have no choice but to follow, do I? I have no way out of this place except where he goes. I think I have an idea how he's doing this, but this is no time to experiment—I have to end Zirae once and for all and get back to my mates and the mess in Manhattan.

Zirae ducks through the rip in the shadow-realm—beyond, blinding light and shades of yellow.

I follow Zirae through the gap and into a world of blinding sun and oppressive heat. I squint, staggering under the sudden assault of light and heat.

At that moment, I catch a glimpse of Zirae, naked but for a loin cloth, swiping at me with his knife. I dodge, but not fast enough—the blade slices across my hip, creasing my blood armor and the skin beneath it. The sudden burning tells me the knife is no normal blade—poisoned, is my guess.

I hiss at the dull ache that sets in.

Zirae wiggles the knife at me. "Like it? Made it myself. Poisoned prana. You'll feel the effects soon enough."

I don't bother answering. I feel the effects already—a sluggishness in my muscles, a dulling of the senses.

I turn part of my attention inward, assessing: my ocean of prana is stained a toxic bright green at the edges. I decide, perhaps belatedly, that trying to fight with a weapon I have no training in is a losing game—I'm not a warrior.

I draw prana, let it surge through me, filling my mind and body and spirit—I feel the taint of the poison, however. Perhaps I can burn it off or use enough prana to bleed out the effects.

Zirae is watching me, his posture deceptively casual and upright. "What to do, what to do, what to do, eh?" He singsongs, bobbing his head side to side to the rhythm of his singsonging speech. "You know, we don't have to be enemies. I could teach you. Make you my apprentice. You have a shocking amount of potential, I admit. You and me, together? We could take over. Who could stand against us? No one. Not even your precious Alpha Prime."

"I'd rather die," I spit.

He cackles. "That can be arranged!"

He lunges, snake-swift, the vicious tip of his poisoned knife slicing toward my belly. I twist to the side, bringing my sword up to block; he stiffens the fingers of his free hand into a claw, palm up, and wrenches his arm upward as if lifting a heavy weight. Beneath me, the earth itself shudders, trembles, and then abruptly rockets skyward... with me on it.

My stomach hurtles to my feet as I'm launched airborne—the wedge of earth he used to fling me up halted after about twenty feet, now a jagged outcropping of granite.

Tumbling and twisting, I windmill my arms, floating for a heart-lurching instant—and then I'm falling, falling, falling. If I don't do something—*now*—I'll land on the uplifted column of rock and be smashed into wet bits.

With panic flaring in my gut and prana seething in my veins, I let instinct take over, closing my eyes and relaxing into thoughtless autopilot.

Help me, Mother, I whisper to myself mentally. *Help me.*

The earth hurtles up toward me, and my stomach is in my throat now, at my teeth. I summon wind, a straight-line blast of hurricane-force spewing skyward. It knocks me tumbling head over heels—I splay my arms and legs out wide like a skydiver, and it catches me, spins me along my long axis, and then I find a sort of balance, on my belly, facing down—a hundred feet above the earth, Zirae staring up at me with amusement.

He bares his teeth at me in a hateful rictus and then lashes out with his fist, eyes flaring with prana. His strike knocks a huge chunk of rock free from the column, and then he whips his knife hand upward, and a gust of wind launches the chunk of rock at me like a cannonball.

Another, and another, and another—four in machine-gun succession. Still precariously balanced on a geyser of wind, I conjure a shield. Just in time—the jagged chunk of stone shatters on the shield, and then the other three follow. With each impact, the kinetic transference shudders me backward and out of balance, and suddenly I'm tumbling downward once more.

Zirae snaps his fingers, eyes flaring green-white, and he whips his arm at me as if throwing a ball—a rippling globule of white mage-flame rockets toward me, aimed to intersect my descent as if I'm a clay pigeon as he's at a shooting range.

I tuck myself into a ball and blast myself with a short gust of wind from the side, sending me spinning and twisting at an angle—I feel the searing ball of mage-flame scorch past my ribcage.

He has me on the defensive, and I'm going to lose. I have to turn it back on him. But how?

Still tumbling down, Seconds pass like minutes—like hours.

From this vantage point, I catch a quick glimpse of the world I've found myself in: a vast, endless, barren wasteland of cracked, parched, hardpan earth, featureless and waterless. A desert, clearly. I wish I'd paid more attention to world geography.

Not that it matters—unless I figure out how to even the playing field against Zirae, I'm going to die, and soon.

A spark of creativity hits, and I put it into motion immediately: conjure a small flat square shield beneath me and summon wind from below—the shield acts like a sail, catching the wind and arresting my momentum. A slight adjustment to the wind's velocity, and now I'm hovering.

Moving slowly and carefully, my focus straining between holding the wind and shield simultaneously, I work to my feet, standing on the shield. It feels like standing on a mattress, soggy and sinking, yet I also feel the precarious balance tipping and shifting with every minute adjustment of my weight.

Zirae gazes up at me, amused. "Now what? Hmm? Going to hover up there until you run out of prana or I knock you off with a fireball?"

He launches another one at me to punctuate his question; it flies wide past my head, but even flinching as it passes by makes me wobble and windmill my arms.

I growl to myself. This is a stupid predicament.

I let the wind drop, and I hurtle downward, crouching on the shield as air screams past my face. Zirae hurls fireballs at me in machine-gun succession, each one sizzling closer and closer. Every instinct tells me to call the wind to stop my fall, but I ignore it. Not yet. Not yet.

Ready an offensive glamour: A line of prana lanced into the earth beneath Zirae's feet—he sees it, but until I engage the glamour, he can't do anything about it.

At the last second, barely a dozen feet above the ground, I shoot to my feet and call the wind in a hard, wide, spewing fountain that halts my momentum so abruptly I'm flattened against the shield like a bug splatting against a windshield.

Zirae laughs at me. "What a delightful performance, WorldBreaker! Where's all your vaunted Secundus power?"

Without moving—because I can't, yet—I send my will surging down the ley line running beneath Zirae's feet.

CRACK! The earth itself splits open like a yawning maw—the rumble and grind of tectonic plates shifting is deafening, shaking the whole world, it feels like.

Zirae screams as the earth he stands upon vanishes, sending him hurtling down toward… what? The center of the earth? I let go of the shield and wind, collapsing to the hard hot cracked ground. Groaning as every bone in my body protests from the sudden violent halt, I release the glamour holding the earth open—it wants to close, needs to close, and I let it.

Another rumble shakes the ground with such violence that my teeth rattle in my skull. I work to my feet just in time to see the six-foot-wide crack in the earth shudder closed, leaving no trace that it ever existed.

A seed of hope germinates in my gut—it can't be that simple, can it?

No. Another, softer, quieter rumble trembles underfoot, this one not of my doing. I gather my prana, still feeling the sickly, sluggish effects of the poison—less, now, thankfully. My armor must have absorbed the worst of it.

A mound of dirt erupts where Zirae vanished—like the old cartoons of a chipmunk tunneling underneath the black and white cat. Or something like that—I was never much for cartoons.

A second later, Zirae crawls out of the earth, caked in dirt so thick only his eyes and teeth show white—the former glaring with hate, the latter bared like an animal.

"Nice try, Once-Mortal Bitch." He spits dirty saliva at his feet. "Time to die."

"You first, you sick, decrepit old monster." I launch a fireball at him out of pure spite.

He deflects it with his bare hand, casually and with an annoyed sigh. "You'll have to try harder than that."

He swipes his hand at me, fingers stiff, palm flat and horizontal, like a blade. A razor-thin disc of solidified air slices at me—I duck just in time.

Fuck the games. I'm done with this cat-and-mouse bullshit.

I launch a battering ram of air at him, but it's just a distraction. He leans into it and lets it knock him skidding backward. Now, I do channel something remembered from a show I used to watch after school in junior high: *Avatar: The Last Airbender*.

Taking a page from Zirae's book—something I'm loathe to admit I do far more than I'd like—I use my prana to rip a chunk of earth free from the ground and launch it at him, hauling at the titanic mass with both hands as if pulling a rope. The ten-foot-high and wide chunk of dirt and rock smashes into him from the left. I'm already jerking a second block out of the ground and screaming as I haul it the other way to smash into him from the opposite side. It becomes a flowing sort of dance, then, like a kata— Toph stomping and punching and hurling, sending mountains of stone and rock flying and smashing and exploding.

Fury powers my movements—fucking Zirae, hijacking me at the worst possible moment. I jerk and redirect, smashing him from every side without pattern until he's sagging on his hands and knees, gasping, spitting blood, coughing wetly.

He collapses to his belly, hands trapped beneath him, eyes vacant, red-shot, blood drooling from his lips.

His knife is stuck point-down in the dirt a few feet

away from him. I yank it free and stalk toward him. His eyes follow me, listless, agonized.

I crouch beside him, gripping his hair in one hand and pressing the knife blade to his throat with the other. I wish I had some witty, biting thing to say to him, some sarcastic superhero one-liner.

But I don't. I'm exhausted, angry, and have no clue where Zirae brought me—or how.

There's a flash of light under Zirae, accompanied by the sharp, sour scent of rotting meat and coffee breath.

I drag the knife across his throat and hurl myself backward.

Too late.

He rolls to his side, even as my knife slices open his throat and his lifeblood sluices down his chest in a thick scarlet river. His hands, gnarled and arthritic and powerful, clamp around my wrists and hold on with vise-like, unbreakable strength.

His eyes blaze with hate even as he dies. "Break... this...World...Breaker."

Light flashes from his hands and his eyes blaze with greenish-white light. Searing heat—or is it brutal, biting cold?—eats through flesh and muscle and into bone, and my wrists grind with agony.

Zirae chokes with wet, gurgling laughter, flopping to his back—his bare feet scrabble at the hard earth. His back spasms. A pool of blood soaks into the thirsty ground, softening the hardpan.

He goes still.

I look down: circling both wrists are a pair of identical bracelets. Fashioned from some oily, tainted metal, gleaming with a sickly rainbow sheen like sunlight on spilled oil or rotting meat, they are slick and featureless. Each one is about the thickness of my thumb and heavier than it should be. There is no closure, no clasp.

"What the fuck?" I yank at them, one and then the other. "No! What the fuck is this? What the fuck did you do to me, Zirae?"

I summon prana—nothing.

A sick feeling swells up in my gut.

I look inside…but there's nothing to see because I *can't* look inside. I can't see my prana. I can't feel it. I'm not blocked from it—it's like it doesn't exist.

I look down: my blood armor is gone. I'm back in my street clothes—a pair of jeans, a forest-green V-neck T-shirt, and comfy, well-worn Vans.

My hair is still unnaturally white, but the glow is gone. My bondmark tattoos are there, too, but dull and lifeless— mere tattoos.

Caleb? Caspian? My thoughts echo in my head and go unanswered. **Stirling? Alistair? Phineas?**

"What did you do?" I whisper. I lurch to my feet and straddle Zirae, shaking him. "What the fuck did *you do*?"

He flops lifelessly. His eyes stare vacantly at nothing. His skin is already cooling.

"*FUCK!*" I kick him as hard as I can.

His corpse should have flown halfway across the desert. Instead, my shoe sinks into his ribs, which crack—my toes throb in pain.

I hop away, screaming. After a moment, the worst of the ache fades—I wiggle my toes. Nothing is broken, but god that was dumb.

I suck in a deep breath and pace in circles around Zirae's corpse. "You absolute *FUCK!*" I whirl and scream the last word at him—the scream is so hard and crazed that my throat scrapes, hoarse.

No prana. No vampiric strength or speed. Nothing. I may as well be mortal. Maybe I *am* mortal.

Who knows where the fuck I am. Where do I go? What do I do?

I can't feel my mates—and that absence hurts worse than any physical pain. I realize—only now that I can't feel them—how much I relied on them, on feeling them in my spirit, in my mind. They're always there. Even the rest of my coven back in England, I *felt* them. I didn't have to talk to them every day to feel their spirits and be comforted by that.

Now…I'm empty. My mind, my spirit—my body. I'm empty. Utterly alone.

Mom? The thought echoes in my head.

"MOM!" I sag to my knees as the featureless wasteland absorbs my plea.

Above, the sky is a barren blue dome, and the sun is scorching and blinding. Around me—nothing but hardpan, cracks zigzagging madly in every direction. Heat waves shimmer.

What do I do?

Even alone under the mountain, I had a goal and something to fight for: freedom. Get my magic back. Get back to my mate and my coven. I had a path forward.

Now? I still need my magic back, and I still need to get to my mates…but how? I can't even sense my prana. Nor can I sense my vampire—the hunger, the bloodlust… it's gone.

I don't feel my mates—or the bond-sickness. I felt that immediately last time.

I yank on the bracelets again, to no avail. Zirae's knife! I grab it from the ground where I'd dropped it and saw at the metal with the blade—after several seconds of frantic sawing I check my progress: not so much as a scratch.

"Fuck," I mutter and throw the knife petulantly at Zirae's corpse.

I turn in circles, scanning the horizon in three hundred-and-sixty degrees for anything, any sign of… anything.

But there's nothing. Just heat haze and cracked earth.

Zirae's right arm is flung out wide, index finger pointing as if urging me to go that way.

So, I do the only logical thing: start walking in the opposite direction.

Chapter 15

THE HEAT IS FUCKING UNBEARABLE. It's like standing in an oven. The hazy shimmer of heat ripples around me, the sun doesn't move, and each step seems to take me no closer to anything because there's nowhere to go; everything is the same in every direction.

I could be on a gigantic treadmill for all the progress I'm making. Once in a while, I look back and see the dark hazy hump that is Zirae's corpse, and for a while, it doesn't change. And then I look back and it's a barely visible smudge on the horizon.

And then there's nothing. And, oddly,

that terrifies me. It was my only marker in the featureless wasteland.

I keep walking.

My feet leave no prints. There's not so much as a puff of wind nor a single scrap of cloud. Not a bush, not a blade of grass, not a speck of sand. Nothing.

I keep walking.

I'm not thirsty, though. That's weird, right?

There's no pain, no bond-sickness. No blood-lust. My skin remains pink and soft—no hardening, no fangs.

Again and again as I walk, I reach for my prana, and again and again I find nothing. It's like touching your tongue to your gum where a tooth used to be.

I walk. And walk. And walk. Slowly, imperceptibly, the sun lowers toward the horizon on my left—which means I'm going…south? Cardinal directions were never my strong suit.

Does it matter? I don't know where I am, so I have no destination, and thus, it doesn't matter which way I go. I'm just walking because it's something to do.

Am I still immortal? I don't seem to be getting thirsty, nor am I getting sunburned or suffering from heatstroke or anything you'd assume I would feel being stuck in an unforgiving wasteland without food, water, or shelter.

So then, what? Just wander aimlessly? Eventually, assuming I am still immortal, I'll arrive somewhere.

Fucking Zirae.

Since I can't solve my magic problem, I think back to how he appeared—what happened and how he managed the things he did.

I was able to enter The Dreaming in my body and exit again. I think I poked a hole in the fabric between the realms or dimensions or whatever. But did the hole I made close? Is it still open up there on the mountaintop, letting the creatures from The Dreaming enter our world? The thought makes me shudder in horror. What if I unwittingly unleashed those mana-eating monsters on the world?

Zirae was able to close the gaps he created. Or, so it seemed. Did they close on their own?

Was the dark, oily nowhere-place part of The Dreaming? Another layer? Or some other realm or dimension? How did he hijack my glamour? I meant to open the earth beneath the column of Mortal Federation machinery, like I did Zirae, here. Instead, Zirae turned the hole in the ground into a hole in reality—a portal to The Dreaming, or wherever that was. And then, somehow, he used a knife, a physical object, to cut open a hole to the other side, which led us here. From New York, through some strange section of The Dreaming, to this place…Death Valley? The Sahara? It's not either of those, I don't think. Death Valley has rocks and mountains and sand and stuff, I think, and the Saraha is nothing but sand dunes. What other large deserts are there? I mean, the North and South Poles are technically deserts, but this very clearly is not one of the poles. There's a desert in South America, but that one is way up on the top of the mountains, where some mysterious ancient people made giant line drawings—the Nazca lines, I think. What does that leave? Australia? This isn't the Outback. Wait! The Gobi! This must be the Gobi—it's the only other desert on the planet that I know of.

Great. So, I'm reasonably certain I'm in the Gobi Desert, which I think is in China. So we went from New York to China via…what? A wormhole? A portal through The Dreaming?

Perhaps the knife is the key. But…he couldn't have used the knife to make the entire half-a-mile-long prana leyline into a portal—it happened instantaneously. The hole he cut with the knife was just big enough to allow us to step through.

I shake my head—I'm no closer to understanding what Zirae did or how. I'd had a thought earlier, but it went out of my head. How could he have gone there in his physical body? I was under the impression—arrogantly, perhaps—that I am the only one who can, due to my unique genetic makeup, my status as a Secundus.

But then, that's how he escaped me the first time, and I was warned that he had that ability—something he should not be able to do.

I startle from my thoughts—the sun has set behind me, leaving me trudging through the soft orange glow of the gloaming. Heat dissipates swiftly, with nothing to hold it in.

With nothing else to do, I keep walking. My legs don't seem tired, and my feet don't hurt. I'm not thirsty. I'm not hungry. I'm not bond-sick or caught up in bloodlust.

Did I die? Is this some weird Purgatory?

I go back to the problem of Zirae and his ability to traverse The Dreaming. Could there be something to that? Some way of using The Dreaming as a means of travel? Did he have some way of navigating? Of knowing where we'd come out?

I ruminate about what he did, and how to replicate it safely. Portals, paths, and possibilities. Instead of relying on airplanes, boats, and cars—and the necessary accompanying materials and resources—we could simply open a portal and go where we want.

The journey itself was simple and easy—there was no disorientation, no vertigo, and no side effects. Just the danger of the mana-creatures. Which, to be fair, is not an insignificant hurdle.

My mind wanders to those things next. What are they? Creatures of pure mana? Creatures that subsist on mana? Both? They didn't have form or substance when they emerged in The Waking, looking like nothing so much as a heat haze shimmer in the vague shape of some kind of creature. But not a creature I recognized, even insofar as I could make out their shape to begin with. I could see something like legs, or arms, or pincers, or claws.

But then, once here, they sort of just…glommed onto things and changed them. One turned a bus into a monster, a living insectile creature that ate people. Another turned corpses into legs and a taxi into a body and became a spider. A third went into an apartment and came out a Cave Troll from Lord of the Rings.

I won't claim to be any great shakes when it comes to logic—in the mathematic, philosophical sense. But it seems to me that if those things live in The Dreaming and eat mana, then they must be drawn to mana in our world. Caleb has told me that mortals, and even immortal Once-Bloods, have and use mana because all living, sentient creatures do, but we produce more than we use. The rest is just sort of…there. Overflowing. Dripping from us. Leaking into our dreams. That excess is what shifters feed off of. But shifters, being denizens of The Waking, must feed on mana in The Dreaming, in their Dreaming forms. The creatures—I'll need a name for them, I suppose—seem able to feed on mana in The Waking and use it to take physical form. Twisted, freakish, magical form.

So what are they drawn to? Thought? Dreams? Creativity? I don't know. All of the above, I suppose. They enter The Waking, find some source of mana, eat it, and become physical. But the bus? Why a bus? Why turn a bus into a bug?

There are no answers.

I become aware of my surroundings again—I've just been sort of trudging forward aimlessly, not really seeing. Sort of like when you're driving somewhere and go on autopilot—you're driving, you're paying attention, but then you get where you're going and have no memory of the preceding trip.

Except I didn't get anywhere. There's nothing—more nothing. Endless amounts of absolutely fucking *nothing*. Cracked hardpan in every direction. Now, above, a dark sky strewn with countless diamond stars.

It's bitterly cold.

Part of me wants to just stop walking and sit down. But I think if I do, I won't get back up. I won't start walking again. I'll just lay there, undying, forever.

I keep walking. I watch the stars shifting overhead, rotating slowly around me—the motion of the planet itself, as if my perception of time has been stretched out.

My legs do not tire. I still feel no hunger, no thirst. I mean, I suppose it could be worse, right?

Wait, forget I asked that—I have no desire to tempt The Fates. You hear me, Fates? If you're real and you're out there and listening to my thoughts, I don't need things to be any worse. This is bad enough.

What *are* The Fates, anyway? Are they real? Are they a group of fae who sit on some mountain somewhere, watching the lives of humanity and toying with us through a glamour writ cosmic scale?

Stars fade and the black blanket sky becomes a dim gray. The bitter cold that doesn't quite bother me lessens to merely chilly. Slowly, the stars wink out one by one as the gray becomes hazy, and then the haze becomes pink stains on the edge of the horizon. The pink turns ombre, layered with orange. And then yellow begins to scar the orange and erases the pink entirely.

I wonder how far I've walked?

Twenty miles? Fifty?

I'm not walking especially fast. I haven't stopped; I'm untiring, and as far as I can tell, I've been walking in a straight line.

So hopefully, I've made at least twenty miles of progress.

Only, what, a few hundred more to go before I find something? How big is the Gobi Desert? What if I was on the edge and if I had picked a different direction, I'd have found something by now?

Maybe I should turn. I could be a few miles away from an oasis, or even a road, or a hotel.

I'm not hungry, but god, I could kill for a cheeseburger, french fries, and an ice-cold Diet Coke.

When was the last time I had a Diet Coke? Will I ever have one again? McDonalds probably won't exist for much longer.

And you know what? I don't understand why civilization ended anyway. Because there are magical people out there who live a long time? So fucking what? Why is that worth killing people over?

But then, we killed each other over the right to own

other people, which is a vile, heinous practice. So it's not a big jump to hating people who are, in fact, vastly different than you. People who don't just look different but can kill you easily and who you can't easily hurt…and you didn't even know those people existed…and then suddenly, surprise! You're surrounded by people who turn into animals, can do magic, and enjoy drinking your blood.

So, I guess I *do* get it.

The sun makes its first appearance on the horizon on my left, a sliver of brilliance.

Something about the sun isn't right. But what? I glance at it—it's the right color. Moving slowly, imperceptibly above the horizon. It's generating heat—I can feel the chill of the night air fleeing before the streaming golden-yellow rays of the rising sun.

Walk, walk, walk.

My feet are moving on their own, I think. I'm not sure I could stop if I tried. I don't bother testing the theory, though. Why bother? I won't get anywhere sitting on my ass. And since I'm immortal enough not to need food, water, shade, or rest, I may as well cover the miles.

"Are you sure you're going the right way, Little Sparrow?" Caspian's voice comes from my right.

I turn my head, and there he is, tall, lean, muscular, and sexy as hell. He's wearing tight black jeans, vintage Nikes, and a fitted red V-neck sweater made from expensive cashmere, the sleeves tugged up around his veiny, powerful forearms.

"Cas!" I turn and lunge for him, intending to throw my arms around him.

I stumble, my arms wrapping around nothing but air. I whirl in place.

"Cas?" I bite back a sob. "Cas!"

"Who are you talking to?" Caleb, behind me.

Naked, sexy, all rippling muscles and hard angles, that huge, thick, perfect cock swaying and dangling…

I prowl toward him. "Caleb."

He grins. "Are you sure you're going the right way, Sparrow?"

"Why do you keep asking me that?"

I blink, and he's gone.

"NO!" I stomp my foot. "No, NO, *NO*!" I feel like a child. "Come back!

Wait. Which way was I going? I spin in place, looking for Caspian. Or is it Caleb?

The sun—it was on my left.

And…when it set last night, it set on my left. But then later it was behind me.

And now it's on my left again, rising.

Which means…

I'VE BEEN GOING IN FUCKING CIRCLES?

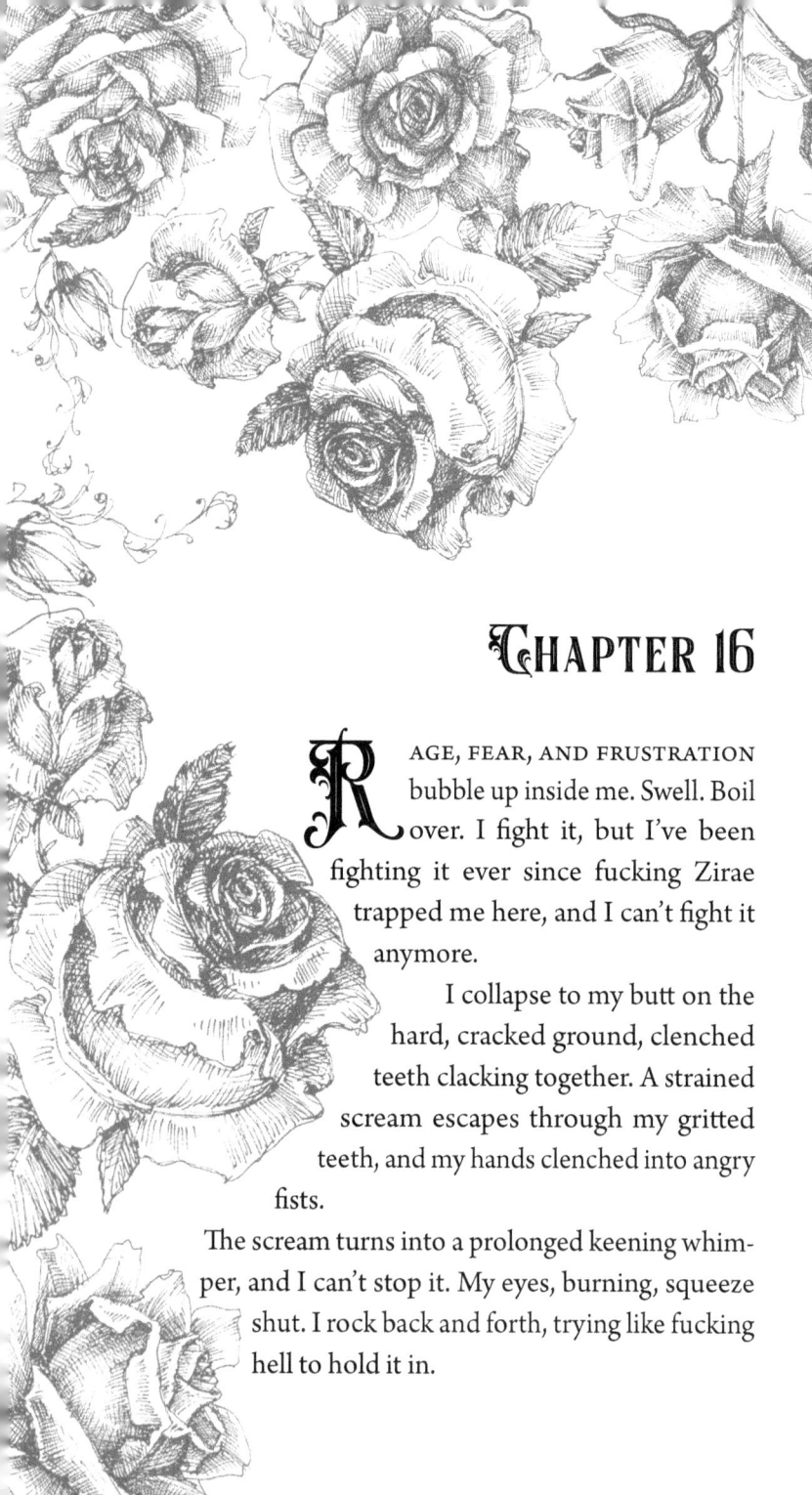

Chapter 16

RAGE, FEAR, AND FRUSTRATION bubble up inside me. Swell. Boil over. I fight it, but I've been fighting it ever since fucking Zirae trapped me here, and I can't fight it anymore.

I collapse to my butt on the hard, cracked ground, clenched teeth clacking together. A strained scream escapes through my gritted teeth, and my hands clenched into angry fists.

The scream turns into a prolonged keening whimper, and I can't stop it. My eyes, burning, squeeze shut. I rock back and forth, trying like fucking hell to hold it in.

But then, I ask myself…why?

Who am I trying to be strong for? Myself?

I let it out.

A wild, throat-scraping scream unleashes from somewhere in my gut, and when I run out of breath to scream, it becomes a sob, and the sob becomes a full-on ugly cry, the type I haven't done since that day in the woods a few months after Mom died.

Collapsing backward, I dig the heels of my palms into my eyes and just let myself cry and scream and kick my heels into the concrete-like ground until I've run out of tears.

The sun blazes overhead. In a distant, impersonal sort of way, I am aware of the heat baking me like a potato in an oven, but it doesn't seem to affect me.

How long have I been here? A day? Two days? How many sunrises and sunsets have I walked through? It's hard to think straight, hard to remember. Without sleep, food, water, or anything at all to mark the hours and days, they've all sort of blurred together. I think it might be only a single 24-hour period, but I can't be sure.

And really, does it matter? Without any physical needs, I'm just a ghost. No one. Nothing. I can just wander this gods-forsaken desert for all of my eternal existence.

Without magic or my connection to my mates, how will they ever find me in this wide, wild world?

They won't.

Out of tears, I just lay there. I can't look directly at the sun, of course, but if I squint and watch it through my peripheral vision I can track its motion across the sky. It arcs downward in not quite perceptible degrees, taking the heat with it.

Evening.

The sky is burned by the setting sun to an orange-red smear that gradually turns scarlet and then purple and then gray. And then the sky is black above me, and the cold wraps itself around me like a blanket of all sharp edges.

The first star pricks the sky directly over my head, a tiny winking speck of salt against an endless black backdrop.

I wonder if I can just pull my hands through the bracelets. I'd have to break my hands to do so, but if I succeeded, they'd heal.

But if I succeeded, would the bloodlust and all the other physical needs I've been denied by Zirea's fucking cursed bracelets all come due at the same time?

I pull the bracelet away from my hand, folding my fingers in as tight as they can go, pushing, pushing, pushing, and pulling, pulling, pulling until my hand pulses with pain in protest, and still I strain until I feel something pop—my thumb. Interestingly, the pain is as distant as my perception of heat and cold. But yet, after another moment of pulling—and some cursing and screaming—it becomes obvious I'm not getting the damned bracelet off that way.

I let go and let my hand flop to the ground with a frustrated huff.

Overhead, a few million more stars have made their abrupt appearance. I fold my hands over my belly and stare, unblinking, up at the sky.

The stars seem to twist slowly. Or perhaps rotate is the better word.

"Giving up, are you?" Caspian, beside me.

"Yes. I am." I know he's a figment of my delirious

imagination, but even that version of my beloved Caspian is a comfort.

"Do you love me as much as you love Caleb?" He asks.

"Fuck you."

"No, really."

"No, really, fuck you." I don't look at him—he's not there. I know I'm talking to myself. But, fuck it. I don't care. "I love you differently but equally."

"The stars are beautiful tonight."

I snort. "The stars are beautiful every night."

"You can't give up. The world needs you. I need you."

"Well, too bad. Zirae wins. I may have killed him once and for all, but he still won. I'm stuck here. I wandered in circles for who knows how long. I got literally nowhere. I don't even have my own tracks to follow."

"Maybe someone will come to your rescue?"

I snort again. "Oh yeah, for sure," I retort, my voice dripping with sarcasm. "Someone is just going to appear here in the middle of the Gobi fucking Desert, or wherever the fuck I am, and rescue me. *I'm* the rescuer, Cas. *I* do the rescuing. I don't *get* rescued."

"Except without your magic and your immortal abilities, what are you? Who are you? Just a lost, weak, scared, pathetic little girl. The only reason you haven't died in this fucking desert is because you literally physically can't."

I finally turn and look at him, set to rage against him and his asshole truth, but he's not there. No one is there. I'm talking to myself. Am I hearing things? Or am I talking for Caspian and myself?

Impossible to know.

Apparently, I'm going crazy. Or already am crazy.

Are crazy? Am Crazy?

Who the hell cares about grammar at a time like this, you daft bitch?

(Am—it's "I already am crazy.")

Incrementally, the stars wink away one by one, and then all of a sudden.

For a while, the sky is stuck between black and gray, just the very thin razor edge of the horizon stained with a hint of what will eventually become light.

I wonder if I can sleep?

I close my eyes, but they immediately pop back open, almost on their own.

Nope.

I guess I'll just be here until…what? Until something happens? Until I go truly whack-a-doodle? I mean, I'm talking to myself and hearing my mates' voices and seeing them…that seems pretty fucking whack-a-doodle to me.

The sun rises. It's on my left, still, so I haven't managed to go in circles while lying down. At least there's that.

The bitter cold is slowly replaced by a savage heat that can't touch me.

There's a faint twinge of something almost like pain in my thumb. Oh—right. I dislocated it.

I lift my hand and stare at it—the thumb is most assuredly very far out of joint. Gripping the thumb in my fist, I yank it away from my hand—another twinge of what under normal circumstances would be agonizing pain, and then nothing. I move my thumb around. Feels fine.

Whatever.

I don't care. Nothing matters.

Ghosts don't have feelings.

Do they? I don't know.

The sun is midway between the horizon and overhead.

What does that convert to in clock time? Nine a.m.? But then, it's relative, isn't it? Nine in the morning here is not the same as nine in LA, Chicago, or New York. And the time of sunrise and sunset is different at different times of the year...

God, who the fuck *cares*? What is going on in my brain?

I close my eyes again because the sun is very bright— maybe because I was staring directly at it.

I feel something. A lessening of the incandescent heat of the sun that I can't quite feel, almost as if a shadow has fallen across me.

I open my eyes, and yes. A shadow has indeed fallen across my body.

It's distinctly man-shaped.

I rotate my head backward and to the left, where the shadow-casting object should be.

It's a male...something. A person. He's standing between me and the sun.

I think.

If he's real.

He's close enough to touch, and the shadow feels real. He doesn't speak. Doesn't move.

He has hair so blonde it's almost as white as mine. Long, thin, perfectly straight, falling past his shoulders. A dry puff of wind flutters the edges of his hair, increasing my inclination to think he just might be physically real. I'm just not convinced yet. He has no facial hair nor any hint of it. Sharp high cheekbones, angular jawline. Pointed ears.

I'd say he's a fae, but there's something *not* fae about him. The shape of his ears, maybe? They point vertically instead of angled backward like fae ears. His eyes are a shocking shade of bright purple. His lips are thin and well-shaped, with a pronounced Cupid's Bow and a deep philtrum.

He stares at me without blinking, standing over me, gazing down, hands behind his back. He's dressed in a voluminous black robe open at the front below the wide black leather belt around his waist—hand-tooled with arabesques and curls and whorls and loops. The robe is open at the chest, revealing pale skin and a hint of defined muscle, and floats around his feet an inch or two above the ground. His legs, when the skirt of the robe billows open in another puff of wind, are wrapped in black trousers—tight, more like leggings. He's barefoot. For some reason, my gaze is drawn to his feet—long, wide at the toes, deeply arched. He wiggles his toes; my gaze flicks up to his, and a tiny hint of a smirk crosses his face.

He sure seems real.

Without thinking, I reach up and wiggle my fingers at him, a gesture meant to communicate *Come down here where I can touch you.*

He squats lithely, elbows resting on his knees, hands dangling by his shins. His hands are like his feet—an unusual mix of delicate and powerful.

He has a sword at his left hip, the scabbard done in the same exquisitely worked black leather. The pommel of the sword is a sharp point of silver metal with a bulbous end at the base of the handle to stop the hand from sliding down. The grip is wrapped in more fine leather and wound with silver wire. The cross-guard is a twisted length of square metal. The blade is straight, wide, and long, tapering to a point.

I reach my hand toward him, and my fingers touch the flesh of his jaw—soft, cool skin over hard bone.

"Hello, little lost one." His voice is low and smooth and musical. "Why are you lying on the ground in the middle of the Gobi Desert?"

I blink at him. "You...you seem real."

He smiles patiently. Taps the tip of my nose with a finger. "I am." His fingertip traces my lips. "I'm quite real. The desert can do funny things to people."

"I saw my mates. I heard them. I talked to them. But I knew it wasn't real."

"Can you sit up?" He asks. "Do you need help?"

I shake my head and sit up. Swivel on my butt to face him. "Who are you?"

"Well, you're in my desert, so perhaps you'll do me the favor of answering that question first. Who are you? And what are you doing in my desert?"

"*Your* desert?"

He shrugs. "My desert, yes. I've claimed it since no one else seems to want it."

"Because it's a brutal, unforgiving wasteland?" I frown. "I thought people did live here? Somewhere. Like, Mongolians, or something. My memory of geography class is somewhat vague, I admit."

He smirks, shrugging. "Oh, they do. Some Han Chinese, too. Just not here. And I avoid them, usually. I stick to the brutal, unforgiving wasteland."

"Why?"

"It suits me."

"Weird."

He laughs. "Indeed. Now. Who are you, and why are you in my desert?"

"My name is Maeve Sparrow. I'm a Vaer—vampire-fae. The only one, as far as I know."

He nods. "I see." A pause. "And how did you end up here in the desert?"

I sigh. "Zirae."

He nods knowingly. "Ah. A real prick. Or at least he was when I knew him. Albeit that was…quite a while ago." He arches an eyebrow. "What happened?"

"It's a long story."

He shrugs. "We're both immortal, and I have nowhere to be."

"Well, I do."

He frowns. "Then why are you lying on the ground?"

"Because I…" I trail off, loathe to admit the truth out loud to a real person. "I gave up," I mumble under my breath.

He assesses me. "I sense no magic in you." His frown deepens. "Well, I do, but…" He shakes his head. "I do not understand what I am sensing from you. I sense great and powerful magic, and none at all."

I lift my wrists and jangle the cursed bangles. "It's these fucking things. Zirae put them on me. It was the last thing he did before he died. They somehow block my access to all magic—including my vampire abilities. I can't sense my magic at all. I feel no bloodlust. No hunger. No thirst. No need for vitality. I haven't gotten sunburned. I don't seem to sleep—I *can't* sleep. I can't get them off, and I can't even sense what they are or how they work. I've been mage-cuffed before, and I can break those." I shake my wrists again. "But these gods-and-blood-be-damned things I can't do anything about."

He blinks twice but otherwise makes no expression. "I see. And when you say Zirae died…"

I shrug. "I mean he died. Stopped breathing. No more Zirae." I wave my hand vaguely at the desert. "He's out there somewhere. I don't know where because I've been walking in circles for I don't know how fucking long."

"How did he die?"

"I suspect it was the several tons of rock I hit him with a good, oh, half a dozen times."

"*You* killed *Zirae*, eldest of the elder fae, in a one-on-one mage battle?"

I nod. "I did." I shrug. "Twice, actually. The first time, he escaped through a weird portal into The Dreaming that he was somehow able to open. He laid low for a few months, and then when I was fighting the Mortal Federation in Manhattan, he somehow hijacked my glamour, turned it into a rift into The Dreaming, sucked me in, closed it, and we fought in The Dreaming, or some other plane a whole hell of a lot *like* The Dreaming, and then he opened another hole, I followed him through, we landed here in this godforsaken *FUCKING SHITHOLE DESERT—*" I'm shouting by this point, "we fought, and I killed the evil, crazy, sadistic old bastard."

The male sinks back to sit on his buttocks and then crosses his legs into the lotus position. "That is a truly remarkable feat, Miss Maeve Sparrow. Zirae was a cunning and powerful mage."

"Yeah, well, the old fuck got the last laugh, didn't he?" I shake the bracelets. "Literally. He died laughing."

"He always was like that."

"You knew him, then?"

He nods. "I did. I knew him as a boy, and later as a

young man, and then again when he was in full possession of his powers. He was somewhat cracked in the head by then, already."

I frown. "Wait, when you say you knew him as a boy… when *he* was a boy, or when *you* were a boy?"

He regards me silently for several moments. "So, without magic, unable to even die, you wandered in circles? At some point, I assume, you realized you were going in circles and sat down and gave up. And then I arrived. Do I have this correct?"

"More or less, yes." I run my hands through my hair. "Well, you have it exactly right."

"I assume you'd like to get out of the desert?"

"God, yes."

He nods. "That I can help you with."

I shake the bracelets. "And these?"

He frowns. "Those, unfortunately, are somewhat beyond my ability to assist you with. But I can help you find someone who can."

I examine him again, more closely. His face is unlined, youthful, and firm. But his eyes, his presence…he exudes age. Immense, mind-boggling age. The way he looks at me feels like he's seen everything there is to see.

He sees into my soul. Into the core of who I am, and without effort. God, I wish I could feel his magic—I bet it's incredible.

The sense of age coming from this male is so palpable and so intense that it's almost scary—scratch that, not almost…it *is* scary.

"What is your name?" I ask.

He adjusts the sword at his hip, tipping the hilt down

and the tip up and rotating the hilt away from his body. "Aeon." *EE-on*.

"Like, eons?"

He nods. "Yes, but spelled with the Latin ligature ash." I blink at him, and he chuckles, not unkindly. "The squished together A-E. So it is properly spelled Ash-O-N, but more commonly in recent millennia, I have taken to spelling it A-E-O-N. Either way, the pronunciation is the same. Aeon."

"Recent millennia?"

He shrugs.

"So, who are you?"

He laughs. "I just told you. I'm Aeon."

"Okay, but…you're not fae, are you?"

He shakes his head. "No, not exactly."

"Or a vampire? Or a shifter."

He shakes his head. "No."

"You're something else."

"Yes."

"And you're not going to tell me what?"

A shrug. "Perhaps." He rises to his feet in a smooth, lithe motion and brushes off his backside. "Come." Without a word, he strides away—if the sun rises in the east, then he's heading south. I think.

I get to my feet. Despite having been lying on the ground for days, or a day, or…I don't know how long… I'm not stiff.

I follow him.

"Where are we going?" I ask, trotting to catch up with him.

He shrugs. "Out of the Gobi, first. Then west. West, west, west. Eventually to your New York."

"It's not *my* New York."

Another shrug. He can communicate a lot in shrugs—this one seems to mean *Yours, not yours, it means less than nothing to me.*

We walk together for a while. He says nothing. He walks straight as an arrow as if he knows exactly where he's going, and I begin to realize why I was walking in circles—I keep bumping into his shoulder. I'm subtly angling to the left. With no landmarks and no trail behind to judge by, there was no way to know, but I was gradually turning leftward. If I had been leaving tracks, I probably would have crossed them.

"How do you know where to go?"

Shrug. "It all looks the same around here, yes? Well, it's not. I've spent a great many years in this desert, so I know every inch of it as well as you know your backyard."

"I've never had a backyard."

He glances at me, puzzled. "Oh no?"

I shake my head. "Nope. My mom and I moved around a lot, and it was always from apartment to apartment. A house with a yard never really figured in."

He makes an expression that doesn't mean anything more than a visual version of "hmmm."

Without a conversational gambit to play off, I lapse back into silence. We walk in what I now assume is a straight line from nowhere to nowhere—or so it seems.

"So, you were just wandering around the desert and happened to come across me?" I glance at him sidelong.

He tips his head to the side. "Somewhat."

"You're pretty evasive."

"I have reason to be."

"What reason would that be?"

He grins at me. "Who and what I am."

I sigh. "Helpful."

"We have a very long walk, Maeve. We have all the time in the world to get to know each other."

"So you *will* answer questions directly at some point?"

He laughs outright. "Yes. At some point, I will give you direct answers."

"But not now?"

He laughs again—he has a musical voice; musical does not mean soft or gentle or delicate or anything. Just… rich, full, smooth, and rhythmic. It's hard to describe. But nothing about Aeon is soft or gentle. Every movement is lithe and graceful in a way not even Caleb or Caspian can equal. He doesn't seem to hurry, but his pace eats up the distance easily. His hand rests on his sword now and then, and his head and eyes are always moving, roving, seeking, seeing.

I suspect he doesn't need magic to be deadly and dangerous.

"Ask me one question. I might answer it." He smirks.

I consider my options for a long time. "Did you find me on purpose or on accident?"

He glances at me, surprised. "Not the question I would have expected." A pause as he thinks. "I felt magic somewhere in the desert. I went looking for the source and found you. So, did I know I'd find *you* specifically? No, I did not. Did I know I'd find something or someone? Yes."

"You felt the presence of magic? From how far away?"

A shrug. "Quite a distance. I'm extremely attuned to the presence of maya in this world." He stops walking, eyes closed, and pivots slowly on one heel, nostrils flaring as he scents the air. He points. "There. Perhaps…

three hundred kilometers that way, someone has a glamour. Low level. Likely a simple ward." A shrug. "Nothing worth investigating."

I stare at him. "You can sense a ward from three hundred kilometers away? I...well, I have no idea what that is in miles because I'm an American, but it's really fucking far."

He furrows his brow and wrinkles his nose in thought—a weirdly and unexpectedly human gesture. "Conversions are difficult because neither miles nor kilometers are native to me. But, if I have it correct, I believe it would be roughly a hundred and eighty-some miles."

"What unit of measurement would be native to you?"

He laughs. "Cubits were the first unit of anything like a standard system, but that was...well...I was well into my immortal adulthood by the time cubits became popular. Before that, it was very localized. But most commonly, you would refer to distances based on a day's travel. So, if I was discussing how long it would take to get to the person using that low-level glamour, I would estimate roughly six days of walking. I can average about thirty miles from sunup to sundown. If I'm in a hurry and I walk the sun around, I could probably make it in four. If I run, two to three days."

I'm getting the impression that Aeon is so old he makes Zirae seem like a spring chicken. Whatever that means. A chicken born in spring, probably—meaning a baby. God, sayings are weird.

I look at him again. And once more, I'm struck by his features. The upward-pointed ears, so unlike my own. His facial structure is different, too. Sharper, more angular, more vulpine. He is no more a fae than I am a shifter.

He's not like any Primi I've ever met. He's something else. Something older.

"Aeon…how old *are* you, exactly?"

He doesn't answer, doesn't show any sign of having heard me, but I know he did, so I wait. "The truth is, I do not know." He glances at me. "I'm certain that answer is frustrating to you, but it is the truth."

"Well, Zirae claimed to be over six thousand years old. From Sumer." I watch him as he listens. "Are you older than Zirae?"

He smiles faintly. Nods once. "I am. " He regards me with a blank expression that I am beginning to equate with him considering how much to tell me. "I and my people, the tribe from which I am descended, were myth to the Sumerians when Zirae was born to the king of Ur and his concubine."

"He was a prince?"

He nods. "The crown prince. His mother was fae, impregnated by the King. He was raised to be the successor, but his mother hated the king. She allowed him to think Zirae would be the king when he died, and then, at the last moment, when the King was dying and had already pronounced Zirae his successor, she absconded with Zirae in the night, casting a glamour on the whole palace. When they woke up, their crown prince was gone, along with a sizeable portion of treasure from the treasury. She left Sumer, used magic to hide their tracks from the mortal king's soldiers, and vanished with him. No one saw them again for several hundred years. When Zirae reemerged, he was a powerful mage with what could be termed a classical education in glamourworking. Where they went and who trained him is something even I have never truly been able to find out. There are rumors, of course."

"Such as?"

"Oh, wild stuff. Atlantis, for example."

"Was Atlantis real?"

He smiles at me. "Oh yes, of course. It was a civilization in the Mediterranean, mostly comprised of immortals descended from my people—or an offshoot of my people, at least. There was a cataclysm—their island was a volcano, which detonated. That detonation caused earthquakes, which caused tsunamis, flooding, and a host of other natural disasters. The island was erased, and those who survived fled and intermingled with the other societies then burgeoning in the Mediterranean region. No great mystery. But since it was so long ago, and since all traces were erased by the cataclysm, there's no solid evidence of it in the mortal archeological record. And, of course, the terms of The Treaty mean current mortals have even less of a clue what really happened since Atlantis was a civilization of immortals."

"But, to mortals, that is the mystery. That would be exactly what Hollywood would say happened—an island nation of magical beings who suffered a great disaster and disappeared."

He laughs. "True, when you frame it like that. And, to be fair, they were quite technologically advanced compared to mortal civilizations of the time. Atlantis was a hub of trade for thousands of years because they created such wonders."

"Are you from Atlantis?"

He shakes his head. "No, I am not." A smirk. "Disappointed?"

I shrug. "No. I would like to know where you are from, though."

He nudges me with his shoulder. "We have to save things to talk about for the fire."

"The fire?"

He nods. "Oh yes. Real conversation is best had around a campfire after the day's travel is done."

"So what you're saying, though, is that you're at least double Zirae's age."

He bobs his head from side to side. "Roughly. Perhaps." He frowns. "Let's just say I stopped trying to keep count after my tenth millennium. After that, counting seemed pointless." He shrugs. "I was only estimating after the first two or three thousand years anyway. Records and histories and such were scattered, sporadic, and inaccurate at best then, for one thing."

I think about trying to keep track of my birthdays for thousands of years, and my mind wobbles a bit. "I can sort of see how you'd stop bothering to count your birthdays after a while."

He nods, and glances at me. "And how old are you?"

I'm embarrassed to answer. "Nineteen?"

He chuckles. "Are you asking me? Because I certainly don't know. Judging the age of a person is beyond me at this point."

I shrug. "No. I'm nineteen. Almost twenty. It's just sort of embarrassing to admit to being nineteen when I'm talking to someone who is literally older than human history."

He stops and turns to face me; his piercing, brilliant purple eyes burn into me, shake me to my core. I can't breathe when he turns those eyes on me—they see too much. Know too much. "Maeve, one's age is beyond one's control. It's nothing to be embarrassed about. You are young. And yes, to me, your lifespan so far represents barely a single heartbeat, you could say. But that does not mean I don't see you. It doesn't mean you are less. Only that you are young. And young or not, you did something no one, in seven thousand years, ever did: you defeated the most powerful fae mage to ever live. Twice. That, my lovely young Vaer, is something you should be proud of. He was… perhaps not evil, but twisted. And I have long felt his influence on mortal and immortal affairs was not a net positive."

"Tell me about it. He and the Tribunal kept immortals from understanding the benefits of procreating with the other immortal races because they were afraid of what would happen to them. It has done possibly irreparable harm, not just to immortals, but to everyone. That damned treaty was a travesty of justice." I hear my voice rising, intensity threading through my tone.

Aeon traces the tips of his middle and ring fingers of his right hand over my cheekbone. "You are not wrong, but you lack context."

"I was raised mortal. So, yeah."

He blinks. "I am not easily surprised, but you continue to surprise me, Maeve Sparrow. I should like to hear more of this at tonight's fire."

My thoughts, however, are not on the fire, or the conversation, or even the promise of more direct answers to my approximately two hundred million questions.

No, my thoughts are on the way my cheek burns. The way my skin tingles where he touched me. The way my heart is doing leaps and jigs.

It feels a whole hell of a lot like…

No.

Nope.

I have five mates. I have no business feeling attraction to *anyone* else.

Especially not an immortal who's neither fae, shifter, vampire, Secundus, or anything I recognize or have ever heard…someone so old he stopped estimating his age at ten thousand years.

Nope.

I felt nothing. Nothing at all.

Funny how I don't believe myself.

CHAPTER 17

AEON PICKS A SPOT AT RANDOM and sinks down to sit cross-legged, back straight. He pats the ground beside him. I sit. This spot is identical to every other square inch of this godforsaken wasteland—featureless, barren, and brutal. The ground is, perhaps, slightly less cracked and hard. There is, perhaps, a thin scrim of dirt or sand.

I glance at Aeon, but he seems to be concentrating rather hard. He's staring at the ground in front of him, his wide, almond-shaped eyes narrowed, his jaw set. I keep silent and wait.

For several moments, he just stares,

unblinking, as if willing something to happen. What, I don't know. Then, he uses his index finger to draw a series of lines in the thin layer of dirt—first, a horizontal line going left to right, and then a vertical line bisecting the first, creating a plus sign, and then a third diagonally intersecting the first two, and a fourth the opposite direction…an asterisk, essentially. Then, he draws a circle around the asterisk. He places his hand, palm down, over the center of the design, not quite touching the earth.

Nothing happens.

And then, something. A faint orange-ish glow from the inch-high gap between his palm and the earth. It's so faint I can't swear it's there. He hasn't blinked, keeping his gaze rigidly fixed on the point where the lines intersect.

Slowly, the faint, almost imperceptible glow brightens until it's definite and unmistakable. Heat emanates from the gap, as well—again, faint at first but slowly intensifying.

And then, all at once, there's a *WHUMP!* as flames ignite. Aeon removes his hand, shaking it as if to assuage a burn. When he looks at me, his eyes are glowing an incandescent azure, quickly fading back to purple.

The fire is blue—a magical blue, the same virulent blue as the glow of his eyes. It dances like normal fire, flickering and casting light and cavorting shadows. The light cast by the fire is a weird, soft blue that soothes something deep inside me.

Aeon shifts back from the fire and lounges backward on an elbow, legs stretched out to one side. The fire emits from the center of the intersecting lines, and while it seems to be reaching higher and higher, it does not extend past the circumference of the circle. It also does not have any fuel source.

I can't help but stare into it. "That's the weirdest fire I've ever seen."

Aeon nods. "The knowledge of it has been lost for a very long time."

I put my hands toward it cautiously. "It gives off heat, but it's definitely not any mage-flame I've ever seen."

He shrugs. "It *is* mage-flame, but my magic is different than yours, or that of fae." He juts his chin at the fire. "It took me an embarrassingly long time to conjure it, but such minor magics are difficult for me."

I frown at him, laying down on the opposite side of the fire from him, resting my head on my hand. "I don't know if that means you're so powerful that minor magic like conjuring flame is difficult, or the opposite."

He smiles, staring into the flames, as I am—there is something even more hypnotic about this fire than normal. "My magic is…somewhat unique, even among my people. It's why I cannot simply glamour those cursed bracelets off you. Simply put, my magic is…" he frowns, struggling to find the right words. "It works on a far larger scale. To understand what that means, you'd need a lot more context, though—which we'll get to. But, well…put it like this, Maeve: a firehose is a wonderful, powerful, useful tool, but not very good for putting out a candle."

I look at him across the strange blue flames. "I see."

We relax in silence for a very long time, as stars wheel and spin overhead and a sharp white sliver of waxing crescent moon slings across the sky.

Aeon finds my eyes. "Can you trust me?"

I blink at the sudden question. "*Can* I? Or *do* I? The former seems more of a question for you."

His lips twitch in a slight smile. "A fair point. Do you? Will you?"

I lift a hand palm-up and let it fall back down to my hip. "I mean, I followed you across the desert. I'm all but helpless, so I don't have much of a choice, do I?"

He scrutinizes me. "Perhaps. But do you?"

I lift my hand again. "I suppose, to a point. It depends on what you're about to ask me to do."

"That's where the trust comes in. It's hard to explain. I'd rather just do it, but I don't want you to be frightened."

I laugh. "After the shit I've been through, Aeon, unless you're about to transport me to Hell itself or turn into, like, some bloodthirsty monster I have no hope of defeating, then there isn't much that will scare me."

He smiles. "Nothing like that." He eyes me for a moment. "You'll have to tell me your story. Will you?"

I smile and flip my hand up again. "Sure. Or, I should say I will if you will."

He nods. "I agree to your terms."

I feel something like static electricity spark along my forehead. Or behind my forehead. It's hard to explain. I touch the spot, frowning. "What the hell was that?"

"We agreed to a pact. It is magically binding. Nothing so serious as an oath, however."

I blink at him. "I'm not sure that was necessary."

He shrugs. "Perhaps not, but I didn't do it. Or rather, not intentionally. One of the things that defines my people is that we must be exceedingly careful about what we agree to and how we phrase our agreements because they are all magically binding, and it is beyond our control. Our magic simply…seizes the agreement and binds it to the parties involved."

"That's weird."

"Perhaps."

"So, what is it I'm trusting you with, Aeon?"

"You'll see. For now, don't worry about it. But when you notice something unusual, that's what you agreed to trust me with. Essentially, yourself. Your physical well-being."

I frown. "That's vague, but I'll play along."

"I need the words, Maeve. If you will, please, tell me that you trust me on this particular, specific matter."

"But I don't know the matter."

"The magic does—my magic does. And so does yours."

"My magic is gone."

"Not gone. Blocked. You cannot access it at this time, nor can you feel it, but it's there." He shifts closer to me, rolls to lay on his back, and moves so we are lying parallel to each other across the fire. He extends his hand to me. "Join hands with me, if you will."

I reach out and take his hand—he threads our fingers together, and I feel a frisson of something sizzle through me.

I ignore it. Not going there. No, no, no.

"Now." His voice is low and quiet and calm. "Try to relax. Breathe. If you have ever meditated, do so now. Eyes closed, slow, even breaths." His voice, already musical, becomes hypnotic, lulling.

He begins chanting or singing. I don't recognize the language, other than to think it sounds related to Arabic or Hebrew, but with slightly less emphasis on the guttural 'ch' sound in the back of the throat. His voice is music. His words, whatever they mean, are powerful. This is no lullaby—it's a glamour. A very, very powerful one. Even without access to my magic, I can feel it. My skin tingles and goosebumps rise all over my body, my fine hairs lift, and my breathing becomes shallow and quick.

I focus on keeping my breathing slow and deep and even. Eyes closed. I listen to his voice and try to pick out the words, but I get lost in the sound, the rhythm. It seems to go on for a very long time, and the heat of the flames and his hand in mine anchor me to reality. Without the heat of the fire and the warmth of his hand, I might just float away on the river of his voice.

Gradually, his singing tapers off, and he falls silent. I don't open my eyes. I can't.

"Tell me about your mother?" He asks, his voice a soft murmur as if he, too, is reticent to intrude on the moment. There's something sacred about what he did—it feels like being in a cathedral, where you just somehow know you shouldn't be loud.

It seems perfectly natural to hold his hand—and to keep my eyes closed.

"She was..." words fail me. "Well, she was magical. I mean, duh, she was fae. But I didn't know that. I didn't know what she was or what I was until after she was murdered by the Tribunal. My whole life, she was all I had and all I needed. We moved around a lot. Like every six months, usually, if not more. Mostly around the south and west. Never anywhere cold—I think she had a secret hatred for cold. She was...gentle. But she had this way of drawing people to her. Everyone who met her loved her. Wanted to be near her. Men especially. Yet she never had to fight men off. They never got violent or inappropriate with her that I ever saw. When she smiled, it seemed like the whole world got brighter. I...I think I was a pretty well-behaved kid because I didn't want to make her sad or angry—it would be like...god, I don't know how to put it. It would be unnatural. That's the best I can do. It would just be wrong. So I always, always tried *so* hard to be good. And she made it easy. She didn't have many rules. Mainly, stay close to her in public. Don't leave the house without her. Don't talk to strangers without her. But at home, she just...she made everything better. I mean, she wasn't perfect. She was reclusive at times. She'd just want to be in her room alone for hours at a time. I could watch TV or read or whatever, and if I needed her she was there, but I just sort of knew to leave her be. I never knew why. I do, now, though."

"Why?"

"She was casting a demense. Or rather, demenses, plural. According to my grandfather, she spent my whole life turning me into one immense demense of her spirit." I snort. "I didn't mean to rhyme, sorry. Anyway. I realized in hindsight that she was doing it every time she brushed my hair at night. That was my favorite time of the day. She would sit on my bed with her back to the wall and I'd sit between her legs and she'd brush my hair. Over and over, for like an hour. And she'd sing. It always lulled me to sleep, and I never noticed that I never understood the words. Sort of like what you just did, but I wasn't aware that she wasn't speaking English. I think. It's all fuzzy, now."

Aeon doesn't respond for a few moments. Even though my eyes are closed, I feel a weird sense of disorientation, sort of like how when trying to take a nap in the sunshine you feel like you're falling or tilting somehow—drifting off to sleep on a raft in a gentle surf. I keep my eyes closed and wait for Aeon to speak.

"What was the effect of your mother's sacrifice?"

"Sacrifice?"

"Well, yes. To cast a demense is to divest a portion of yourself, your soul, your essence. Putting that sliver into an object which you then carry around? That's a selfish act, because a portion of your soul is outside of your body, which means a part of you will live on as long as that object is intact. But what your mother did? Sliver after sliver, day after day, putting those slivers into *you*? That was the ultimate act of sacrifice. Even had she chosen to die directly so you might live, what you say she did with the demenses is a far greater and more noble sacrifice."

"Why?"

"Well, first, answer my question, if you will. What was the effect on you?"

"I...well, you have to understand, first of all, that when I was born, she and my...well, not my father but the man my mother loved who thought of me as a daughter—they cast a glamour on me that suppressed my immortal nature. It didn't just hide it, like a mask, but suppressed it so it was impossible to tell, for anyone, even me, that I was anything but mortal."

"I apologize for the interruption, but why?"

"Because my mother was kidnapped by her father and subjected to a reproductive experiment meant to solve the immortal reproduction conundrum."

"I assume you mean cross-race mating?"

"Yes," I answer. "But against her will. Forcefully. For months."

Silence. "By her own father?"

"Unfortunately, yes. Now, he was under the gun—head of the committee dedicated to solving the problem, which up until then was focused on every other solution *but* mating with the other kinds of immortal—the other Primi."

"Primi?"

"Oh, yes. That's Zirae's word for Fae, shifters, and vampires. Primi. I, a vaer, am a Secundus. Aeshir and Fomori are the other Secundae—fae-shifter and shifter-vampire, respectively." Pause. "The terms are logical and useful, so we've continued to use them even though they were created by a creature as vile as Zirae. Anyway. My grandfather didn't have much of a choice—or no good choices, at least. Succeed or be executed—and probably his wife and my mother with him, simply to be thorough. So, he chose. And it succeeded. She conceived me with a vampire, escaped, and went on the run. Cast the glamour to hide my nature. When I was eighteen, she was caught and executed by the Tribunal, and that sort of triggered everything. Andreas, my mother's lover, came to get me and told me he was my long-lost father—which was believable since she never told me one single thing about my father or anything about her past. But then I was drawn to Caspian and his coven, discovered the immortal world existed, and it eventually became clear I was *not* mortal. This is the Cliff's Note's version, by the way. Eventually, it became clear I wasn't just *not* mortal, I wasn't a normal *im*mortal—I was both vampire and fae, somehow."

Aeon squeezes my hand. "Go on."

"I was pursued by the Tribunal and the IRRC—the Immortal Reproductive Research Council. They didn't want me to go public—fully public *or* just within the immortal community—about my nature. It would threaten their hold on power, you see. I mean, sure, they were worried about what, um, is happening out there, but I think it was going to happen anyway, and now, at least, it's happening somewhat on our terms."

"Pardon, but what's happening?"

I snort. "You don't know?"

"No. I have been in a reclusive period. I go through them every few centuries. I get tired of people, mortal or immortal, and choose somewhere to get away for a while. Thus, my adoption of the Gobi. I've been here wandering the Gobi for, oh…a hundred years or so. I do occasionally pop into a city just to take the temperature of the world and sort of just… assimilate a bit, so I don't seem and sound so anachronistic. But I've not done that in, oh, a year or so."

I clear my throat. "So you've just been…walking around the Gobi Desert, alone, for the last century?"

"Yes."

"Weird."

"Perhaps, I suppose."

"So, what's happening is that the mortal world discovered, sort of by accident and sort of my fault, that we exist. The Tribunal and IRRC cornered me, my mate, and my coven in New York, and a battle broke out because I refused to go with them and be their prisoner and lab rat. I refused to be silenced. Well, some mortal livestreamed the whole thing, and it went viral." I hesitate. "Are you familiar with those terms?"

"Yes," he says, sounding amused. "I know what livestreaming and viral mean."

"Well, you just told me you've been out here for a hundred years. It's a logical question."

"It is, but I did also say I spend time in cities just to stay abreast of such things." He pauses a moment. "I assume mortals didn't take it well."

"Um, no. It's…well, it's bad. The American government has all but shut down because so many of the officials in the highest positions were immortal, and the fear and divisiveness that resulted just meant chaos everywhere. It's global, though. I admit I don't know what things are like in every country because I've been focused on mine."

"I see. Not surprising. Mortals have never been fully able to accept our kind. But it comes and goes. In some periods we are more tolerated, and in some less so. This most recent period after The Treaty, however, is different than the others that have come before because of the glamour cast to make mortals forget—not just that generation, but all mortals, forever going forward."

"Yeah, that's the part I've never gotten clarity on. Who decided that? Who agreed to it? Who cast the glamour? How? What was it supposed to solve? I know The Treaty ended the war and the loss of lives, but it also doomed immortals to a slow extinction."

"Indeed. There is much that has been forgotten."

I consider the weight behind that statement. "So it would seem." I resist the urge to look at him. "It seems to me like you know a lot of what's been forgotten."

"I do."

"Don't you owe it to people to share that information?"

"If I thought it would have done any good, I would have. I still would. And now that mortals are aware of what they don't know, the world might be ready for what I know. Accompanying you will serve to help me assess that." He squeezes my hand. "Now. Back to my very first question: what were the impacts of your mother's demenses?"

"A sense of her spirit within me. In moments of extreme danger or need, I would suddenly be able to perform wildly advanced feats of magic that I shouldn't be capable of. And usually, it would just happen without me intentionally trying to do anything. I just seemed to know things despite having zero magical education or training. It wasn't until I met my grandfather and learned the truth from him that I understood what was happening—my mother had infused so much of herself in me that there's almost a second spirit inside me. At least, that's my theory. I spoke to her in The Dreaming once, but only once. As I learn to control my magic I've had to rely less and less on Mother's Spirit, which is bittersweet because once I knew what it was, it felt like a way of being connected to her."

"Remarkable," he murmurs, awe obvious in his tone. "Truly, your mother was a remarkable woman."

"So it would seem. I mean, I know she was—but it feels like I didn't know her."

"Do children ever really know their parents?"

I laugh. "I wouldn't know. I just know I didn't really know my mother—at all."

The sense of tilting, twisting, floating disorientation has subsided. Aeon squeezes my hand.

"Open your eyes," he says.

Slowly, I open my eyes. Stars—an infinite wash of stars, shaded blue by the flickering fire between Aeon and me. Something is off—what, though?

I glance at Aeon. He's washed and shaded in delicate, soothing blue, looking at me with eyes slowly fading back to purple from having glowed brilliant azure.

He did something magical, then.

I blink and examine my surroundings. The flat, endless vista of cracked hardpan has been replaced by low, rolling hills—in the dim light of a fresh rising dawn they're little more than sharp-edged shadows against the backdrop of gray morning on the horizon. The blue mage-flames dance merrily, twisting and shivering and bathing me in delicious warmth.

I sit up. Grass surrounds me, damp with dew everywhere but where I was lying. Aeon sits up beside me, releasing my hand. Watches me, waiting for my reaction.

"Where are we now?" I ask.

A one-shoulder shrug. "Hard to say for sure, but a good distance north and west. Out of the Greater Gobi. Probably somewhere in northern Mongolia or southern Russia. That kind of travel is…imprecise at best."

"What kind of travel is it?" I ask. "And if you shrug and give me another vague non-answer, I shall be extremely displeased."

He grins. "We wouldn't want that, would we?" God, his smile is disorienting. His teeth are white and straight, and his lips are…kissable, is all I can say. The smile, though…it transforms his ageless features. Creases at the corners of his mouth, smile lines at the corners of his eyes, the brilliance of it is intoxicating and nearly as hypnotizing as his eyes.

STOP IT, MAEVE!

This is ridiculous. It's mere physical attraction. Nothing to act on. Nothing to worry about.

"You can't give me that stupid smile and think it'll erase the question, Aeon." I hold his eyes without blinking, without smiling, without expression. It's all an act, and I think he knows it.

He affects me. It's not cool.

I have mates. Five of them. I neither want nor need a sixth, and honestly, I'm not sure I can handle another colossal male personality.

I don't want Aeon. Not in any way.

He stares at me so intently I wonder if he can read my mind. Eventually, he nods, once.

"Very well. I shall uphold my end of the agreement. You shall receive your answers." he places his hands, palms down, index fingers together, thumbs overlapping, above the flames. They reach up and lick at his hands, and then the fire seems to lift up and off the ground and absorb into his hands. The blue glow fades and dissipates, and the natural, normal dawn haze blankets us.

He rubs his hands together as if to warm them up, and faint blue sparks dance around his hands and wink out so fast I wonder if I saw them at all.

He rises to his feet in a lithe, liquid motion. He unbuckles his belt, rests it on one shoulder, adjusts his robe and re-belts it, adjusting the sword. "Come. Let's make miles."

I get to my feet, brush grass off my butt, and rake my hand through my hair. "I'm guessing you can't just travel us like that back to The Enclave?"

A shake of his head. "Alas, no. It has a limited range, and I can only work the glamour every so often. I won't be able to do it again for a few days."

"But what is it? How does it work?"

"In the mortal world, there is a form of written

entertainment known as science fiction. I assume you're familiar with it."

I laugh. "Yes, I'm familiar with science fiction, Aeon."

"One mustn't assume. Anyway. Certain writers have posited a theory of travel known as wormholes. One theory in particular works upon the premise that wormhole technology folds space-time and pokes a hole through it, allowing one to travel great and impossible distances in a short period of time. Do you follow?"

I shrug. "More or less."

"What Zirae did—the portal you described—is a version of what I did. Zirae's wormhole was…messy. Self-taught based on fragments of ancient texts from my time. Because he didn't have the full text or a qualified instructor to teach him the correct techniques, he did it incorrectly—and very dangerously. The technique has a name in the language I spoke as a youth, but even the name of the language has been forgotten for over ten thousand years, so knowing it would do you little good. Think of it as…" he looks up, frowning. "Transverse Relocation." Another pause. "Well, no. Relocation is misleading. Hmmm. Transverse, I like. How about telelocation? Tranverse telelocation."

I snort. "That's a mouthful. Sounds like something from Star Trek."

He lights up. "Yes! I met Gene. Wonderful chap."

"The way you talk changes constantly."

He shrugs. "Well, yes. I suppose it would. I pride myself on my facility with language—learning to speak and sound like a native. But I've learned so many languages and dialects and accents over the millennia that they sort of migrate around in my brain willy-nilly. English has been my go-to for several centuries."

We've been walking as we talk, a few feet separating us. Aeon is a tall dark shadow with white hair, his voice seeming to emanate from the shadow. Around us, the hills gain features as the light blooms—waving short grass, the occasional wildflower.

We walk in silence for a while—a long time. Wind blows constantly, a steady stream of cool air from the west. It sends Aeon's hair fluttering behind him like a flag—mine, too.

"Does the…whatever you called it—transverse telelocation…does it cross The Dreaming?"

A thoughtful pause. "In a way, yes. It's not The Dreaming as you would know it, however. It's…well, that's not entirely true. It *is* The Dreaming. Just…a different form of it. Or a different part of it. It's hard to discuss in English. I don't suppose you know Sanskrit?"

I laugh. "Prana, rakta, mana, and maya. That's about it."

"Ah. Well, never mind. Essentially, you're entering The Dreaming through a different door, which changes the essential nature of The Dreaming. Transverse Telelocation—and you know, that *is* a mouthful?—it brings you into The Dreaming, but sort of…across the top. Are you familiar with the term meniscus?" I nod, and he continues. "It's sort of like traveling along the surface of the water, within the meniscus but not truly beneath the surface. So, the things that live in the depths below are still there and can find you and eat you, but you're not really *in* the water. What Zirae did was akin to jumping into the water from a dock and then attempting to swim in the meniscus from there. The correct technique is more subtle and precise—it takes longer but is safer and more accurate. It is more like gliding along the meniscus from shore without ever truly penetrating the surface. No splash, no altering the hungry residents of the dark deeps."

I nod. "Interesting. Could I learn it?"

"Certainly. With ease, I would think." He rests one hand on the hilt of his sword. "Now, if you would, allow me some time to think so I can order my thoughts—what to tell you, how, and in what order."

And so, we walk in companionable silence for several hours after that. The sun rises behind us, and the rolling hills unfold before us and wrinkle away behind us.

The sun is past its zenith and is on its way back down before Aeon clears his throat and begins speaking.

CHAPTER 18

"FIRST, THE QUESTION OF *WHAT* I AM. As you may have guessed, I am neither fae, nor shifter, nor vampire, nor any kind of heretofore unknown hybrid like yourself. If you absolutely *must* give me a name, call me an elf. As from Tolkien." A pause. "A lovely and wonderfully interesting man, Tolkien."

"I suppose that makes sense," I say.

"I thought so. My people predate what Zirae has termed the Primi—shifters, fae, and vampires. We are the forebears of the Primi. I'll get to that later. For now, consider this a basic overview. As you have noticed, I do have magic, and as I have said, it is not like yours. And to be clear, my magic is not like that of anyone else among my people either—I've always been a bit of an outlier. A black sheep, you might say. Or, a freak. For one thing, even among my people, immortality is a bit of a misnomer. We *do* age, just as fae and the other Primi do—just very, very slowly. I, however, for reasons I cannot explain, do not seem to age—at all. When my body reached thirty linear years of age, I simply...stopped aging. I cannot explain it. Like all others, however, I can be harmed by violence but not by illness."

He walks in silence for a while. I walk and wait.

"My magic, then. I told you, I believe, that it works on what you might think of as a larger scope or scale than you may be familiar with. When you look within, how do you see your magic?"

I shrug. "Like an ocean. A vast, turbulent ocean of golden-white light."

A nod. "Ah. I cannot see my magic when I look within, but it's a matter of perspective. When you are on the mountain, you cannot see the mountain, yes?"

I nod. "Well, yes. You're too close."

"Just so. My reservoir of magic is so vast that I cannot see it in total. But that vast potential comes with limitations. You see, when a being such as you or myself or Zirae possesses great power, it must come in a package. Being fallible creatures with a limited grasp on dimension and even more limited creativity, we cannot have raw, unformed power. All that magic *must* have a shape. You understand?"

I nod and shrug. "Sure."

"Essentially, it becomes specialized. One develops an

affinity for or a skill in something particular. Zirae's was that…oh gods, what did he call it? Something ridiculous. Loop of undeath or something?"

"Coil of Undying Death." I shudder. "Fucking horrible."

"He subjected you to it, then?"

I nod. "Oh yes. He did."

"He could do other things, of course. But that was his specialty. He devoted a lot of time to perfecting it. And it *was* quite effective. I allowed him to practice it on me, once. A rather unpleasant experience, I must say."

"You think?"

He glances at me. "Are you familiar with the Fates?"

I bob my head from side to side. "A little bit. Immortals discuss them as if they're real people out there somewhere, watching and manipulating the lives of mortals and immortals. But I'm not sure if they're real or a legend or just a myth. People tend to blame a lot of things on them, I've noticed." I look at him. "Why?"

"Well, for one, they're real. They, along with me, are the last survivors of our race. They, like me, possess power of such immensity that it must be specialized to a very, very specific thing. For the Fates, their power is one of perspective. They see lives as threads in a tapestry. Instead of seeing each person as an individual, they perceive lives as threads. This impersonality is what allows them to do what they do. Which is to manipulate events—they are *not* omniscient or omnipotent. They provide guidance…nudges, you might say. And they do so with detached, observational benevolence. They are not good or evil, but impartial, with a general bent toward goodness. They do tend to focus on the lives of mortals, however, mostly because immortals can feel their influence—we elders especially—and we don't like being influenced like that. Mortals cannot feel the touch of the Fates."

"Can you give me an example?" I ask.

He tips his head to one side. "I can try. Think of…a man. A mortal male. He's lonely. He desires a mate. He wishes for companionship, physical and emotional intimacy, someone to trust and share life with. This man is walking down the street. His view of his life, necessarily, is limited. He cannot see past the moment in front of him. But the Fates can. And they see that if this man turns left at the upcoming intersection, he will trip over something on the sidewalk and, in so doing, bump into a beautiful woman—or man. This interaction will set him along a path of discovering the love he's been seeking with that person. If he had gone straight at the intersection or turned right, he would not have encountered that person. The Fates, then, nudge him to turn left."

"But they can't see *everyone* in the whole world all the time?"

"Of course not. As I said, they're not all-knowing or all-seeing. They just see, know, and can do vastly more than anyone else."

"Except you."

"No. Not except me. They cannot influence me because I know them and I know the feel of their magic, but I cannot see as they do. My magic is different, and personal to me."

"What do you specialize in, then?"

He smiles. "A good portion of my magic is dedicated to memory."

I frown at him. "Memory?"

"Yes. Being as old as I am, and having lived a life among

the mortals, except for my regular hiatuses away, without magic I could never retain all of the knowledge, skills, and memories I have acquired. It's part of why most immortals get age-sick—their minds are full. They cannot ingest any more experience. I have had to learn an alternative because I, for good or ill, am addicted to living."

"Well, you're gonna have to elaborate, then." I smile at him. "But, I do like that you're still addicted to living after, what, ten, twelve thousand years?"

He smiles, shrugs. "Perhaps closer to thirteen, but it's impossible to know for sure. And it doesn't matter. What's a millennium against eternity?"

I cackle. "To someone who hasn't made it a quarter of a century yet, a fucking lot."

"Fair." He goes silent for a minute and then continues. "So, my memory storage structures. Silos, you might think of them. Over time, I've devised a system of off-loading memory. Sort of like compressing a computer file and storing it in the cloud."

I blink at him. "You're familiar with computers?"

He shrugs. "Sure. They're fascinating. As much magic to me as my magic would be to a mortal. I love them. Anyway. You might think of my mind—" he taps his temple, "as a library. And, like a library, there is an organizational system. So, if I would like to access a memory from my youth, I would enter my memory—it would look like meditation to you—and go to the section dedicated to personal memories. I haven't got everything stored, of course, just the important stuff. Things like the endless days of walking where nothing happens, or eating a meal without any significance, or other such meaningless detritus I allow myself to forget. Meeting you, for example, will be stored in the important memory area." He smiles at me.

"Other sections," he continues, "include magic—meaning glamours, spells, skills, and such. Physical skills like construction, medicine, combat, and the like are another section. I have a whole section dedicated to notable quotes, another to geography—memories of specific places, and mental maps of places I've been."

"So when you want to remember something, you can't just 'remember it,' you have to intentionally find it and recall it."

He nods. "Yes. It's not a technique I invented, I just added magic to it. But holding the structure and retaining the organization requires a good deal of constant magical drain."

"Is it something you have to focus on all the time? Or is it, like, just running in the background?"

"It's more in the background. I've been maintaining it for so long at this point that I'm not even aware of it. It's not like casting a glamour or telelocating. It's subtle."

"You mentioned physical skills like combat, medicine, and construction."

"Yes. I live among mortals the majority of the time. Like modern fae, I use a mask to hide my features. I assume an identity—whatever interests me at that time and in that place. I've been many, *many* things over the years. A healer, a doctor, or a surgeon, depending on the terminology of the time. I've been a soldier—it's the simplest path, usually, because most quirks and oddities are overlooked in warfare as long as you kill the enemy effectively. I've been a trader, a merchant, a mercenary…there isn't much I haven't done, at one point or another. I've never been a king or emperor or a lord or any other kind of ruler—such things do not suit me. I have no interest in ruling people. I've seen what it does to even the most well-intentioned person."

"That's interesting to me," I say. "I'd think you'd want to take a stab at being king at some point."

"I have been offered a throne on more than a few occasions and have been tempted, I admit. But your turn of phrase, to take a stab at, is an apropos one. When one is in charge, you will earn the hatred of someone, and inevitably that someone will try to take a stab at you. And if I'm going to fight, I'd like to know who my enemy is, keep them in front where I can see them, and defeat them on my terms. A king cannot do that. So no, no crown or throne for me."

"Out there," I say, "the immortals call me the WorldBreaker and the Once-Mortal Queen. I'm sort of being looked to by the immortals to create something out of the chaos. But it comes with built-in enemies— immortals who don't want to be ruled and mortals who hate immortals."

Aeon glances at me. "WorldBreaker and Once-Mortal queen? That's you, eh? That old prophecy?"

"So it would seem. You know about it?"

He nods. "Well, certainly. Galenova, the woman who gave the prophecy, was a good friend of mine. Galenova was never wrong, but her prophecies were often rather vague and could be quite difficult, if not impossible, to make sense of."

"So far, all it's done is put me in an impossible position."

"Galenova would tell you to ignore it and just live your life. You cannot influence the future—you can only live in the now. Of course, every action you take changes the future, but that's unknowable—even for seers like Galenova. Even the Fates can only see into the very near future. She would always warn her listeners not to place too much stock in prophecies. They're often only of any value in hindsight."

I bark a laugh. "That actually helps, Aeon. Thank you."

"Glad to be of some small service." He looks around us—our surroundings are not much changed. Rolling green hills, a blue sky dusking into orange and red and purple as the sun sets.

"Tell me more about the Fates," I say.

He nods. "Very well."

He lowers himself to the ground cross-legged and cups his palms over the ground, concentrating. An orange glow blossoms between his palms and the ground and then grows and grows, brightens and brightens—remaining orange-yellow rather than the delicate, hypnotic blue. When he removes his hands, the flames dance and lick and reach for the sky, looking for all the world like normal fire.

I eye him. "It's not blue."

"Well, no. It's not mage-flame. The blue comes from my magic—part of the telelocating glamour. This is just regular old fire."

"But then…what is it feeding off of? There's no wood."

A grin. "Magic."

I roll my eyes at him. "No shit, Sherlock."

"Oh, you wanted technical details? Essentially, I create a dense, compressed ball of maya, plant it just under the surface of the soil, and then ignite it. It burns slowly, and, by nature, only consumes the magic, so it won't spread to our surroundings. I'd hate to cause a grass fire out here."

I nod, thinking through how I'd do it if I had my magic. "Neat. I bet I could figure that one out on my own."

"I'm sure you could."

"Yeah, if I could get rid of these fucking things." I shake my wrists.

"That was Zirae's other specialty—constraining magic. He created mage-cuffs, you know." He taps the bracelet on my left wrist. "I've been examining these. I think I know how to solve the issue, but as I've said, my magic doesn't work that way. But once we find someone who can do what must be done, it should be a simple matter."

"Where will you find the right person?" I ask.

He shrugs, smiles. "Oh, we will. I have a few individuals in mind. We just have to get to them."

"By crossing *the entire world*…on foot?"

He nods. "Well, yes. How else? I'll telelocate us again when I can. Tomorrow or the next day. It has a range of a few hundred kilometers. A thousand, at most. And as I've said, it's imprecise. I cannot specify where we emerge, so it can be dangerous. I could bring us out in the bottom of the ocean or the top of a mountain, and we'd be in a worse position. I can only do it in open areas like this, never in a populated area."

"I see." I sigh. "So, we walk."

"So, we walk." He considers in silence, watching the fire. "So, the Fates. It's a good way to introduce our next topic—a broad overview of immortal history, specifically the parts that have been forgotten by modern immortals."

"Zirae is modern to you?"

He nods, shrugs. "Well, yes. I was already several thousand years old when I met him as a child. He was a devious, obnoxious little shit. A spoiled brat with more power than sense who had never been told no. At the core, he was never anything but a bully."

"Damn straight," I say. "When I was about to beat him,

he ran away. I mean sure, I suppose discretion is the better part of valor and all, but…it just seemed like a bitch move."

"A bitch move," Aeon echoes, grinning. "Exactly. Most of his moves were bitch moves." A wave of his hand. "Anyway. The Fates predate me by a thousand years or so. A generation, essentially. They are the last of what you might call the direct descendants of the Nephilim themselves, whereas I am descended two generations removed."

"Nephilim?"

He nods. "I must go back." He holds his hands over the fire and wiggles his fingers—the fire flares, crackles, sparks, and jumps several feet higher, giving off intense heat and bright yellow light that casts dancing shadows behind us. "This is my personal belief, mind you—even we, of that time, never knew the truth—not for sure. It was nearly forgotten even by our time. But I believe that all immortals are descended from a single stock—angels who bred with the first humans. This is mentioned in passing in the mortal Bible. When the angels procreated with the humans, they created a new species—humans with superhuman abilities granted by their partially angelic heritage.

"As time went on, the Nephilim continued to make children, and those children of the Nephilim intermarried with each other and with mortals. Eventually, six distinct tribes were formed. They had names for themselves, and I knew them once, but I've forgotten—or, if I do retain the knowledge, it's somewhere in the library and it would take too much time and effort to retrieve, and it wouldn't mean anything you anyway since it's a long-dead language, like my own first tongue.

"Centuries wore on, and then millennia. Mortals came and went, formed civilizations and societies, merged, mingled, and died out. The children of the Nephilim began to realize that with their great powers and long lives came a caveat—limited fertility. Children were rare. For every immortal who was born, there were a thousand mortals, if not more. It was a kind of balance—nature's way. It became clear that they were all dying out. Fewer and fewer children were being born. Why? Studies were conducted by the learned ones, and the answer became clear quite soon: the tribes refused to interbreed or marry across tribal lines. Inbreeding exacerbated the infertility, and so the tribes shrank and shrank until the learned ones gave the tribes an ultimatum—or rather, presented the truth everyone had been ignoring. Die out, or procreate across tribal lines."

"Sounds familiar," I say.

"Exactly. What modern immortals face is an age-old choice. Get over yourselves or die out."

"I assume they chose door number one."

"Correct. The six tribes began to intermarry and interbreed, and eventually, the six tribes were reduced to three—what you now know as fae, shifters, and vampires."

"The original six—were their abilities different?"

Aeon nods. "Of course. With every crossing of tribal lines, the resulting children possessed different abilities and changing powers. Increasing, usually, with counterbalancing limitations. The original six tribes were divided by their unique properties." He lists them, ticking them off on his fingers. "Elemental, with subdivisions by element; magic, somewhat akin to modern fae, focusing on creative glamours and spells; combat, or offensive magic; healing; divination, or seers and prophets; and heightened physical ability, or supernatural strength, speed, healing factor, and such."

"I can see where the intermarriages created the Primi as we now know them," I say.

"Indeed, indeed. Some abilities mostly died out, such as divination. A few Primi possess the ability in a minor way, but nothing like those original children of the Nephilim. But there was a trade-off—a seer, for example, usually did not have any other real powers. No strength, speed, ability to wield combat magic, or healing. Modern fae have a lesser potential in one thing as a trade for greater potential in many things."

"And the Fates, then, are Seers?"

He nods. "Yes, but they are the first generation produced by intermarriage—the divination tribe with the glamour tribe."

"And you?"

"I am from the interim period before the tribes merged into three, but after they began intermarrying. My mother was from the elemental tribe and my father from the glamour tribe—both were among the most powerful ever born to those tribes, and I am the result." He waves a hand. "More on me later. You asked about the Fates. They are, like me, truly ageless—I assume it's a fluke, a genetic oddity. Their powers, as I have said, are the ability to see and manipulate the threads of lives of mortals and immortals. There are three of them, sisters. Their names are lost to the fog of time. But more so, because their other great ability is… call it a…" he frowns. "Hmmm. I suppose 'distortion field' is the best I can come up with."

"Distortion field? Also, it sounds like you don't *know* very much about them—I thought you said you knew them."

He smiles, tipping his head to one side. "I believe I have met them, have had conversations with them. What

I have termed a distortion field is a passive magical ability they have little or no control over—I feel, without any real evidence, that they can probably reduce or increase the power of the effect field, but I do not think they can negate it entirely. Essentially, you might run into them, talk to them, see them, and even know them for who they are, and while you're with them, everything is normal. But once you leave and you're no longer in their physical presence, you forget. It's a sort of passive, involuntary memory-phage."

"Memory-phage?"

"That's a glamour that erases memory. Immortal glamourists have been using it to cover up evidence of our existence since time began. There are different versions and different methods, but essentially they are all the same, downstream—cast a spell, and the subject, or victim if you prefer, will forget certain things. Depending on the power and skill of the caster, the effects can be precise or general, narrow or sweeping. The trick with a memory-phage is that the glamour must be intentionally ceased or it will simply keep going, eating away more and more memory. Theoretically, if left unchecked, a memory-phage could erase a person entirely—make them unable to form any memories at all, leaving them…well, a vegetable, more or less."

Something clicks. "Oh!" I snap my fingers. "That's what happened!"

He blinks at me. "Hmm?"

"Oh, um, well, I told you about my fight with the Tribunal and IRRC forces in Manhattan. And how it was livestreamed by a mortal and went viral. Well, the mortal who recorded the video was eventually tracked down, but she's like you said—catatonic. Mortal doctors couldn't figure it out—there was no obvious trauma, no illness, no discernable reason for her condition. I don't know if she was examined by immortal doctors —if she was, it was never publicized. But a memory-phage makes sense."

He nods. "The Tribunal uses them quite frequently, yes. In the case of a large-scale event as you describe, standard operating procedure would be to send shock troops in to deal with the problem, supported by mages for defensive reasons and to supplement the offensive measures, followed by a single or a pair of mages whose role is to cast a memory-phage so the mortals won't' remember what happened. It's a specifically calibrated glamour that has been carefully designed and attuned to erase only a very narrow window of memory, so the affected mortals will just have a fuzzy notion of something having happened, but not what—and eventually, unable to remember, they choose to ignore the hole in their memory. But, if that glamourworker is interrupted by, say, death or injury before he or she has a chance to finish the glamour, it would simply keep phaging. It is rare, but it does happen."

"And the Fates have this thing happening all the time?" I ask.

He nods. "Yes. I think it is quite a burden for them. The moment you leave their presence, you forget them. They cannot marry. Cannot take lovers. Cannot be apart from each other for even one hour. It makes them truly impartial and objective, I suppose, but it seems a very lonely life."

"God, that would be…" I try to imagine it and shudder. "Awful."

He nods. "I have much sympathy for them." He looks away into the night, and I think he is seeing the past.

"You've never had a mate?" I ask, after a while.

A slow, soft sigh. "Mate? No, no." He is silent again for a while. Looks at me. Considers. "Truth?"

I nod. "Always."

"I believe I was mated to one of the Fates. I deduce this by a long gap in my memory. There is a period of...." another long sigh, this one thoughtful, ruminative. "Oh, probably two thousand years where I have no memory." He taps his temple. "The library up here is also organized chronologically. I've spent, oh, decades at a time, sorting through my memories surrounding that period, and the gap is undeniable. I can trace languages learned, wars fought, notable figures met, advances in technology, and major historical events from before and after it, and the gap is quite large. At *least* two thousand years. The only explanation that I have ever come up with that explains it is that I met the Fates, became lovers with one of them, and remained with them constantly for the duration of the memory gap. My memory suddenly and inexplicably picks up with me in a desert, alone. Here, as a matter of fact."

"Ahhhh," I singsong. "The truth comes out."

He glances at me. "What truth?"

"The reason you have claimed the Gobi as yours."

He blinks at me. "What?"

I laugh. "Oh, come on, Aeon. You can't be *that* dense."

He blinks. Seems almost offended. "I've no idea what you mean."

I stare at him. "Twelve thousand years old, ageless, magic so immense and powerful you can't manage a simple pair of magic-restricting cuffs, yet you're *that* unself-aware?"

"Maeve." He looks away, jaw hard, eyes narrowed. "If you have a revelation for me, please share it."

I lean close to him, shoulder to shoulder—the sizzle

of endorphins and hormones searing through me is disorienting. "I'm not mocking you or teasing you, Aeon. You're just so wise and ancient it seems weird and implausible that you could be so lacking in self-awareness." My head droops until his shoulder is supporting me. "You came back to this desert because it's the last place you were before your memory goes out. You hope to find them again. Or maybe get your money back."

He goes very still and silent for a very long time. "Gods and blood," he whispers. "You're right. How could I be so obtuse?"

"We all have blind spots, Aeon. And sometimes we willfully dupe ourselves into believing things, or we refuse to admit the truth because it is inconvenient or painful. Because that seems easier. I was in a kind of numb denial for a long time after my mom died. I couldn't mourn. I could barely admit that she was dead." I lift my head to look at him from a few inches away, noting the frown lines between his eyes, the creases beside his mouth. "I can see how if you spent two thousand years with someone and can't remember any of it, you might go seeking the place you last remember being with them, or as close as you can come. But it's too painful to think about too much, so you don't. You just find comfort in the desert."

"Who's wise now?" He asks.

He turns his head, and now his eyes, amethyst and endless, fix on mine. See into me. For a moment, the ageless, almost god-like immortal is gone, replaced by a mere man. A male who has loved and lost, who has been much alone, and perhaps even feels hesitancy to admit his loneliness. I see a being who has wandered this earth for twelve thousand years…most of it alone.

But why?

"Don't," he murmurs.

I frown. "Don't what?"

"Ask me the question I see in your eyes."

"Why not?"

He brushes the pad of his thumb over my lips, sending sparks shivering down my spine, making my nipples stand on end like diamonds, my core heat.

From one simple, innocent touch.

"Because I know the answer, and you're not ready for it."

The urge to take his thumb between my teeth and taste his skin is overwhelming. The urge to bury my fingers in his hair and yank him to me and kiss him until we're both breathless is overpowering.

"Maeve, don't. I'm warning you." Despite his words, his eyes tell a different story. As do the way his fingertips dance over my cheekbone, my temple, curve behind my ear.

If I didn't know better, I'd say the way I'm feeling is magical. I mean, there's no way I can feel this way naturally, right? As in mere human attraction?

I've been denying it and repressing it and refusing to examine my feelings because they scare me and I don't want them and I don't want another mate and I don't want the complication that I know must come with being with a man like Aeon.

Cat's out of the bag, now, though.

Now that I've admitted I want to kiss him, it feels like I've opened Pandora's Box.

His jaw is sharp and hard and angular under my palm. His lips are soft against the pad of my thumb. His skin is smooth and naturally stubble-free.

"You can't grow a beard?"

He huffs a laugh. "That's your question?"

"Mmmm," I acknowledge, too taken in by the counterpoint of his soft skin and hard jaw, soft lips and sharp eyes. "Yes?"

"No, my people don't grow beards. I could glamour one, but it wouldn't be real."

"You can perform a transverse telelocation. You can conjure mage-flame. You can organize your memories in a physical library in your mind. You can glamour yourself a beard…"

"Yes, he says, leading. "But?"

"But you can't get these off me?" I shake my wrist in front of his eyes. Firelight glints off the sickly, oil-slick, color-swirling metal, diffusing and refracting and casting unnatural reflections on the grass at our feet.

"My magic doesn't work that way."

"It sure seems to, except in this."

"You don't understand."

"No! I don't! And you won't explain it!"

"I can't!"

"Can't? Or won't?"

"Is there a difference?"

"Yes!" I shout, scrambling away from him and to my feet. "Yes, there fucking is! If you physically, magically, are unable to speak about it, *that's* 'can't.' If you are simply unwilling to for whatever reason, that's 'won't.' Seems like a pretty obvious distinction to me."

"Maybe it's bigger than that, Maeve. Maybe it's bigger than you."

"What could be bigger than me that requires you to not tell me why you can't or won't help me?"

"I *am* helping you!" He shoots to his feet, eyes blazing,

shifting from piercing purple to luminous blue. "I took you from the desert. I'm taking you to someone who *can* work the magic needed to get you out of those cuffs."

I turn away, squeezing my eyes shut against tears. "I don't…" They fall anyway—normal tears, no glow, no blood. "I don't know what's happening to me. I went from a normal girl to not a normal girl. Then from thinking I'm a normal immortal to realizing I'm not even a normal one of those! And now the whole fucking world is depending on me and looking at me and watching me and placing expectations on me and hating me and fearing me, and I barely know the first thing about my own people! I know nothing about our history. I know nothing about ruling or about leading! I'm *nineteen*! I was raised in the modern mortal world. I should be wearing pajama pants to eight AM. Civics classes at a university somewhere. I should be worried about joining a sorority. I should be studying for tests in some library and drinking too much and having a pregnancy scare." I fling an arm at the world at large. "I should *not* be carrying the weight of the future of the entire race of human beings on my fucking back!"

I stomp away, digging the heels of my palms into my eyes.

I feel him behind me. "Don't, Aeon."

"Don't comfort you?"

"No."

"Why not?"

"Because I shouldn't be attracted to you. I shouldn't want you. I don't! I *don't* want you. I don't *want* to be attracted to you. You're fucking complicated, and you're a major fucking complication on my life, and if you can't tell, my life is fucking complicated enough as it is." I whirl in place, and my hair slaps him in the face—he gathers it in his fist, wrapping the length of it around his palm, and steps into me. "Aeon, *please*—don't."

"Don't what, Maeve Sparrow?"

"Kiss me."

"I'm not. You're kissing me." His lips move against mine. Damn it.

He's right. I'm the one who lifted up on my toes.

I wrench myself away from him with a high-pitched gasp of effort, hating the arousal so obvious in the sound. Hate the way my sex clenched when he wrapped my hair around his fist. Hate the way his lips, for a split second, felt so right against mine.

I start walking, not caring which way I go—it doesn't matter. Just away.

"Maeve," he calls out. "That way." I glance back at him, and he's pointing ninety degrees to the way I'm going.

I adjust my direction, but otherwise. ignore him.

I walk for hours. I feel him behind me, but he gives me space.

CHAPTER 19

I WALK THE SUN UP AND BACK DOWN, AND I walk the stars out and the moon high, and then the sky gray and starless once more, and then another dawn.

I feel Aeon behind me. I feel him trying to find something to say and failing.

I can't bring myself to stop. I can't bring myself to break the silence.

The last time I gave in to my feelings for another male, I caused Caspian untold pain. The pleasure and joy of a new mate were burdened by the sorrow of the pain I caused Caspian, who loved me first and forgave me and accepted Caleb.

How can I go through that again? My mates must think I'm dead. The thought cuts me like a knife.

Once more, even knowing it's futile, I struggle with the cuffs, pulling at them, straining, screaming. I spy a sharp rock on the ground and pick it up and smash at the cuffs with it, but I miss and hit my wrists and pain slashes through me and blood wells and drips into the grass at my feet. There's not so much as a mark on the metal.

I collapse to my knees, sobbing. Aeon takes my injured wrist in his hand, closing his large, slender, strong hand around my injury. Blue light glows, flares, and subsides.

When he removes his hand, my injury is gone.

"What the fuck!" I yell, ripping my arm away and lurching to my feet. "You can heal me, but you can't fucking *FIX MY GODDAMN MAGIC?*"

"I can't fix your magic because there's nothing wrong with it!" he shouts back. "I'm not holding out on you! My magic *DOES NOT WORK THAT WAY*!"

"Well, you're gonna have to explain because I don't believe you. You can do all sorts of 'minor' glamours that are not at all minor. But this? Somehow *this* is beyond you." I shake my wrists at him again, a gesture even I'm getting sick of.

He sighs. "Damn it." He pinches the bridge of his nose. "Fine. I am not magically bound to silence, only honor-bond. But for you, I'll accept the tarnish on my honor."

"I…I don't understand what that means."

"I know." He sits cross-legged in the grass and cups his hands, palms down, a few inches above the earth.

Yellow light blazes, and then morphs green, and then fades into blue, and then brightens. A few moments later, he moves his hands, and the weird, soft, hypnotic, soothing blue fire dances and casts long, shifting shadows across the wild rolling hills behind us.

I recognize the beginning of his telelocation glamour and lay down as we did the first time, with the fire between our bodies, midway between hip and shoulder, arm extended. When the fire is burning strong and the magic is washing over us, he lays down as well and takes my hand, after a hesitation.

I'm the one to tangle our hands. "I'm sorry," I whisper. "I know you're helping. I'm not your responsibility, and I'm not your problem. You have no obligation to do a damn thing for me, and I'm being ungrateful. I apologize, Aeon."

"There's nothing to forgive and no reason to apologize, Maeve. I cannot fathom being suddenly cut off from my magic. It is…it is an integral part of who I am as a person, and I cannot imagine being without it. I would go mad. I would not know who I am without it."

"Exactly," I whisper. "I don't know who I am without it, and that scares the hell out of me. Who am I?"

"I do not mock or belittle, Maeve, please believe me. But you're nineteen. Almost twenty, as you said. And at that age, you should be still figuring out who you are. You carry a burden too heavy for anyone, mortal or immortal, at an age when you can barely be expected to know yourself."

"It's too much. And now I'm lost, and without my magic, and my mates probably think I'm dead, and my cause is probably suffering and maybe even falling apart without me, and everything I've done will have been for nothing, and yet here I am worrying about feeling some *tingles* for you. Being attracted to you is the *last* thing I should be worried about. But…" I groan a sigh. "It's all so complicated, and if I could just get my magic back, that would be one less thing to worry about, and then maybe I could figure everything else out."

"When I tell you my magic doesn't work that way, it really is true. It doesn't. It never has. The minor glamours and magics I've done are just that, minor. Minor healing, minor conjurations. Telelocation isn't minor, but it does fall under the major category in terms of how my magic *does* work. But the truth is, there's another reason I can't get Zirae's cuffs off you."

I open my eyes and turn my head to look at him. It's a mistake—above, the stars are spinning as if the Earth is a top that has been set to twirling on a tabletop. The blue glow of magic from the fire is so brilliant and vivid it strains my eyes, so intense it washes through my brain and into my soul. Yet, overlaid beneath and behind the blue glow is the vacant black void of The Dreaming, the sense of nothingness, of chasmic space, endless dark, and hungry shadows. Yet, too, I see the rolling green hills bathed silver by starlight and the waxing moon—now a half-moon. Time is distorting, I think. Just last night—was it last night?—the moon was a waxing crescent.

"Close your eyes," Aeon admonishes. "You'll make yourself sick."

I shake my head, trying to sort out the information my eyes are giving me. "It's confusing, but…" I shrug. "It's not so bad."

"Very well."

"What's the reason, Aeon?"

"The reason is that I'm using most of my magic on something else, and the glamour Zirae used to create those cuffs is not minor magic. It will require a lot of power and a lot of skill. And while I have the raw power, I simply do not have the bandwidth available. And truthfully, such a thing is beyond my skill. It's just…" a shrug. "It's just not how my magic works."

"Your library?" I ask. "Is that what's taking up so much of your bandwidth?"

He shakes his head. "No, that's…. that's perhaps thirty percent of my magic. There's a good, oh, fifty-five, perhaps sixty percent used for… something else."

"So everything I've seen you do has been using less than ten percent of your ability?"

"At a rough estimate, yes."

"What's the rest being used for?"

A long silence. I look at him—he's thinking. Weighing. Choosing words, choosing which information to share. Or perhaps just finding the courage to simply say it.

Shadows move, dancing on his face, casting his features into sharp shadow. Overhead, the stars spin, blurring into silvery streaks of light, as if I'm trapped in a long-exposure photograph.

"Two hundred and thirty-eight years ago," he murmurs, almost to himself, "a treaty was signed, establishing a lasting peace between the rulers of the mortal factions and the elders of the immortals. It ended a long, bloody war that cost the lives of tens of thousands of immortals when we could already scarcely tolerate the loss of one immortal."

"Aeon…"

He squeezes my hand and I fall silent. Close my eyes once more and let his words wash over me.

"The war was sweeping. It was, truly, the first world war. Mortals remember it differently, of course." A pause. "And that's where I come in."

"You were part of the Mortals' War?"

"Everyone was," he murmurs. "Mortals remember the French Revolution, the American Revolution…the other conflicts and wars going on elsewhere in the world at the time, but they don't remember that all over the globe, mortals were rising up against immortals. Slaughtering us. Hating us. Drawing us into war. Using any excuse—like that pathetic little faction of extremist godhoodists who started things in the Colonies."

I snort. 'the Colonies', Aeon? Your age is showing. No one has called the US 'the Colonies' since the seventeen hundreds, I think." I frown. "Also, godhoodists? Never heard that one."

"The immortals who claimed to believe we immortals were meant to rule over the mortals because of our divine nature, our godhood. It was a handful of egotists, narcissists, and hedonists who used that as an excuse to take what they wanted. The immortal elders and the mortal leaders all knew the godhoodists weren't a major movement, but the mortal politicians used it as an excuse for warmongering."

"Sounds like what mortal politicians are *still* doing."

"Yes, well, it's one of the things the mortals are obnoxiously consistent about." He sounds remarkably sour on the topic.

"Where do you come in?" I ask.

A sigh. "I'm working up to that. It's difficult to talk about for reasons you'll come to understand." A long, long pause; I can almost hear the earth spinning, almost feel the warm tingling rush of magic on my skin. "I was there when the treaty was signed. I was masquerading as a fae elder at the time. I'd been all over the world, telelocating to the utmost of my abilities—and what I saw was suffering. Immortals being hunted by mobs and faced with the choice to either use their abilities and slaughter them, reinforcing the mortals' fears, or let themselves be killed. I watched wars break out, watched it spread over the whole world, bit by bit, over months and then years. For six years, I wandered the earth, watching us slaughter each other. Watching mortals grow more and more fearful of us as they drove us to worse and worse violence. And we were not innocent. We committed atrocities, same as they did. But the mortals could afford to lose their children to war. They could replace their numbers in a generation or two—and then some. We could not. Even then, before the Treaty, our numbers had been declining for centuries. The war had to end. It *had* to."

"I've heard some of this, but I didn't realize it was global."

"Few do, even among immortals. See, what isn't widely known, even among immortals, is that the glamour that changed the mortal world's knowledge of immortal existence also affected immortals to a degree. The glamour was designed and implemented in such a way that certain amounts of memory loss were inevitable for *everyone* involved—except the person who cast the glamour."

My stomach sinks. "I was told it was a group of six fae. They died casting it or something like that. That's what Alistair told me."

"Alistair Taylor?" He asks.

"Yes. He's my mate and the leader of the coven into which I mated."

"I knew him. I worked with him during several campaigns in the Colonies. An excellent soldier." A musing hum. "He'd not know me now, though. I was masked to look like a fae."

"You mask yourself even among other immortals?" I ask.

"Yes. Just as immortals mask themselves among mortals to avoid questions and conflict, so too do I among immortals for the same reason."

"So, the glamour that erased knowledge of immortals was cast by *one* person? God, the amount of power that must have required. Who could be capable of such a thing?"

I know the answer.

I open my eyes, turn my head, and look at him. His eyes glow azure, casting almost as much light as the fire. He regards me steadily and evenly, his emotions carefully hidden.

"Aeon—what? No." I hold his eyes. "*No.*"

He smiles weakly. "Yes. It's my glamour."

I shake my head. "Bullshit."

He laughs, but the laughter doesn't reach his eyes. "Truth."

"Why? Why would you do that?"

A ragged sigh. "I didn't see much alternative at the time. The war was showing no sign of stopping. Immortals were dying. One immortal could take on a dozen, or two dozen, or even three dozen at a time, and in previous wars, swords and spears and bows and even trebuchets and the occasional firearm wouldn't change the outcome, even outnumbered. It was armies of men armed with muskets and cannons that changed the calculus of warfare. Coordinating shields with offense was proving difficult, and even the best shields will fail sooner rather than later under sustained fire. And mortals are far from stupid—they learned very quickly that if you concentrate fire on a specific location, the shield will fail that much faster." He sighs, long and bitter. "And there was also resistance among the elders to allow certain tactics and strategies that would have allowed us to…well…kill far more of the mortals at once than we were currently using. Sort of a magic version of nuclear warfare."

"Angelfire," I murmur.

"That's one. It's very inaccurate and doesn't just kill people, it kills *everything*, including the ground, the earth itself—nothing will grow or live where Angelfire has burned." Sadness and sorrow weigh down his voice. "There were others that were discussed. Violent, destructive magics. Things that, once unleashed, cannot be undone. And the elders, whether right or wrong, chose not to go down that path. It would have won us the war, but at what cost? It would have decimated mortals. Erased entire cities. Wiped tribes and families and whole villages off the map. It would have made us the villains in a very real sense, and it would have made us gods, as the godhoodists wished—by merit of having killed off the vast majority of mortals, leaving the rest essentially slaves.

"It was that, or sign the treaty."

"Like a…what's the phrase…Pyrrhic victory?" I ask.

A shrug. "Not exactly. A Pyrrhic victory is where one side technically wins the battle but in doing so loses so many of its soldiers that it barely counts as a win. What the immortal elders faced was a far worse dilemma: win but become evil, or lose and face the consequences. It's the same choice immortals have faced throughout history when confronted with an angry mob of mortals who hate you and want to kill you simply for who and what you are: prove them right in being afraid of you, or suffer."

"I never understood it in that context before."

"Because very few have the context," Aeon says.

"So, how did you end up being chosen to cast the glamour?"

"The peace talks were falling apart. The mortals insisted on a reproductive restriction meant to stop mortal women from dying in childbirth. Understandably, the immortal elders balked at this. Neither side could agree, and it was looking more and more like the war would just continue. And if it did, we would just die out. We'd end up going extinct as a species. And not eventually, but in a matter of years, not decades or centuries or millennia." He halts, sighs. "I revealed myself, my true nature, to the elders. I implored them not to accept that condition—we had to be able to reproduce. And there was an obvious alternative: mate with each other…across tribal lines."

"I'm guessing that suggestion went over like a lead balloon."

"Exactly. Flat-out refusal. I explained the cycle, how immortals have faced this dilemma already—and the only conclusion that anyone could come to is that marriage across tribal lines is the only way." Pause, a groaning sigh. "They wouldn't even consider it. It would be the end of immortals, they feared. We'd just mingle and water down the bloodlines. Not so, I told them. Bloodlines change, powers change, traits and features and abilities change, but immortal-kind lives on."

"They're a bunch of stubborn old farts," I say. "Stuck in their ways, addicted to power, and afraid of irrelevancy."

"So, they're human."

I laugh. "A fair and true point, sir."

"It was a mortal politician who suggested the glamour. Jefferson? Franklin? No, no. Someone obscure, at least according to your mortal histories. I can't remember—the name is in there somewhere but it's not worth the effort to retrieve it. It was a passing comment, almost a joke. Something like, 'Too bad you can't just make us all forget you ever existed.'"

"How would that help? Being invisible to the mortals…what does that do? It's just putting your hands over your eyes so you can't see the problem—the problem hasn't gone away just because you can't see it."

"It would help if they'd listened to me. What I suggested was that immortals go back to living among the mortals, hidden and masked. I hated even suggesting it, but it was better than our whole race dying out. Don't agree to reproductive restrictions, I said. I'll cast the glamour, and we'll be forgotten by mortals forever. It'll buy us time, at the very least. Mortals have short memories, except when they don't. In a couple hundred years, we can re-negotiate the treaty."

I frown, thinking. "Is that a possibility?"

"Well, sure. I think it would require a summit, like NATO or G20, where the few world leaders who *do* know the secret of our existence negotiate with the immortal leadership. Or, it would have been. But you disbanded the Tribunal, killed Zirae, the de facto leader, and then our existence went public anyway, causing a rift—the glamour is trying to erase their memories, but technology makes it impossible. It's part of what is driving the conflict, actually. They are confused and afraid of the dichotomy in their brains. They feel lied to, and that makes them angry, and on top of that, there's suddenly a whole new race of beings that live longer and have actual magic. It's a shock. And it's made worse by interactions of magic and technological dissemination of information that even magic can't keep up with."

"So…you cast the glamour anyway?"

He shakes his head. "No. They lied to me. They didn't want me on the council—I'm not a fae, or a shifter, or a vampire. I'm a relic of a bygone age—Zirae's words. They'll summon me when they make a decision. I told them I would not cast the glamour if they didn't make a provision for the future of our people. They're not my people, they told me. Very well, but my offer stands, as do my conditions."

"How could they have forced you? How could they have lied to you? Can't you tell?"

"I'm not infallible. And magic works on me, too. You see, my magic works best on large-scale effects. Global weather patterns. Conjurations that affect a large area. It's very, very difficult for me to focus on something so minuscule as healing or summoning fire. It's…" he trails off, thinking. "It's a matter of perspective, but my perspective, in this case, is not something I can easily change. I see from twenty thousand feet—I see the landmasses, the continents, the mountain ranges. I do not see the towns, the people, the cars. Does that make sense?"

"Sort of."

"So, yes, I could cast a lie detection glamour—but doing so is as hard for me as it would be for you to attempt the memory-phage glamour I cast. They lied to me and manipulated me. Zirae, the cunning old fox he is, knew somehow that we—my people—have the oath effect. Zirae manipulated me into promising to cast the glamour, and I, occasionally a fool, did not include the caveat of reproductive rights. You see, the elders were so afraid of the peace talks failing and the war continuing that they were willing to sacrifice our future for our present. Live now, die later. But they're not mortals—it wasn't a problem for a later generation. I think they assumed they'd be able to get out of it. To work around the issue—or solve the reproductive issue scientifically." Aeon sounds more human than ever—angry, embarrassed, frustrated. "By the time I realized how thoroughly Zirae had played me, I was locked in by my oath—I *had* to cast the glamour."

"God, Aeon."

"Do not pity me. It was hubris at play. I assumed because I was so much older and more powerful than the likes of Zirae, whom I'd known as a babe in swaddling clothes and then a snot-nosed brat tramping around the palace bullying everyone and then as an arrogant, hot-tempered young buck terrorizing everyone with his newfound powers. He outmaneuvered me. Got me to agree to cast the damned spell and lied to me about the contents of the treaty. They signed away reproductive rights. There wasn't a damn thing I could do." I hear pain in his voice—deep and bitter. "It is the worst failure of my life."

"Aeon…"

I open my eyes again; the stars are no longer spinning but seem to be…folding. Merging? The four quadrants of the heavens are moving inward toward each other, and where they meet, directly overhead at a point directly above the flickering blue fire, the stars seem to blur and distort into a single point of muted and filtered light.

His eyes glow blinding blue, and the void sings to my soul, and hills ripple in a long wind.

"You wanted to help," I whisper.

"Yes. And instead, I made things worse. Our people

are dying out, still—or, perhaps not my people. I don't know anymore."

"Why not undo the glamour?"

"I almost have many times over the years. But…I couldn't bring myself to do so. The chaos that would ensue from the whole world, suddenly and apropos of nothing, remembering the existence of immortals?" A harsh bark of laughter. "No. That would not help. So, the glamour stays."

"But you *could* undo it."

"Of course." He goes silent. "It would be a relief."

"A relief?" I ask. "How so?"

"Well, it's just a memory-phage, Maeve. A very, *very*, very big one, with specific parameters. Forget immortals, past, present, and ongoing. Do not forget anything else. But anything to do with the existence of mortals is forgotten, and a convenient lie is slotted into place."

"How do you fabricate the lies?"

"Oh, that's the beautiful part of a memory-phage," he says. "You don't. The subject's unconscious mind does."

"So the relief would be…what?"

"A memory-phage isn't a set-it-and-forget-it glamour, like a ward or a conjuring. It's more like a shield—you have to focus on maintaining it."

I frown at him. "You're saying you've been constantly, intentionally, and consciously maintaining a memory-phage glamour over the whole mortal population of the globe for 238 years?"

"Yes."

"So just…let it go, Aeon. The world is ready. We're outed."

"It's not that simple."

"No?"

"No." He points up at the sky. "It would be sort of like that. A bifurcation. Memory would return—everything. All the knowledge that was erased would return, all the history. The books would all be wrong. There would be… confusion isn't even the word. Minds could splinter, Maeve. The chaos you're talking about? It would get *so* much worse because there's history that in some ways might be better left forgotten."

"History is *never* best left forgotten, Aeon," I snap. "Never. We can't let ourselves forget, or we won't learn. We can't forget 9/11, Vietnam, the Civil War, The Trail of Tears, the Japanese internment camps, Auschwitz. We can't forget any of that, so we don't repeat it. And we can't forget that we *did* kill who knows how many mortal women so we could have babies. For *thousands* of years, we did that because we were too scared and selfish to do the right fucking thing. God, not even the *right* thing—the only logical, *possible* thing for our self-preservation."

He's quiet for a long time. "Yes. You're right. But the fact remains that if I undo the memory-phage, chaos will ensue—and according to you, the world is already in a state of chaos."

"Exactly. It's already chaos. Governments are already toppling. The face of human civilization is already irrevocably altered and will only go through more upheaval before we find any kind of equilibrium. What better time than now?" I turn my head to look at him. The glow of his eyes is so fierce it's disconcerting. "Things are already bad, Aeon. Mortals are already angry and feel lied to—they don't care about the Mortals' War—to them, shit, to *me,* it's something that happened a quarter of a millennium ago. Having the true history suddenly and literally magically appear in everyone's heads all at once…yeah, that'll be a shock. But we have to rewrite the history books anyway."

"I don't *know* what will happen," Aeon says. "Not for sure. It's never been done before."

"Do all memory-phages have to be maintained like that?"

"No. Normally, you have to time it—so many seconds for so many minutes of memory erased, or something like that. But this is a vastly different thing than causing a couple of dozen mortals to forget that they saw a shifter turn into a wolf in the middle of Walmart. It's not even similar to making a few hundred mortals forget they saw a fight between immortals. It's the whole world. All mortals. All memory. Written, verbal, public, private, past, present, and future."

"What is it like?"

He hums. "Sort of…sort of like holding a glass of water in your hand. But the glass is full to the brim, you can't spill it, and you can't ever put it down. So you have to learn to sleep, walk, talk, eat, and do everything with it in your hand. You can't ever use that hand. Your focus is always split."

"Sounds miserable."

"It hasn't been fun. But I've long known that an end was coming, one way or another. I'm no seer. But I just… feel it. Perhaps the Fates, whichever of them was my lover, told me something. Perhaps I didn't forget it entirely. I don't know. But I knew I wouldn't have to hold it forever. And in the scope of eternity—gods and blood, in the scope of my life so far, two hundred and forty years is an eyeblink. Barely two percent. It's nothing."

"But it has drained you to almost nothing for two hundred and forty years."

"Perhaps. But I couldn't just unleash the truth simply because I was tired of maintaining the glamour. I was bound by my oath to cast it and honor-bound by my agreement with the council of elders, what you call the Tribunal, to keep silent about it. I gave my word to them. But, you disbanded them and ended their authority over immortals, which I have taken to mean my promise to remain silent is ended." A laugh. "A liberal interpretation of honor, to be sure."

"They lied to you and tricked you! You don't owe them anything."

"Honor is for you, not others. You do not keep your word to impress other people with your integrity—you keep your word so you can live with yourself." His eyes meet mine, and the glow is less intense, and the whirling spinning folding of the stars slows, and the echoing hollow void of The Dreaming subsides into mere shadow, and the rolling green hills seem to dissolve into the gray light of dawn. "I did not maintain the glamour because I promised to. I maintained it because it was the right thing to do."

"But it's not, anymore. It *was*—you *did* do the right thing. But now things have changed."

He nods. "Things have changed, yes." He searches me. "I will release the glamour. But not until we get those cuffs off you."

CHAPTER 20

SIT UP, HEEDLESS OF MY surroundings or the still-fading effects of the telelocation glamour. "Why?" I demand. "Why wait?"

"Because without you, the whole thing will fall apart."

I shake my head, groaning—more in denial than disagreement. "How do you know? You've been wandering the Gobi for the last century."

"Because of *who* you *are*, Maeve. You are the WorldBreaker. The Once-Mortal Queen."

"I thought you didn't believe in that shit?"

"Not what I said," Aeon says, rising to his feet. "I said you can't rely on prophecies because they're best understood in hindsight. But in this case, I spent time with Galenova discussing this particular prophecy."

I stare at him, stunned. "And you're just now telling me this?" I ask. "What did you talk about?"

He sighs. "Galenova was no more able to translate her prophecies than anyone else. Especially things so far in the future—she received your prophecy eleven thousand years ago—she had no way of understanding the large majority of what she saw. And I certainly had nothing to add. But she…" he trails off, thinking. "She *did* understand that the term WorldBreaker would be misunderstood. That term is the key, she said. The Once-Mortal Queen business was more of just an additional identifier. WorldBreaker was the key to the whole prophecy."

"Well, please elaborate, Mr. Informational Tightwad."

"Tightwad?"

"It means—"

"I know what it means, Maeve." he sounds annoyed. "Information is power. I haven't survived twelve millennia by playing fast and loose with the things I know. I did not keep it from you for any reason other than holding back things until such a time as it becomes necessary or beneficial to share them is a very, *very* long-ingrained habit. And my discussion with Galenova isn't going to do much for you."

"Anything will help," I mutter. "I feel like I'm drowning, sometimes."

"To Galenova, the gist of what she saw in the prophecy was that you—and there is no doubt in my mind that the prophecy is about you—would be an impetus for change and the linchpin for progress. But, being an agent of change is not an easy burden to bear. People don't like change. We never have, we never will. The notion that you would break the world comes from the idea that you can't make an omelet without breaking eggs. It did not mean that you would be responsible for destruction, only that you, your appearance, and your choices would set things in motion, which it sounds like has already happened. The whole prophecy has been lost, as I'm sure you're aware. And no, I do not have the whole thing anywhere in my memory. If I did, I would share it with you—please believe that. But what I do have is what Galenova told me off the record. Which is that after you've set certain events in motion, you will continue to be vitally important in how the future plays out. Your choices will change the future. It wasn't a prophecy so much as a private feeling she had after ruminating on the prophecy as a whole."

"Great," I mutter. "More pressure."

He moves to stand in front of me and takes my arms in his hands. His eyes revert to merely shocking purple instead of the disconcerting, soul-searing maya-infused blue. "Maeve—you are equal to the task. I have known many, many, many people throughout my life. Few of them have been your equal."

I laugh. "You barely know me. You only know me as a helpless quasi-mortal lost in the desert, without my powers, without my mates, frustrated, angry, scared, and alone. How could you possibly know the first thing about whether I'm up to the task of saving the whole fucking world?"

"Exactly because you think of it as your job to save the whole fucking world. It's not. But you've taken on that burden and you're driving yourself crazy trying to get back to where the work is." He cups my jaw in one long-fingered, slender, powerful hand. "You are not your powers, Maeve. Fae, vampire, immortal, former-mortal... lover, mate, queen—you are many things. And I believe in all of them."

"I just...I need my magic back, Aeon," I whisper, catching his wrist in my hand and holding on, unable to stop myself from nuzzling my cheek into his palm.

"It would be a grave mistake for me to undo the memory-phage before you have your powers back, before you're back where you need to be to do the work in front of you. I cannot explain why because I don't know—it's a feeling, and I have long since learned to trust those feelings."

"Like the feeling of knowing somehow that you wouldn't have to hold the glamour indefinitely?"

He nods. "Sort of. That's a little different."

"How so?"

He shakes his head. "That's a topic for later." He smiles at me, rubbing a thumb over my lips, his eyes following the path of his thumb as if wishing his mouth were there instead. "For now, we have miles to cover." He turns and takes in our surroundings.

I gasp. Put my fingers to my mouth, eyes wide.

We're on a mountain—not the peak, but midway down, on the side. I glance up and behind and see the bulk of the mountain looming, a colossus of snow-capped jagged bare rock. All around us are towering pines blanketed in fresh snow. To either side of us, the mountain range reaches and sprawls, peaks scraping the bare blue dome of the sky. Before us, a valley. Studded with trees and rippling with grass and wildflowers, a blacktop road winding and switchbacking its way toward a sprawling city spiked with towers and glinting with sunlight off of glass, suburbs divided by a cross-section of streets.

"Where are we?" I ask.

"Chimgan Mountain," he answers. "That's Tashkent, the capital of Uzbekistan. Settled in the Third Century BCE, it was declared a sovereign nation by the Soviet Union in 1991. The mountains you see around us are the Uzbek Mountains, an arm of the Tien Shan range."

I can't catch my breath, so beautiful is the vista. "Uzbekistan." I glance at Aeon, if only so I can get a breath. "As an American—a well-traveled one, I always thought, if not in an international sense, Uzbekistan was always just a name on a map, a weird, exotic idea of a place. I never even wondered what it would look like. And now, here I am. It's wild, Aeon."

"The world is a wild, wonderful place," he says. "I have seen…perhaps not *all* of it, but a vast majority. And even after twelve thousand years of wandering, it never ceases to amaze me. The wonders of it still take my breath away."

The descent down the mountain is an incredible hike. Not feeling any fatigue makes it that much better. There's no trail, or at least we're not following it. Unsurprisingly, Aeon's sense of direction is unerring, bringing us down the mountain and into the foothills by sunset. We keep walking through the night and reach Tashkent as the stars shine and the moon—now a waning crescent—sheds liquid silver on the world.

I'm not sure what I was expecting from a city as exotic-sounding as Tashkent, but…it's a fairly modern city. Three- and four-lane roads, much wider than those in most American cities, are mostly empty at this time of night, with a few busses trundling past, groaning and rattling.

Squat tenements and shops and restaurants line the roads. The architecture is an eclectic mix of styles—nothing I'm knowledgeable enough to identify. It's distinctly *not* Western in ways I can't quite pinpoint.

"What's our plan here?" I ask.

He shrugs. "Catch a train west. If you were truly mortal, I'd suggest a hotel, a shower, and some food, but since you're not, we could just keep going. Without a need for rest or sustenance, we are only limited by our motivation to continue."

"You don't require food or rest?" I ask.

"Mmmm, not as such. Not sleep. It's more of a meditative state than anything, and I only truly *require* it every few days—once a week, perhaps, at most. I do enjoy food, but I do not require it. Or at least not in the way that mortals do."

We are walking down a silent, empty, tree-lined street. A white wrought iron fence separates the sidewalk from an open grassy field on our right. Across the street on our left are older apartments of three and four stories, each window with an air conditioner unit.

"How do you differ from fae in terms of the balance of the Three Sisters and the Fourth God?" I ask.

A man on a ten-speed bicycle zips past us; I catch a glimpse of an Asiatic face, eyes wide with surprise, mouth a shocked O before he's gone.

Aeon considers my questions for a long time. "The balance of the three tribes you say Zirae called the Primi is a recent development—a natural limitation to their overall greater powers. The requirements, physiologically, of fae and shifters in particular are an oddity. The original Children of the Nephilim were unimaginably powerful, truly godlike. Their genetic proximity to the angels gave them nearly unlimited power. The trade-off, however, was stark. They could perform wonders of magic even I can only conceive of—but the toll, physically, was atrocious. The cost of such magic on their non-angelic body was tremendous. The more they used their magic, the shorter their lives—by orders of magnitude. A single major glamour could knock a thousand years off of a life. So, using their magic became a matter of necessity. Their children, the six tribes as they became, were the first to develop what you might understand as genetic limitations as a form of natural balance. Instead of the power to literally pluck a star from the heavens and hold it in one's hand, they wielded less raw magical power but healed faster. Prana, mana, rakta, and maya were not yet understood concepts. There was just magic—Life, Blood, and Death. Subsequent generations, up until the Great Reckoning, saw further genetic adaptations as the tribes began to separate by ability and then began to breed intentionally to hone those powers. Seers began to use more mana, the power of dreaming, the power of sight, and creativity. The greater requirement of mana meant their bodies had to learn to use more and draw more—which downline turned into shifters.

"Similarly, hunters and combat tribes prized physical prowess—quicker healing, better eyesight, greater strength, faster reactions. This is in the blood—the muscles, the fibers, the cells themselves. These became vampires."

"And mages and such became the fae," I cut in. "Where do you fall?"

"In between. I do not draw any one form of energy more than the other. I require them all in balance. Except perhaps blood—But then, a modern vampire is far more physically powerful than I am. Magic itself provides a natural increase in physical ability, which is why all immortals are faster, stronger, heal faster, and see better than mortals. My body draws mana and prana from the world around me. That is, I believe, the reason my powers are of such a large scope—I draw more and can store more. But I can only use it in direct proportion—I can't force a waterfall through a drinking straw." He hesitates. "My greatest weakness, if you must know, is claustrophobia. I cannot be indoors for very long, or I weaken swiftly. To be imprisoned for longer than a few years would kill me—years at most. More if I am allowed outside, less if I am in solitary confinement, away from the sky and sun and moon and stars."

"I can't imagine anyone being able to imprison you."

He laughs. "Well, thank you. It hasn't happened often, but it has. If I take enough damage, I am as vulnerable as anyone else. I just heal fairly fast, and as long as I can get outside and see the sun and feel the wind, I will heal and regain my powers and escape."

"I see."

"So now you know my weakness—that's a secret I've long held close, you know."

I look up at him, and I'm somewhat shocked to see something like worry, fear, or nerves on his face. I take his hand. "Your secret is safe with me, Aeon."

"I know it is." His voice is quiet—and when I steal another glance at him, the worry is gone.

"You said something a bit ago, and now I can't stop thinking about it," I tell him.

"And what's that?"

"A shower."

He grins. "Ask and you shall receive."

Thirty minutes later, we're in a hotel room. He paid with an AMEX black card, which he produced from some hidden pocket of his garment.

As we enter the room, I glance at him. "You have a credit card?"

He laughs. "You think I've existed for twelve thousand years without accumulating wealth?"

I frown. "Well, I suppose not." I gesture at him. "It's just…that outfit says 'ascetic monk warrior' more than it does 'wealthy playboy.'"

He laughs again, striding to the single king-size bed, where he divests himself of his belt, which he wraps around the sword, and then the outer robe, revealing a bare torso above black…leggings. Hose? Trousers?

His body is, unsurprisingly, rock hard, shredded, and mouthwatering. He's…well…he's so beautiful it's making my determination to ignore my stupid attraction to him that much harder to stick with.

I turn away.

"Have you ever watched any movies about spycraft?" he asks.

I sit on the edge of the bed, as far from him as I can get, and start taking off my shoes for the first time in…I have no idea. A long time.

"I mean…James Bond?" I answer.

He snorts. "Not what I mean. Regardless, my point is that I've tailored my approach to public identity after spycraft. I have many identities which I use in various parts of the world. Here, my identity is little more than a credit card and a fake passport. An excellent fake, but a fake." He laughs. "Well, all of them are fake, obviously. But I have money stashed all over the world. In banks, post office boxes, investments, and, in some cases, literal buried or hidden treasure. The world runs on money, Maeve. Wealth, no matter the era, is wealth, and wealth speaks. Wealth moves. It is a sad reality, in some ways, because the world would be better if we were all equal, but alas, that is not how the world works. So, I accumulate wealth wherever and however I can. Usually via legal means, although I have moonlighted as a pirate, brigand, and outlaw on occasion."

I toss my shoes and socks aside with a sigh of relief. "That feels amazing." I glance at him. "I bet you have some stories to tell, huh?"

He nods, shrugs. "Well, yes, I suppose I do." He removes his sandals and reclines on the bed. "Take your shower, Maeve."

It's the longest, hottest, most luxurious shower of my life, despite the mediocrity of the accommodations—it's not a particularly upscale hotel, but it's near the train station Aeon intends us to use, and we're not staying long. All that matters to me at the moment is that the water is hot and the stream powerful.

I wash and condition my hair and scrub my body. One thing I don't miss about being mortal is the body hair— no shaving of the legs or armpits. A weird side effect of immortality that no one told me—immortals don't have body hair. I've just been too busy to appreciate it, honestly.

I dry off, wrap a towel around myself, and exit the bathroom in a belch of steam.

"Feel better?" Aeon asks from the bed—his eyes are closed, hands folded on his diaphragm, feet crossed at the ankle.

He's never seemed so human.

My eyes rake over the sharp, inhumanly beautiful planes of his face, the high cheekbones and plump lips, the hard jaw, the broad shoulders…the anvil of his chest, and the carved blocks of his abs.

When my eyes go back up to his, he's looking at me. And the look in his eyes is…

Hungry.

There's no other word for it.

"Don't look at me like that, Aeon," I whisper.

"Then stop being so fucking breathtaking."

"I have mates."

"I know."

"No matter how I might feel, I can't go there with you."

"No?"

"No."

"Why not?"

I shake my head, swallowing hard—my damp hair flings side to side and sticks to my shoulders. His eyes roam my face, then drop to my thighs—the towel is small and ends at mid-thigh. I have to clutch it closed because it's not big enough to fully wrap around me and stay closed.

It gaps open at my side, showing him a whole hell of a lot of thighs and the side of my ass.

"I can't. I mated with Caleb, and it damn near killed Caspian. And the others. I can't take a new mate every time I vanish."

"Who said anything about a mate?"

I frown at him. "I'm not a casual kind of girl, Aeon. If you think I am, then you've taken the measure of me most incorrectly."

"Apologies. I did not mean it in that sense."

I snort and shake my head. "How else could you have meant it?"

He rises from the bed and stalks around the foot of it. Prowls toward me.

I back away from him and catch up against the wall. He stops in front of me, blocking out the room and everything else with himself. His eyes blaze purple—flare blue.

"Don't," I whisper.

"Don't what?"

"Seduce me."

"I'm not."

"Then what is this?" I breathe. "What are you doing?"

"There are things I haven't told you." He inches closer until his chest presses against my breasts, and I smell his sweet breath and the scent of sand and wind and pine trees and starlight. "Things about... you. And me."

"I have a feeling there's a lot you haven't told me."

"This is somewhat relevant to this current issue, however."

"What is it?" I ask.

He swallows, draws in a deep breath. Searches me with his eyes, which flare blue, subside to purple, flare blue. "I shouldn't tell you. Not until you have your magic back."

"Why?"

"It wouldn't be fair to you."

"Nothing about my life since Mom died has been fair. It's all been a constant stream of chaos and intensity and changes and surprises. So just tell me."

He doesn't answer immediately. Instead, he pinches a lock of my hair between his forefinger and thumb; his eyes flare a soft shade of blue, and he drags his fingers down the lock of hair from my scalp; where his fingers touch, the hair dries. A small, private smile ghosts across his lips as he touches my hair. His eyes scan and search my face, and all I see in his eyes is hunger. But even that is mostly hidden, as if he's doing his best to bury it but his hunger is so potent it cannot be contained.

He gathers my hair in his hand, and his eyes flare azure, and he passes my hair through his fist, and when it flutters back around my shoulders, it's perfectly dry.

And glowing white with power.

"What?" I breathe. "How?"

"Your power responds to mine."

I feel it—almost. A tingle in my belly, static electric shocks buzzing my fingertips.

"That's a thing?"

"With me, it is."

"Aren't you just full of surprises?" My voice is breathy, and dammit, all I feel is the boiling of need, of attraction.

I can't blame this on a mating bond. There's nothing magical about this. It's just plain old-fashioned lust.

He gathers my hair in his hand again, and its golden-white glow flares like a lightbulb being turned on. The sizzle in my belly becomes heat, impossible and wild. With his other hand, he cups my jaw. Unblinking, he stares into my eyes, and I cannot look away. The blue of his magic is fucking hypnotic, a blue so deep and complex it defies description, luminous and burning—almost…angelic.

Where he touches, my skin burns, tingles, and aches. The ache drives down into my belly, turns my nipples to diamond points, and makes my core pulse with desire.

I swallow hard. "Aeon…what aren't you telling me?"

"I don't want to. Not yet."

I catch his wrists—both of them, and I swear I can

feel the magic pulsing in his veins louder and harder than his heartbeat.

"Why?"

"It'll change things."

"So?"

"You're not ready for what it will become."

"How do you know?"

"You told me."

"That I'm not ready?"

His index finger traces my lips. I taste the salt of his skin and the tingle of his magic. It's intoxicating.

"For another mate."

"You said I'm not your mate."

"You're not." A heavy pause. His finger dips into the groove of my philtrum, down my lips to my chin, down my throat…breastbone…to the edge of the towel. "Yet."

"Yet?" I breathe, gulping.

He doesn't respond. His hands press against the wall beside my face, and his forehead touches mine, resting, leaning. His breathing is labored.

"Aeon?"

"At the end of the day, Maeve, I'm just a man. A strange one. A unique one." Thick, sharp pause. "A frequently lonely one. I've been alone, without a friend, without a companion…without a lover…for a very, very long time. And you…Maeve. You tempt me, tease me, torture me."

"I…I'm not doing anything." My hands lift, and my fingertips find firm flesh, hard muscle.

"You don't have to." He circles my wrists with his hands, lifts them over my head, and pins them to the wall. "It's just you. The color and the scent of your hair. The soft cream of your skin. Your mind. Your magic. Your courage."

"Aeon…" I breathe, struggling weakly against his hold on my wrists.

"Don't speak," he murmurs. "Unless it's to tell me to go."

I can't. Damn me, I should. But I can't. My tongue is stuck to the roof of my mouth. My lips are parted, my breath short and quick. My skin tingles and my nipples are hard and achy.

"Your body, Maeve. Fully clothed you're a temptress. Like this, naught covering you but a flimsy bit of cloth?"

I try to speak, to think, to demur, to deny, but I can't. His luminous blue eyes blaze with wild potent magic, and I know the volcanic need taking over me like wildfire is all me—no magic needed to seduce me.

I'm doing fine all on my own, letting him seduce me, falling under the spell of his magic—but this magic is far more prosaic than any glamour. It's just him. His easy confidence. His swaggering power. He's masculine but gentle. He is confident in himself without being arrogant, even though he has every right to be.

"I've awaited you for ten thousand years, Maeve. Can you comprehend that? I was truly never mated to the Fates because I have always been promised to another." His eyes fix on mine, searing into my soul with truth so bright and bold and piercing that I cannot look away, can only lock my knees to stay upright under the assault of his eyes, the ravaging brutal beauty of his body, the hunger—the desperation—for me, written in every line of his face and every mote of light in his eyes. "That conversation with Galenova? She saw many things in that vision. She saw the prophecy of you—the WorldBreaker, the Once-Mortal-Queen. She saw your coming, your ascent to power, your struggles, your mates—the wolf and the vampire. But there was more. It wasn't in the prophecy as written. She never understood why, but she knew she couldn't write the other part down. She saw me, Maeve. She saw me walking in the desert. She saw me find you. She told me of this in whispers over a campfire of mage-flame on an island in the Aegean, in a time when mortals were still figuring out fire. She told me of you. Not the being who was prophesied, but the woman. My mate, she said." He goes silent, and his lips touch my temple, and sparks fly, threatening to set me alight, to ignite the dry tinder of my desire into a conflagration.

"Would you like to know what she said?" He asks.

"Yes." I breathe it, a bare whisper.

His eyes turn the blue of mage flame, of the steady burn of a gas range. The blue of stars. "'She will be your mate.'" His voice is not his—it is the soft, dry, raspy, papery voice of an old woman, singsong, musical, delicate, strong. "'You will wait for her, Aeon. An age, you will wait. Through storms and wars you will wait. Civilizations will rise and fall, and you will yearn for her. She will come to you in the desert. You will know her, and you will feel her. But even when you find her, Aeon, she will not be yours. You cannot take her as your mate until the binding is broken. She will not know you until the binding is broken. When the mate-bond is fulfilled, her stars will be complete, and the seven will be aligned.'"

The searing blaze of his eyes dims to merely blinding, and the hot wash of magic subsides.

"We are meant to be mated?" I ask.

A single nod.

"And you've known it all this time?"

Another nod.

"And you're just now telling me?"

Nod.

"Why?"

"I felt your birth nearly a century before it happened. Why, I don't know. Perhaps one of my ancestors was a seer, and I have a touch of the sight. I don't know. All I know is I knew your birth was imminent. I was drawn to you. If I had allowed it, I would have found your mother and watched and waited. I would have watched your birth. Your life. I would have stopped the experiment. I would have done many things which I knew I could not, should not do. So, I fled. I hid in the desert as far from you as I could get, and I stayed there. Where I knew you would come one day. I was wandering that desert for a hundred years, waiting for *you*, Maeve."

"Aeon," I gasp. "I…"

"I can't have you." He's tortured—I hear it in his voice. See it on his face. "Not yet."

"I don't understand."

He shakes his head. Keeping my hands pinned overhead, he nuzzles his nose against my ear, behind my ear, the line of my jaw. Inhales my scent.

He transfers both of my hands to one of his—and even with my powers, I couldn't break his hold. Yet, his touch is gentle. A word, a thought, and he'd release me.

One finger traces a line down my temple, past my ear, down my jaw, over my chest and to the edge of the towel once more.

"I've dreamed of you," he whispers. "Vivid dreams. I've seen your face in a thousand fantasies. I know you. I've tasted you, loved you, devoured you until you forget your name—a thousand, thousand times. I know your scent, Maeve. I know every curve of your body."

I gulp. Gasp. Shake. My knees are weak, and a hurricane of butterflies rages in my belly.

That touch, that finger, it carves over the towel, down my front, to my hip, where the towel gaps open. How it hasn't fallen, I don't know.

The blue glow of his eyes dims until his eyes are purple once more, and the towel drops to the floor.

He was keeping it in place with magic.

I'm naked.

Bare for him.

Bared to him.

He draws away, and his eyes devour my nude form— my breasts, my belly, my thighs, my sex. "My goddess. My mate."

"Aeon, fuck." I struggle against his hold, but it's futile. "Why? Why can't we…why can't you—what do the cuffs have to do with our mate-bond?"

"We can't be mated until you have your magic back."

"And you can't undo the cuffs."

"If I could, I would have already." Anger burns in his voice. "He designed the glamour with me in mind, I'm sure. He knew the blind spot in my magic—I can manage minor glamours or massive ones. There's nothing in between, and this glamour is exactly in the middle. Easy for any fae of middling power. Impossible for me. I've tried. Every moment since I saw you lying on the ground and knew you as the one I've so long awaited, I've racked my brain and searched my magic for a way to break the glamour." He shakes his head, a growl escaping. "I could terraform the whole planet with a snap of my fingers. Reduce the Himalayas to a bit of rock. Turn the Pacific into a puddle. Put a second moon in the sky. I could make every man, woman, and child, mortal or immortal, dance until they die. I've made every single mortal for two hundred and forty years forget an entire race of humans ever existed. But I can't break this stupid, ridiculous, absurd, gods-and-blood-be-damned glamour!"

"Aeon," I whisper again. "You're torturing yourself. And me."

"Fuck—I know!" he snarls, head hanging.

His eyes meet mine again, and the ravaged, wild, desperate need for me is all-consuming, a kind of madness in him. "Ten thousand years I've waited for my mate. And now I have you, here, in front of me, naked, wanting me— and I can't fucking have you."

"What would happen if—"

"Something bad. I don't know. Or perhaps nothing. Perhaps I simply can't—something would prevent us from mating. I don't know."

His hands rest on my naked hips, and where he touches me, I burn. I feel his breath on my skin, his eyes on my breasts.

He sinks to his knees. He grips my hips in both arms, and his forehead rests on my navel. His hands slide around to my buttocks, and my breath stutters at his touch there.

"Aeon, please. Don't torture us this way."

His head rolls against my belly—a shake of his head. "One kiss. One taste."

"Aeon…"

He looks up at me with pained purple eyes, his face savaged with need so fierce it frightens me. His chest rises and falls with heavy breaths as if the effort to restrain himself is physically draining. His hands slide to my hips once more, to my belly. My breath catches in my lungs. I watch his hands inch upward, higher and higher. A gasp slips past my lips as his hands cup my breasts and lift, fingers caressing the soft skin, thumbs brushing over my erect nipples.

Without taking his eyes from mine, he brings his lips to my navel. Kisses.

Another kiss, an inch lower.

"Aeon?" It's a fraught, breathless whisper.

"One taste, my mate, my moon and stars."

"We can't. You said—"

"I know. But how can I not? I'll die without you now that I've found you. One taste of your beauty, it's all I ask."

Thoughtless within the spell of his words, his presence, his need, I've kept my hands overhead as if still pinned there. Now I remember them and bury them in his hair.

It's all the permission he needs.

His mouth goes to my sex and I feel his hot breath and the wet search of his tongue along my folds. He flicks his tongue against my clit, and I scream, head flinging back, eyes closing. I arch, and press myself against his mouth.

Scream.

Blue glow floods the room, and heat blisters through me. Sensations, already heightened, become well-nigh unbearable. Every flick of his tongue sends rockets of orgasmic bliss through my body. Each cup and caress of my breasts makes the hot line between my nipples and clit sing and sear. The rub of his face against the tender silk of my inner thighs is madness. The hot huff of his breath is wild intoxication.

"Aeon," I breathe.

He only growls against my sex in response. A pinch of my nipples makes my knees quaver and give out, and I feel magic hold me up. His mouth works faster and faster, with ever more ravaging desperation, until I'm dipping at the knees and screaming through gasps and knotting my fingers in his hair and feeling an orgasm welling up inside me like magma inside a volcano.

Wind swirls around us, my hair fluttering—I can see its glow merging and clashing with the blue of Aeon's magic. The walls around us fade and there's only darkness and nothingness and us, his mouth, his hands, and my body. I feel stars crash past me, hear the god-scaled roar of their flames, and something titanic coils around us and I feel its hunger and sense its fear, and it flees. Planets and galaxies rage around us, flung past and soaring above, and his tongue drives me to madness, and my orgasm goes nova within me, and I lose myself in the screaming heat and the smashing ecstasy.

For a split second, I feel them—my mates. Alistair, Caspian, Fin, Caleb, and Stirling. I feel their minds and their souls, and their bodies, and I know they feel me, feel this, and I feel their relief and confusion and worry and joy and need and anger and love, above all love, love so potent and fierce and wild it dissolves all else until there's only love, the touch of mind to mind the sweetest caress.

The universe twists in on itself and the walls revolve around us and my butt and shoulders settle on the bed and Aeon is above me and his skin and muscles are hot and hard under my hands and I grasp his manhood over his clothes and I find his mouth—I kiss him. He tastes like

me, like my sex, and like the stars themselves—life and fire
and wonder and time.

I find flesh and the waist of his pants and dig under
and grip his naked erection and it's hot and thick and huge
and mine—

He rips himself away with a savage snarl. "FUCK!"

Gasping, panting, dizzy and trembling and still shaking from the orgasm, I pry my eyes open to see Aeon across
the room, raggedly gasping, hunched over, hands on his
knees, shoulders slumped.

"Aeon?"

He shakes his head. Holds his hand out, palm to me. A
shred of blue smears across his eyes, and his robe, belt, and
sword blur, suddenly in two places at once, and then he's
shrugging into his robe, winding the belt around his waist.

"Aeon?"

His eyes flick to me, and he takes a step toward me,
reaching. Stops, shaking from head to toe. "Ten thousand
years," he breathes. "And I must wait yet more." His eyes
close softly, slowly. "I need a moment, my goddess."

Before I can say a word, he draws his sword and slices
horizontally through the air—blue magic flares and I see
The Dreaming. He lets the cut turn him in a pirouette, and
he dances through the gap, somehow gripping the edge
of reality and yanking it shut behind him like a door—
the slice, spin, step through, and closure are all a single,
fluid motion.

I gape and then lurch to my feet, staggering across the
room to the window. I'm just in time to see him emerge on
the sidewalk below, naked blade resting on his shoulder.
He rakes a hand through his hair. Looks up and sees me.

My goddess. I almost hear the words in my head—perhaps I do.

I stare down at him. Trembling, knees quaking, I hold his eyes as the blue fades to purple.

I look down at the star tattooed on my chest, from whence the lines of my mate bond radiate.

The center, bare of ink before, glows with faint, dim white light.

And I know what will happen when Aeon and I mate.

The bond will be complete.

The seven will be aligned.

CHAPTER 21

THE TRAIN ROCKS GENTLY FROM SIDE to side. I'd expected to hear a steady click-click-click, but the cars are so well insulated that the sound, if it happens at all, is too faint and muffled to hear anymore.

We've been on one train or another for three days and counting. Our first leg was from Tashkent to Samara, Russia—a journey of over forty-eight hours nonstop. It was breathtaking, rugged, wild, and everchanging. Over mountains and through valleys, lowlands, and highlands, past villages where life probably hasn't changed much in centuries and towns where modernity has caught up to some degree. I don't recognize any of the cars. The languages on street signs and storefronts gradually shift to being largely Cyrillic, and then entirely.

Aeon spends most of the trip meditating—eyes closed, sitting upright with his hands on his knees, chin on his chest. His breathing slows until he only takes one breath every thirty seconds. No one, at any point, questioned the giant sword on his hip or looked askance at his unusual garb; when I ask, he shrugs.

"A mask," he answers. "Somehow, the glamour in those cuffs prevents you from seeing the mask or any evidence of the magic." A shake of his head. "He really outdid himself with those, I must admit. A viciously clever bit of magic."

"Hard to appreciate when it's affecting you," I say.

All I get is a nod and a shrug.

We arrive in Samara in the middle of the night, with the next leg not leaving till the following morning.

"There's nowhere to go," Aeon informs me. "We don't need sleep, so there's no point wasting time finding a hotel."

So we pass the time in the station on hard plastic seats, with the lights overhead flickering intermittently. A bored clerk behind the ticket window watches something on his phone, the volume up, no earbuds—the chatter and laughter and shouts in Russian soon become merely background noise.

Aeon resumes meditating. His version of sleep, I suppose.

With nothing else to do, I attempt meditation as well. More accurately, I turn my attention inward. Look for any hint of magic, any suggestion of the glamour Aeon claims is blocking my access to my magic.

It takes a long time and a headache-inducing amount of concentration, but I reach a point where I can *almost* feel a faint tingle of something in my belly. I can't see anything, but I know the touch of magic. I know the effervescence of it in my veins. It's there but so faint it's essentially undetectable. Funny, though: the harder I focus on feeling it, the more my fingers tingle, as if they've been asleep and are waking up—pins and needles tickling and tripping beneath my fingernails and around my knuckles and making my palms itch.

Here, I see few signs of the larger chaos in the world. The riots haven't come this way. I've not seen a single magical person, or at least not anyone open about it.

"Are there no immortals in this part of the world?" I ask.

Aeon's eyes remain closed. "Of course there are."

"There's no fighting, no riots, no mobs hunting down immortals."

"It will come here, eventually. Such things take time to spread from the large western cities to places like this, remote and largely disconnected from the goings on of the wider world." He pauses. "It's why I like places like this. Peace lingers here. Lives are simpler. Harder, in many ways—and in ways that, if I'm being brutally honest, I don't think you can understand. But, simpler."

"And you can understand, can you?"

His eyes slide open. "Of course not. I have spent much time in remote regions, living with the locals. So, in that sense, yes, I do understand. But I also cannot because I can leave whenever I wish and begin a life somewhere else. For the local mortals, this is the only home they and their ancestors have ever known and will ever know and have no such luxury."

"If you had to pick one life to live, and that was it, forever, what would you choose?"

He stares at me. "That's like asking me which finger is my favorite. I'm rather attached to them all." A snort and a shake of his head. "I have lived countless lives, Maeve. I spent an entire human lifetime—a long one, a hundred years—as a fisherman on the Isle of Skye. I lived in a stone hut and saw no one for months at a time. That was delightful. The sea, the sky, the storms, the solitude? Just me and my boat, the nets, the seals and the whales and the birds?" His smile is calm and wistful. "It was lonely but lovely."

"Have you ever taken a mortal lover?"

He stares into nothing for a long time. "Yes. When I was young—toward the end of my…second century? Third? She was a Neanderthal. But you must understand that mortals completely misunderstand what their earliest ancestors were like. Dress her in modern clothes with a modern haircut and makeup, and you'd be hard-pressed to know the difference. Facial structure, a bit. Gait and posture—but those are effects of lifestyle as much as physiology. She was wonderful. Caring. Affectionate. Peaceful and gentle. Animals of all kinds were drawn to her. Wild deer would approach her and eat out of her hand. Birds would land on her shoulders. Mice would make nests near our bed. We didn't share a language, but it didn't matter. We communicated through sign language, which was her primary language anyway. I found her injured and left behind by her tribe. I healed her and ended up staying with her. She brought me peace. Our cave was small and warm. We hung furs on the walls and spread them on the floor. She made a kind of broom out of a branch and rushes and kept the floors free of dirt. I gave her a small knife as a gift and taught her to whittle. Her favorite way to pass the evenings was to whittle animals out of wood."

He reaches into a pocket of his robe and produces a carving. It's small enough he can close his fist around it. The wood, probably once pale and almost white, has been stained by the ages that have passed and by the oils of his hands. It's a squirrel, balanced on its hind legs, an acorn in its paws, bushy tail arched high and drooping low. It's a stunning work of art, full of intricate detail.

I gasp when he reverently places it on my palm. "My god, Aeon. It's incredible."

He nods. "It is." A sigh. "I have carried that with me ever since. It reminds me of her and the time I spent with her. Fifty years. I avoided all magic except for the mask that made me look less elvish and more human, and to age myself along with her. I loved her very much."

"What was her name?" I ask, my voice quiet.

"Agana. At least, that's what I called her. I think her actual name was much longer and meant something like 'She Who Wanders The Sky.'" His smile is private, burgeoning with memory. "She was a dreamer. She would sit at the entrance of our cave and just watch the sky. The clouds, the birds. She was fascinated by it." He swallows hard. "When Agana was on her deathbed, moments from her last breath, I took her into the sky. I summoned the wind and let it carry us up into the clouds. I held her and showed the place where we lived from a bird's perspective. Her last breaths on this earth were filled with wonder as she finally saw what she had spent her whole life dreaming of."

My eyes burn. "That's beautiful, Aeon."

"After that, no more mortal lovers. It's too hard." A ragged sigh. "I wouldn't trade away those years for anything, but I wouldn't live through her death and the grief I felt afterward for anything, either."

Samara to Moscow, another thirteen hours. Moscow is enormous, and much warmer than I expected. It's fast-paced and a place of contradictions. Elaborate architecture, new buildings and old, wealth, laughter, arguments, and kindness and rudeness.

Here, the conflict does exist. I see a fae, unmasked, marching down the sidewalk, being trailed by a swarm of shouting, cursing teenagers. The fae, a younger male, ignores them even when they begin throwing stones and bricks and water bottles and old food—he has a shield up, and the detritus bounces off, which only infuriates them more.

I see a car burning in an alley.

A troop of soldiers marches past, armed and uniformed and stern—a coven of vampires, huddled in the shadows of a tall high-rise, vanish in a blur at the sight of the soldiers.

Aeon brings me to The Red Square with the Kremlin and St. Basil's Cathedral with its bulbous spires and soaring minarets and the vast expanse of open space where so much history has occurred.

Moscow to Prague—it's a complicated journey with a lot of stops and transfers. Another full day.

We are on a train pulling into Prague's Main Station. The train pulls to a stop under a high, soaring tunnel of latticework metal and glass. Mortals scurry off and away—fearful, furtive. Gunfire echoes, staccato chattering, and isolated rifle cracks. Something explodes in the distance with a whump.

"Amazing that the trains are still running with all this going on," I say, as we follow the crowd into the station's lobby.

"Europeans are very serious about their trains," Aeon says. "They'll be the last thing to stop running."

I wish I had more time and that I was visiting this city under different circumstances and at a different time. It's incredible. Bridges and buildings were built by artisans who took pride in their work and built things to last. Narrow, winding avenues and quaint streetside cafes. Window flower boxes hanging from brightly colored apartment buildings open directly onto the street.

Alas, however, the trip from the train station is a chaotic blur—Aeon manages to snag a taxi despite the crush of humanity all trying to find one. He rattles off an address in Czech, and the taxi driver—an older male wearing sunglasses despite the gloom of the early morning hour—nods.

As we're pulling to a stop with a noisy squeal of brakes, the driver glances around furtively and then removes his sunglasses to reveal a pair of void-black vampire eyes.

He says something in Czech.

"He wants to know if you're her," Aeon translates. "The Queen."

The driver is twisted in place, one arm along the back of his seat, searching me with his eyes.

"What do you sense in him?" I ask.

Aeon shrugs. "Curiosity. Fear. Hope."

"Then tell him that I am she."

Aeon relays my words. The driver's eyes widen, and he reaches for me with one hand. Speaks in rapid Czech, my hand in his.

"He blesses you by the old gods and the new, and by old blood and the new. He says you are a beacon of hope for immortals. He has no hate for the mortals, but only wishes to live in peace and harmony with them." Aeon pauses, listening, and then continues translating. "Your mate, Alistair, has called for many of the old ones, like him, to join your growing court in England, and he wishes to travel there, but his coven has chosen to stay here, in Praha, where they have lived for many centuries." Another pause. "He says the whole world is watching as your people build The Enclave. He wishes to ask you for a blessing."

My throat is thick. "A...a blessing?"

Aeon nods. Holds my eyes. "Correct."

"What kind of blessing do I give to a vampire?"

He glances at the ceiling. "Recite something—anything. Put your hand on his shoulder. I know of something. I'll tell you what I said after."

The first thing to come to mind is "Mary had a little lamb," but I discard that. I wrack my brain.

And then...my fingers tingle. My palms itch. And

something bubbles up in the back of my mind and trickles into my mouth.

"May the blood guide you. May shadows comfort you. May the sun hide its face and the night last forever. May your death be swift and your life eternal."

Aeon's eyes betray his surprise, but he hides it swiftly and relays my words. The vampire covers his mouth with his hand, visibly moved. He kisses my hand, and then pricks the ring finger of his right hand with his fang and extends the digit to me, blood welling at the tip.

Panicked, I look to Aeon for help. He clamps a hand, out of sight of the driver, on my thigh. He closes his eyes to hide the flare of blue, and I feel a surge of something rush through me—cold, or hot, swift, or sluggish…it's hard to understand, let alone explain. I feel my fangs lengthen. I prick my finger, the ring finger of my right hand, and extend it to him in turn.

He pinches my finger gently and guides it to his mouth and smears my blood along his lower lip. I mirror his action, recognizing the ritual in the gesture, even if it's new to me.

He licks his lip, and his eyes pulse once, revealing pale brown irises for a brief moment before they revert to blackness. I lick my own lip and feel sparks burst in my skull— the moment Aeon releases my thigh, the sparks cease, and my fangs retract and the bizarre sensation vanishes.

Aeon produces a wad of cash from somewhere, but the driver shakes his head, chattering excitedly in rapid Czech. His eyes are smeared with bloodtears as we exit the car. He waves at us, shouting what I assume are farewells.

When he's gone, Aeon shoots me a puzzled frown. "How did you know that blessing?"

My turn to shrug. "Mother's Spirit."

He nods thoughtfully. "Even through the glamour holding your magic hostage, a mother's love wins."

My eyes, already hazy from the old vampire's emotional words to me, sting with tears. "So it would seem," is all I can manage. I clear my throat and wipe my eyes with the heels of my palms. "Where are we?"

"Visiting an old friend—a mutual acquaintance shared by Andreas and I."

"You know Andreas?"

A shrug—so many damn shrugs. "Not directly. We both knew people who knew each other. This was during the Greek war for independence. I was posing as a war correspondent for a Greek newspaper attached to the unit he served in. We met a few times, briefly, but he—" here, Aeon gestures at the building in front of us, a graceful, lovely, old apartment block, "was close to both of us. He was the commanding officer to whom I reported, and Andreas reported to him as well. After the war, the three of us exchanged letters—or, well, Andreas and I both exchanged letters with Leonidas, who tended to share with us what the other was writing. It was always an odd triangle."

"When you say Leonidas," I hedge, "You don't mean…"

Aeon laughs. "Gods, no. Not *that* Leonidas. *He* was a mortal, and he did indeed die with his men at Thermopylae."

"I see." I see a curtain twitch. "And this Leonidas can help me?"

A nod. "He is a powerful glamourworker, one who specializes in what you might call magical lockpicking."

"Well, then, let's get on with it. I need my magic back."

My fingers buzz and my palms itch as if I've got a handful of old television static. "The longer I'm blocked, the worse it'll be when I get it back. I'm starting to feel like I might explode." It's not something I've realized until I say it.

Aeon winces, nods. "I can see it building up, as a matter of fact."

Aeon presses a button on the intercom labeled "L. Demetriou."

A short silence, and then a rough, gruff voice. "It has been a long time, Iannis."

"It has," Aeon returns. "I need your help."

"You or the girl?"

"The girl."

"I saw the block from the window. It's a real nasty fucker."

"It is. And she's no mere girl."

"I know this too." The intercom buzzes. "Come up."

The stairs are narrow and steep but clean and well-lit. We ascend to the third floor; a window facing the street lets in sunlight, bathing the faded and well-worn but clean gray carpet, muted ochre walls, and plaster tray ceiling with a line of ornate plaster rosettes marching down the hallway.

Dust motes swirl and dance in chaotic, mathematical orbits in the ray of sunshine. A door at the far end of the hallway creaks open.

Aeon and I meet Mr. L. Demetriou at his door. He's a tall, broad, barrel-chested fae with a vicious scar running vertically down the left side of his face; the scar claimed his eye, and in the socket is a miniature sun—a glowing ball of white mage-fire. His hair is salt-and-pepper, cropped to a military high-and-tight. He wears dark-wash blue jeans and a faded gray T-shirt. A short sword is buckled on his left hip, and a gargantuan revolver on his right.

He grins, showing white teeth. "Iannis. I've not seen you since—when was it?"

"Italy, 1945."

The old soldier—for that's what he is, from head to toe, every inch a career warrior—guffaws, clapping Aeon on the shoulder with a huge hard paw. "Ahh, yes! Roma, my old lover. We drank a barrel of old red wine and told fish stories."

Aeon laughs. "I've not been that drunk since, old friend." He wraps an arm around my shoulders and guides me closer to the old soldier. "Leonidas, it is my great honor to introduce to you Maeve Sparrow, Once-Mortal Queen and the WorldBreaker. Also of note, her mother was Andreas Bouras's mate."

Leonidas assesses me with frank, open hazel eyes… or, eye. Although, the mage-flame eye does seem to regard me as well, and to move in synch with the other.

"Andreas Bouras, eh? A good man, a great soldier, and a better friend."

I smile, nodding. "He's like a father to me. He's in Manhattan, leading the army there fighting the Mortal Federation."

Leonidas nods. "So I've heard. The whole world watches the events there. The recent victories bode well, and the reports I'm hearing of advances in magic-technology hybridization give us all reason to hope."

"I've been…involuntarily out of touch," I say. "I'd like to hear what you've heard."

"There have been reports of your disappearance but no official announcements." He slaps the doorframe. "Here

I am, leaving you standing outside like the mannerless boor that I am. Please, come in."

He ushers us in. His apartment is small and tidy, befitting a soldier. The walls are white, adorned with clusters of photographs arranged by period: daguerreotypes and tintypes of Leonidas in various uniforms, posed and candid—I don't know enough of uniforms to know when the photographs were taken and where; there are early black and white photographs, heavily shadowed and grainy from what appears to be World War One; better photographs of him with a unit from World War 2 and/or Korea; color photographs from Vietnam, the first Gulf War, somewhere in Europe…he appears to have fought in just about every armed conflict there's been in the last couple hundred years.

His appearance is consistent through them all—a mortal male in his forties, grizzled, hardened, scarred, with an eyepatch and short hair; his mask doesn't change much, it seems, other than his ears and to age him down.

There's a threadbare brown couch, a low, scratched oak coffee table with an ashtray, a thick paperback novel open face down, and a half-empty bottle of ambrosia. A bookshelf opposite the couch—where a TV would be—is overstuffed with a myriad of books of all subjects, sizes, and conditions. A cell phone rests on the arm of the couch where he was sitting and reading before we arrived.

"It ain't much, but it's home, for now," Leonidas says, noting my appraisal.

I gesture at the array of photographs. "Quite a story told, there."

His eyes scan the photographs. "Sure is. Fought in a

lot of wars." He turns back to me. "You, my girl, have a serious problem."

I hold up my wrists. "I certainly do. Ae—Iannis tells me you can help?"

He frowns, and his good eye flares as he uses magic to peer at me. He hums and nods, scans me from head to toe, and then takes my hands in his and turns them palm up, palm down, edge up, edge down, and then runs his fingers around the circumference of one cuff and then the other.

His eye dims to normal, and he releases my hands. "This is a nasty bit of business." He frowns again, more in puzzlement. "I recognize the work, but I can't place it."

"Zirae," I answer.

He nods. "Ah, yes. I knew it looked familiar. But even for him, this is vicious."

I shrug. "He really hated me, I think. Or feared me, or both."

"Hated? Past tense?"

"Past tense. I killed him. These damned things were the last thing he did on this earth. And damn him to all the hells for it." I can't help a growling sigh. "He hijacked my spell, dragged me through some portal, and dropped me in the Gobi. We fought, I killed him, and as he died, he slapped these fucking things on me. I can't access my magic at all—I can't even feel it. Even my vampiric nature is suppressed—no bloodlust, no sun sensitivity, nothing. I'm almost mortal, except I don't need to eat, sleep, or rest."

He nods. "Yes. It's a hell of a glamour. I doubt I'll be able to break it on my own—Zirae's powers were far beyond my own, and this…this is a work of art, as much as I hate to admire anything about that venomous old scorpion."

"So you can't help?"

He bobs his head to one side. "Now, I didn't say that did I? I said I can't do it on my own. I'll try, but my feeling is that you'll have to jump in and finish it off. I think I'll be able to interrupt it long enough for you to grab some prana and finish the fucker off."

"How does it work?" I ask.

He takes one of my hands again and draws a line from my hand up my arm to my shoulder and back down to my heart, never quite actually touching me anywhere but where his hand holds my wrist.

"The Three Sisters and the Fourth God flow inside you within your blood." He tilts his head to one side. "Not *in* your blood, exactly, but close enough—it flows along the same channels. A regular mage-cuff operates on two levels: one, a glamour to prevent the cuff from being unlocked. It is essentially a very simple but effective ward. The second part of the cuff is an insertion point for the magic, allowing the glamour, which is, in essence, a parasite, to enter your body and do its dastardly work on your magic."

"I understand," I say, knowing I sound bitter. "I was a prisoner of the Tribunal for several months. I broke out of the mage-cuffs, so I am intimately familiar with how they work."

He regards me with shock and respect. "You *broke* out of mage-cuffs? It was thought to be impossible."

"For a Primi, yes. I am no ordinary immortal, however. It still required…a lot of power."

He taps the bracelet around my wrist. "This is different from a mage-cuff but operates on a similar level. There is a glamour—single use only—that closes the clasp, fuses it, and makes it impervious to physical manipulation. A nuclear bomb could go off in this room, and those things would be untouched."

"So I discovered," I say, wry and bitter.

"I imagine," he says. "The insidious part is how it affects your magic. Instead of introducing a parasitic glamour that attacks your magic much the same way white blood cells attack a disease, these devious little bastards are much simpler and much more elegant. They produce a glamour that acts like a dam at your wrists. Essentially, they halt the flow of magic, damming it at your wrists. The magic still exists, but without the flow, you can't feel it, can't see it, can't use it. But your basic nature cannot be changed—you are not a mortal. The bloodlust, the prana hunger, all that is a byproduct of the magic on your body. Without the flow, those things cease as well."

"So what's the plan, then?" I ask.

"Simple. I should have enough juice to temporarily block or interrupt the glamour in the cuffs. You'll have to act fast, though—and I mean *fast*. You have to be ready to strike the moment you feel your shit turn on, got it?"

I nod. "I understand."

He moves to the couch and sits, patting the seat beside him. He looks at Aeon. "Iannis, you're on containment. The magic in her needs to flow. It needs expression. I have no way of knowing what will happen once we break this thing. She could detonate, go feral, who fuckin' knows. So you gotta make sure whatever happens stays in this room."

Aeon nods. "I understand." His eyes flare blue. "We are warded. You may begin."

Leonidas takes my hands in his, his huge paws circling my wrists with the bracelets under his fingertips and palms. His good eye flares white, and his magical one blazes brighter than ever—his skin glows a searing white, and I feel heat surge through me.

My fingers tingle like mad and my palms itch worse than ever.

"Be ready," he murmurs.

Silence.

Heat increases, feeling like pressure on my hands.

The tingling and itching spread to my forearms, my biceps, my shoulders—and then, all at once, scorching blistering heat turns my heart into a sun gone nova, pounding with a raging fire that surges through my veins, burning me up from the inside. It blazes down to my toes and up to my scalp, my eyes, my hair, my skin, my fingernails. Everything burns.

Someone is screaming—me.

And then I feel it—my magic. It's a blessed, beautiful burst of bliss, a sweet rush of familiar strength; my nostrils are filled with the scent of sunlight and honey. I look within and see my magic, but now it's not just a boiling ocean, it's…a tsunami, a fifty-foot-high storm surge of wild power, frothing and smashing and churning.

I strike with all possible speed, throwing my entire mental being into the oceanic maelstrom. I fill myself with prana, suck in and absorb, drowning myself until I'm glutted and leaking with raw power.

Milliseconds have passed—they feel like hours.

I send my attention to my body, and immediately I see the glamour. It—or they, because the two bracelets function separately—appear as opaque, white-glowing discs bisecting my hands at the wrists. The flow of energy slams against the barriers and reverses flow, eddying at the dams, where it appears dull, lifeless, and sickly, blazing brilliant and blinding in my chest. Too bright.

Which is when I fully comprehend the dastardly deviousness of Zirae's cuffs. They are a death sentence. Worse, they turn me into a walking time bomb—each day that passes, the clogged, dammed flow of magic congeals and compresses and coagulates in my veins, much like clogged arteries causing an eventual heart attack. Only, instead of merely dropping dead, I'll involuntarily vent burst.

A being with the sheer amount of raw energy inside, like me? I could very well level an entire city.

"*HURRY*!" I hear Leonidas say through gritted teeth. "I'm losing it!"

I smash the glamours with a twin burst of prana; the glamours spiderweb but hold. I hammer them again, and again, and again, harder each time.

I feel Leonidas's grip on the part of the glamour hiding my magic from me weakening, slipping, causing my access to slacken. The glamours are nearly broken, chipped, and cracked.

With a last desperate assault, screaming, I lash out with every ounce of power I have left. The strikes hit as I feel Leonidas lose his hold, and the gate slams down and my magic vanishes once again.

For a moment, I'm back to what I was—powerless, helpless, and doomed.

I open my eyes—Leonidas is slumped forward on the couch, hands on his knees, panting as if he's just sprinted a hundred yards all out.

"Did—did it work?" He gasps.

"I…" I start, about to tell him it didn't.

But then…a tingle in my fingers. An itch at the bend

of my elbow. A tremble in my belly. A flutter in my chest as my heart lurches.

A burning ache flares in my chest and my wrists are gripped by pulsing pangs of agony. The bracelets glow red-hot, and the scent of burning flesh fills the small apartment.

I can't breathe. My muscles twitch and contract involuntarily—seizures.

My eyes shutter closed, and searing white light blasts my eyelids. A guttural sound scrapes out of me, becoming a gurgle and then a hoarse rasp.

And then—the world goes utterly white.

Silent.

Still.

White becomes black, a swift slide down the spectrum of visible light. Heat becomes cold, and I'm swallowed by nothingness.

CHAPTER 22

"Maeve?" The voice is low, worried

Light filters through my eyelids, and then Aeon's face appears above me. For a moment, my mind is vacant, thoughtless, emotionless.

And then it all comes back, all at once.

I blink once, twice, three times.

I smell something—blood. It's…intoxicating. Ocean brine, hot sand, cinnamon. Saliva floods my mouth, and I feel my fangs prick my lips, and a ripping, vicious snarl rattles my chest and rasps my throat.

"Careful, Iannis." Leonidas, wary. "That's bloodlust if I've ever seen it."

"Yes." His eyes are purple, watchful, brimming with emotion. "You're okay, Maeve. It worked."

Hunger.

Thirst.

Need.

My vision narrows, black obscuring everything around me except Aeon. I can almost see his blood pumping in his veins, and I *need* it.

Bloodlust is all-consuming—I have no thoughts but thirst, no instinct but to drink. To take. To taste.

"Blood," I seethe, my voice inhuman and dark and boiling with violence.

"Maeve, I know you—" Aeon begins.

It's too late.

I feel my body tense—I feel something hard beneath me…the floor? And then I'm airborne, body lightened as my muscles propel me upward. I slam into Aeon, and the scent of blood is all-consuming—brine and sand and cinnamon. His muscles are firm and his skin is warm and everything in me is starved for him. My legs hook around his waist and my hands claw at his arms and chest and shoulders, and the *thrum-thrum-thrum* of his blood in his veins is a deafening, delicious symphony of tympani, pounding, pounding, pounding in my ears.

My sex is flooded with the liquid heat of my need, my desperation for him, my mate, my bond. I must taste him, my lust feel him, must know him, must entwine him into my being, my self, my body, my soul.

I lash his throat with my tongue and I feel him tense all over and hear him groan—his cock unfurls, hardens, and presses against my core through our clothing. His hands cup my ass with a brutal grip that has me spasming with arousal, and I taste magic in the air, his magic, Leonidas's, mine, but mostly Aeon's.

I pierce his skin with my fangs and his blood surges into my mouth and fuck, it tastes exactly how it smells—complex and wild and sweet; cinnamon, brine, and sun-warmed sand.

I rip at his clothes as I drink. Hot solid flesh and rippling muscle fill my hands—chest, arms, abs.

"Maeve—"

Sweet hot blood—I'm insatiable.

His prana tastes much like his blood, and I pull at that too, great deep quaffs of his magical essence restoring my ocean's equilibrium, refilling its reserves.

More.

His hands push at me, pull at me, unbutton my jeans, rip at my shirt.

Fuck this.

I coat my body in prana and set it alight; mage-flame licks over my skin and turns my clothing to ash, leaving me naked. A cool shiver ripples down Aeon's body, and then he too is naked.

"Maeve—"

I've had enough blood that I can form coherent thoughts, even if I'm not entirely in control yet—now, I'm in the throes of a mating frenzy like no other, a need for Aeon so potent and undeniable I can't breathe until I have him, can't think until he's inside me.

"What?" I gasp, clutching his cock.

Gods and blood, he's well-endowed. Thick and

straight and long, pulsing with heat, rigid and iron-hard, silky skin slippery with precum.

"Are you sure you want this?"

"Want, no," I pant. "Need, yes."

"You said you weren't ready for another mate."

"I'm not." I stroke him, feeling him shudder, feeling his belly tuck in with each slide of my hand down his shaft. "But you're my mate. I know it. You know it. There's no choice. But also…" I force my eyes open and meet his—mine are white-gold and his sunlit Aegean blue. "I want you. I've wanted you since you saved me from the fucking desert. I don't know how my other mates will react, but we'll have to handle that later."

Aeon's eyes burst so brightly blue that I have to squint, and then there's a sense of movement, and a cushion of air beneath us, lifting us. I add mine to it, lightening my body, and we soar upward.

Endless blue sky surrounds us, a few puffy clouds here and there, and a quick glance down shows Prague laid out beneath us, and then I snap a shield around us, obscuring us in a white haze.

Aeon's mouth finds mine and his tongue lashes mine and his teeth nip at my lips, and his fingers find my sex. A touch, a tweak, a twirl, and I'm riding the edge in seconds, gasping his name and clinging to him.

"I need you, Aeon," I whisper into his ear, and he shudders.

I nestle his cock in my slit, and he groans, his mouth pressing against the side of my throat.

He pulls back. "Look at me, Maeve." I meet his eyes. "I've waited ten thousand years for this moment, my goddess, my mate. I won't rush it."

I cup his cheek. "Make me yours, Aeon. However you wish." He searches me. "I can sever the mate-link if you want out. You don't have to do anything you're not ready for."

"I didn't know that was a thing."

His eyes darken. His jaw tightens. "It has only been done a few times that I know of, but it can be done, and I know how."

"You'd do that? For me? After everything?"

"I've felt you across the years, my goddess. I told you, I think I have a touch of the sight because I have seen you. I knew when you were born. I saw your dreams—I saw you and the shifter circling each other in the Dreaming before you mated with him. I saw you and the vampires. I saw you in the Tribunal's mountain. I saw the child you lost. I see the love you share with your mates. I know you, Maeve Sparrow. The weeks which have passed are a drop in the bucket. We will love each other for a true eon—-an astronomical eon, meaning a billion years. I've seen it. I've seen our future. I've seen your belly grow with my child." A pause. "But yes, if it's what you want, I will sever the bond and let you go."

I hold his eyes, clinging to his neck with one hand and caressing his cheek and lips and eyebrows with the other. "An eon, with my Aeon." I thrust down to take him inside me, and my mouth drops open and my lips shudder as he fills me and stretches me to an aching burn. "Does that answer your question?"

He cries out in a hoarse voice as my pussy swallows his hardness and wraps around him, and he buries his face in the crook of my neck and clutches my hips where my thighs bend up to my waist, and he pushes me down onto his upward thrust.

I feel him drive home, our hips colliding, bellies touching, my breasts crushed flat against his chest. The shield is a smooth, cool, semi-solid surface beneath us. Aeon wraps my hair around his hand and yanks my head back and claims my mouth with rough, forceful possession, tongue invading, teeth slashing, a desperate hunger over-taking him. His fingers find my clit and press and swipe and circle between our bodies, sending me over the edge.

I come, hard and fast, quaking and spasming around him; I feel magic flare and taste it in the air and feel it rush-ing and tingling through me, and then I feel Aeon in my mind, feel him in my soul, feel him in my body. But this isn't the mating bond, not yet. This is something else.

My orgasm, instead of subsiding, only burns hotter, and my shaking turns to near-seizures, and my screams turn breathless, and he's driving up into me and each thrust sends me to a whole other plane of pleasure, ecstasy that peaks and peaks higher and higher with every union of our bodies.

"Aeon!" I whimper, too breathless to even scream, now.

"I…" he groans, arching, thrusting. "I have to let it go now, Maeve. I have to let go."

I bite his earlobe and squeeze around his cock as hard as I can and wrap my limbs around his hard lean body and meet his desperate thrusts.

"Give it to me, Aeon. Come for me."

"No, not—not that. Not yet." He releases my hair and cups the back of my head. "The memory-phage. I have to let it go, now."

"Do it."

"My magic might…flare up a bit."

"I trust you. Let go, Aeon. I can take everything you are."

He takes my mouth again, licking my lips and my teeth and biting and kissing. "No matter what you see, hear, or feel, just remember that you're safe. I've got you."

"I know."

He drives into me, slowing his pace to a lazy rolling thrust, tenderly cupping my nape, teasing my clit. "Let go of your magic. The shield, the wind, everything."

"Did I…did I hurt you with my bloodlust?"

He laughs. "Not at all. It felt amazing." He brushes a thumb across my lips. "Now. Let go of your magic and hold on to me."

I press my face into the hot smooth column of his throat, clinging to him with my arms and legs, letting him fuck me slowly, gently, lazily; I release all magic. The wind subsides and the shield dissipates and suddenly the globe is a plaything beneath us, continents and oceans and polar caps—we're miles high. I feel the icy bite of the thin atmosphere, but it feels good on my hot naked flesh.

We're falling. My stomach launches up into my throat, but I don't scream, or feel any fear—only perfect trust in Aeon.

I feel a bolt of energy pulse out of him—and then I see it, a shockwave of magic bursting out of him and racing around the earth at the speed of sound, maybe even the speed of light. It's hard to tell. It's there and gone, a white-blue-gold warping rippling line of magic sweeping out of Aeon and around the planet.

We hurtle earthward.

I cling to Aeon, gasping as each thrust pushes me to a higher plane of orgasmic bliss—each one heretofore unknown, each wilder and hotter and more intense than the last. Wind rushes past us, and we pass through clouds that feel like a cool wash of damp nothing.

And then Aeon roars and his skin burns beneath me, and his eyes blaze with such intense, searing blue light that even with tightly shut eyes I'm blinded. I feel magic detonate out of him. Force my eyes open.

Black thunderheads form beneath us, snarling and swirling and shot through with lances of lightning flashing blue, purple, yellow, white, and green.

We tilt downward and hurtle into the center of the storm, and rain lashes us and wind thrashes us and lightning sears and spears above and below and behind and before, yet nothing touches us, and thunder cracks and booms like a cannonade.

White light bursts and our downward fall is arrested.

Darkness all around, and crushing pressure. Aeon's eyes provide the only light: we're on the sea floor, and jellyfish pulse past and things move in the shadows beyond the eyelight. The sea floor is not sand or rock. Here are structures. A temple looms before us, cast in blue-white stark relief, sending sharp shadows slicing at odd angles away. A house, here. Buildings, everywhere, all kinds, ancient and fully intact.

We float amidst the ruins of the sunken temples of Atlantis, and Aeon makes love to me slowly, delicately, desperately. He kisses me, and we taste brine on our lips, and nothing can touch us. The cold is nothing, the pressure is nothing. There is only us.

Here, we mate in twisting throes, and my screams

of ecstasy send bubbles upward, and I cling to him and move with him.

I feel the mate-bond. I feel it building. Aeon touches my clit again and thrusts deep, and I come and come, and white heat shatters through me and light bursts behind my eyes and in my skull. I feel Aeon pull at my mana, my prana, my maya—he presses my thumb to my fang, loosening a cloud of red blood, and he brings my thumb into his mouth, taking my rakta as well, and I follow suit, pulling at his prana and licking his throat and sizing his jugular and drinking his blood.

MAEVE! His voice tolls within me, in my head and my heart and my soul.

AEON!

I am yours, and you are mine. He whispers this in my ear with his voice and speaks it into my mind, and my heart fills with him, my soul floods with him, and I feel him pounding into me with mad abandon, and I know he's about to come.

I squeeze around him and drink his blood and draw his prana and meet his thrusts with my own, and now I feel him stutter, shudder, and shake. Gasp. Groan. Shout. And then he unleashes inside me, a hot wet flood of his seed and my body accepts it and I taste him, see him, feel him.

I see his youth—riding horses and training with swords and strolling through palaces and blue skies and sand and heat and concubines and servants; his mother, a woman with white hair like his and eyes purple like his and brown skin and quick laughter and soft hugs; I see his whole life in a fast-forward blur, snatches of an endless parade of lives. I see him as a warrior, a healer, a trader, a peasant, a fisherman, a tanner, a scholar…too many lives to decipher or enumerate; I see Agana, She Who Wanders The Sky, a strong, lovely, powerful yet strangely delicate woman with a high forehead and deep-set eyes; I even see the gap in his memory, white space of nothing like an eyeblink; I see him fighting and running, wandering and loving, roaming the earth, forever restless. I see him, all of him, through the ages.

The sea shivers and a grumble echoes beneath us.

Atlantis is rising.

The sea churns and froths and bubbles, and all around us Atlantis rises from the depths. The pressure subsides and the crushing dark lightens, and then waves crash and thunder cracks and lightning spears and rain slants in a hurricane wind.

Aeon twists and puts his back to the wet stone steps of the temple, and there we worship each other beneath a frieze of ancient gods lost to history. The hurricane dissolves and the sun shines and warms us, and still we move together in perfect union, loving and writhing and twisting and arching. I cry his name, and thunder rolls out of a clear blue sky, and he whispers mine and lightning answers.

This is more than sex, more than mating, more than mere bonding.

I feel my chest spark with a burning line of sharp pain that steals my breath and I open my eyes to see the star at the center of my tattoo blaze with incandescent white light.

Aeon rolls us so my back is on the now warm, dry stone of the temple steps, braces himself on his hands beside my face, leans down to kiss me, and drives into me relentlessly, still hard after coming inside me, and I've come so many times I've lost count—to be honest, I barely notice the orgasms now, too lost in the wild magic of this moment.

He slashes his hand in front of us, and a black line appears in the air before us, and we're sucked forward into the black void of The Dreaming, and we stream through the nothing and cold and heat and then he slashes again and my breth catches.

We're all together, somehow—all of us: Alistair, Caleb, Aeon, Stirling, Caspian, Phineas, and me. I don't know where we are. The light comes from nowhere and everywhere, a diffuse warm light like an Edison bulb bathing us in a soothing amber glow. There's nothing around us, and it is somehow everything—a gray haze that swirls like fog, and through skirling eddies, I see London and Manhattan and Hong Kong and Paris and deserts and mountains and rolling prairies and pristine white snow lit into a million diamonds by a dawn sun.

"Maeve," Caspian whispers, his lips at my ear. "I thought I'd lost you."

"I know," I whisper back. "I'm sorry. Zirae—"

I'm still wrapped up in Aeon, shuddering at the edge of an endless orgasm, and Caspian nips the back of my neck and licks behind my left ear and then my throat my pulse point, and then he's drinking from me and I'm gasping and whimpering as I feel my mate, my love, my beloved Caspian swallowing my life and filling my soul with his essence.

Caleb is on the other side, nibbling my earlobe and caressing my ass—we're weightless or suspended in nothingness, I don't know and don't care; all I know is that Alistair is beneath me and Aeon is above me, framing me, and Caleb is on my right and Caspian on my left, Caspian drinking and Caleb touching and kissing everywhere his hands and mouth can find; Stirling guides me to sit up, and my hair floats around my head in a weightless halo, an impossibility that I do not question, and now Stirling and Fin are licking my breasts and their fangs are digging in and piercing and they're drinking from me and whispering my name in my mind and moaning as they drink.

Caleb moves behind me and his weight presses on my back and shoulders and his lips touch my ear and he whispers his love, and now magic provides all the preparation I need—he slides into me, filling me to bursting with his impossible cock, stretching me apart with pain that burns so beautifully and becomes purest pleasure as both entrances are plundered by my mates. I taste Alistair's cock and swallow it and his groan of relief is everything.

Aeon slides out of me and Caspian is there, taking his place and Aeon has my hair in his fist and he guides my mouth down Alistair's shaft and there's not enough of me for all of my mates, but damn me if I'm not gonna try.

Fin licks my wound closed at my breast and Stirling does the same, and I fill my hands with them and caress them to straining hardness and everything is in synch. Caspian thrusts in as Caleb pulls out and Alistair glides through my lips and Stirling and Fin push into my hands.

"Mine—" I gasp. "My mates. My everything."

I feel Aeon everywhere, in every movement, every taste of flesh every slide of skin, this place is him, somehow. I open my eyes and meet his and his joy is effusive and overflowing, his eyes blazing with magic and love and awe and contentment—he's in love with me, not just mated to my magic and by the Fates. Watching me be loved by and returning love to my mates is enough, more than enough—it fills him, completes him. He hasn't said it, but I don't need the words from him—I feel them in everything he does, everything else he says.

I'm overloaded by sensation, glutted on my mates. Caspian drives into me in time with Caleb, trading, alternating, and I rise to the cusp of orgasm and together we detonate, Caspian first and then me and then Caleb, and as the men find their release, they unite in their thrusts so I'm filled with them both at once, and they come, and it sends mine into a shattering of climactic ecstasy.

As Caspian finishes, a pulse of power bursts out of me—familiar, wild, potent.

It comes from my womb.

My eyes fly open and meet Caspian's; no words are needed. Bloodtears fill his eyes and trickle down his cheeks.

Time ceases, or has never been.

Phineas is beneath me, driving up into my sex, and Stirling is behind me, and everything else falls away but them—Stirling's calm cool depths and Phineas's wild strength. I feel them both in my soul and my heart and my body all at once and our whispers of love are silent and spoken and we twist together in the haze of everything and nothing everywhere and nowhere.

Magic washes and now it's just me and Alistair, as it is always with us. His sweet soft manner and kindness and intelligence fill me, and there are no words with him either, as no words are necessary with anyone—my mates all know me and this place reveals all.

I open myself as Alistair and I writhe together, and I show them all where I've been and what's happened—I give them access to my mind and everything I am—the fight with Zirae and the cuffs and the timeless time wandering the desert alone, and Aeon finding me. Our journey. Leonidas. Everything.

Alistair releases with a quiet gasp, his cheek against my ear.

Aeon has a bondmark tattoo as well. A blue line of ink, the blue of his eyes when they blaze with magic, running from the middle fingertips of each hand up his arms and down to his chest, to the star that all of us have, now filled in.

Wind blows.

A blue sky arches overhead.

There's grass beneath me. Sunshine.

Alistair's stomach is my pillow. Fin's head is on my left breast, Stirling on my right. Caspian lays beside me, our hands linked. Caleb lays perpendicular to me at my feet, my feet on his chest, his hands massaging and kneading. Aeon rests his head on my naked lap.

I feel and smell clean, as if I've bathed. I'm deliciously sore all over with reminders of our love.

But yet, we've been here in the grass forever, it feels like. Making love in a field, beneath the endless blue sky, cooled by a long breeze, warmed by the sun.

Laughter rings out somewhere.

I look down at Aeon. "Where are we?"

He smiles lazily, cockily. "Central Park."

"As in Manhattan?" I blink at him.

"Yes."

"How...wait, before *how*—where *were* we?"

He shrugs. "Hard to explain. A place I discovered... oh, about the time when the Christ walked the earth. It's a pocket between The Waking and The Dreaming. Out of time, out of dimension. It's a strange place, hard to access. I couldn't do it until I released the memory-phage."

"It's done then?" Alistair asks. "The glamour that erased memory?"

"Yes. It's done. It didn't *erase* memory, it just… blocked it. Changed it. It's not exactly a phage, more of a bastard version of one that doesn't devour memory, only consumes and holds."

I roll my eyes. "Your stories always have one more dimension to them that you didn't mention the last time."

"Old habit," he answers. "I may not tell the whole truth all the time, but I never lie. But, I will promise to do my best to tell the whole truth."

"I'd appreciate it. Lying by omission is still lying, in my book."

"Noted," he says, his voice wry.

"We cracked the energy problem," Caleb says. "Well, Elias and his team did."

"It works?" I ask. "Tell me! How?"

He just chuckles. "Elias will have to explain it. It's beyond me. Some clever combination of engineering and magic."

"And plumbing?"

He presses his thumb into the arch of my foot. "Almost there."

"And the Mortal Federation?"

A long pause. "Down, but not out," Caspian answers. "We drove them out of Manhattan, but they're still out there. Their numbers are way down—it turns out most mortals, once they are shown the truth, don't hate us. They're just afraid. Once they see that most of us aren't interested in harming anyone, the problem goes away."

"The damage is done, though," Stirling says. "Governments all across the world have collapsed. Infrastructure is crumbling. The world is watching how we set up the Enclave."

"Unfortunately, Stirling is right," Alistair says. "Things will not ever go back to anything like normal. We are responsible for establishing a new normal."

I glance down my body at Aeon again. "Did you actually raise Atlantis, or was that, like, a fever dream?"

His smile is amused and arrogant. "I did."

"Why?"

A shrug. "When I released the memory-phage, my magic returned to me all at once in a rush. It was a lot like holding a rubber band stretched out and then letting it go. It snaps back, yes? Same thing. I wasn't maintaining a spell that continuously ate memories; I was holding their memories at bay. Or, if you'd like to be pedantic, I was holding the *information* at bay rather than their memory's ability to remember our existence. The energy used in holding all that information at bay had to be redirected. I felt raising Atlantis would be better than leveling Athens or something, which was the other alternative."

I decide to address the elephant in the room. "I'd just like to say thank you to all of you for being so understanding and accepting of what happened with me and Aeon." I look at Caspian. "You in particular. I didn't go looking for anything."

Caspian only smiles. "I know. It was weird—you vanished into that portal or whatever it was, and we all knew it was Zirae. There was the fear that something had happened to you—meaning, the worry that you'd died. But we'd have felt it if you had, and we didn't feel that. Losing a bonded mate is not something you can mistake. So it became an exercise in trusting you. We knew—*I* knew—you'd come back in one piece. And then, suddenly, we were all transported into that pocket realm or whatever it was, and…" he frowns. "It's hard to explain. But the moment we saw you and Aeon, we understood. Even before you opened your memories to us, we understood. Or at least, I did."

Stirling tilts his head to kiss my sternum. "The fact that there was no bond-sickness sort of explained things, in a way."

"So, you're not jealous? Or upset?"

"It was mostly the timing, with Caleb," Caspian says. "I was bond-sick and forced to feel your pain and everything you went through without knowing what was happening and being unable to do a damn thing about it, and then you were feeling pleasure and it turned out to be the very person who, as I understood it at the time, had captured you and turned you over to The Tribunal. So, it wasn't about you taking another mate—it wasn't jealousy. It was who, how, and when. This, with him?" he indicates Aeon. "It's different. So no, no jealousy."

"She resisted it until there was no other choice, until the magic of the mate-bond took over," Aeon says. "She was worried about you all. She didn't want to and refused to do anything that would hurt you. You were all she thought of."

"And just so everyone is on the same page," I say, "I'm pretty sure Aeon is the last one. Six mates is…a lot." I laugh. "Not that I'd trade any one of you for the whole fucking world."

Alistair runs his fingers through my hair. "We should talk about the other thing that happened."

Caspian rolls to his side and reaches over Stirling to place his palm on my belly. "I didn't imagine that?"

I rest my hand on his, smiling at him with tears welling. "No, my love. You didn't. I conceived."

He looks at me for a long time, his face carefully blank. And then, very slowly, his expression crumbles and blood-tears trickle down his cheeks. "After..." he swallows hard, sits up and wipes at his eyes with the heels of his palms. "It was too hard to think about, but I...when I felt them do to you what they...what those fucking bastards did, I..."

I dislodge everyone and move to sit behind Caspian, straddling his hips with my thighs, crushing my breasts to his back and wrapping my arms around him, resting my cheek on his nape. "Tell me, my love. Let it out."

Fin takes one of his hands and Stirling the other. Caleb leans toward him, thunking their foreheads together with his hand on the back of Caspian's neck; Alistair rests his hand on his shoulder, squeezing.

"I was just starting to wrap my head around the idea of being a father." He sniffs, and his shoulders shake. "My mom. She was about my age when she had me. And I was just...I was thinking about her and wishing she could be here to meet her grandchild. I was just starting to...not be scared of failing, starting to really want it, you know?"

"I couldn't think about it," I whisper. "I mean, there was so much happening anyway, but really, I was terrified. Deep down, I was so fucking scared of being pregnant. I'd just become immortal, and I just...I wasn't ready. But I would have been. I just needed time to accept it, to think about it, to feel it. I didn't get that. It was taken from me." I let my blood- and prana-tears fall. "In some ways, I didn't know how strongly I felt about being pregnant until it was taken away from me."

"It's a good thing you destroyed them all already," Aeon says, "or I'd raze that place to ashes and salt the earth where it was."

Caspian takes a deep breath, holds it, and then lets it out slowly and shakily. "It's going to be different this time around."

"Yes," I whisper and kiss his back. "It will be."

CHAPTER 23

THE ARMY OF THE MORTAL Federation is bivouacked on the road on the Jersey side of the Lincoln Tunnel. The abandoned cars have been removed and pushed further west and crushed and stacked to create a blockade across the entire freeway. They've created a checkpoint at the mouth of the tunnel, complete with razor wire and sandbags and a machine gun emplacement, manned by a least twenty soldiers. A manually operated boom arm is complemented by a spike strip.

Dressed in clean jeans, sneakers, and a

forest green V-neck sweater, I stand alone in the tunnel, just out of range of the mortal's senses.

I'm gathering my nerves and my anger.

In the three months since my return to the Enclave, the Mortal Federation has harried and harassed us on all sides, sending squads to raid one bridge or tunnel while the main force attacks the rest.

They accomplish nothing other than wasting mortal lives, not to mention equipment and resources. We've learned to deal with their obnoxious attacks in stride: throw up a shield, draw them in close, and attack—they give up quickly, because the mortals, most of them, are losing their belief in the cause.

Even the most hard-headed of racist, bigoted mortals has seen, time and again, that we will defend ourselves, but that we have no interest in a war. Leave us alone and we'll leave you alone.

We don't pursue. We don't press the attack. When forced to attack, we do our best to preserve life. We bring the wounded in, tend to them, feed them, heal them, and show them what we're building.

No mortal, once within the walls of the Enclave, has ever gone back to the Federation.

Bridgestone leads the attacks himself, and the word from defectors is that Bridgestone and his closest lieutenants force the army to obey through fear tactics. Rumor has it, in fact, that the whole army is on the verge of mutiny.

Therefore, I've decided to speed the process along a bit.

You're sure about this? Caspian says, across the group link.

Not at all, I answer. **But it's worth a try.**

Say the word, my goddess, Aeon says. *I'll send a storm to wipe them off the map.*

That won't be necessary, I don't think, I say, laughing mentally. **But thank you for the offer. I'll keep it in mind.**

Caleb is in wolf form nearby, prowling the perimeter. Any sign of trouble and he can be at my side in seconds.

The rest are scattered around the area in a wide circle, surrounding the army—and by the rest, I mean my entire force of immortals and mortals—nearly ten thousand strong. Bridgestone's Federation is down to five thousand at best.

So, either I can find a way to end this myself, or I give the word to attack, and we end it the hard way. Either way, I'm done with the fucking Federation. We have more important things to do than waste time and resources fighting assholes.

I let out a breath and shake my hands. I've practiced this endlessly over the last few weeks until I'm confident in the process.

Time to try it for real.

Overhead, a hawk screeches. I close my eyes and tune into the pack link: Caleb has added Emily to the pack, and we've discovered a way to let her project what she sees across the link. I can tune into it and see what she sees, now.

We've gotten to the point that Emily, scouting from above, can focus on a particular location, providing me with enough detail to let me cast a portal to that spot. I can rip through the pocket realm as Aeon has taught me and arrive in the exact spot Emily is focused on. We've got it down to a science, now, or perhaps an art form—I can dial in on a location as small as a single sidewalk square, no matter how far away it is, as long as Emily can see it and I can link to her mind.

Emily is soaring overhead, watching. She's located Bridgestone—he's in the command tent with his cronies.

Descending, standby, Emily says.

I see New York laid out beneath me in remarkable acuity. The soldiers are mostly relaxed, their rifles set aside, cookfires burning on the blacktop, working out on make-shift weight equipment, lounging, chatting, laughing, roughhousing, throwing footballs and baseballs.

My view suddenly warps downward as Emily stoops toward the earth. My gut lurches, and then she hauls up and lands on something—a telephone pole, maybe. Her perch gives her a direct line of sight right into the command tent's open doorway, giving me a clear view of Bridgestone and his six commanders.

Commanders, lieutenants, whatever—I don't know the first thing about military command structure and care even less.

I let out a breath, and shake my hands. Focus hard on the image Emily is providing—a huge green tent, the flaps tied open, a cot in a far corner, a big folding table in the middle, around which the men are clustered, pointing here and there at maps, planning their next assault.

I draw prana into my hands, visualizing the interior of the command tent. I stab my hand forward, fingers stiff-ened into a blade, now holding two images in my mind—the command tent and the pocket realm, gray haze and swirling fog and diffuse directionless light. My hand meets resistance, and then something pops, and my hand bursts through the skin of reality. I grip the edge of the hole—it feels like trying to grasp a bar of soap at the bottom of a tub of water, slippery and all rounded edges. Once I've got a good grip, I pull downward, expanding the hole—it requires a shocking amount of strength to do so, as the fabric between the realms is incredibly stretchy, reaching with something very much like sentience to close the hole. I step through, keeping my grip on the edge, and then help the edges knit back together.

If you don't, Aeon warned me endlessly, you could allow things into The Waking that don't belong here. And again, I think of the hole I must have made and left gaping open at the top of the mountain, back in Switzerland.

For a moment, I'm in the pocket realm. The fog swirls around me, and in every direction I see a different scene shifting and rotating and blurring. You can get anywhere from here, as long as you've seen it with your own eyes. Or, apparently, if you have a pack-link to a hawk shifter.

Ahead of me, the breaks in the swirling fog mirror the image I'm holding in my head of the command tent's interior. No need to tear a hole, here. Simply step forward, keeping the image of your destination firmly in your mind's eye.

Gray light and hazy fog dissolve, granulate, swirling with shadows and light. And then the light is greenish, filtered by the tent walls, and male voices murmur.

I release my prana, standing at the entrance of the tent. Behind me, the camp is noisy and chaotic.

A cigarette smolders between the lips of one of the commanders. One of the men laughs. Bridgestone's voice carries over all of them. "One last push, gentlemen. We feint on two fronts and send everything we've got south down the Hudson Bridge."

The men are all facing away from me, Bridgestone in

the center, three of his subordinates on each side. I spend a moment just listening to them talk strategy, squad assignments, loadouts, and which trucks, tanks, and APCs will support which advance.

"I just have one question, sir," a commander on the far right says, sounding hesitant. "I don't mean to…errr… play devil's advocate or whatever but—"

"Spit it the fuck out, Nelson. Jesus." Bridgestone grabs a cup from the table in front of him and spits into it—chewing tobacco. Nasty.

"Just…as we're approaching, you've specified that your orders are to shoot to kill. But, um…how do we know who is who? Our intel, such as it is, reports that there are ever-increasing numbers of mortals choosing to live in the Enclave with the…um, enemy. If we go in and kill a bunch of our people, mortals I mean, and it gets out? Public opinion, which is already not entirely in our favor, will turn against us."

Bridgestone spits into the cup again; one of his commanders on his immediate left turns his head to the side and suppresses a retch. "If they choose to live among those freaks, then they've made their choice. They're not collateral damage at that point, Nelson, they're enemies who have been eliminated." A pause. "So tell the men to spread the word to anyone else who may have that concern—*anyone* on that island is an enemy." He leans forward to catch Nelson's eye. "And Nelson? It's *not* the fucking *Enclave*. It's fucking Manhattan, part of the United States of fucking America. You got me?" His voice is an enraged snarl by the end.

"Sir, yes sir."

I've heard enough.

I throw a coil of prana around the seven scheming mortals and condense it into hardened air, pinning their arms to their sides and their legs together. I reach out and close the flaps of the tent, plunging the interior into darkness lit only by a single bare bulb, the electricity for which is provided by a noisily rattling generator just the tent. The men are shouting and struggling. I ignore them and reach up to unscrew the light bulb, letting the cool, pleasing shadows engulf the tent.

I move around to the opposite side of the table, letting my vastly superior vampiric night vision adjust.

"Gentlemen," I say. "Good morning."

"Let me go, bitch queen." Bridgestone, breathing threats and epithets, as usual.

I muzzle him with a mouthful of icy air, reducing his protests to confused, muffled grunts. "I'll get to you in a moment, Mr. Bridgestone."

I lighten myself and bolt through the shadows to stand next to the rightmost commander—Nelson. I suppress the pheromone instinct, grab Nelson's hair, and nick his throat without the benefit of saliva to negate the pain, such as it is. He gasps in surprise and stiffens; I take a tiny taste of his blood and prana, purely to get a sense of the man.

"Matthew Alan Nelson, age fifty-two. Born in Red Hook, New Jersey. Mother, Eileen Nelson, deceased; father Roger Nelson, living. Elder brother is Sean Nelson, a retired insurance adjuster with three children and six grandchildren. Younger sister is Abigail Nelson, a secretary for a naval officer in Annapolis, mother of two; her husband is deployed as a senior officer on a carrier. You are married to Annie, father to Connor, Caitlin, and Craig—star students and athletes at prestigious universities."

"All publicly available information," he mutters.

"Mmm, true." I touch his earlobe and send a bolt of cold through him, making him shiver—for effect. "You cheated on your wife, Matthew. Twice, in fact. Once with a petty officer named Jennifer. It lasted for six months until she requested and received a transfer. To get away from you, but you've only ever suspected that, never knew it for sure. The second time was….ohhh, Matt, you're a naughty boy. The second time was with one of your daughter's close friends. To be fair, she instigated it, but you didn't shut it down. Did you, Matthew?"

"It was just once," he whispers. "I swear."

"You don't have to swear to me, Matthew. I already know. I know you wet the bed till you were eight. I know you cheated on several exams at West Point." I put my lips to his ear. "And I know you are starting to sympathize with my people."

He stammers a few times, but can't get anything coherent out, and falls silent.

I move to the next in line and repeat the process, divulging a few of each man's more embarrassing secrets.

I continue to ignore Bridgestone.

Move around to the opposite side of the table and conjure my mark of fealty, letting it hover, glowing incandescent golden-white above the middle of the table, providing a ghostly illumination.

"This, gentlemen, is a mark of fealty. Touch it, and you are swearing fealty to me, to my army, and to my cause. Betray that oath and you die a horrible death. Take the mark of fealty, gentlemen. You know what's right and what's wrong, each of you. I can taste it in your blood. You know damn well that what you are doing—what you're forcing your men out there to do—is wrong. Each man or woman who goes out and dies at our hands in the name of your vile, bigoted cause is murder. Their blood is on *your* hands. We are defending ourselves, our home, our rights, and the rights of all marginalized, oppressed, and ignored people."

"And…and if we don't?" asks Nelson.

I shrug. "If the situations were reversed, the choice you'd give me is to convert to your side or die or be imprisoned. Well, gentlemen, I'm not you. What I'm offering you is a way out. An excuse to listen to your consciences. If you pursue this idiotic crusade of yours against my people, you will lose. I won't kill you here and now, regardless. But if you come against me and my people, I will not show mercy. You have been warned. Your troops I shall show mercy to at all possible opportunity, for they are mostly innocent. I will provide them all the same choice you face now."

Silence.

"Nelson, you asked a wonderful question, a few moments ago. How are your soldiers to know the difference between mortals and immortals? I mean, a vampire, if he or she is unblooded, is easy to spot. A fae, unmasked, can be determined by his or her ears if nothing else. A shifter, well, you'll never know unless and until he or she shifts in front of you. But, how do you *know*? Which makes one wonder, I should think, whether your crusade is predicated upon a faulty premise to begin with: that we immortals are freaks and inferior beings. That we are inhuman."

Continued silence.

"I'll leave you with the mark and your thoughts, gentlemen. The mark will stay. Taking it will not harm you, and will not otherwise bind you to me or any other immortals except through your magically binding word of loyalty to me and my cause. There is, typically, a formal, ritual oath spoken when one takes the mark, but I don't expect that of you, and it isn't necessary anyway." I release the bonds around them, re-wrapping Bridgestone so tightly he can't move; I allow the gag to warm up to room temperature—wouldn't want his tongue to get frostbit. He'll need it shortly.

I leave the mark hovering over the table, move around behind Bridgestone, grab him by the collar and shove him roughly toward the exit. Rip open the portal and shove him through. Close it behind me, and shove him through again to the other side, now exiting in the middle of Times Square.

A crowd is gathered, upon my orders—mixed mortals and immortals. All the immortals are unmasked, but without scent, it'd be somewhat difficult to pick one immortal out of the crowd of thousands.

Times Square is dark, now. The iconic marquees and signs are blank. The stores are darkened, most of the glass broken and boarded up and the wares long since stolen. The bleachers are stuffed with people, and more crowd around the section I cordoned off as my stage for the next act.

Bridgestone is gagging around his, well, gag—the transition was abrupt and likely disorienting for the stupid mortal asshole. But that's his problem—the gag, being nothing more than a ball of swirling, condensed air, will allow vomit to pass through, should he puke. No risk of choking.

Although I'm tempted, I must say—I really do loathe this man even more than I did Zirae.

We emerge from the portal, Bridgestone stumbling, gagging, and then shuffling in a befuddled circle.

"Wheh—mmm—hiii?" he grunts.

"Where are you?" I translate. "Where does it look like you are, Mr. Bridgestone? Times Square. The heart of our Enclave."

"Geh-eh-wuh."

"Bullshit. You're no general. Not anymore. The moment you led troops against peaceful American citizens, you lost that privilege. You do not represent anyone or anything but yourself and your racist beliefs." I gesture around at the crowd. "Look around you, Nathaniel. What do you see?"

I allow the gag to dissolve. He spits, works his jaw. "Freaks and traitors."

"The only traitor here is you!" A man shouts somewhere to my right and pretty far back. "I'm no freak, and I'm certainly not a traitor! I'm a red-blooded mortal American. I fought for my country in Iraq and Afghanistan. I joined you because you said we were fighting a threat to our country, and I believed you! More the fool, me. You're nothing but a bully and racist!"

"I'm no racist!" Bridgestone says, whirling to face the voice as best as he can determine, although the speaker remains hidden in the crowd. "I accept all mortals, regardless of race, gender, sexual orientation, or religion. What I don't accept are perversions of nature!"

"Which makes you a racist!" the same man shouts. "The people you claim to hate are as human as the rest of us. They're just different. You're the perversion, you asshole!"

"Say that to my face, coward!" Bridgestone snarls, struggling against his bonds.

The crowd jostles, and a man emerges. A very, very large mortal male. Six and a half feet tall, muscular, tanned, wearing fatigues and carrying a shotgun. He stomps up to the cordon—rope fixed to orange traffic cones—and climbs over. Shotgun on his shoulder, he swaggers up to Bridgestone and stares down at him.

"You…" he shoves Bridgestone backward; hurriedly, I release the bonds around him so he can move freely. "Are." Another shove. "An *ASSHOLE*!"

Bridgestone, immediately sensing the release of the bonds, reaches for the sidearm at his right hip as he stumbles backward upon the man's last hard shove.

The man bats the gun aside and slugs Bridgestone in the gut, doubling him over. "*That's* for sending me into a fight you *knew* we'd lose against people who weren't our enemy."

The man turns his back on Bridgestone and swaggers back to the crowd; Bridgestone, being who he is, brings the gun up to bear.

"Ah ah ah," I admonish, moving in front of Bridgestone with my finger to the barrel. "I don't think so."

His finger tightens on the trigger.

"Remember what happened last time?" I ask, my voice sweet. "Think hard, mortal, before you pull that trigger."

He hesitates. Let the gun droop down. "What do you want?"

I laugh. "A broad question, Nathaniel. I want a lot of things."

"Why am I here? What do you want from me?"

I circle him. "Why are you here and what do I want from you? Excellent questions, Nathaniel."

I sweep a hand at the crowd in a 360-degree gesture. "What you see around you is a mixed group of mortals and immortals. I called them here. There are no disguises, no magical masks, nothing hidden. Fae are fae, vampires are vampires, and shifters are in human form."

"Okay? And?"

"Can you tell who is who?" I step up to the cordon and place my hand on the shoulder of a young woman—a fae with brown hair loose around her shoulders, conveniently hiding her ears. "What about her? Fae? Vampire? Shifter? Vaer? Aeshir? Fomori? Mortal? What is she?" I smile at him. "If she is immortal, I invite you to try to shoot her. I need not interfere—she can protect herself against one measly mortal with a stupid little gun." Before Bridgestone can speak, I interrupt. "From there. No questioning, just look at her and decide. Shoot or don't. But if you shoot, and you're wrong..." I reach out and accept a shockstick. "I poke you with this." The prongs arc and spit viciously. "It won't kill you, at this setting, but you really, *really* won't enjoy it. And yes, if she is a mortal, she will be protected from your bullet."

He blinks at me—I can see him thinking. He grips the gun tighter, finger outside the trigger guard, the barrel aimed at the ground a few feet in front of him. His eyes shift to the woman.

She's young-looking—older than Stirling but younger than Alistair, appearing late twenties to a mortal eye. She's wearing a pair of jeans, a well-worn *Reading Rainbow* shirt, and a loose white cardigan. Her hair is tied up messily and she wears no makeup. She's gorgeous, but so are any number of mortal women.

Bridgestone frowns. Looks at me and then at the woman. He grips and regrips the pistol.

I squeeze the woman's shoulder and weave through the crowd until I come to another person. This one is an elderly male. Black. Elegantly dressed in a pinstripe suit and fedora. Mortal. And one of the engineers who helped crack the energy solution.

I sling an arm across his shoulder. "I've got you," I whisper.

"I know it," he mutters back. "Ain't scared'a that racist old fuck."

"What about him?" I shrug. "Mortal? Immortal?" I send some prana into the shockstick, making it spark. "Gonna shoot him?"

Bridgestone is getting upset and confused. His eyes scan the crowd, looking for someone to hate.

I move to someone else—a male shifter of Asian descent, and a recent emigree to the Enclave. Rest my hand on his shoulder. "And him?"

To a mortal female, middle-aged and pretty, stocky with short hair and multiple piercings and tattoos on her hands and forearms. "And her?" I whisper in her ear. "I hope I didn't incorrectly assume anything."

She chuckles. "Nah, but I appreciate the thought, ma'am."

"Ma'am," I scoff, snorting.

She stands tall and proud, chin lifted, eyes blazing with defiance. "Gonna shoot me, Bridgestone? Come on, pussy. Shoot me. See what happens."

Another person steps forward. "Shoot me, Bridgestone. Try it, asshole."

And another. "How many bullets you got, prick?"

Pivoting in circles as more and more people step out of the crowd and cluster closer to him, daring him to shoot them, Bridgestone quickly becomes overwhelmed and panicked. "ENOUGH! I get it!"

He ejects the magazine and jacks the round of the chamber—it clatters to the ground with a soft tinkle of metal on stone.

"Okay, everyone, back up. Give him space." I step through the crowd and into the cordoned-off area. I stop in front of Bridgestone. "You get it? You've changed your ways, have you? Just like that?"

He doesn't answer.

"Aeon?" I call. "Will you please deposit this mortal somewhere far, far away? We aren't murderers like him, so not a mountaintop, desert, or the bottom of the ocean."

Aeon slips through the crowd, white hair fluttering in an invisible wind. He grabs Bridgestone by the arm, murmurs something to him, and then portals him away. A few moments later, Aeon returns.

"Where'd you leave him?" I ask. "And what did you say to him?"

"I left him in the bush outside a small village in Kenya. If he is humble and kind and gracious, they will care for him and bring him to a larger city. If he is not? Well, they'll just let Africa deal with him. His fate will be up to what kind of man he is." He grins. "I told him he's fortunate you're making the decisions and not me because I would have ripped his spine out through his rectum." A wicked grin. "I feel like he believed me, seeing as he piddled his pants."

The last thing to deal with, then, is the remains of the Federation.

Only, according to Emily's aerial reconnaissance, the army quickly discovered Bridgestone's absence—and the fact that the six ranking commanders all vanished...having taken my mark. Within twenty-four hours, the army is gone. Most return to wherever home was, but over a thousand of them join the enclave.

Now?

All we have to do is rebuild society.

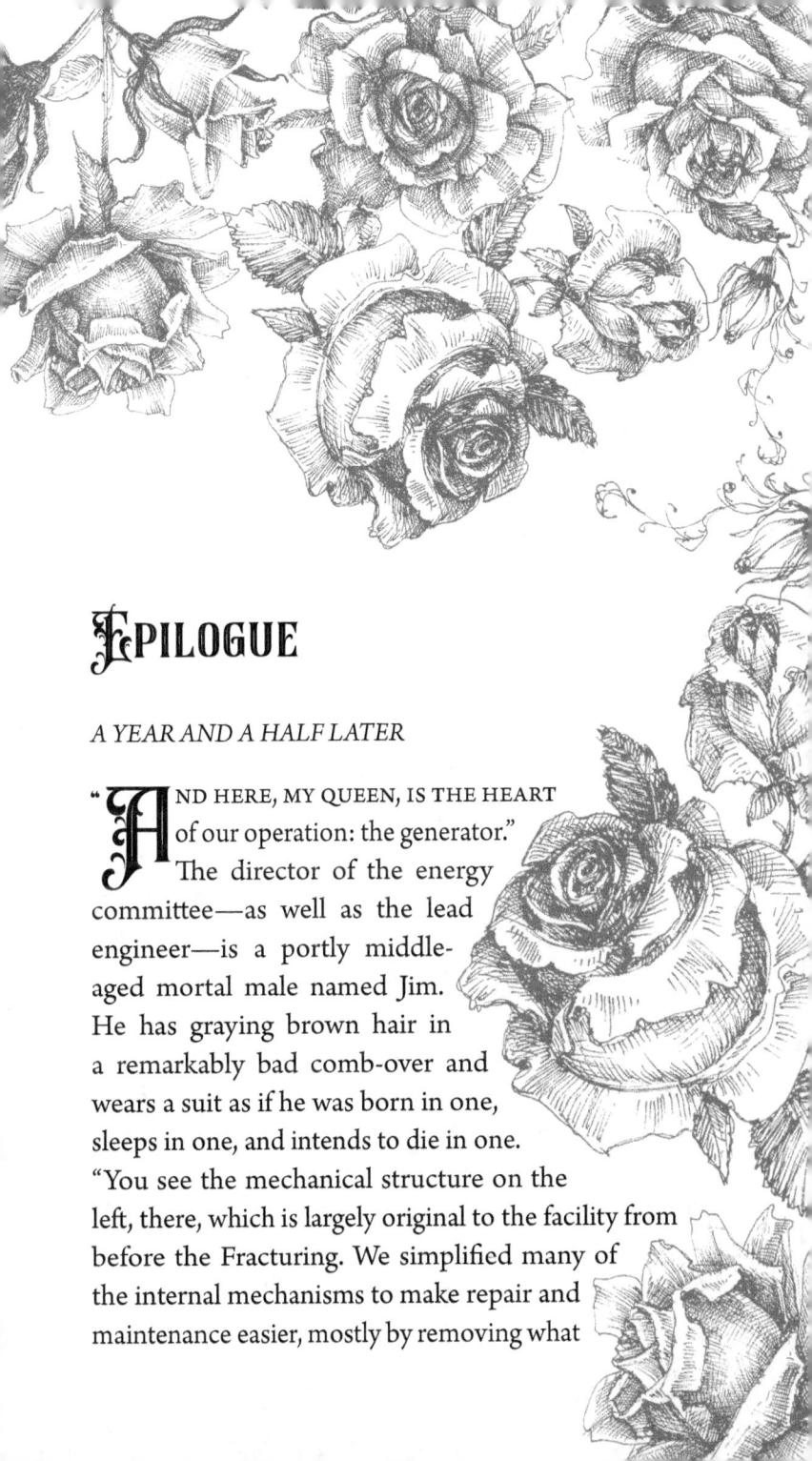

EPILOGUE

A YEAR AND A HALF LATER

"AND HERE, MY QUEEN, IS THE HEART of our operation: the generator."

The director of the energy committee—as well as the lead engineer—is a portly middle-aged mortal male named Jim. He has graying brown hair in a remarkably bad comb-over and wears a suit as if he was born in one, sleeps in one, and intends to die in one.

"You see the mechanical structure on the left, there, which is largely original to the facility from before the Fracturing. We simplified many of the internal mechanisms to make repair and maintenance easier, mostly by removing what was no longer necessary. The magical mechanism is on your right, powered by glamours provided on a volunteer basis, as you're aware."

I scan the setup. It truly is ingenious. The original turbines, formerly powered in this case by coal, churn deafeningly, even on this side of the thick, sound-deadening glass. They're enormous, each the size of a three or four-story apartment building. Tubes and pipes and conduits run to and from it, varying in sizes. Where the power used to come from burning coal, however, the mechanisms have been entirely re-designed and re-built, making the bulk of the facility unnecessary. There's a small room, insulated, sound-proofed, and stocked with a variety of supplies. A volunteer—any immortal capable of producing even a small glamour—will spend an eight-hour shift maintaining the glamour that provides power to the turbines. The glamour is a simple one. An electrical storm, more or less—an indoor lightning storm created by Aeon. The lightning strikes a metal ball, and the energy is transmitted by a combination of magical and mechanical means to the turbines—the exact science of it is a bit above my understanding, but I'm told it functions along normal physics guidelines, albeit given a magical assist.

The net result is clean, endless energy. Not free—it costs round-the-clock manpower to maintain the glamour Aeon created, but that's the beauty of it. The manpower is done on a volunteer, rotational basis. For every shift you work maintaining the glamour, you are given a thousand credits, which is not currency, exactly. There is still money in the enclave, gold-backed, but it sees little use. Most people prefer to trade. The credits from a shift at the plant give the bearer purchasing power at the markets, and each vendor marks their goods or services with a credit cost.

The same system is applied to the waste transfer plants, where magic is again used to facilitate the processing of liquid and solid wastes, magic taking the place of electricity, all else functioning the same. Plumbing, as well.

Trash removal is wildly different now. It turns out that the Weavers, as we have begun calling the creatures who reside in The Dreaming, have a penchant for our trash since to them it is positively dripping with residual mana. The garbage removal carts are simple two-wheeled light metal handcarts drawn by individuals paid with market credits. Instead of collecting the trash on the street and hauling it away to a dump or whatever, the cart interior is a mobile portal to The Dreaming, into which the trash is tossed. The Weavers eat it, which serves to keep them sated and less likely to bother travelers using the portals.

You see, Aeon, after some tinkering, figured out how to create stable, always-open portals through The Dreaming—or, more accurately, through the pocket realm, which is somewhat like the very surface of The Dreaming, the meniscus, as Aeon explained it, what feels like so long ago.

These portals can go anywhere, providing free, clean, instant travel. They're guarded and monitored, of course, and all travel is sold and registered; the proceeds—goods, promise of service, or credits—are property of the Manhattan Enclave. There are portals to the other major Enclaves: LA, Atlanta, Chicago, Milwaukee, Indianapolis, Houston, New Orleans, San Diego, and Seattle, as well as international destinations like Paris, Berlin, Prague, Hong Kong, Beijing, Sydney…all the largest of the major cities have become Enclaves designed after what we have built here.

The Enclaves are independent city-states. Most national governments collapsed in the wake of the Fracturing—the term given to the revelation of immortals and the subsequent chaos. A few places have retained a central government, but those are mostly the smaller, poorer, and more remote areas where life never really changed all that much to begin with.

The internet failed, and despite work by the best minds in the magical and mortal communities, it hasn't returned. Most agree this is a good thing.

International shipping ceased when global oil and gas supplies dried up, and without those, manufacturing ceased…the trickle-down effect was massive. Electricity, now supplied by magical-mechanical hybrid systems, is used only for lighting, heat, and climate control. The system cannot distribute beyond a certain distance from the source—some kind of innate limitation of the magic. This means outlying communities have to rely on either natural renewable energy and storage solutions—which have become a major focus of magical and scientific research—or they simply do without. In those places, life has returned to a strange amalgam of modern and pre-industrial revolution. Horses, mules, and oxen once again provide transportation and hauling, but often they haul repurposed vehicles. Agriculture is once again the purview of the individual rather than corporations.

Part of the Enclave design is to utilize vertical space in the high-rises for urban agriculture. Skyscrapers, empty now that so many industries have gone extinct, are gutted and turned into gardens tended by a mix of full-time

Enclave employees and volunteers. Abandoned buildings and unnecessary structures are demolished and used for agriculture or simply as parks.

Returning, momentarily, to the power plants: the smokestacks and the rest of the facility formerly dedicated to using coal for power have been converted as well, and here is one of the truly world-changing inventions. Instead of sending pollution into the atmosphere, the smokestacks have been converted to pull smog out of the air and clean it. This is another magical-mechanical hybrid system, invented by—or at least by a committee of scientists led by—my grandfather, Elias Sparrow. The system of smog scrubbers is hellishly complex, and we've only managed one working example, but now that we have the system in place, the other Enclaves are clamoring for the design.

It's not all hunky-dory.

Outside the cities, life is much, much harder, if simpler. Food can be scarce without a central government, and road maintenance and such things are long gone. Law enforcement is a local issue, and in the rewilded areas between Enclaves, local communities, and non-Enclave cities, lawlessness abounds. Some immortals have designated themselves vigilantes, dedicated themselves to roving the roadways and stopping robbers and outlaws from preying on mortals.

I often have to arbitrate disputes between the various magical communities, as queen, which requires traveling from Enclave to Enclave, although I return to my home in Manhattan as regularly as possible.

My other home, the estate in England, remains a far-off dream—somewhere I'd like to more or less retire to when things have settled more. There's still too much upheaval and chaos, now, though, and I'm needed too constantly to spend much time there.

To mortals, those who don't live in daily proximity to me in the Enclave, at least, I'm a bit of a curiosity. There's a good bit of hubbub and fanfare wherever I go, which has taken some getting used to. Curious mortals flock to wherever I'll be just to get a look at "A Real Queen." I don't have the heart to tell them I don't have an actual royal bone in my body and that I don't even really believe in royalty anyway, and that I view my position as a kind of public servant. It won't matter because they'll see me how they want to see me. I just do my best to make sure that my words, actions, and policies are as morally aligned as possible. To that end, I surround myself with people—mortal and immortal—who will give me good advice and keep me humble.

My mates certainly don't help in that last regard. They treat me like…well…like you'd expect.

My first child was born on the new year, exactly at midnight. Fireworks celebrated her arrival.

Eliza Andrea Sparrow is the first Tertius, the first child of a Secundus. With a vampire father and a Vaer mother, Eliza is still too young to show much by way of what her powers will be. She has my ears—fae ears. Her father's hair, coal black, glossy, thick. Her eyes flash gray when she's crying—luminous from within, looking precisely like a thin layer of cloud cover in front of the sun. Otherwise, they're pale blue, like chips of a glacier, like mine and Mom's. Her skin is pale as porcelain and in direct sunlight almost seems transparent. She doesn't cry often. Aside from her daddy and me, Aeon is her favorite. She sits on his shoulders and rides everywhere with him, tugging on his hair and calling him "Eenon."

"Go fast, Eenon! Go high, Eenon!" she screeches.

And Aeon, tilting his head back to look up at her with a dry, droll expression, says, "Must I, Littlest Sparrow?"

"EENON GO FAST! EENON GO HIGH!" This is with a resounding sequence of smacks with both hands upon Aeon's head.

"Very well, then. Hold on tight."

And so Eliza clutches his head with her arms so tightly it would choke a mortal being, but Aeon, being who he is, tolerates it without a word. He summons air swirling beneath him and they rocket upward into the blue sky, Eliza's joyful shrieks of laughter receding.

We all gather in the bright open field of Central Park, watch Aeon dart this way and that, blasting himself upward and side to side, letting them fall before catching them again.

Caspian, of course, spoils her rotten. She clings to his shoulders as well, and he takes her on long runs through the Enclave, leaping from roof to roof, balcony to balcony, streetlight to streetlight, while Eliza's laughter rings out and echoes off the glass.

It's such a common thing that Enclave residents are used to it, often pausing to look up as Eliza's laughter catches up to them, a smile on their faces as the daddy-daughter pair blurs past.

There are other marriages and other Tertius children; Eliza was simply the first. We actually have quite a creche, over a dozen children ranging from newborns to toddlers Eliza's age. We, my family, have chosen a former office building near Times Square, which is the official gathering place for announcements, celebrations, meetings, elections, and speeches. We renovated it, gutting it from top to bottom and creating a comfortable, spacious home on the top two floors, the rest dedicated to the administrative endeavors necessary to running the Enclave.

As queen, I endeavor to be little more than a figurehead, and I'm constantly seeking political ways to reduce my power. Initially, I was it—the end of the line, all decisions being my purview. But it was exhausting and stressful and at the end of the day, I'm still just a girl barely out of her teen years. I wasn't raised to be a politician. Aeldfar says I make a good queen precisely because I don't want to be one, and everyone else seems to agree. But, being queen, I get my way.

I researched, discussed, questioned, and polled, and came up with a system.

Each tribe—we have taken to referring to the various kinds of immortals as tribes, in deference to Aeon's historical authority on the subject—chooses by popular vote a pair of representatives. Policies and decisions are made on behalf of the tribal constituents by the representatives, and when the entire panel of representatives gathers to make a decision that affects the entire Enclave, a simple majority wins, with me as a tiebreaker.

The representatives are elected each year—if no challenger arises for either slot, then the process is expedited—each voter chooses to keep the rep for the next year. If no challenger arises but the rep is not kept, a new election must be called. Once the individual Enclaves have chosen their tribal representatives, an Immortal Summit is convened here in Manhattan, wherein the tribes from across the globe discuss, vote on, and decide larger factors affecting immortals as a whole.

Throughout the entire process, mortals are welcome

to observe and question, although they do not receive a vote on tribal matters. Mortals do, however, have representatives for Immortal Enclave Summits.

Overall, the system works well. I'm sure over time it will evolve, but for now, it works. People have a voice. Mortals, within the Enclave, at least, accept the immortals.

The funny part of it all is that the Enclaves, designed by, run by, and made possible by magicals—the increasingly more popular term that is rapidly replacing immortals—are the only places where life is truly anything like what it was before the Fracture. Elsewhere, it's a shitshow. Places where mortals—non-magicals—are in charge? No power, no plumbing, no modern amenities. Or, very little. Gasoline is all but gone—the entire infrastructure that produced gasoline has collapsed and does not show any signs of resuscitating. And that's just one facet.

Outside the Enclaves, there's still plenty of anti-magical sentiment and bigotry. There are still "militias" dedicated to hunting down magicals…and it goes as well as you can expect.

I generally don't bother myself with the world beyond the Enclaves—my responsibility is magicals and those mortals who choose to live under my care in the Enclaves for which I am responsible.

I am the ultimate tiebreaker at the Immortal Summit.

I lounge in the grass in Central Park, my head on Caleb's chest while he rubs my belly, marveling at the little shifter-something growing in there. I think about how strange it is, how far I've come from that day in LA in the car with Mom—the last time I saw her alive, the last conversation I had with her.

Andreas leads a band of vigilantes dedicated to

preserving law and order in the boroughs around our Enclave. They patrol the streets and provide a sense of safety for the mortals still living there—we're working on expanding the reach of our services, but it's a slow process since it's all new technologies and magical-mechanical manufacturing is still in its infancy. Beyond the borders of Manhattan, life is still tough for the mortals—the non-magicals. We do what we can, and we welcome new mortals in every week, but eventually, we are going to run out of space and the Enclave will have to expand to include the outer boroughs.

It's a work in progress, the kind of thing that will likely never be totally complete. Will our hybrid systems be able to replace the systems and infrastructure as they used to exist? Will other cities become Enclaves? How will the more remote and isolated communities adapt and adjust to this new no-central government reality? Will new borders, countries, and governments crop up?

There are too many unanswered questions, and I'm not the one to answer them.

Not now, at least.

Caleb bolts upright. "Holy shit! She moved! It moved? He moved? The baby moved!"

I laugh, placing my hand on his and guiding his hand over to the side where the baby is currently doing gymnastics—I've felt the movement inside me before now, but this is the first time Caleb has felt it on the outside. The joy and wonder on his face are truly something to behold. I mean, sure, he felt Eliza moving around and reacted similarly, but I guess for daddies it's a little different—more moving and wondrous when it's your child. Not that Eliza is any less loved by him—but she calls Cas "Da-da" and everyone else by their name, or at least, the one-year-old version of it: Eenon, Stirring (the exact flavor of mispronunciation varies widely), Fin is always just "Fin", and "Stair" or "Alstir", and "Cay-eb."

I think just knowing the child will emerge and one day call you "Daddy" changes things.

Well...it changes everything, to be honest.

Being a mother has changed everything. I've started trying to see the larger picture when making decisions, especially regarding the world she's growing up in.

In fact, that was the catalyst behind nudging Aeldfar to work on a smog-scrubber—wanting to improve the world—not just politically. It turns out that magic makes some things possible that weren't before—seems obvious, perhaps, but the process of learning how to combine magic and non-magical engineering is much, much harder than one would think, requiring a lot of creativity and ingenuity to make the two extremely disparate modalities work in unison to achieve a single goal. Where non-magical engineering was still a long way off from making CO_2 conversion facilities a reasonable, achievable reality, magic has made it not just possible, but wildly effective. The biggest hurdle now is the simple fact of how hard it is to manufacture mechanical materials without automation and all that comes with it. Everything must be made by hand, and even in that, we're learning, slowly, how to mix magic in to make things easier and faster.

Non-magicals are adapting to life with magic—some better than others. In our Enclave, for example, there are magic-free zones. Magicals are welcome, but magic is not. No glamours, no use of powers. Shifters are welcome in their animal forms as well as human. The idea, laid out by the non-magical representatives, is to create some pockets where non-magicals can feel like things are the way they used to be—to a degree. Unexpectedly, most magicals embraced the idea wholeheartedly—to them, the Null Zones, as they're called, are places where they can just *be*. You can sit and have a conversation with someone, and it doesn't matter who or what they are. Something about knowing no one is going to use magic—even for something minor and harmless, or even good—seems to take some kind of pressure off of everyone. Null Zones have become the go-to place to meet people, magical or not.

Masks are a thing of the past.

Schooling in the Enclaves is different now—a hybrid of old and new. Enclaves are divided into districts of no more than a thousand school-age children, and each district is subdivided into one-room schools of no more than fifty students taught by a single teacher. Districts are managed by a single district director, and beneath the director is a regional manager, overseeing clusters of ten to twelve individual schoolrooms, ensuring no schoolroom is overpopulated, and that each room has enough supplies and such. Students are encouraged to self-direct their education, with their academic independence growing as they do, so by the time a student is eighteen he or she will be largely responsible for their curriculum, guided and facilitated by the teacher and regional manager, leaving the teacher free to be more hands-on with the younger students. One of the core subjects each schoolroom is required to teach is a magical history class. The curriculum was designed by Aeon and supported by a panel of elders from each tribe.

Schoolrooms are not divided by magical nor non-magical, but rather, students are assigned a room by location, with no student traveling more than a few blocks. Attached to each schoolroom are a handful of volunteers who watch kids below school age so the parents can work.

What has surprised me most is the spirit of volunteerism that drives the Enclaves. Not everyone volunteers in something, of course, but most do a few times a month—working the glamour rooms, watching children, street cleaning crews…the list of volunteer jobs is nearly endless and ever-changing. By providing market credits, everyone wins, because the vendors who provide the goods or services for credits are benefits of volunteers—they have kids in a school or creche, their homes are powered by fae glamours, their trash collected, their plumbing…permanent positions are paid a wage in hard currency, but those positions are limited to the most important. When we— the governing body, meaning myself, my mates, and the panel of reps—discussed the idea of volunteerism being a basic tenet of how the Enclaves function, most of us were skeptical it would work. But when we held town halls in various sections of the Enclave and took votes and polls on the subject, it became clear that most people supported the premise. And when we rolled out the first programs— glamour-rooms at the power plants, plumbing, and waste plants—it was a resounding success, and non-magicals wanted in; where could they volunteer? Volunteer support groups proliferate—many new couples meet while volunteering.

It's not perfect, of course. Many programs are always short-staffed and overworked, and things break down before volunteers can be brought in to get it going again.

But when you're building something brand new, there's bound to be hiccups, right?

It's not Utopia. There's still crime. People still steal, and people still get in fights. Someone calls someone else a slur. People have been killed. Someone uses magic in a Null Zone and is temporarily banned. People struggle to make it while others succeed. Some have more; some have less. Couples break up. Students fail or don't show up. Teachers end up with too many students and not enough resources.

It's life.

Magical, non-magical, we're all just trying to make it one day at a time in a world that is, somehow, both new and old. We face the same struggles humans have always faced. Bigotry still exists. Hate still happens. Suffering happens. But so does love, and compassion, and generosity.

Call me an optimist if you must, but I think the Enclaves are an improvement over the old ways, in general. Not having a central government anymore is both a boon and a bane and in ways we probably can't see from here, only a year and a half out from the Fracturing. Some call it the Collapse, but Fracture has increasingly become the new favorite, as it more accurately describes what happened—sure, governments collapsed when fear and confusion spread and led to infighting and civil war, but really, it was a fracturing. Political leaders moved to lead Enclaves and city-states rather than counties, states, and countries. After all, city-states were the norm for a very, very long time—in fact, according to Aeon, countries with borders and central governments are a relatively recent invention, and he always assumed it would break down and return to a decentralized system eventually.

God, my mind is everywhere today.

Probably because I don't have any meetings or

decisions—it's Sunday. People have begun taking Sundays off from just about everything—another return to old ways.

It's my favorite day of the week. I sleep in late with my mates. Eliza always ends up in bed with us at some point. We have a dog, Bob, a fat basset hound Caleb found wandering the streets and adopted. Bob likes to wake us up by sitting at the foot of our bed and howling his hoarse, funny little howl until someone gets up and feeds him.

Eliza and Bob are best friends. She likes to hand-feed Bob his kibble and usually takes a bite for him and a bite for her. No amount of scolding or saying no can prevent Eliza from sharing Bob's food, so we just go with it.

After breakfast, we take a walk. Caleb and the pack shift to wolf form and spend the morning running and circling and howling while the coven, Eliza, and I stroll to the park. Eliza spends the day playing with friends while we watch and lounge. Someone brings lunch and we have a picnic.

Eliza takes a nap and we adults…play. Or just relax with books.

I haven't felt Mother's Spirit in a very long time. Perhaps I used up all the magic. Perhaps I don't need her as much as I once did. Or maybe, somehow, her spirit simply found a new vessel…her namesake.

Eliza is a magical child. I mean, obviously—she's a magical. But I mean it in a more colloquial sense. She's joyful, cheerful, easy to please, and largely self-soothing. But more than anything, her eyes shine with a gleam that seems to just be…*Mom*. I can't explain it. Maybe it's me inventing things, seeing things because I want to.

But I don't think so.

Aeon sees it. Caspian sees it. Aeldfar sees it—and he, being Mom's father, knew her perhaps better than I did, and he sees it.

Either way, it's a comfort to me. Knowing that Mom lives on, one way or another. In me, in Eliza, and in the world we're building. She sacrificed herself for me, to give me the power and strength to do what was necessary— what I did.

Not that I did it alone—far, far from it.

Where would I be without Caspian, Alistair, Stirling, Fin, Caleb, and Aeon? I shudder to even consider. I thank the Fates for putting my mates into my life. I doubt I've ever met them and I doubt I ever will, but if I ever do I'll thank them for their manipulation of the threads of my life.

The baby kicks again.

Stirling watches Caleb's eyes light up with wonder, and I see…not jealousy, just…wistfulness. Desire.

And I think I know who's going to give me my next baby.

Stirling must have caught my thought because he smiles at me. *Damn right I'm gonna give you a baby.*

I can't wait.

He laughs mentally, his lips twitching. *I mean, you have to have this one first.*

Details, I say. **Good thing we have plenty of time, huh?**

It took 127 years, but Aeon finally told me he loves me. I knew—he's shown me in a million, million ways. But Aeon has always held things close, has always taken time to process things, to communicate. Thirteen thousand years of habit is hard to break, I suppose. I've never minded. I know he loves me, and I was always content to wait—I have time.

He told me he loved me when I told him I was pregnant again…with his baby, this time. Of all my mates, he was the most hesitant to allow that. Apparently, he has some way of controlling the potency of his swimmers—a minor detail he neglected to tell me. I knew he wasn't ready, and again, I was okay with that. My other mates have given me sixteen children over the last century and a quarter—and almost thirty grandchildren. Since I don't age, or very, very, very slowly, my womb remains fertile. And my love for my mates waxes stronger than ever, so we continue having kids.

Aeon has his ear to my belly. He says he's listening to her heartbeat. Her, he says. The child will be a girl. He has a touch of the sight, you know, he tells me.

I know.

I haven't told him yet, but I've decided to name her Agana. She Who Wanders The Sky.

Four hundred years after the Fracture, my mates and I have decided it's time to retire to the England estate. The Enclaves are strong, and new ones apply for registration and admittance to the Immortal Summit every decade or so. Infrastructure is stable. Remote communities have power, plumbing, and trash removal.

There are no cell phones and no internet. But with

the proliferation of portals, it's not needed. Goods can be shipped via portal, allowing international trade.

I'm no longer needed, except for official duties at yearly summits and the occasional tiebreaker vote.

My clan is thousands strong, now.

Eliza is a director of education at an Enclave in Scotland with her mates and children. My other kids are all over the place, but they all come back to Mama frequently.

The world is in good hands, I think.

We stroll through the portal, a private one going from our home in Manhattan to the front door of the estate.

Harry stands waiting, vampirically pale, eyes void, back straight and proud.

"Welcome home, my queen," he says with a bow.

"Thank you, Harry," I say, already looking forward to a splash in that amazing bathroom with my mates. "It's good to be home."

THE END

About the Author

Jasinda Wilder is a *New York Times, Wall Street Journal,* and *USA Today* bestselling author of more than 100 titles including the #1 Amazon bestseller Falling Into You, the Audie Award-winning (best audiobook) Alpha, and the beloved, 17-book Badd Brothers series.

She and her husband Jack Wilder have sold more than 7 million copies and have been translated into more than 20 languages worldwide. You can find them at their fairy tale cottage by a lake somewhere in Michigan with their 6 kids, 5 dogs, 2 cats, 2 bunnies, and way too many ducks and chickens.

ALSO BY JASINDA WILDER

If you enjoyed this book, you can help others enjoy it as well by recommending it to friends and family, or by mentioning it in reading and discussion groups and online forums. You can also review it on the site from which you purchased it. But, whether you recommend it to anyone else or not, thank you *so much* for taking the time to read my book! Your support means the world to me!

My other titles:

Forbidden Fruit

Wild Ride: Biker Billionaire

Delilah's Diary

Big Girls Do It:

Big Girls Do It
Married
On Christmas
Pregnant
Rock Stars Do It
Big Love Abroad

The Falling Series:
Falling Into You
Falling Into Us
Falling Under
Falling Away
Falling for Colton

The Ever Trilogy:
Forever & Always
After Forever
Saving Forever

From the world of *Wounded:*
Wounded
Captured

From the world of *Stripped:*
Stripped
Trashed

From the world of *Alpha:*
Alpha
Beta
Omega
Harris: Alpha One Security Book 1
Thresh: Alpha One Security Book 2

Puck: Alpha One Security Book 4
Lear: Alpha One Security Book 5
Anselm: Alpha One Security Book 6
Sigma
Gamma

The Houri Legends:
Jack and Djinn
Djinn and Tonic

Dad Bod Contracting:
Hammered
Drilled
Nailed
Screwed

Fifty States of Love:
Pregnant in Pennsylvania
Cowboy in Colorado
Married in Michigan
Christmas in Connecticut

Billionaire Baby Club:
Lizzy Goes Brains Over Braun
Autumn Rolls a Seven
Laurel's Bright Idea

Club Sin:
Rev
Kane
Chance
Silas
Saxon

Blood Heir
Blood Heir
Blood Bonds

Standalone titles:
Yours
The Cabin
The Parent Trap
Wish Upon A Star
Big Hose

Non-Fiction titles:
You Can Do It
You Can Do It: Strength
You Can Do It: Fasting

Jack Wilder Titles:
The Missionary

JJ Wilder Titles:
Ark

To be informed of new releases, special offers, and other Jasinda news, sign up for Jasinda's email newsletter.

www.ingramcontent.com/pod-product-compliance
Lightning Source LLC
Chambersburg PA
CBHW070831260626
47170CB00007B/2332